I0817871

ALAS, THE BEST LAID PLANS

Vol. III

of

THE STEWARD

M.D. IRONZ

Also by M.D. Ironz

THE STEWARD
Domaine Delafaire
Realms Of Possibility
Alas, The Best Laid Plans

Standalone
Dire Covenants

Original Publication in the United States of America

Professorial Holdings

professorialholdings@gmail.com

CH 1

THE UNEXPECTED KNOCK upon the front door of Ellen's Delafaire Farm home was only the first in a series of surprises. This night would prove to be interesting, and to a large degree enlightening.

Ellen's unlikely visitor was Lady Leanan of the Sidhe, an elder vampire from the Realm of Shadow.

Somewhat shocked and understandably wary, Ellen maintained a calm demeanor despite her flaring curiosity. *What is this all about? I suppose I'm expected to play the role of amenable host? We'll see.*

However, before permitting Leanan to pass through the home's protective wards, Ellen demanded and received a binding oath from Leanan to ensure she meant no harm or ill intent.

The Sidhe surprised Ellen by calling forth another person from the darkness, Miska, originally from the Realm of Were. Leanan urged that he, too, be granted passage through the protective wards.

Of course, Ellen and Miska were well acquainted; but, prior to this night, Leanan had been unaware of that fact.

Ellen could not help but smile at the image of hulking Miska gently cradling her purring cat, Smokey, against his massive chest.

Lady Leanan noticed as well, smirking at the incongruous display of tenderness.

Ellen noted that her dogs, the Chows, Max and Sophie, remained quiet and relaxed at her side, unruffled. Somewhat reassured, she sighed and lightly scoffed to herself.

Hmmph, I see you guys aren't worried—and you know I trust your judgment.

I suppose I should get used to surprises like this. Inheriting this farm and the Stewardship of the Grand Portal of the Realm of Man was bound to have unanticipated consequences, like unexpected visitors at any and all hours. Who knows what else?

And now I'm about to invite two people, who most would call supernatural creatures, into my home. One, Miska the werebear, I know I can trust—and thankfully he's in man-form tonight—the other, Leanan the vampire? Well, we'll see.

My life has become interesting, indeed.

Ellen stood to one side, and held the screen door open. "It's good to see you, Miska. Please, enter and feel welcome in my home—and pursuant to your oath, you as well, Lady Leanan."

The dogs moved off to the far end of the hall, as if they were waiting to escort Ellen and her visitors.

As Ellen closed the door, Leanan asked, "Forgive my impatience, but would you mind explaining how it is that you and Miska know one another?"

"This story may take a little while to tell," Ellen cautioned. "Can I offer either of you anything to eat or drink?" She looked at Leanan and blurted, "Oh—I am sorry. I didn't think! I mean—"

Leanan chuckled. "Be at ease, Ellen; I am not offended. The vast majority of folklore and mythology your people rely upon regarding my kind is dated, confusing, and for the most part simply *wrong*. Some dreadful Hollywood films have even further muddied the waters. Does it surprise you that I know of motion pictures? It should not, for I have spent much time in your realm. And, I will admit to having developed a taste for the fine wines found here.

"I also have no doubt that Miska is hungry—although he is too polite and courteous to admit it. So, we will take advantage of your graciously offered hospitality."

Feeling equally cautious as likely gracious or hospitable, Ellen nodded. "Uh-huh, follow me."

"Of course, please lead on. For what it is worth, I am sorry I was unable to bid you farewell when I was last your host. I understand your departure was not without issues, no?"

"You could say that. In fact, it would help to explain how Miska and I met. Come, the kitchen is the best place to tell this tale."

ELLEN SERVED MISKA a platter of cold cuts, cheeses, and fresh bread. She poured glasses of wine for herself and Leanan; but, Miska declined, opting instead for sweet tea.

Once settled, Ellen began her narrative, recounting how she, Mark, and Hawk had come to the Realm of Shadow in search of their missing friend, Stacy, leading to their initial encounter with the Sidhe at the crossroads inn, the scene of recent carnage. Once it was determined that Leanan's quarry, Salidar, was in fact with Stacy, a tentative understanding had followed to include Leanan's suggestion of mutual assistance in search efforts and the offer of accommodations at her castle within the Shadow Realm.

Ellen was aware that much of this information was already known to Leanan. However, it soon became clear that the Sidhe was very interested to hear how the Lady Sabrina's familiar, Gunther, had interfered with their departure from Leanan's castle, and subsequently attempted to capture them by force. This, of course, had led to the encounter with Miska in his bear form, and dealing with Gunther.

Ellen did not comment on Gunther's injuries.

Leanan listened without making any interruptions.

As her story wound to a close, Ellen asked Leanan, "Now if you don't mind, how is it that Miska is with you this night?"

Leanan sipped deeply from her glass. "To be succinct, he came to my castle seeking to see the body of Boltar, suspecting that it was actually his lost brother, Ivan. Such was the case—Boltar *is* Ivan."

Pausing she took a long sip from her glass, draining it.

"Now, as to why he is with me tonight, that will take some time to explain. A bit more wine, please? I rarely drink the wine of my own realm—dreadful stuff, has been for generations. But, the wines of your realm—ah yes, they are far superior."

Ellen refilled both their glasses. Miska was more than satisfied with a refill of the sweet tea.

"Miska," said Ellen softly, "I am sorry about your brother."

"Thank you, Lady Ellen. I-I not sure what to do. I thought take him home, but—"

"Miska," interrupted Leanan, "I will explain the circumstances to our hostess. There are some things of which you are unaware, such that you need not concern yourself. You have been through much of late. Perhaps you should rest?"

"As you wish, m'lady," he acknowledged and sighed heavily. "I tired; my heart heavy."

"Ellen," Leanan said, "I was going to explain things first, and then ask you to let Miska stay here with you, in the Realm of Man, for his own safety. It is very important. Could you accommodate him, and perhaps send him to rest now?"

Hmm, another surprise . . . what next?

"Of course, Miska, come with me. You can use Mark's room; he's in New York right now."

Ellen led Miska upstairs; Smokey followed.

THE CHOWS STAYED IN the kitchen with Leanan, and watched her placidly.

She waited until Ellen was out of earshot, and then spoke to the dogs.

"I bid you greetings, loyal guardians. I have not seen you for many years, and yet you have not changed one iota. Be at ease—you may rest assured that I shall honor my oath. I intend no harm to the new Steward, or those she holds dear."

The dogs, unblinking, did not respond.

IN A FEW MINUTES, ELLEN returned.

"You were right, Leanan. Miska was lightly snoring by the time I got him settled and bid him 'good night'. Now, please explain *what* is going on."

"Ellen, to put it simply, Miska's life is in danger. But I am unsure at this moment just who is the threat—perhaps Lady Diere, or even Queen Mab—"

"What? Of the Dark Elves?" Ellen blurted.

"Yes, it is likely," the Sidhe confirmed. "You may as well get comfortable; this may take a while."

For the next hour, Leanan articulated her suspicions and concerns that something sinister involving the Realm of Dark Elves would impact the Unseelie Court, if not the Council of Realms itself. Clearly she suspected her home Realm of Shadow would be mistakenly implicated; and now, thanks to Boltar, the Realm of Were was in similar jeopardy. However, Miska and his story might be sufficient to prove otherwise.

Ellen asked a few questions, but for the most part, just listened.

When Leanan had finished, they sat quietly sipping their wine.

"So," Ellen began, "I am to hide Miska here, for how long? And just how many people know that he and Ivan are brothers? And more importantly, who else will know he's here?"

"Fair questions, all. " Leanan sighed. "Firstly, no one, other than me, knows he is here. Far too many now know that Miska and Ivan—Boltar—are brothers; and, that knowledge will only spread. Unfortunately, that is assuredly inevitable. Regrettably, I do not know how long he must be kept hidden, for I am not yet certain what game is afoot. But I *do* sense that the stakes are very high; the peace and balance of the Unseelie and Seelie Courts—perhaps even that of all eight Council Realms may be in jeopardy." Leanan downed most of her wine in one draught.

Ellen considered Leanan's words as she sipped from her own nearly full glass.

"I see, although I'll admit I may not fully appreciate all the political ramifications. So now, assuming that Miska is safe, what will you do next?" Ellen asked, reaching for the wine bottle.

"I must return to my castle and comply with the Council's request; I must release the body of Boltar to Queen Mab. I really have no choice. Then we shall see what happens. But I must be wary, for all is not well within my own realm."

"What do you mean?" Ellen probed as she topped off Leanan's glass.

Leanan paused and sipped, her gaze seemingly distracted.

"It is strange, Ellen, how problems within my House somehow involve you; I find that curious indeed."

Ellen simply shrugged. How was one supposed to answer that?

Leanan stared into her glass and sighed in resignation.

"Very well, Ellen, I will share with you some things you must keep to yourself."

"Such as?"

Leanan glanced around and leaned forward.

"You should know that I was instructed to prevent you from leaving my castle in the Realm of Shadow; but, I did not do so. More to the point, I did not see any value in detaining you and your friends, only potential problems. So, once you were reunited at my castle with your friend, Stacy, you were permitted to leave unhindered."

"Not quite *unhindered*—Gunther tried very hard to prevent our departure, followed us, and tried to employ force, as I told you."

"True, but not on my instructions. He believed he was acting on behalf of his mistress, the Lady Sabrina. He paid dearly for such initiative. He had not yet regained consciousness when I departed Shadow with Miska.

"But I must warn you—when he *does* sufficiently recover, notwithstanding the loss of an eye and severe scarring, Sabrina plans to bestow upon him the *Dark Gift,* raising him to the status of a *vampire lord.* Make no mistake, he will neither forgive nor forget those who caused his disfigurement. You and your friends have made a very dangerous enemy of Gunther."

Silence hung heavily between them. In that moment, Ellen sensed that her guest was unsettled and somehow hesitant—something about this warning?

"But that's not all, is it?" Ellen pressed. "There's more to it—isn't there?"

Leanan's shoulders slumped. "Alas, tis all too true. I objected, of course, to Gunther's proposed elevation. He is a very poor choice after all; quite obsessed with his mistress, given to emotional outbursts, and spitefully vindictive. Worst of all, he is not overly bright. He is even foolish enough to insist being called by his *true name* while serving as Sabrina's familiar.

"However, my concerns were generally ignored. I fear it is evident that my influence has suffered somewhat, no doubt as a result of my failure to follow the instructions of the senior-most elder of my House—"

"Ah, you mean," Ellen interrupted, "to stop us from leaving?"

"Precisely," the Sidhe admitted. "I should add that none within my House know of my visit here, or its purpose."

Ellen's surprise shone in her voice. "So, you intend to unravel the mystery of Ivan/Boltar *alone?*"

"No, not alone," Leanan assured her. "There are a few who share my concerns—well, at least one other whom out of necessity I have come to trust, Lord Addecus of the Were. But I think it would be best that you not know more at this point—perhaps later."

"Well, can you at least tell me if there are any other vampires here in my home realm, and whether or not they are involved in this *conspiracy?*"

Leanan's eyebrows rose. "That is insightful, Ellen; it may well be a conspiracy. But I do not know the identities of any other conspirators—not yet.

"Now, are there other vampires in your realm now? Possibly, but I think not; at least I know of none from Shadow. In fact, most of the wiser, more traditional of my kind vacated the Realm of Man by the middle of the twentieth century. By then mankind had developed methods of detection that were simply too efficient. Some occasionally visit, I am sure, but it is foolhardy in the extreme for them to *hunt,* especially since *hunting* in the Realm of Man is forbidden by Council decree. But then again, it happens."

"You said that the vast majority of folklore—*our* folklore—related to your kind was 'simply wrong', right?" Ellen probed. "So, what's wrong about it?"

Leanan shook her head. "Oh, child, where to begin? It would be easier to admit what is correct; and, that would be very little.

"In truth, we are not so dissimilar from you. We do have an aversion to sunlight; it is uncomfortable. Prolonged exposure can be deadly to some of us, as can fire, cardiac impalement, and gross dismemberment, to include decapitation. Nor do I know of any normal human who could survive such things."

"Wait—cardiac impalement? I thought the undead didn't even have heartbeats," Ellen blurted.

Leanan rolled her eyes. "Oh ye gods! *Undead* is an unfortunate term, and has been long corrupted. Consider this: undead quite literally means alive, does it not? By literal definition, even you are undead at this very moment. How the term came to refer only to vampire-kind is murky at best. I blame certain creative writers and Hollywood for persisting in such semantic slander. Ah, forgive me; I digress.

"Yes, we have hearts, and heartbeats. Admittedly, these beats are faint and slow by comparison to your own; but remember, our metabolisms are vastly different, as are our lifestyles."

"So," Ellen reasoned, "you're not immortal?"

"Of course not! We are very, very long lived—but not truly immortal."

"Wow, there's a lot we got wrong. What about mirrors? Do you cast reflections?"

Leanan shrugged. "We do cast reflections, even in silvered mirrors, or at least most of us do."

"Silver," remarked Ellen. "Yes, what about silver, and crosses and such?"

Leanan gave her a tired smile and shook her head. "More superstitions and misconceptions, I fear, perpetuated by some truly regrettable and cringe-worthy films.

"Silver is indeed the bane of most Were, but it has little to no effect on my kind. In fact, I am quite fond of silver jewelry. Then again, there are certain exceptions, like those few among us who are extremely well versed in the dark arts, and are capable of shape-changing."

"But I thought all vampires could change their shape," Ellen interjected. "At least, that's the popular folklore—you know, that they can use *black magic* or something, to change into bats or wolves, or even mist and smoke."

"Black magic?" Leanan chuckled. "How utterly pedestrian and judgmental! Forgive me, but I've not heard that term for some time.

"Ellen, magic is neither black nor white; it has no intrinsic morality. One need only look to the intent of the user to determine the nature of the specific spell—and even that observation is open to interpretation. Indeed, by what measure is an act of magic good or evil? Who is empowered to so judge?

Ah, but I digress once more—my apologies. May I trouble you for some more wine?"

Ellen carefully refilled her guest's glass, draining the bottle, and waited politely as Leanan sipped slowly.

Once more composed, the Sidhe continued.

"Where was I? Ah, yes, silver. You must understand, Ellen, that all vampires use what most would call magic to varying degrees. For example, with a few simple spells, many are capable of simple levitation, and even flight in some realms. All are capable of some level of defensive magic. However, only the most adept magic users among us are capable of changing form—a skill the Were enjoy from birth. And like the Were, these vampiric shape-changers become vulnerable to certain inherent perils of the metamorphosis—"

"Really? Like what?" interrupted Ellen.

"Well, there can be cumulative effects. For example, over protracted time the actual result of the *change* can appear somewhat less than complete; recognizable characteristics of the other form may linger as part of the new form. While rare, it is not unknown, particularly among the most senior elders of the Were, who are still capable of the metamorphosis but are distinctly hybrid in appearance. Lord Addecus, whom I mentioned previously, is one such Were elder. In man form he displays serpentine features; whereas, in snake form he can manifest human-like expressions.

"As you might imagine, such manifestations, this alteration in one's appearance, takes considerable time and a high number of metamorphic events—many, many changes. Vampires are certainly long-lived enough, but tend to be too vain to gamble with any degradation of their personal appearance. I know I would have no such interest."

Ellen shuddered. "Me neither! No thank you!"

Leanan nodded. "So, you see, alteration of one's appearance and the perils of silver—questionable trade-offs, in my opinion—may be the price paid by shape-changing vampires. These are the vampires who have issues with silvered mirrors. It is thought that their reflections are *swallowed* to some degree by the silver. But as I said, such vampires are very rare."

Ellen sipped gently at her wine, her thoughts cascading in turbulent comprehension. *There was so much to learn—so much to know. Whoa, I think I'm feeling this wine; I need to slow it down a bit—but I'm still so curious . . .*

"Well then, um, what about the crosses—you know, crucifixes?"

"Crucifixes?" Leanan paused, tilting her head. "Oh, you mean symbolic objects, perhaps talismans? Well, there *are* differences. A talisman is intended to hold, focus, or possibly transfer the power of an enchantment. Now, as for mere symbols of protection or faith, crosses and the like, they have no inherent protective value; unless, of course, like a talisman, they can hold a deliberately cast spell. However . . ."

"Please, go on," prompted Ellen.

"You should understand that the strength of any individual's commitment to a cause or belief is effectively a manifestation of personal power—or personal magic, if you prefer. And sometimes, if that power is focused and channeled through a symbolic object, or even a talisman, it can have an effect—possibly quite a powerful effect. Of course, each case is different."

"That makes a sort of sense," Ellen acknowledged, "but does that hold true for things like good luck tokens—you know, like a horseshoe over a doorway or finding a four-leafed clover?"

"A horse? Wouldn't the horse eat the clover?" Leanan smiled. "Oh my, forgive me; I couldn't resist!"

Ellen pursed her lips, the corners of her mouth turning up. "Glad to see you have a sense of humor. So, what about good luck tokens?"

Once more composed, Leanan tilted her head and laid a finger along her jaw.

"Good luck tokens and belief? Hmm, I had not thought about that as such, or in those terms, but I see no reason to discount the possibility of a link. Although, there are those who might suggest that the *finding* of such a token might be subtle yet deft manipulation at the hands of the Fates. Whereas, the *use* of a horseshoe—typically an object of *cold iron*—is said to have a more ominous origin."

"Really? How is that?"

"There are certain denizens of Faerie who have an inherent aversion to cold iron. They are the more mischievous types who find great amusement in the playing of tricks and annoying others, especially in the Realm of Man. Mankind soon discovered that the presence of cold iron tended to keep the pranksters at bay—*good luck indeed!* So, a common object of cold iron, a discarded horseshoe for example, became such a token, displayed above a doorway thus barring entrance to those unwelcome miscreants. Of course, this happened a very long time ago."

"It must have," agreed Ellen. "Good luck tokens and charms have been around throughout recorded history."

"To be precise," Leanan cautioned, "*charms* are, or were, actually spells attached to a talisman or amulet. Oh, I know that over the ages the term has come to refer to the object; however, the genesis of the term, its intended reference, was to the enchantment, typically a minor spell of some sort. No doubt the original meaning has faded and been forgotten in the fullness of time."

"That's interesting," noted Ellen. "Do all spells fade?"

"Most do, with time. However, some are extremely powerful and may be considered, more or less, effectively perpetual—or at least such are their *effects.* Unless, of course, they are deliberately altered or tampered with, a most dangerous proposition in any sense."

"I can imagine," Ellen mused aloud. "But that aside, I must admit I'm more curious about *you.*"

"Me?" Leanan remarked in surprise. "What do you mean?"

"I think we got off track a bit. We were discussing the nature of vampires. The magic is fascinating and all, but I'm curious about the more mundane stuff."

"Mundane?"

"Yeah, like what about eating and drinking? Well, I mean, here you are, drinking wine—I see we need another bottle—and I think you like it."

"Oh, I do," Leanan readily admitted. "I like it very much—and no, I am not subject to inebriation. The taste pleases me; however, I gain no sustenance from it, nor would I from common foods. Yes, I can eat if I so please, but it would be an empty, futile gesture that would require digestion and ultimately elimination."

Ellen winced. "Oh, sorry, didn't mean to go there."

Leanan gave a little shake of her head and waved a hand dismissively.

"So, it has to be the blood of the living," Ellen deduced, removing a dark *merlot* from the wine rack. "But blood, like this wine, is mostly water; so, that means—oh, never mind."

Leanan raise a lone eyebrow in mild disapproval and waggled her empty glass. "Can we move along, please, Ellen?"

"Yeah, sorry, lemme get this open—ah, there we go. Your glass, please?"

Leanan smiled warily, placed her empty glass on the counter.

Ellen poured, ignoring her own glass. *But not for me; it seems I can't keep up with you—and I'm not gonna try. Unlike you, I get a little tipsy after my third glass.*

Sliding the refilled glass forward, Ellen nodded. "There you go. Now, bear with me, Leanan, I'm still a bit confused. I was under the impression that all vampires drink blood, yet I have heard of something called *psychic vampires.* Can you help me to understand?"

Ellen thought her guest seemed to be wrestling with a personal decision.

"Ellen, whatever I tell you in this regard must be held in the strictest confidence; only you may know, unless I tell you otherwise. I will have your oath on this."

Ellen paused momentarily in thought, then agreed. "Very well. By the Powers of Air and Earth, Fire and Water, I, Ellen Doyle, promise not to share this information, without your approval. Will that suffice?"

"Admirably so," Leanan responded, and sipped deeply from her refreshed glass.

"Well?" Ellen prompted.

"Please understand," Leanan raised a cautionary finger, "that divulging this much information, even amongst younger vampires, is strongly discouraged, and largely prohibited outside our culture. However, I have often found myself somewhat frustrated with such inherent institutional paranoia, so much so that I have publicly questioned the efficacy of the prohibition.

"As might have been expected, raising such an issue did not exactly endear me to certain elders of my kind. Their rationale is simple; it serves to keep others from any comprehension of vampiric nature, thereby keeping the populace ignorant and frightened. Do you see?"

"Sure, I get it. Accurate information may disclose, um, vulnerabilities, right?"

"Precisely," Leanan acknowledged. "Right now, I need you as an ally, Ellen. I must trust you—as you must trust me. There really is no other way."

"If you'll keep your oath," Ellen declared, "I'll keep mine."

"Very well," Leanan confirmed and sat back.

"Ah, where to begin? Ellen, as I have already said, you may be surprised to learn that we, you and I, are not so dissimilar. You survive on the energy you derive from food and drink, your sustenance, do you not?"

"Yeah, so?"

"Have you ever considered the fact that everything you consume *is* or *was* alive? Even water teems with life. It is quite true; the food of life *is* life—or *life energy*. Do you understand?"

"Well, I never thought about it in those terms," Ellen admitted, "but yes, I do understand."

"Then you must understand that we vampires are also sustained by *life energy*. Most acquire it through the drinking of blood. The blood of the living is *flush* with life energy. Yet, to take too much can result in the death of the donor.

"Blood is not the only means to transfer life energy; some take it during sex—the incubus and succubus for example. Some among the more adept and skilled, typically the senior elders, can draw life energy directly from the living by simple touch. Of course, among the very rarest are those few who can sustain themselves by merely being in sufficient proximity to mortals, or even other vampires. Yes, there are those, the most powerful, who can feed off of us at their whim. My mother, Lamia, is such a one—"

"Your *mother?* You were *born* a vampire?" Ellen blurted, and just had to ask, "You weren't *turned,* uh, so to speak?"

Leanan's face clouded; she pursed her lips. She tapped her empty glass with a long and elegant scarlet fingernail, prompting Ellen to pour another refill.

"I find *turned* a distasteful term." Leanan scowled, and held up her hand to forestall Ellen's apology.

"Yes, I was born a vampire, a long time ago. No, do not ask—I will keep *some* secrets," she insisted, smiling wryly.

Chagrined, Ellen shrugged. "Sorry, I meant no offense. I'm just trying to understand."

"Hmmph, *turned* . . . so be it. Occasionally, a person, a mortal human, is given the *Dark Gift* through the transfer of a vampire's blood. That person then goes through a protracted transformation process that can last as long as several days and nights. Reborn, in a sense, as a *fledgling*, and experiencing an unfamiliar and demanding thirst, each newly made vampire must be taught how to acquire sustenance, *life energy*.

"The drinking of blood is the first lesson; the other techniques and their commensurate disciplines follow in time. However, not all new vampires rise above their baser natures. The level of individual skill in the taking of life energy is dependent upon that person's ability to assimilate a new lifestyle, and the personal dedication to improvement. By far, most fledglings succumb to the seductive lure of blood drinking and never bother to perfect any of the more advanced techniques; whereas, those born into the culture have a more *structured education*."

"I see," Ellen murmured, mildly repulsed, yet nonetheless fascinated. "So, anytime a vampire takes too much life energy, no matter the technique, death of the donor can result? And those who receive the *Dark Gift,* as opposed to those who are, uh, born into the culture, are more likely to be predominately blood drinkers?"

"Yes, that is correct," Leanan agreed. "But you must understand that all vampires enjoy the drinking of blood, notwithstanding that many need not do it to survive. And it is those who can drain and consume someone's life energy without the shedding of blood—and routinely do so, via contact or proximity—who are considered *psychic vampires*."

Ellen barely managed to suppress a shudder.

"Ellen, you asked earlier if there were other vampires in your realm, and I told you that I knew of none from Shadow. Know that not all vampiric beings reside within the Realm of Shadow. Examples can be found native to almost all realms; and, I do not refer to just the Council Realms."

"Do you mean, that even here . . ?" Ellen hedged.

"It would be rather naïve of you to think that your realm has not produced something of a native equivalent," Leanan cautioned.

Ellen felt her mind opening to the possibility, as the Sidhe explained further.

"Your human history is rife with examples; and, I mean beyond your mythology and folklore. The historical legacy of humanity has been quite sanguine, indeed. Surely, you do not hope to blame such blatant carnage entirely on denizens of Shadow?"

"No, not at all. I am well aware of mankind's capability for cruelty and horror," Ellen replied meekly.

Leanan shrugged. "I do not mean to imply that your *native vampires* are all bloody rapacious fiends—some, no doubt. But in my experience in this realm, I have met more than a few individuals of very unusual charisma, magnetic personalities who thrive upon the energies of their devoted followers. In my view, that is a rather esoteric and quite advanced technique, in other words, a very high level of psychic vampirism."

Ellen felt a sudden chill. More questions bubbled up in her mind but she was instinctively reluctant to give them voice. However, her curiosity got the better of her.

"Leanan, just how advanced are *you?* I mean, uh, in terms of the techniques?"

Leanan looked into Ellen's eyes, and responded in a dead voice without rancor or pity.

"Trust me, Ellen, you do not want to know."

PADRAIC THE ROGUE SQUATTED in the solitary cone of light and started going through Salidar's pack. Alone for the moment, he knew that *she* could arrive at any time. This was Lady Diere's favored location for clandestine meetings, and if his memory served, the occasional tryst.

As he rummaged through the knapsack, his disappointment grew. He could find nothing of intelligence value here; some clothing, a cat mask, dagger, traveler's hardtack, water flask, and a folded cloak. Salidar apparently traveled light. Nonetheless, his things could not be left aboard the *Xanthippe*;

had they been found, the ruse may have unraveled prematurely and their plan fail.

Her voice was cool and clear, and lightly veiled in subtle sarcasm.

"Oh my, are your circumstances so poor that one of such esteemed status is reduced to pilfering through another's property?"

He winced at her tone, and sadly shook his head; but, he did not rise.

"Well, I see you still never miss an opportunity to be petty, my dear Lady Diere. These belong to Salidar, who served you—and me—rather well, but was regrettably left behind."

"I am aware of that, Padraic. He was acting on my instructions."

Padraic began to slowly replace Salidar's things back in the pack, casually avoiding looking at her. "As I understand it, he was to deliver your *invitation,* and remain in the Realm of Mer to await your pleasure. Is that not correct?"

"It is. Why are you even concerned—what difference does it make?" She made no effort to hide the smugness in her voice. "You are here, now, as I intended."

He shrugged and glanced up.

"I can see you do not understand. I was in a bit of a bind, as it were—pirates, bent upon collecting this absurd bounty. He found me and helped me escape. He planned on escaping himself at a later time. He has earned my gratitude; I do not forget those who help me."

Diere smiled thinly. "Then it is *I* to whom your gratitude should flow, for *I* sent Salidar to find you, and aid in any escape if necessary. Oh yes, I will have my ring back, if you please."

Padraic studied Diere for a moment. The Dark Elf loomed above him, resplendent in a sleek black velvet gown that seemed to shimmer in blue and violet highlights. A front panel of midnight blue silk dropped from an elaborately braided bodice of black lace. A sable hooded capelet rode her delicate shoulders, dropping nearly to her wrists. An onyx necklace adorned her pale throat, a stunning counterpoise to her darkly intense eyes.

Standing slowly, he faced her. At almost the same height, they were nearly eye to eye.

"In that case," he said evenly, dropping the topaz ring into her open hand, "I am most grateful for your *intercession*. But now, tell me why I am here."

"Oh, Padraic," she cooed coyly, dropping her chin to her shoulder. "Cannot old friends just visit with one another?"

"Come now, Diere—we both know there is a reason for this meeting. What is it?"

"Do not be so brusque, my dear, there is really no need. After all, Padraic, we once had something *special* between us."

"That was years ago. What do you want?"

"Do you not grow weary of constantly being hounded? Everyone speaks of the escalating price on your head. You do know it is not just Duke Briar who would see you brought down—or your head on a platter! Besmirching the honor of his duchess embarrassed him no end—he is still livid! And worse, you have eschewed swearing fealty to either court of Faerie, so you have neither patron nor protection. What sort of life is that?"

Padraic sighed, and let his shoulders drop in apparent resignation. *Hmm, I believe I might know where this is going. Tis best that I play along and learn whatever I can.*

"Aye, there is some truth in that. It makes for an *interesting* life; but, it does grow a bit tiresome."

"Padraic, hear me," she leaned slightly forward, her eyes zealously bright, "I will soon be in a position of considerable authority and *power*. Do not ask, for I can say no more at this moment. Suffice to say that I will be able to offer you both patronage and protection—of such a nature that none would *dare* to offer offense!"

"Diere, what are you talking about? Why would you think I need, *or want,* such patronage and protection?"

"Oh come now, Padraic," she said reasonably. "We both know there was a time when no one would have been capable of making you a prisoner; and yet, it has happened. While you persist in tawdry affairs and seductions, the price on your head continues to rise, as does the interest in your eventual, and inevitably tragic capture. It has become entertaining theater among the Council Realms. Or perhaps you actually want to spend the rest of your life running and looking over your shoulder?"

"What do you want from me?" he asked, with a deliberate hint of defeat in his voice. "What must I do to benefit from your *proposed benevolence?"*

"Not that much, really," Diere said coyly, as she seductively stroked the sable edge of her capelet. "Merely swear fealty to me, and assume your rightful place at my side—as consort."

Stunned, he stiffened. *"What? Swear fealty? Consort?* Diere, what are you planning? You know I have always resisted swearing fealty to either of the Faerie Courts—and I would not do so now!"

"Padraic, dearest," she soothed, with more than a trace of condescension, "You are not *listening.* I said you would swear fealty to *me*—not the Faerie Courts. Trust me—you will come to realize it would be well to your advantage."

"Diere, I cannot fathom what you are up to. But I can understand that it must be significant; after all, the swearing of fealty *to an individual* smacks of royal prerogative. But I am intrigued. What would be expected of me in this role of *consort?*"

She turned her face slightly away. "Being at my side, as would be expected, at certain times and functions . . . and in my bed, when I require."

He smirked. But his brows knit as she jabbed a stiffened finger at his face.

"I am no fool, Padraic! I know you only too well! You can still have your little dalliances—provided you are *discreet*. I am sure you can understand and appreciate my point."

Padraic was beginning to understand very well, very well indeed. However, he would need more time to confirm his suspicions. For now he needed to barter some sort of delay.

"Hmm . . . As I said, I must admit that I am intrigued by your offer; it is certainly becoming more attractive to me. I need time to consider. Surely, you can understand?"

"Oh, I do indeed," Diere responded. "But take not too long in accepting my offer. I would have your answer by the waxing crescent moon—five days hence—no later."

Padraic nodded in agreement. "Within five days then."

But Diere was not yet through with him, and she raised an elegant finger in afterthought.

"One parting consideration, my dear Padraic . . . Even if you do not fully appreciate the scope of my patronage and protection at this time, you should consider complying with my request for the sake of your *daughter*. My benevolence could extend to her as well. And of late, I understand she could use some protection."

"Daughter? I have no offspring!" exclaimed Padraic, clearly shocked.

"Oh, do you not?" She snorted spitefully. "It would seem that you should keep better track of your sordid little affairs! When you deserted me to have your fun with that mousy little woman in the Realm of Man, you fathered a child on her! But then, how would you know? You disappeared into the Realm of Mer shortly thereafter."

Padraic could not even speak. His mouth hung open, and his mind raced. *A daughter? In the Realm of Man? But by whom? Millie? Yes, it must be Millie—it had to be! How long ago—a quarter century? Is all of this true?*

One glance and it was clear to him that Diere took great satisfaction in his discomfort and shock. She appeared absolutely delighted that he had not known.

However, her tone was even and emotionless.

"I would wager that you are now wrestling with the possibility of truth in this matter. I can assure you that it is so. You have a grown daughter; and furthermore, she is the new Steward of the Grand Portal of the Realm of Man. Her name is Ellen Doyle; she may be in danger. It seems there were attempts upon her life, prior to her ascension to the Stewardship. I can offer her my protection as well—*if* you accept my terms."

His thoughts whirling, Padraic strove for calm and found his voice.

"Lady Diere, you have given me much to consider. I must take the time to contemplate what this all means. Tell me, please; the Steward, is she in any danger at this moment?"

"I am not certain. Perhaps not at this moment; but who can say what lies in the future? It may not be wise to procrastinate in making your decision."

"I shall not," Padraic assured her.

"Five days, Padraic, within five days."

CH 2

THE STATELY HOUSE STOOD dark and quiet on the bluff overlooking the Toledo Bend reservoir. The merest sliver of the new crescent moon cast feeble light on the placid water and the darkly shrouded landscape surrounding the stone and cypress home. A light breeze rustling through the trees served as counterpoint to the nightly chorus of tree frogs and crickets.

A transit globe softly *popped* into existence on the front lawn; the nearby insects went silent. Two hooded figures, short in stature, came forth, turned to face the orb, and watched as it faded into invisibility.

Turning their attention toward the house, they began to approach the front entrance. They didn't exactly *walk;* they exhibited no gait, but rather appeared to *glide*, almost as if they were not in contact with the ground. Their long dark robes smoothly skimmed across the uneven grass.

They floated up to the front porch and stopped before the stout cypress door. One produced a short, yet elaborately carved staff from beneath his robe and used it to firmly rap three times upon the door. They waited patiently.

After a few moments, a pair of porch lamps flared to life. Curtains in the windows to either side of the door were sequentially pulled slightly to one side as someone within peered at the visitors from either vantage point. The light from the lamps did little to disclose any details. The visitors' faces were obscured within the shadows of their hoods; however, it could be clearly seen that their hands were gloved.

The sounds of sliding bolts heralded the opening of the thick cypress door. The interior of the house remained dark in sharp contrast to the illuminated porch. Ling, attired in black, stood at the threshold with little more than her face visible, a stoic, yet cautious mask suspended in the gloom.

She did not speak; there was no need. She recognized who these visitors were—*bogies*, a type of highly intelligent hobgoblin who served the Council.

They were messengers, for the most part, but had been known to serve in other capacities as well. She knew they would formally announce their intentions. The Council was deeply steeped in protocol; its messengers were expected to follow it to the letter.

The robed figure without the staff decreed in a guttural yet even voice, "On behalf of the Council, we seek the man, George Papadolis of the Realm of Man."

Ling nodded once and said, "One moment, if you please."

She stepped back into the darkened room and found George almost within reach, wearing a robe and slippers. He held a short shotgun in his hands.

"You heard?" she asked. "You were expecting them?"

George rubbed sleep from his eyes and yawned before he answered her.

"Aah-yahh . . . Sorry, yeah, I expected something—just not this late at night." He winced at his watch and mumbled, "Damn, it's just past midnight. Yeah, I'll see them. Give me a minute to get dressed. Turn on some lights; and then let `em in."

He started to turn around, but Ling grabbed his arm.

"Respectfully, sir," she whispered firmly. "Do not let them cross your threshold. Go to them, on the porch, and conduct such business there. The sooner they are gone, the better."

"Keep `em outside?"

"Yes, sir." She pointed to the shotgun. "You won't need that; I am here."

He stared at his bodyguard in the dim room, grinned and nodded.

"All right, don't let `em in; keep `em on the porch. Just give me a minute. You can tell `em I'm coming."

He disappeared, headed for his room.

MOMENTS LATER GEORGE returned, dressed in slacks and an open shirt. He slipped a small automatic pistol into his waistband at the small of his back, and then nodded for Ling to let him pass.

He stepped out on the porch and was vaguely surprised to see that he towered over the visitors—they stood only slightly taller than waist-high. Their faces were still not visible, deeply shrouded in their dark hoods. A quick glance over his shoulder assured him that Ling stood nearby, just inside the threshold.

He faced the diminutive pair, and cleared his throat.

"Ahem, I am George Papadolis. You wish to see me?"

"Indeed, good sir. We serve the Council. If you are truly he, you are summoned to appear before the Council upon the fullness of the moon."

The speaker produced a small silvery cylinder from beneath his robe, twisted an elaborate jeweled cap on one end, and opened the tube. A small scroll slipped out. Holding the scroll upright, he continued to speak.

"This is your summons, and an agenda of the meeting. Hold out your left hand—and be very still."

George found this a bit ominous, but he complied.

The bogie seized his fingers with surprising strength and bent them slightly down, thus splaying his palm open wide. The other bogie twisted his short staff somewhere near its middle and separated the rod into two pieces; a gleaming silver blade was revealed.

Before George could react, the blade flashed twice across his palm. Blood welled from the shallow cuts that formed an "X" in his outstretched hand. He yelped and jerked as bright pain seared across the wounds.

Nonetheless, his captor did not release his cramped fingers. Instead, the bogie began a barely audible incantation. The other messenger sheathed the blade, rendering the staff whole once more. He then took the bejeweled end cap and pressed its base into the blood pooling in George's palm. Lifting the cap, he placed the scroll in George's outstretched captive hand.

As his fingers were finally released; they immediately grasped the scroll—an involuntary reflex.

The two bogies stepped back. One replaced the end cap upon the now empty silvery cylinder and tucked the tube away under his robe. The other tucked the staff under his robe. They regarded George in silence.

George forced himself to open his wounded hand. The scroll was stained with his blood; but, the only evidence of the cuts was thin white lines of scar tissue—his hand had already healed. His jaw dropped in astonishment; words failed him.

One of the bogies looked up slightly, raised a gloved finger, and pointed at the scroll.

As George's eyes followed, he thought to steal a glance within the shadowed hood. He instantly wished he hadn't. Twin flat reflections of a pale phosphorescent green shone deep within a narrow skull, and the tip of a long and sharply angular nose twitched as it receded into shadow.

The other bogie spoke, drawing George's attention back to the scroll.

"Good sir, you have received the summons and agenda; we have your blood in receipt. In a fortnight, after the sun sets and in the fullness of the moon, draw a drop of blood from your left thumb and hold the scroll in your left hand. Focus on imagining a transit globe in your mind. A spell now contained within the scroll, and activated by your blood, will produce the globe to transport you to the site of the Council meeting. This will only work for you, and only at that time. You are to travel and attend unaccompanied, without escort or companion. This is a Council requirement. Do you understand?"

"Uh . . . Yeah, I understand."

Without another word, the bogies turned and descended from the porch. George watched wide-eyed as they literally *floated* away, disappearing into the velvet darkness beyond the front lawn.

Moments later, a soft *pop* seemed to come from the same direction, only to be slowly replaced by the tentative refrains of the normal nocturnal chorus of insects.

George returned to the front parlor, staring at the scroll in his hand.

Ling stood to one side, expressionless and inscrutable as always. She locked the door and extinguished the porch lights.

"May I suggest, sir," she offered quietly, "that we not speak of this to the others? And that you secure that scroll somewhere safe?"

"What? Oh, yes . . . of course," he responded, obviously distracted. "I will; but then, I'm going back to bed. Keep an eye on things. I don't think we need any more visitors tonight."

"Of course . . . Good night, sir."

AS THE MORNING SUNLIGHT warmed the Chantilly Parish Sheriff's Department CID squad room, Hawk strode directly to the brew pot and poured his first cup of office coffee. Blacker than crude oil, he guessed that the captain had brewed this pot; the boss just loved strong coffee, and could drink it all day.

Once at his desk, Hawk saw Trey exit the captain's office, a stack of files in one hand and a steaming mug in the other.

"Morning, Hawk," boomed Trey, good-naturedly, as he placed his burden upon his partner's desk. "Nice of you to join us.

"Listen, we got the lab results back on that stuff in that vial you got from your *source*. It is definitely the same concoction in the syringe we found in the failed attempt on the life of Ellen Doyle at the hospital. Hold on a second.

Oh yeah, here it is; 'digitalis, amanita muscaria, and mertensia virginica'. So, it appears that your *source* might be involved in that open case. Care to tell me about it?"

"Sure, a little later," Hawk replied, casting his eyes around the squad room as other detectives milled about. "What else have we got this morning?"

Trey plopped down in his chair and opened another open case file.

"Ah, the *casino homicides* . . . Well, it looks like our esteemed CSI colleague, Cassie, found the e-mail links she was looking for between our decapitated hit-woman, Suzi Origami, and the U.S. Marshals' fugitive parole violator, Theodore Rasmussen, AKA 'Teddy Pots'."

"I'm sure Todd and Willis will be glad to hear that," Hawk remarked. "That'll further corroborate their information, and should help their federal fugitive case on Teddy."

"Yeah," agreed Trey, opening another file, "although Cassie hasn't decrypted all the text just yet."

Handing Hawk a pair of mug shots, he sipped from his mug and pointed to the photos.

"Now, in the original *Doyle case*, behold our suspects' family portraits, Wilson 'Bubba' Cutler and Ignatius 'Iggy' Simpson, complements of the New Orleans PD.

"The first attempt on the life of Ellen Doyle—the pickup truck and taxi collision, and subsequent arson on the cab that cost the driver, Orlando 'Ratso' Ratalondo, his life—is now part of an assault/attempted murder/arson/homicide package to be presented to the grand jury. The District Attorney has decided to move forward and charge Bubba and Iggy with Ratso's death—even though we don't have the body. Mel was right; the DA thinks the tissue samples taken on the scene by CSI will suffice to convince a grand jury to return an indictment."

Hawk swallowed a mouthful of coffee and nodded appreciatively as his partner continued.

"However, in the Perry Wilkerson case, due to the body's state of decomposition, it seems the DA might have to consider waiting on the DNA ID confirmation before seeking an indictment. He was told it might be several weeks to a month or more. He wasn't too happy with that; he might change his mind. I wouldn't be surprised if he had a press release already formatted and ready to go, you know?

"Anyway, the last thing the captain said was that we should go ahead and do our notifications in the Wilkerson case today. There's no next of kin, so that leaves his former law partner, Claude Fornier, and his former defrauded client's surviving family, which means your friend, Ellen Doyle."

"Right, she's Maude Delafaire's niece. I should call her first," Hawk said, "before we go out there."

Trey nodded. "Good idea—you do that, and I'll call Claude Fornier's office. Sheriff asked that we go by there first. He wants to go over there once we've made the official visit. You know he and Claude pretty much grew up with Perry; they were childhood friends. It'll be tough on both of them."

Hawk grimaced. Death notifications are among a detective's least desirable duties. Someone's death has been confirmed; the next of kin, or person closest to the deceased, those with a need to know, must be officially notified. You can never be sure how people will react to the news. Emotions can run the gamut, from silent shock and mute acceptance to shuddering hysterics. It was never easy, for the bereaved *or* the police officer, but it had to be done.

THERE WAS AN AWKWARD moment in Claude Fornier's office when Trey and Hawk softly delivered the sad news.

They had begun by asking Claude and his long-time secretary, Miss Mavis, to take seats on a couch in the quiet office. Miss Mavis must have anticipated the reason for this official visit; she began to tear up even before the detectives disclosed the information. She, too, had known Perry Wilkerson for most of his life.

Upon hearing the inevitable, Claude offered Miss Mavis his handkerchief, wrapped a beefy arm around her slight shoulders and did his best to comfort her. Even his eyes reddened as he sighed in resignation.

It seemed to the detectives that the news did not register so much as a shock, but rather the complete and final loss of any hope, however slight. It clearly took its toll on both Claude and the fragile Miss Mavis.

Claude assured Trey and Hawk that all would be well. "I'll stay with Miss Mavis, and see that she gets home safely."

"The sheriff will be visiting shortly, Claude," Trey advised. "So, we'll be going. You have our deepest condolences."

As they approached their cruiser, they saw Sheriff Frank Tatum walking down the street. The big man's stride was noticeably listless. They acknowledged each other soundlessly as the saddened man turned and resolutely entered the law firm's office.

THE DETECTIVES DROVE in silence for most of the ride to Delafaire Farm. Death notifications tend to engender a lingering sense of disquiet, a harsh reminder of one's own mortality that clings unbidden, clouding the mind with the inevitability of death. The dismal mood hung about the car like an uninvited passenger.

Finally, never taking his eyes from the road, Hawk spoke, breaking the grip of the morose spell.

"Damn, does it ever get any easier? I guess maybe it shouldn't. I hope I never get that callous."

Trey sighed in agreement and stared out the passenger window.

"Yeah, I know what you mean. I've had to make more than enough notifications, and the truth is that it doesn't really matter what the cause of death is—violence, traffic accident, suicide, natural causes, whatever—it never gets any easier.

"But I'll tell you this; the ones I find the hardest are when the victim is a child. Those get to me the most."

Hawk paled at the thought. "Oh man, I haven't had to deal with that yet. I hope I never do."

"Me, too," Trey concurred, "for your sake; but, if you're in this job long enough . . ."

"Yeah, I know." Hawk could barely suppress an involuntary shudder.

Staring out the windshield, Trey added, "Well, we only have one more notification to make this morning. It shouldn't be too bad with your Miss Doyle; she's never even met Perry Wilkerson."

"Yeah, she's fine, uh—*should* be fine. I mean, uh, I *hope* she'll be fine." Hawk stumbled over his own tongue.

Trey smiled. "You sure are spending a lot of time with her, aren't you, youngster? You know, you should be careful; she *is* the victim of a crime *and* a potential witness. There could be an inherent ethics issue here, not to mention certain departmental regulations. You know what I mean?"

Hawk was quiet for a few minutes. Trey had made a valid point; it was both unprofessional and unethical to get involved with the victim or a potential witness during the investigation.

But he was torn—there were extenuating circumstances involved, to say the least.

Trey changed the subject. "So, on another note, is this a good time to tell me about your '*source*'? You know—where you got that vial that you gave to Sgt. Melancon on our road trip to New Orleans to have his CSI techs analyze?"

The question did not make Hawk feel any better; it just reminded him of the layers of secrecy with which he felt burdened. He knew he owed his partner some sort of explanation—he had to tell him *something*.

"Yeah, okay . . . Let me describe a *hypothetical* situation. Let's suppose that this guy's name is *Gunther*, and he's not from around here—or anywhere even close to here. He's not real cooperative; in fact, he's really pretty hostile toward me. Maybe he wouldn't exactly *give* me the vial; I would sort of have to *take* it. But as it happens, suppose he was fixing to hurt someone, who was defenseless at the time, so I sort of stopped him, and then got the vial from him—like *disarming* him. You follow?"

"Hmm, go on," Trey prompted.

"And, well, he was unconscious when I left. I gave him first aid, of course; but, I did leave him there. The problem is that it all happened outside of our jurisdiction—*way outside* our jurisdiction, so to speak."

Trey cleared his throat. "Well, that certainly is an interesting *hypothetical* set of circumstances, Detective, especially since the CSI analysis matches that of the substance recovered from the syringe in that incident where Ellen Doyle appears to have been targeted while a patient at the hospital. I'm not sure what to make of it—*hypothetically*—or that I want to hear any more at this point."

Hawk winced and glanced askance at his partner, who was smiling wryly.

This conversation was far from over; and, they both knew it.

Trey pointed down the road and effectively changed the subject once again.

"There's the turnoff for Delafaire Farm."

Hawk turned into the drive and stopped while Trey got out and opened the gate. At least Ellen was keeping the gate closed, he thought. They drove the rest of the way in silence, enveloped in the healing majesty of the old forest.

ELLEN WAS LOUNGING on the porch, reading the ad inserts from the Sunday paper, and nursing a mug of coffee, with the dogs lounging at her feet, when Trey and Hawk arrived.

"Welcome gentlemen! Can I offer fresh coffee?"

"Coffee? Yes, ma'am," Trey answered grinning as they climbed the front steps.

"This way," she offered, pulling the screen door open and smiling at Hawk.

FRESH MUGS STEAMING, they sat around the kitchen table and talked. All the while, Hawk couldn't take his eyes off her.

As Trey had predicted, Ellen took the news of Perry Wilkerson's death in stride. She expressed polite concern for his family and close friends, of course, but she was otherwise unaffected. After all, Hawk reminded himself, this was the lawyer who had persistently stolen funds from her unaware aunt.

"The other reason we are here," Trey explained, "is to keep you informed of the investigation into the incident in which you were injured when you first arrived in LaBorde a month ago. Do the names *Wilson Cutler* and *Ignatius Simpson* mean anything to you?"

Her brow drawn in puzzlement, Ellen shook her head.

"No, I can't say they do. Who are they?"

"How about some nicknames, *Bubba* and *Iggy*?" Trey pressed.

"Nope, sorry. Are those the nicknames of the same two you first asked about?"

"Yes. We have evidence that these two men are directly responsible for the collision in which you were injured, and a man lost his life. We have secured warrants for their arrest charging them both with the attempt on your life and the death of the cab driver. You should understand that at some point you may be called upon to testify in court."

"Oh, I fully understand," Ellen assured him, "and I have no problem testifying."

Trey smiled. "Somehow, I had no doubt that you would do so. Thank you for your time, and your hospitality. Your coffee is much mo' better than what we have available in our squad room, I guarantee!"

He winked at Hawk, who could only smile.

"Why thank you," she responded with a smile. "Would you care for some more?"

"Thank you, but no. We really have to be getting back to the office. I have a pile of reports to review, and my young partner here has a few to write. So, we'll bid you a good afternoon."

"I'll walk out with you," she said as she rose from the table.

As they made their way through the house, Ellen put her hand on Hawk's arm and asked softly, "Could you call me later, or maybe come by after work? I'm going to fix some red beans and rice for supper, if you don't have plans. We need to *talk.*"

Before he could respond, she tightened her grip, bringing him to a halt in the front hallway, while Trey proceeded onto the front porch.

"Listen," she whispered hastily, "Lady Leanan showed up here a few nights ago—*with Miska!* She asked me to hide him here because his life is in danger. He's staying at the cabin. Look, we *really* need to talk. So, please come over for supper, okay?"

"Uh . . . Yeah, of course, I will. Can I bring anything?" he asked as she released his arm.

"Nope, just yourself. You'd better go—Trey's already outside."

"I'll call you when I'm ready to leave the office," he assured her, and then added, "Be careful."

She smiled and nodded her assent.

He smiled in return, fighting the urge to kiss her, and crossed the porch.

She stood on the threshold holding the screen door open and called out, "See you later!"

Hawk waved as he descended the porch steps to catch up to Trey who was already waiting patiently at the car.

As they strapped on their seat belts Trey said, "Hawk, I'm only going to say this once more. You'd best be careful; that young lady is sweet on you. I know you're mighty fond of her. But you have to keep it professional—at least as long as she's a witness. Understand?"

"Yeah," Hawk sighed. "I know you're right. So, let's hurry up and catch these guys!"

"Now, that, young man, is the proper attitude. There may be hope for you yet."

IN THE MINISTRY BUILDING in the Realm of Storm Haven, Padraic the Rogue sat before the Guildmaster's wide desk and idly swirled the brandy in his glass to absorb the warmth of his palm. He stared across the wooden expanse at the Guildmaster who leaned back in his chair and steepled his fingers.

No gloves hid the Guildmaster's calluses and scarred knuckles, the hands of a man who had either known a lifetime of hard yet skilled labor, or combat—perhaps both. Reaching forward he scooped up his own brandy glass, swirled and slowly sipped the fiery amber liquid. The hood of his robe still hid his face behind a shimmering pattern of iridescence.

The two friends regarded each other in silent communion.

Padraic sipped from his glass and sighed. He could contain the question no longer.

"So, even as Guildmaster you never knew?"

"No, I did not. I gave up trying to keep track of your escapades long ago, my friend. Even the amusement of a fine bawdy tale fades if told too often. To be painfully honest, I am as surprised as you appear to be. Are you certain it is true?"

"Aye, I can sense the truth of it. I just cannot believe that I was never told, or somehow never learned of the truth until now. I should be more careful, and pay more attention to what is happening."

"Oh, now *there's* an understatement," the Guildmaster chuckled. "I have met her, you know—"

"What? You have? When? What can you tell me?" Padraic was overly insistent.

"Patience, old friend . . . I must admit that it warms my heart to see you so concerned. I was worried for a moment that your empathy, and perhaps even your conscience, may have atrophied entirely. Forgive me, but I am finding just a bit of humorous irony in this situation—after all, you never struck me as the paternal type."

Padraic frowned. "Please try to contain your unbridled amusement. I would much prefer that you enlighten me."

"Oh, very well," the Guildmaster acceded. "She visited about ten days ago, at my invitation. I intended to take her measure, for she is the new Steward."

The Guildmaster swirled his glass about and downed the last of his brandy. Staring across the desk at his old friend, he nodded once.

"Padraic, you should be very proud. She is a fine young woman; very intelligent, quick of mind, and quite pretty. She has the knack of seeing to the heart of a matter with apparently little effort.

"I sensed a determination in her, a sense of purpose. She has barely begun her tenure in the office of Steward and has already traversed the Realm of Shadow—at night, no less, in search of a missing friend. She is coming into her own, and grows in skill, craft, and wisdom. You would be impressed; I certainly was. I think Maude chose her successor to Steward of the Grand Portal of the Realm of Man very well, indeed."

Padraic chewed on his lower lip and asked, "Did she speak of her mother?"

"She did not. However, I had the opportunity to spend some time with one of her closest friends, a young woman called Stacy—who, by the way, exhibits the natural skills and rapport of a *wood nymph*. Stacy told me that Ellen's mother, Millie, is fine and had been visiting with Ellen at Delafaire Farm."

"So, they are both, Millie and Ellen, well?"

"Yes, Padraic, they are well."

Padraic stared into a blank distance that only he could perceive. He finished his drink and slumped back in his chair. His thoughts were scattered and disjointed. He just let his mind roam and free-associate; he found that often helped whenever he was confused. But this situation was far beyond his experience or expectations. His befuddlement showed no signs of abating.

The Guildmaster broke into his guest's meandering reverie by asking the one question Padraic could not yet face.

"So, my old friend, what are you going to do?"

Padraic looked up, his face blank of expression. "I-I just don't know."

The Guildmaster reached for the decanter and refreshed both glasses. Without looking at his guest, he cleared his throat and raised a finger.

"Forgive me, if I should overstate the obvious, but surely you see that Lady Diere would not have revealed to you that Ellen is your daughter were it not somehow to her advantage."

The Rogue nodded. It *was* rather obvious, knowing the *Mad Elf* as he did.

"This offer she has made to you—protection in exchange for fealty and becoming her consort—your acceptance is obviously very important to her. I suspect that divulging the information about your daughter was intended to push you past the tipping point, and secure your compliance.

"And, to further intimate that Ellen would benefit from Diere's protection—well, that is just beyond ironic since we have ample reason to believe that Diere is ultimately responsible for the attacks upon your daughter."

"Aye," agreed Padraic, "it smacks of thinly veiled coercion and extortion—comply with her demands or my daughter will suffer. But what can Diere hope to gain by my cooperation? What is really going on?"

The Guildmaster grunted. "Harrumph, now therein lies the crux of the matter. We know that Diere is up to something. We also suspect that Queen Mab has instituted a pogrom to rid herself of any suspected traitorous elements. Are these two working in collusion—or are they adversaries? We simply do not know."

He leveled a finger at the Rogue. "Nor can we speculate how you may fit into this convoluted tapestry of treachery and intrigue; but, I strongly suspect you will be somehow involved.

"Of course, it is possible that Diere's motivation in regard to you is entirely a selfish manifestation of her bruised ego. You do realize that it is well known that you are the only male to ever leave her side on his own initiative. She no doubt perceives that insult as a tarnished blot upon her carefully maintained image. Elves can be quite vain, you know."

Padraic rolled his eyes at the blatant understatement, and shrugged.

"I left her because she was becoming increasingly petty and self-absorbed. Being with her was no longer *fun*, to be perfectly candid."

"You need not explain your actions to me," the Guildmaster assured him. "It is more important at this time to focus on the greater scope of events—the big picture, as some call it. It may be that circumstances are ripe for Diere to try to manipulate you purely as a collateral pawn in a far more comprehensive scheme."

"I fear you are right, old friend. And, I suspect my daughter may be a pawn as well."

"Perhaps . . . But for now, can you put this matter regarding your daughter aside for the moment? We have another issue before us, as you know."

"Oh, of course, Salidar." Padraic rubbed his temples and sighed.

"Yes, he is in the Realm of Mer, in the hands of pirates; and, it appears that there he will remain, at least for the time being."

"That was not the plan. He was to transit out at his earliest opportunity. What happened?"

"From what we have been able to ascertain, he was subject to some sort of enchantment, and has thus been prevented from transiting out. He is now aboard the *Doom Wind*, and is held captive—for ransom, of course—by her master, Captain Bloody Bane."

"Ransom? But who would pay?" Padraic opened his palms. "Of course, Lady Diere! They'll approach Diere."

"They already have. A sea witch known as Circe sent a cryptic message to Lady Diere, a message that we, ah, intercepted briefly. It indicated that Captain Bane demands the usual swag; gold, silver, and implements of magic, for Salidar's release—or he would suffer the usual threats; pain, torture, and a horrible death."

Padraic smirked. "Let me guess; Diere refused to pay any ransom, right?"

The Guildmaster chuckled and leaned back.

"Oh, more than that! She said that she meant to dispose of him anyway, so they would be doing her a favor! Which I must admit I thought was a bit of a shame, of course, because he would probably make a pretty good pirate."

Padraic nearly choked with laughter, but he quickly regained his composure.

"I, too, have to admit there may be some truth to that. He is quite resourceful!"

"Yes, he is indeed," agreed the Guildmaster in amusement. "Thus, I have arranged for him to receive a message that will warn him of Diere's expressed intention, and strongly urge that he survive as best he can, at least until some way can be found to extricate him from his present predicament. But, I must admit I am not overly optimistic at this point."

"Do you have assets aboard the *Doom Wind*?"

"No, but she must put into port periodically; and, Captain Bane has developed a somewhat habitual pattern that we can hope to anticipate and exploit."

"Salidar helped me, when I was a captive; I would help him break his chains," Padraic said firmly. "Is there not something that I can do?"

"No, not at the moment. Our people are watching for the *Doom Wind* to make port—*any* port. However, we know for certain that she will eventually put in at New Port Royal, an infamous pirate den, where we already have assets in place."

"Ah, I see." Padraic nodded approvingly, the genesis of a plan forming in his mind as the Guildmaster continued.

"And considering what Diere may intend for him, he may in fact be better off in Mer—out of sight and out of mind. By the way, I am informed that Salidar is not kept in irons; Bane has put him to work as a common seaman. If he can adapt, of which I harbor no doubt, he may well be safest where he is. Of course, we will know more with time."

Feeling mixed emotions, Padraic sagged in his chair. "You will keep me informed?"

"Certainly, old friend—provided I know where you are. Have you any plans?"

"No, not presently . . . I must confess, I am preoccupied with the idea that I have a *daughter*. If you don't mind, I think I'll stay here for a few days, to learn all that I can. I would very much like to speak to anyone who spent time with her, especially her friend—*Stacy*, was it?"

"Padraic, I understand. But do you not think it may be wise to keep your parentage a secret? Do not forget the *bounty*. There are those who would gladly do you harm, and the less scrupulous among them might well consider harming Ellen to get to you."

Padraic blanched. That had not even occurred to him.

"Ye gods! I had not thought . . . I *am* slipping. But this is—I don't know—so overwhelming in some strange and novel way. What am I to do? What is your counsel, old friend? You are the wisest man I know."

"Bide a while here, with us. Let us ponder these things more deeply, and consider the options. When does Lady Diere expect your answer to her offer?"

"By the waxing crescent moon—three days from now. I feel I have wasted time in my confusion these past two days. Have you any pertinent thoughts?"

The Guildmaster sipped from his glass and mused aloud, "I have."

"Go on, please," the Rogue prodded.

Placing his glass down, the Guildmaster splayed his hands on the rough tabletop.

"Padraic, have you considered a *partial* or *tentative* acceptance of her offer?"

"What? Are you serious?" His shock was obvious.

"I am, indeed. Listen, we know she has an agenda; and, to some extent, she needs your cooperation. That may be the means by which we might extract information relative to her plans. You might only need to appear to cooperate, even in a limited capacity, to learn more. For example, you could take the position that you would be more comfortable with her proposal *if* you knew more about her plans—which I seriously doubt she would honestly confide in you. Think of it as a negotiation position; you would agree to accept the position of *consort*, yet withhold the swearing of *fealty* pending further assurances—*by her actions*—of her intentions."

"I would *never* swear fealty to that *evil, Mad Elf* for any reason!" Padraic interrupted vehemently.

"Well, I should hope not—nor am I suggesting that you ever would," the Guildmaster soothed. "But *she* must not know that! You must stay clear in your purpose, and discreet in both word and deed. You must work to prolong the situation—a paced negotiation. This can work to your advantage. You should insist that Ellen be afforded Diere's *benevolent protection* in the interim as well; which may effectively forestall any further threat to Ellen, at least for the time being, from Diere."

Padraic pondered his friend's words, and found his heretofore chaotic thoughts and concerns coalescing into a manageable configuration; a series of logical perspectives and potentials crystallized in his mind.

"Guildmaster, your words have great merit, and I am grateful for your counsel. I can see the wisdom of your suggestion. Such a negotiated compromise would give Diere initially what her ego may subliminally demand; it would appear that I have returned to her side. She places great emphasis on appearances.

"Yes, I think this strategy is sound—and it buys us time. I think I should stay here until the time she granted me to consider her proposal nearly expires; then I shall answer Diere's offer."

The Guildmaster stood and extended his hand, which Padraic clasped.

"Then we are of an accord," the Guildmaster intoned firmly, "and shall employ this strategy. I cannot help but feel these are dangerous times. We know something significant, and most likely perilous, is underway. I have no doubt that we shall all have our roles to play."

Placing both hands upon Padraic's shoulders, the Guildmaster added in a serious tone, "Now heed my words—you must play your role true to form. The persona of the Rogue must be seen to act accordingly, as would be typically expected, in self-interest and without pangs of conscience. And most importantly, you must become a convincing consort—no matter how distasteful the role, or unpleasant you find Lady Diere. There may be far too much at stake. "

Padraic sighed in resigned determination.

"As you wish, old friend."

CH 3

THE BODY OF BOLTAR had finally been relinquished to the Realm of Dark Elves. It now lay far to the distant north of Queen Mab's castle, within a hidden chamber, deep beneath the mountain retreat of Magus Atrellan. The ensorcelled mortal remains rested upon a large grey slab of stained stone, hewn from a massive granite boulder and chiseled into an altar-like shape by unknown hands, untold ages ago.

A pantheon of worn runes, forgotten symbols of an ancient and arcane dialect, girdled the sides of the soiled sarsen in an unbroken chain. Queen Mab's alchemist, Daegon, strongly suspected that the stone had once held great power; however, it appeared that Atrellan had come to regard it as only a convenient worktable in his lair of metaphysical study and divination.

Daegon stood to one side as Atrellan directed his two acolytes in the placement of four skulls upon the slab at specific cardinal points around the body. The novice attendants dripped wax from four thick guttering candles upon the crowns of the skulls, and then pressed the base of each flickering taper into the cooling wax. In the increased illumination, Daegon could see that each skull was different, representing different races; Dwarven, Vampire, Elfin, and Human.

Curiosity overcame Daegon; he dared to ask, "Atrellan, what are—"

"Silence! Do not interrupt me! The only reason you are here, is that my queen has so commanded. You will *not* interfere in the workings of my spell detection protocols. This is a delicate and protracted procedure that is well beyond your comprehension, and may well take several days and nights.

"While I am fully capable, indeed, even accustomed to such requirements in the practice of my most esoteric art, I realize that such stamina is not within *your* ability. So, there is a resting chamber prepared for you in the level below us; the acolytes will provide food and water should you so desire."

Daegon remained calm and expressionless as he bowed slightly and offered his apology.

"Magus, I beg your forgiveness. I intended no interruption or distraction. However, I was under the impression that Magus Jalash-el of the Shadow Realm had already found a stasis spell and a hidden mind-wipe spell."

Atrellan scowled in distaste and waved a hand dismissively.

"Harrumph, and that is all he *could have found!* He may be considered the finest mage of the Shadow Realm; but, his skills pale in comparison to *mine!* I am the most accomplished and powerful of the Dark Elf mages! *I* shall determine what enchantments adhere to this body!"

Although Daegon remained outwardly passive, he was growing weary of Atrellan's arrogance. For a moment his pique got the better of him; he dared to remind Atrellan of Queen Mab's words.

"Magus, surely you recall that Her Majesty was quite specific in commanding that I, too, examine the corpse, *and* make a full report—*to her*."

Atrellan audibly ground his teeth. He clearly fought to hold his temper in check, and respond in even tones, despite the tightness in his jaws.

"And so you shall, *after* I have conducted my examination—which I have already indicated may take several days and nights! Now, I must insist that you not engage in further interference or interruption!

"I will inform you when I am finished. You may return to my redoubt above; I have an extensive library there which may contain some works that even you may comprehend. Or, you may take your rest in the place prepared for you on the level below. A word of caution, I would strongly advise against venturing below that level; the lowermost dungeon levels are very old, unsafe, and of little interest."

Producing an elaborately engraved ceremonial dagger, his *athame*, from within his robes, Atrellan gestured with its point at Daegon.

"Heed my words—I will have your full attention. I must now invoke a protracted litany of protection and inquiry in an ancient elfin tongue that you would not understand. Should you elect to linger here, I shall insist that you remain silent—and stay out of my way."

Daegon's demeanor appeared placid as he acknowledged Atrellan's warning; but, his anger was a glowing ember that would smolder, carefully shielded from the pompous and condescending elf.

"Of course, as you wish, m'lord Magus."

Daegon elected to stay, and took the opportunity to more closely examine the chamber. Walls of smooth natural rock rose in graceful arcs to a point high above lost in shadows. Reflected torchlight danced along bright veins of metallic ore that webbed the walls in curious flowing patterns. Shadows of empty niches swayed in the walls like the open mouths of wailing supplicants, as if in memory of token offerings placed there in times long past. The floor, equally smooth and dust-free, appeared to be a mosaic comprised of thousands of small, dull-colored stones; however, Daegon could not discern any sort of readily identifiable design.

The centerpiece of the chamber was the *altar stone*, as Daegon had begun thinking of it. Between the foot of the altar stone and the near wall stood a round pedestal about waist-high, its diameter about the length of his forearm. Faint shadows of runes were visible upon the shaft of the pedestal—runes much like those around the altar that Daegon found vaguely familiar. The pedestal's top was perfectly concave, as if scooped out for some specific purpose. Whatever it had been intended to hold was now replaced with a black liquid that reflected no light.

Was this a sort of divination device—Atrellan's scrying bowl?

Hours ago, when they had first descended the winding stairs from the small castle, perched precariously on the side of a mountain crag, Daegon had noticed the smoothness of the stonework. The staircase had been hewn from the raw rock of the mountain and the workmanship was exquisitely precise. And now, looking about the chamber, he was convinced that this was ancient

Dwarven work, of that there could be no doubt. Yet, the runes appeared to be very early elfin, ancient and obscure to be sure, but elfin nonetheless.

Three arched doorways were set equidistant from each other into the smooth rock walls. One led to the winding stairs that descended from the castle above and continued below to another landing and beyond. The second led to a staircase that also appeared to access the lower levels. The third drew Daegon's interest.

He stepped away from Atrellan, who stood swaying rhythmically, his eyes rolled up in his head, holding his athame aloft, all the while incessantly droning on in an obscure elfin dialect.

Taking a torch from a sconce, Daegon slipped through the third arched doorway into a large antechamber. A number of tables, laden with books, scrolls, and clay containers, were arrayed along the far wall. Broad charts of astrological import hung from wooden frames. Tall bookcases that seemed to groan under the weight of their tomes rose against the other walls; but curiously, the center of the room appeared to be vacant.

Moving further into the chamber, he raised the torch and saw that it was not so. A large brass circle was inlaid in the center of the floor; silvery runes were further inlaid within the brass. These runes were similar to those he had seen on the pedestal and the altar stone.

Familiarity nagged at him. *Have I not seen runes like these before today?*

Then it hit him—he *had* seen such runes before, and the realization thoroughly shook him. He had once found an ancient scroll in the pursuit of his personal, *and secret,* quest for knowledge and power within the forbidden arts. This obscure scroll, at least to the extent that he could translate its contents, described the liturgy and practice of worship of those beings known as the *Old Ones.*

This place, that Atrellan now uses as a workroom, had once been a temple of some kind? Was it dedicated to the worship of the Old Ones? Perhaps a place of sacrifice? That would explain the stains upon the altar stone, and the trace rem-

nants of power that I sense. Does Atrellan even know? I seriously doubt it—the fool probably doesn't know the origin of the runes. He likely thinks they are some older form of familiar Elvish. But they are far more ancient than he could possibly know or realize. Indeed, when was the last time Dwarven master craftsmen willingly performed such fine stonework for any Dark Elf?

On the other hand, perhaps he knows very well what old powers linger here—I would do well not to underestimate him.

Yet, I would see more of this place. However, I must be patient, and draw no suspicion. He still insists that this procedure of his will take several days. So be it; I will explore this place within that time, and ferret out what secrets it holds.

His resolve now firm, Daegon left Atrellan to his thaumaturgic endeavors and sought out his assigned rest chamber. He would begin his explorations after a good night's sleep, when Atrellan and his acolytes were drained and weary. The supercilious elf's conceit and arrogance would work to Daegon's advantage.

HAWK ARRIVED AT DELAFAIRE Farm just before sunset. He had come right after work, directly from his office in response to the urgency he sensed underlying Ellen's invitation. He knew only that Lady Leanan had visited, and that Miska was now there.

Ellen met him at the door and ushered him to the kitchen, where he was greeted by the sight of Miska happily wolfing down a serving of red beans and rice. Hawk could not help but smile as Ellen scolded Miska for slipping slices of andouille sausage from his plate to the dogs lounging at his feet.

"Miska! I told you not to feed the dogs from the table—put it in their bowls. I don't want them learning bad habits."

"Yes, m'lady," the big man acceded, appropriately chagrined.

Of course, Max and Sophie were undeterred, eagerly expecting their next forthcoming treat.

At the sight of Hawk, Miska rose and bowed. “M’lord Hawk, I am most pleased to see you. You are well?”

“I am quite well, thank you,” Hawk replied grinning, “and it appears that you are, too. It’s good to see you, Miska. But I’m confused—why are you here?”

Ellen held up a hand. “If you don’t mind, I’ll explain. But first, I did offer you supper, so let me fix you a plate. Miska, would you care for more?”

The big man nodded enthusiastically, and as Ellen turned, he winked at the dogs and pointed to their bowls. He showed no surprise when they winked back and went to sit by them. All the while, Smokey lounged upon a window ledge, the very picture of passive unconcern.

Over supper Ellen recounted the events surrounding Leanan’s visit and Miska’s extended stay in the Realm of Man. Hawk listened attentively and only asked a few questions to clarify a point or two. He found her account concise, comprehensive, and enlightening.

“So, I went through the upstairs closets and I found some clothes that fit Miska fairly well. We’ve got him settled in the cabin. It now has power and a phone, although I haven’t been too successful at explaining how it all works.” Ellen sighed and shrugged her shoulders.

Miska just smiled and said, “But I *do* understand—*tis magic.*”

Hawk chuckled. “Not exactly, Miska. For the moment, let’s focus on teaching you how to use the technology—the phone at least. You know what might be helpful? How about a television? That would expose a lot about our culture. On second thought, maybe that’s not the best idea.”

Ellen laughed and agreed, at least in principle. “Maybe, but I think the idea has *some* merit. We could . . . ” Her voice suddenly trailed off and she sat stiffly upright.

The dogs were on their feet in an instant, and Smokey dropped to the floor and trotted toward the front of the house.

"What is it?" Hawk asked, turning his head and straining to hear anything unusual.

"I . . . I just *felt . . . a transit globe.* I *know* it just appeared near the front of the house." The surprise was evident in her voice. "I'd almost forgotten that I could sense these things. I have to go look."

She headed for the front door, the dogs at her heels, and both Hawk and Miska in her wake. Smokey leapt to a front window ledge and stared silently into the gathering night.

Hawk flipped on the porch lights, and he and Miska peered through the window. At first they saw nothing; then Miska pointed.

"There! Two of them—*bogies*—messengers from the Council!"

Hawk saw the two diminutive figures, robed and hooded, approaching the porch just as Ellen pulled the door open. "Ellen! Wait!" he hissed. "We'll go with—"

"No! Just you, Hawk," she whispered. "Miska must stay hidden!"

Hawk grabbed Miska's arm and said, "She's right! You have to stay out of sight! Is she in any danger from these, uh, *bogies?*"

"No, they are only messengers," Miska replied cautiously. "But, if they are not wearing gloves, do not let them touch you."

"No touching—right!" Hawk said, as he followed Ellen and the dogs onto the porch.

The bogies stopped at the foot of the steps, almost as if they were unable to proceed any further. One spoke in a clear but somewhat guttural voice. "Good evening. We serve the Council; and we seek the Lady Ellen Doyle, Steward of the Grand Portal of the Realm of Man."

The two dogs to either side of her, and Hawk at her shoulder, Ellen stood tall and replied formally. "I am Lady Ellen Doyle, Steward of the Grand Portal. Why do you seek me?"

"We bear an invitation to the next meeting of the Council, a fortnight hence in the fullness of the moon." He produced a scroll from beneath his robe and offered it in a gloved hand.

Ellen descended a few steps and gently took the scroll. The bogie bowed and stepped back. Ellen returned to the porch, and the other messenger spoke.

"Lady Ellen, you have received the invitation and the agenda for the Council meeting. After sunset and upon moonrise on the appointed day, focus on the invitation and call forth a transit globe. You and your escort will be transported to the meeting site. Have you any questions, m'lady?"

"Yes," she responded. "How large an escort am I to be permitted?"

"No larger than befits your station, m'lady. Four personal guards would be acceptable. That is in accordance with the custom."

"Very well, I understand; and I thank you for your service," she acknowledged graciously.

The two messengers bowed and took their leave, slipping into the darkness. A moment later there was a soft *pop* as their transit globe winked out of existence.

Hawk held the door open for Ellen, who led them back to the kitchen.

As they walked, Hawk asked, "Miska, why did you warn us to not be touched by them if they wore no gloves?"

The big man grunted. "Hmmph, bogies . . . They are strange beings, and usually solitary when not serving the Council. They do no physical harm, but they can feed off the fear in others. Their naked touch can bring on nightmares the next time one falls asleep—the most frightful of nightmares, whatever one fears the most. They can travel anywhere, not just among the Council Realms, and are thus well suited to their role as Council messengers. They have been employed in the distant past as executors of punishment by the Council, administering an unsavory penalty indeed—to never sleep restfully again. But now they only perform messenger duties, or so I have been told."

"Like delivering an *invitation?*" Ellen asked.

"Indeed, or serving a *summons*—a more unpleasant command to appear before the Council," Miska cautioned.

"*Unpleasant*, how?" Hawk probed, pushing the door to the kitchen open.

"Upon being served, a receipt in blood is taken and returned to the Council. Not much more than a few drops is required, but failure to appear as commanded invokes a curse of relentless misery and terrible luck."

"That sounds awful!" Ellen winced. "I'm glad I was merely *invited*."

Seating themselves once again in the kitchen, Hawk remarked, "Forgive me if I seem insensitive, Miska, but I find you far more articulate than when we first met."

Miska smiled. "A benefit of remaining in man-form for a protracted time, you see? Of course, I must revert to bear-form for a brief period monthly, roughly corresponding to the lunar cycle; but it does not have to be in concert with the full moon. And I intend to minimize my metamorphosis while a guest of Lady Ellen—although she has generously offered me free roaming privileges within her forest. Of course, I have forsworn hunting and taking of game while I abide here."

"Don't worry, Miska," Ellen remarked, grinning. "We'll keep you well fed."

Miska smiled broadly. "I have no such worries, m'lady. But, tell us of this invitation to a Council meeting, if you please."

Breaking a small wax seal, she opened and unrolled the scroll. As she smoothed the curling parchments, she explained.

"I knew to expect something like this. It is generally considered a required protocol that I appear before the assembled Council and formally introduce myself as the Steward. It's just a formality, but it carries a lot of weight with the other realms."

The scroll held two rolls of parchment, each lettered in an elegant calligraphy. One was the invitation, simple and to the point; the other, the agenda, listed several items of interest. And one item was glaringly ominous—the proposed election to the Chair of Man of one *George Papadolis*.

Flattening the parchment out upon the table, she said, "Hawk, you'd better have a look at this."

Staring at the document, his jaw tightened. "So, my wanted murder suspect, Papa George, will be there. Well, this does corroborate what Lady Leanan told us about him and the Chair of Man thing. When is this meeting, exactly? Have you got a calendar?"

"Yeah, somewhere." She began rummaging through a drawer. "Got it! Let's see, that would be in about two weeks. The full moon is on the eleventh—Sunday, the eleventh."

"And you can bring an escort, right? Up to four people, right?" Hawk's mind was racing.

"Why? What do you have in mind?" Her voice rose slightly.

"It's really very simple," Hawk assured her. "There's a warrant out for Papa George's arrest naming him as a *material witness* in a double homicide; so, I can take him into custody and bring him back here. Well, uh, I mean, rather, that you can *send* us back here. He goes to jail and we've effectively prevented him from being elected to the Chair of Man. Don't you see?"

Ellen did not appear convinced. "Could it really be that simple? Can you handle him by yourself? I don't mean, uh . . . Look, I don't doubt you, but wouldn't that be dangerous?"

"Ellen, it *is* what I do for a living, you know."

"I-I know, but," she stammered, "but shouldn't you have some help? You know what I mean."

Miska spoke up, "I would be most happy to be of service."

Ellen and Hawk turned to him simultaneously, and said, "No!"

Ellen put a hand on his massive arm and said, "Miska, for the time being, you *must* stay hidden. And you mustn't worry—I'm sure Hawk has other resources he can call upon for assistance."

"Yeah, don't worry about it, Miska," Hawk echoed. "I have a feeling there will be ample opportunity to get into a little mischief together. Now, if there's any red beans and rice left, I believe I could find room for another helping."

Miska grinned. "There's cornbread, too!"

Ellen smirked and rolled her eyes.

THE GENTLE KNOCK UPON his office door interrupted the Guildmaster's train of thought. Looking up from the papers on his desk, he saw the senior Storm Haven mage, Gallenius, poke his head in and apologize for the intrusion.

"Please forgive me, Guildmaster, but Padraic has returned. He would like to see you at your earliest convenience."

"Padraic?" repeated the Guildmaster. "He only left us a few days ago—he has already returned?"

"Quite so, Guildmaster," acknowledged Gallenius. "I am told he is on his way to your office as we speak."

"Very well. Show him in as soon as he arrives; and please stay nearby. His sudden return does not bode well—I have no doubt that something is amiss."

"As you wish, Guildmaster. I shall wait without."

Moments later, Gallenius ushered Padraic into the Guildmaster's office, and gently closed the door.

The Guildmaster rose in welcome. "Please sit down, old friend. I certainly did not expect to see you again so soon. Would you care for refreshment, some brandy perhaps?"

"No thank you, Guildmaster. To be candid, I did not expect to return so soon either, but, here I am."

"Please, take your ease," urged the Guildmaster, indicating the nearby chair, "and tell me what has happened."

"Of course, please bear with me. As you know, on the final day of the time Lady Diere had allotted for my decision, I went discreetly to her castle in the Realm of Dark Elves, only to find that she was not in residence. I was told she had been summoned by Queen Mab. No one knew how long she would be gone, so I elected to wait. I was kept incognito, but treated quite well, afforded the hospitality of her house, and given guest quarters. I was seen to by a noble fosterling, Malvana, who had been told to watch for me. You may know of her father, the Earl of Tanist, Queen Mab's avatar to the Council?"

"Oh yes, that would be Darius, Earl of Tanist," the Guildmaster answered. "A powerful Dark Elf from an old house, Tanist—and a staunch Mab loyalist. I knew he had sons, but I did not know of a daughter. So, she is of an age to be a fosterling in the House of Hawthorn; that is interesting. How did you find her?"

"Oh, I would say she is typical of any young adult elfin maid; a bit haughty, and rather pleased with herself. Fortunately, she is quite attuned to household gossip and intrigue, and, of course, somewhat susceptible to charming flattery and attention."

The Guildmaster chuckled and observed, "My word, but you are *ever* the rogue! What did you learn from her?"

"At first, she could only confirm that the queen's summons was quite sudden—it was certainly not expected by Lady Diere. Rather, her ladyship had been expecting *me.* Later the next morning, Malvana told me that she had learned from the household gossip that the queen's summons had something to do with the recently published *agenda* for the next Council meeting; but unfortunately, she did not know any details."

"I see. I assume you *did* meet with Diere upon her return?" inquired the Guildmaster.

"Yes, but not immediately upon her return," Padraic replied. "It was hours later that she invited me to her chambers to share the evening meal."

"You were alone with her?"

"But for the comings and goings of her personal servants, we were alone. But I see your point—I cannot be certain that we were not observed or overheard."

"So, how did it go?" prompted the Guildmaster.

"Surprisingly, very much like you and I had anticipated; but then again, perhaps not." Padraic sat back in his chair and spread his hands openly. "As you know, Lady Diere does *nothing* that is not to her advantage. Yet, she readily accepted my proposal of a *limited* agreement; essentially that I assume the role of consort, but defer for the time being from the swearing of fealty, pending further gestures of good faith."

"So, a fairly amenable negotiation, despite our concerns, eh?"

The Rogue leaned forward in earnestness and shrugged, his hands thrust upward.

"Guildmaster, it was hardly a negotiation at all; she agreed all too readily. It was as if she was preoccupied, perhaps even distracted. The only point at which she balked was my insistence that her protection extend to my daughter, Ellen. For some reason, that issue garnered her full attention—she was very reluctant to agree. I had to take an adamant position in this regard, and remind her that this was an integral aspect of her original offer. Only when I threatened to withdraw from the entire agreement did she relent. I still do not understand her reluctance."

"I may have a theory in that regard," commented the Guildmaster, "but before I get into that, how is it that she allowed you to depart her side? After all, are you not now her consort?"

"I found that curious as well. But it appears that she does not want my *new status* to be common knowledge; she said 'the time is not yet right'. But as I said, she seemed preoccupied and distracted. So, the following morning, I essentially told her the truth; that I have to tie up some loose ends, business matters, and collect a significant debt I am owed in the Realm of Mer."

"A debt? Please, go on."

"Before I fell into the hands of that damned pirate, Captain Bloody Bane, I had recently made delivery of a shipment of smuggled amulets in Derinseum—through a broker, of course—but had not yet collected my payment. Thus, I have unfinished business to attend to in that realm. Diere did not raise any objection, although she no doubt expects that I shall return to her thereafter."

The Guildmaster nodded in agreement. "No doubt she does. So, you intend to go to Mer to check on Madam Iris, do you not? You need not concern yourself; our assets report that she is well, and back to business as usual."

Padraic shook his head and smiled.

"Well, I should hope so—she's my broker. And don't worry, old friend, Storm Haven will get its cut, once I collect."

"Ah, incorrigible as ever—the Rogue once more!" The Guildmaster laughed. "Now, let us consider my theory regarding Lady Diere. One moment."

The Guildmaster stood and went to the door. Opening it, he held a brief conversation with the mage, Gallenius, who handed the Guildmaster a document. Returning to his desk, the Guildmaster handed the paper to Padraic.

"This," he indicated, taking his seat, "is a copy of the agenda for the next Council meeting. We managed to acquire a copy. Please, read it thoroughly."

A moment later Padraic announced, "Ellen's name is here; she is to appear before the Council as Steward. Is that what you want me to see?"

"Yes, in part . . . Look more closely, near the bottom of the agenda. Do you see the reference to a potential candidate for the Chair of Man vacancy, George Papadolis? We have it on good authority that he is rather notorious, a wanted criminal in the Realm of Man. Ellen plans on denouncing him before the Council; and, she has been quite open about it.

"And I must confess that, as it happens unfortunately, I am responsible for her name appearing on the agenda, notwithstanding that it was her request that such an invitation be arranged. We did not anticipate the coincidental timing of agenda points in the *same* meeting—but alas, what is done is done."

Padraic started to speak, but the Guildmaster forestalled him with a gesture.

"But more to the point, we may clearly assume that this publication has now alerted someone—whoever sponsors this man's candidacy—that Ellen will attend. It may be wise to assume that her intentions, beyond her introduction as the new Steward, are suspected—if not *known*.

"Furthermore, we now believe there is little doubt that this man, George Papadolis, is but a pawn. But the question is *whose?* Lady Diere, Queen Mab—or both?" The Guildmaster shrugged with open hands, his question hanging like an unwelcome cloud between them.

"So, if Ellen formally denounces this criminal," Padraic deduced, "she will effectively frustrate someone's plans, as this George Papadolis will be deemed unacceptable by the Council. And if this sinister someone suspects Ellen's intentions, this person may act to protect such plans."

"That is my thinking as well," conceded the Guildmaster. "This sudden summons for Lady Diere to attend Queen Mab, purportedly in response to this published agenda, suggests that the appearance of Ellen's name may be the basis for their concern. Furthermore, your insistence that Ellen be 'protected' by Diere seems to have presented some complications for Diere. I am now more strongly suspicious that Diere and Mab are working in collusion, and that could not be more dangerous."

Padraic suddenly stood, placed his hands flat upon the desk, and said urgently, "We must warn Ellen! She should not attempt to appear before the Council!"

"I would wager that is exactly what Diere and Mab would have you say; it is certainly what they would intend," observed the Guildmaster. "In all candor, I do not believe that anyone could dissuade Ellen from doing what she believes she must."

"I will go to her—I must! I am her father! Surely she will listen to me."

The Guildmaster laughed sympathetically and shook his head.

"Forgive me, old friend, but this *paternal prerogative* is a novel facet of your *rogue persona.* Yes, you are her father; and yes, she *might* even believe you. But she is a force to be reckoned with, an adult woman of clear resolve. You would not dissuade her from attending that Council meeting."

Padraic resumed his seat, at a loss for words, frustration and concern distorting his countenance.

"Padraic, were you and Ellen's mother, *Millie*, is it? Were you ever married? Did the two of you have some sort of ceremony, in any realm?"

The Rogue took a moment to focus on the question, his slight disorientation obvious. The Guildmaster remained patient; he knew this could be significant.

"As best I recall," Padraic answered, his brows knit and lips pursed, "she insisted on going to some small office in a courthouse in the Realm of Man. We had to repeat some words and sign some paper. So, I would say *yes*, we probably were 'married' according to her custom. I left for the Realm of Mer some weeks after that. Why do you ask?"

The Guildmaster folded his arms. "Because someday, it may become important that Ellen knows that she was not born the *illegitimate* offspring of a fay father and a human mother. Someday, it may matter to others as well. And someday, you may be asked by Ellen, if not Millie, to explain why you left."

"As you know, marriage is more of a human institution," Padraic pointed out. "Few in Faerie even consider it, as you *well know*, old friend. Besides, I never even knew Millie was with child."

"All true, perhaps—but now moot," observed the Guildmaster. "Ellen may be *your* daughter, but her continued well-being and her personal security in her capacity as the Steward of the Grand Portal of the Realm of Man is *our* mutual concern."

"Yes, of course, please continue. You have something in mind—you always do."

The Guildmaster nodded and raised a finger in emphasis.

"I think we may have to take steps to see to her protection—whether she is aware of it or not. In truth, it would not surprise me were she to decline any overt assistance."

"In that case," Padraic suggested, "how about *covert* assistance?"

"That would certainly be playing to our *strengths*," noted the Guildmaster dryly. "I will convey a message to her articulating our concerns and offering our assistance. However, regardless of her response, we will take appropriate steps to insure her safety—covertly, if necessary."

"If there is anything I can do, I am at your disposal," insisted Padraic.

"As it happens, old friend, your *unique proximity* to Lady Diere may prove invaluable. You and Gallenius must work out a clandestine communications procedure, so we can keep each other informed. But be careful; do not jeopardize your position, or your person. Am I clear on that point?"

"Crystal clear, my old friend. Now, I really must get to Mer—I am expected, you see."

"Not before you and Gallenius confer. Remember—be careful."

ELLEN HAD DEVELOPED the habit of walking the dogs in the morning before it got too warm. If they ventured anywhere near the cabin, Miska would join them; he had done so this morning. So, Ellen had taken the opportunity to show him the caves and the hidden still.

The avoidance spell was still in place, but it had no appreciable effect on Miska, although he did notice it.

"I sensed it, m'lady; but I, and my people, are generally immune to most common magic. However, strong sorcery—especially that of a dark nature—can be another matter altogether. Is all well here?"

"Yes, I believe so. The caves are as I remembered them, unmolested. There have been no intrusions since I was last here."

"I am impressed," he confided. "These are fine caves. This stonework is obviously Dwarven. I must admit I like the large, more natural outer cave—tis perfect for a bear's lair."

"Really?" she responded in amusement. "Then, Miska, you must make yourself at home there whenever you feel the need to be in your ursine aspect."

Miska was delighted. "Lady Ellen! You are too kind! Thank you, thank you!"

UPON RETURNING TO HER kitchen, Ellen saw the red light on her answering machine winking at her; a message waited. Pulling her cell phone from her jeans pocket, she was chagrined to see that she'd neglected to turn it on.

Oh, well . . . Let's see who called—maybe Hawk?

Pressing the *play* button was followed by a soft whirring, and then Stacy's voice bubbled forth in excitement.

"Hi, Ellen! It's me! Surprise! Your mom and I are coming back to the farm! We're in the Dallas-Fort Worth airport waiting on our connecting flight. I wanted to just show up and surprise you, but your mom said that wouldn't be a good idea. So we compromised; I'm surprising you now! Now don't worry—everything's fine. It's about an hour flight, and we're getting ready to board in a few minutes. We should get into LaBorde a little after one o'clock. If you can't pick us up, don't worry—we'll take a cab. Oh, I can't wait to see you! There's so much to talk about! Huh, what? Okay, I gotta go—they're boarding! See you soon! Bye!"

Ellen was stunned, pleased, and a little concerned all at once.

Stacy and Millie were returning—already? They'd only been back in Los Angeles a few weeks. Was something wrong? Stacy didn't sound like anything was amiss; and, she'd said that everything was fine.

Realizing she'd have to wait for her answers, she glanced at the clock—almost noon. If she left right away, she could get to the airport in plenty of time.

She didn't have to worry about Miska; he was planning on spending the afternoon fishing off the cabin's dock. She poured some fresh water in the pets' bowls; they wouldn't need any food until time for supper.

On an impulse, she picked up the kitchen phone and dialed Hawk's number; the call went to voice mail. Guessing he was in court, she left a message asking him to call her cell phone.

She retrieved her cell phone and started to stuff it in her pocket, but hesitated—making sure she turned it on this time. Picking up her truck keys, she turned and faced the pets.

"I have to go to the airport. Stacy and my mom are coming back. You guys stay here. You've got plenty of fresh water. I should be back in about two hours. Y'all be good now."

Smokey and the dogs regarded her placidly, as if they understood every word. Ellen had no doubt that they did.

She'd found herself frequently holding one-sided conversations with them. It may have looked strange to others, but to Ellen it was now completely normal and a comfortable routine. Sometimes she even held deep discussions with them after spending time on the phone with her mother; it was so great to share your thoughts with someone who always listened and was never judgmental.

Especially since recently, Ellen sensed that her mother had become somewhat moody, perhaps even a bit depressed since her return to Los Angeles.

In her calls to Ellen, Millie explained that there were big changes on the horizon at her job. The restaurant had been sold and was to be demolished and then rebuilt as a fast-food franchise. Ostensibly, the employees were to be offered jobs with the new owners; but, it would be several months before the new eatery would open. Few people could afford such a prolonged period of unemployment. Besides, Millie just couldn't picture herself in the fast-food game; she'd have to find another job.

Whenever Ellen asked what her mother's current boyfriend, Earl, thought about the issue, Millie would deflect the question and change the subject. Ellen did not press. All she could really do was try to be supportive and be a good listener. Of course, Ellen never missed an opportunity to remind Millie that she always had a home with her.

The irony of the offer did not escape Ellen—the formerly rebellious teenager offering the parent a secure and stable environment.

Telephone conversations with Stacy were not as frequent once Mark had returned to New York; but that was something Ellen intuitively understood. She smiled—for the both of them.

On the other hand, Ellen understood that Stacy was no longer quite as happy in *her* job either. The government contract was winding to a close, and the company had not been successful in securing another contract. Stacy's promised raise and bonus were in jeopardy—the simple truth was that now she was *bored.* Stacy kept raving about how much fun she'd had visiting Ellen, and how exciting it had all been. *"Once you've been in such a fantastic other world—even Los Angeles is boring!"*

Ellen could sense that Stacy was more than ready for a change. She had repeatedly said that if Millie ever agreed to try some sort of home-based herb and flower seed business, that she'd throw in with her and handle the online marketing and sales. It was evident that Millie was mildly flattered and somewhat intrigued. Ellen was supportive. Trying not to appear too eager, she agreed that it wasn't really a bad idea at all, and of course, Delafaire Farm was ready-made for that kind of cottage industry.

In fact, Ellen and Mark held several long-distance conversations on this very subject, and they had done a fair bit of research. If they were to broaden the scope of the business, it had the propensity to be reasonably profitable. Heirloom seeds were fine, but herbs and flowers might be too seasonal. However, if they were to include jellies, jams, and canned preserves they could be assured of a year-round operation. Ellen knew that Mark and Stacy had been discussing the concept as well.

The problem was that Ellen didn't know how to approach her mother with the idea, without sounding like she wanted Millie to leave Earl, the latest in a succession of boyfriends Millie tried to *fix*. That was too close to old scar tissue covering the rift that had sundered them so many years ago; Ellen did not want to open that old wound. She very much wanted her mother to move back home, to Louisiana; but, it had to be Millie's idea, and on Millie's terms.

ELLEN MADE PRETTY GOOD time driving to the airport; but it wasn't quite good enough. Stacy and Millie's plane benefited from a strong tailwind and landed almost twenty minutes earlier than expected. She spotted them just leaving the luggage return area of the terminal and heading for a line of parked taxis.

Ellen got their attention by beeping her horn and waving excitedly. She pulled to the curb and grinned broadly as they hefted their luggage into the truck bed. Millie and Stacy piled into the Ford's cab, laughing and pushing like schoolgirls. Impossibly trying to hug one another, all three were talking at once.

Ellen's cell phone rang.

"Hello? Oh, hi, Hawk, is everything okay? Good, listen, I can't talk right now—I have to drive. I'm at the airport. My mom and Stacy just got in. Yeah, a *big* surprise! Oh, the airport policeman is waving me off the curbside. I have to drive—"

"Give me that!" Stacy demanded, grinning as she reached across Millie and snatched the phone away from Ellen. "Now, you can drive—I'll talk to Hawk. Hi, Hawk! Did you miss me?"

Ellen and Millie erupted in laughter as the truck pulled away from the curb and joined the departing traffic. Once clear of the airport, they made excellent time.

Ellen and her mom chatted away as they drove home. Millie described their trip in detail, and spared no criticism in regard to the dearth of decent airline food.

Ellen was not very surprised; Millie remembered when airlines served something resembling a true meal on long flights. She was even less impressed with the fare offered in airport restaurants—hardly real restaurants, rather crowded counters touting inflated prices for mediocre fast food. She compared the experience to the hustling midway at a county fair. Ellen could tell that her mother was more than a bit sensitive about the fast-food issue.

Stacy interrupted to hand Ellen's cell phone back to her. "Here you go, Ellen. I invited your boyfriend over for dinner tonight—I hope you don't mind," Stacy teased.

"He's not . . . uh, not my *boyfriend,*" Ellen stammered.

"What?" squealed Stacy with delight. "Who are you kidding?"

Even Millie was smiling. "So you two are what—just *good friends?*"

"Mother!" Ellen exclaimed in exasperation, but she couldn't contain her own smile. Soon she was laughing along with Millie and Stacy.

Catching her breath, Millie asked, "Have you heard from Mark?"

Ellen nodded. "Yeah, we talked, uh, last Tuesday, I think. He's wrapping things up in New York. In fact, he's talking about coming back sooner than he thought, too."

"Yeah!" interrupted Stacy. "Like *Monday!*"

"This *coming* Monday? Are you kidding? Today is Friday!" Ellen exclaimed.

With tongue firmly in cheek, Millie remarked, "It may come as no surprise that Mark and Stacy have been on the phone with one another daily—and nightly. So, her information might be just a little fresher."

Ellen grinned from ear to ear. "Oh my, so they're an item now? Any wedding plans?"

"We-e-elll," wheedled Stacy coyly, and then suddenly burst out in laughter, pointing at Ellen. "Omigawd! You should see your face! Gotcha!"

Millie playfully swatted Stacy's arm. "Behave, young lady, Ellen *is* trying to drive."

"Okay, okay . . . Hey, we're almost home—there's the turnoff!" Stacy pointed to the open gate.

As Ellen turned up the drive, she asked, "You haven't told me why you decided to visit again so soon. Is everything all right?"

Her passengers looked at one another, and finally Millie sighed.

"Ellen, this isn't just a spontaneous visit. I know it's kind of a surprise, but we, Stacy and I, just had to sit down and talk with you face-to-face. This isn't something I'd feel right about doing on the phone.

"It's about a business, and your offer to let me live here. It's been on my mind; and well, Stacy and I have been talking, off and on, about this business thing ever since we went back to Los Angeles. Remember when we were all talking about running an online herb and garden business? Well, we've put our heads together—and I mean Mark, too—taken stock of our skills and resources, and decided that we really could do it. Mark said he could help us incorporate. Of course, this all depends to a large degree on you, or rather your approval, and participation."

Stunned but pleased, Ellen carefully asked, "That's great, but what about your jobs, your lives back in California? Mom, what about your *boyfriend?*"

Millie folded her hands in her lap and spoke softly, "What Earl and I have, *had* actually, was more of a relationship of convenience that we'd both grown comfortable with. And the truth is that he was occasionally seeing his ex-wife—he didn't think I knew. I did, but I never let on. Why rock the boat? But who was I kidding? At best, that sort of thing is never fulfilling—half the satisfaction smothered in all the denial and guilt. So, he and I talked it out. It was a friendly parting—after all, we always were friends.

"And now, I'm kind of forced to consider a career change, too. The restaurant will never be the same, and I just don't see myself in that kind of place—it's not for me. I think I kind of lost an anchor with the restaurant closing. That led me to seriously look at what Earl and I were really all about; and well, now you know all the rest.

"So, I've got no real reason to stay there, in Los Angeles, you see? And the truth is that I really enjoyed the time I spent here with you, more than anything I've done in a long time. I didn't—I don't want to give that up."

Ellen felt an unaccountable sadness, a heart tugging empathy for her mother.

So, it turns out that Earl was just another man Millie couldn't fix. Now there's an observation I'd best keep to myself. At least leaving Los Angeles is her idea.

In her heart, Ellen readily admitted that the time they had recently spent together was among her happiest. She had really come to appreciate her mother, her trials and accomplishments. Perhaps this could work out after all. An affirming sense of relief washed over her.

"As for me," piped up Stacy, "I went back to my *boring* job. Remember that I'd been promised a raise and a bonus if we closed out this contract on time and under budget—which we *did,* right? Well, Mr. Rosedale, the general manager, babbled some rhetoric about the state of the economy, and then denied all raises and bonuses for the rest of the fiscal year. *Then* he dropped the bomb about staff cuts—*'furloughs'* he called them. Half of our department would be affected; and, *he* would decide who would stay."

Her lips thinned and a scowl fleetingly fled across her face.

"Well, I'll make it short. So, he, Mr. Rosedale, called me into his office and hinted that he *might* let me stay—*if*. . . But I read between those lines, and volunteered to be *furloughed.* So, here I am. I'm ready to work for myself for a change, or at least give it a trial run."

"So, we're back to the original plan?" Ellen asked. "We grow and prepare herbs, and what, flower bulbs? And then market them online?"

Stacy and Millie smiled and bobbed their heads in unison, and Millie added, "We think it may be a little more involved than just that. Refrigeration would be an issue with shipping of fresh flowers and such, so we're also thinking about dried herbs and spices. And maybe having some local stores carry some cute little jars of fancy potpourri, jellies, jams, and such. You see what I mean?"

"You gotta remember we talked about this," Stacy insisted. "We could collect and sell the seeds, too. You know design little seed packets, cute ones! Identify heirloom seeds in special little packets, right?"

"You know, that's just simple enough to work," Ellen admitted, delighted to hear her mother and Stacy so invested in the concept. "Mark is on board with this?"

"Don't you remember, Ellen?" Stacy asked impatiently. "He was there when we first talked about this when we found the coins in the cave; Mark thought it was a *great* idea! He explained how you had to have, and *show* a legitimate cash flow. After all, it *is* a farm."

"Yes, I remember. It does make sense," Ellen agreed, trying to contain her elation and relief as she pulled up in front of the house and parked the truck.

Millie stared up at the house, smiled and sighed. "I admit it took me a while to adjust to the idea. You know how big changes are hard for me. But I do have a life to live—and I'm not afraid of some hard work."

"Mom, I couldn't be happier," Ellen exclaimed, wrapping her mother in a hug, and squeezing Stacy's hand. "You know this is gonna be a lot of fun!"

"We know," said Stacy smirking, as she opened the Ford's passenger door and climbed out. "Of course, we'll have some details to work out—'logistics' as Mark would say, even for a *trial run*. And I'll have to make one more trip back to L.A. I'm going to sublet my apartment until the lease expires. My car is leased, too, but that's almost up anyway. Say Ellen, you should sub-let your old apartment, too! And your old furniture, if you don't want any of it, I could sell it for you with my stuff."

Ellen retrieved her purse from behind the driver's seat and shut the door, "That's not a bad idea. My apartment lease is almost up; and the furniture was secondhand to begin with. I haven't even given that stuff any thought. I think I will let you sell it. How about you, Mom, anything you need to get rid of?"

"Trust me, Ellen, I've already taken care of it. I only need the rest of my clothes, and Earl has agreed to ship those when I ask him."

Millie helped Stacy unload their luggage. Ellen took two of the bags and started for the porch steps.

“That’s great, Mom! Then you don’t even have to go back! Oh, I almost forgot—we have a guest, Miska! He’s staying at the cabin actually, but he’ll be joining us for dinner.”

“Miska is here? Cool!” exclaimed Stacy, clapping her hands. “Um, in man-form, I trust? Oh, this is going to be an interesting dinner! You *will* be explaining just what’s been going on around here, right?”

Ellen nodded affirmatively.

“Miska?” Millie asked. “Isn’t he the man y’all met who can become a big bear?”

“Oh yeah,” answered Stacy, “but he’s a big old sweetie. You’ll like him!”

“Well then,” said Millie, “we’d better see what’s in the pantry for supper.”

CH 4

ATRELLAN AND HIS ACOLYTES had labored at their task for three full days and nights. Despite their best efforts, the ensorcelled body of Boltar yielded no further secrets. A weary Atrellan had more than exhausted his considerable repertoire of elfin thaumaturgy, employing every spell he knew—sometimes in multiple combinations. However, he could discern nothing more than the two spells that Jalash-el had already found.

He was loath to admit that he could do no better than the Shadow Mage—especially to the likes of Daegon. The bitter taste of failure soured his palate and stuck in his craw.

In the steady light of a dozen thick candles, Atrellan sat hunched over his notes at a rough table in the room off the main chamber that held Boltar's body. Several dusty scrolls lay open on the tabletop in an apparent haphazard fashion. However, to the elfin mage's eye, these were carefully placed examples of arcane references, that when arrayed just *so*, offered obscure insights and revealed an ordered series of incantations that he had stumbled across years ago, but had never mustered the courage to try.

Evidently the remnants of a great store of sorcerous knowledge relating to the Old Ones, a pantheon of ancient and dimly remembered gods, these ancient scrolls were not actually composed of parchment, but rather the carefully flayed, stretched, and tanned skins of some forgotten beast—or being. These documents were among the oldest Atrellan had found here when he took possession of this lonely redoubt upon his assumption of the office of the most Senior and Preeminent Magus of the Dark Elves, following the *coup d'état* orchestrated by the former Lady Celeste, now the reigning Queen Mab LIV.

His deposed predecessor, the former Magus Primus, had refused to answer any questions regarding these scrolls—even when subjected to the most strenuous persuasion in the dungeons below. Unfortunately, the former senior adept did not survive Atrellan's impatient questioning. At the moment of his gasping demise, the dying mage mumbled a dire warning which Atrellan chose to ignore.

Consequently, Atrellan learned nothing useful from the aged adept. Nonetheless, Atrellan sensed that keys to great power were contained within these forbidden scrolls. He spent years trying to decipher and comprehend the obscure runes, but was only partially successful. That he had now resorted to these proscribed ancient texts demonstrated just how desperate he was growing. Unfortunately, Atrellan found nothing that would aid him in probing any deeper into the mystery of the bespelled remains.

Which is not to say that he failed to find anything of interest—oh yes, he found something that put him in mind of Daegon, that *annoying alchemist.* He glanced up at the doorway to be assured that he was not being observed, and then resumed copying a passage in runic text from two of the closer scrolls.

ONLY A FEW PACES AWAY, in the main chamber, the two spent elfin acolytes sat slumped over, leaning against the side of the altar stone. After the last spell-casting session conducted by Atrellan, they had collapsed right where they stood, utterly exhausted. Much younger than the adept, these apprentices had nowhere near the stamina of their lord and teacher. They fell into a deep sleep as soon as the mage retired to the other room to record his notes, as he did after every failed session.

Daegon had watched a few of these sessions from the shadowed doorways, mindful of the mage's warning, always careful to remain unobtrusive and out of Atrellan's way. Daegon soon lost interest when it became apparent that Atrellan was out of his depth, repeating ineffective spells in newly contrived combinations, with no effective results—or worse, having ill-conceived incantations bounce back at the startled mage in a shower of harsh sparks.

Daegon would learn nothing new by continued observation, so he elected to spend more time exploring.

His assigned sleeping accommodations were one floor below, but both stairwells continued well beyond, down into a stygian abyss. Ignoring Atrellan's warning, Daegon took a fresh torch and descended one set of stairs.

On his first foray, he found two lower levels; each was a warren of chambers of varying size, and all were empty but for dust and minor debris. The stonework was similar to that of the chambers above, very old yet precise, and no doubt Dwarven as well. There seemed to be no further access below; the further descending stairwell abruptly ended in the rubble of an ancient ceiling collapse.

It was on his second expedition into the lower chambers via the other, still intact, stairwell that he found the hidden stone door. It was barely discernible at the end of a long dark passage. Had it not been slightly ajar, and its shadow swaying slightly with the movement of his torch, he'd have missed it. Its face was smooth rock with a small notch for one's fingers to pull it open. The quality of the door's workmanship was obviously Dwarven, but the short passage that lay beyond and the descending stairs were rough-hewn and spare. This section was obviously far older, carved by unknown primitive hands.

Below he found the dungeon, and the implements of torture one would expect. The chamber may have been ancient, but someone—no doubt Atrellan—kept the tools of the torturer's trade in complete working order, and ready for use.

No rust stained the massive iron maiden, suspended gibbets, or wickedly hooked chains drooping from an overhead rack. An ominous collection of tongs, brands, and pokers lay across a flat stone slab that jutted out like a natural shelf from the rough wall. Smaller devices hung from hooks driven into the wall above the rudimentary shelf. Daegon recognized thumbscrews, clamps of various shapes, and an assortment of *flagellae*—scourging and whipping implements. A pile of dry firewood and a basket of charcoal lay at the ready beside a large iron brazier.

So, the old elf has a sadistic streak. I suppose I should not be surprised.

A heavy iron-strapped door stood half-open on the far wall, a dubious invitation to an open maw of pitch black.

As he approached, Daegon was surprised to see his torch waver in the eddy of a fragile air current coming from within that dark abyss. He paused at the threshold and thrust the flame forward; another rough set of stairs was revealed. These steps were quite wide, descending into utter darkness.

Casting a wary eye over his shoulder, Daegon started down the wide staircase, his feet, ever so cautiously, finding the worn depressions in the ancient stone. He descended for at least a dozen steps and noticed a perceptible drop in the ambient temperature. Cool and dank, the rough walls oozed a chilling dampness that glistened in the torchlight.

At the base of the stairs he found a long and wide hall with a number of moldy wooden doors standing open on either side. Thrusting his torch into each opening as he passed, his suspicions were confirmed—*prisoner cells*. He found none of the cells occupied. He heard small frantic scurryings, vermin, no doubt fleeing from the invasive torchlight.

At the end of the broad hall, he found a huge door, twice his height, standing slightly ajar. The gap was about the length of his forearm. He hoisted his torch for a better look. This door was quite stout, nearly two hand-spans thick, bound in iron, and incongruously inlaid with wide strips of tarnished silver. Daegon pulled on the massive door, but it didn't budge. Determined to see what lay beyond, he thrust his torch past the door's edge and with a modest effort managed to squeeze himself through the opening and into a large space.

What's this—another cell?

His breath caught in his throat and his eyes bulged! There, in the far corner, something stared at him!

He shoved his torch forward, but only succeeded in momentarily blinding himself as he couldn't see beyond the flare of the flame. He quickly recovered his wits, stepped to one side, and held the torch up and out to his right.

A massive sightless skull grinned at him.

By the gods! That thing is huge!

His composure regained, he carefully stepped forward, his flickering brand held high, and examined the skeletal remains. The bones, still intact, were very large. In life, it must have stood almost twenty feet in height; but in death, sitting slumped against the cell wall, the shape seemed somehow diminished. The large eyeless skull sprouted twin tusks thrusting up from a jutting lower jaw. There was little evidence of a neck but for a tarnished silver collar between the head and bones of the wide shoulders. A drooping loop of stout links chained the collar to the wall.

Looking more closely, Daegon saw that the wrists were bound in wide silver manacles linked by a long chain to an iron ring set high in the wall. A tattered hide encircled the desiccated waist, almost completely covering the blackened silver belt whose huge silver links were affixed to the wall as well.

A giant mountain troll? It must be! That would explain the silver restraints. And this one has been dead a long time—a very long time. Is this Atrellan's work—or some ancient elfin sorcerer?

For just a moment, Daegon was tempted to call upon his *secret knowledge* and have this corpse divulge its secrets; but, he discarded the idea almost immediately. It might prove foolish in the extreme to perform a spell of necromancy in this place.

Who knows what sinister energies might linger here?

Holding the torch before him, he looked around the large cell and saw the walls were damaged. Rubble was piled haphazardly in the opposite corner. As he cautiously approached, his flame began to waver. The closer he got to the corner, the more the fire danced about the head of his torch. There was definitely a draft emanating from the pile of debris.

Holding the torch near the walls, he could see that large rusty rings of iron had been forcefully pulled from the walls, and now lay twisted among the shards of broken stone. A short length of stout chain was still attached to an iron ring, its final link broken. Daegon rubbed at the tarnished metal of the chain and found it to be silver.

So, another was imprisoned here as well—another mountain troll, perhaps? And somehow tore loose of his bonds, and made his escape?

Holding the torch closer to the debris pile, the flame fluttered on the draft. He stepped back a few paces and estimated the broken debris to be piled higher than a man could easily reach.

This is fresh air streaming in here—a passage, a fault in the rock, an earthquake? Who knows? There is too much debris here to have come from simply pulling the restraint rings from the walls. I suspect a cave-in may be responsible. I will likely never know.

At the thought of a cave-in, Daegon remembered the collapsed stairwell he had encountered. Casting a wary eye across the unstable ceiling, he decided it would likely be wise to depart these lowermost regions.

Retracing his steps, Daegon returned to his sleeping chamber.

ATRELLAN WAS WAITING for him, restlessly pacing back and forth. The old mage seemed impatient, yet distracted.

"Ah, m'lord Magus, can I be of some service?" Daegon asked, careful to mask his surprise with mildly indifferent courtesy.

"Where—" Atrellan began haughtily, but then sighed in weariness. "Never mind. I have just received a messenger from the queen; she grows impatient for results. I have concluded my examination of the body, and found the spells I expected to find. I must now prepare my final report and make the necessary preparations to deliver the remains to Her Majesty."

"But m'lord, I have not yet—" Daegon started to point out.

"I know," Atrellan interrupted. "You may examine the corpse now. Be quick about it! I am to send a messenger with my report to the queen before sunset this day."

"I shall do so at once, m'lord," Daegon assured the mage. "May I ask? Were the spells you found the same as the Shadow mage, Jalash-el, found?"

Atrellan clenched his jaws, audibly grinding his teeth.

Daegon could almost sense the old elf's bile rising in his gorge.

"M'lord?" the alchemist dared. "Are you unwell?"

A slight tremor of the senior adept's shoulders betrayed his barely successful struggle to maintain control as he seethed, "I am fine! Yes, I found the same. I can see no reason to delay in complying with the queen's request. She shall receive the body as soon as possible. Now, do as she has commanded—quickly!"

"As you wish, m'lord," Daegon replied, bowing slightly, and biting his tongue. Careful to display a placid demeanor, Daegon followed Atrellan to the chamber in which Boltar lay.

Atrellan sent one of the two exhausted acolytes to the upper redoubt's library in search of an obscure tome; the other he set to sweeping the staircase landing. As they turned to their respective tasks, Atrellan went into the adjacent room to work on his notes.

His final comment to Daegon was terse and, as always, condescending.

"Do not disturb me until you are prepared to confirm my findings—or admit your failure to meet even that simple task."

Daegon made no response to Atrellan's back, but the ember of resentment smoldered deep in the pit of his gut. He cleared his mind of such distractions and prepared himself for the task ahead.

DAEGON WAS QUITE METHODICAL in his examination technique. It took him less than two hours to find the spells that Jalash-el and Atrellan had found. But he sensed that there was something else, something more deeply hidden, something that faded away if he tried to focus on it. Such a mysterious and nebulous phantasm, hovering just beyond the edge of his perception, intrigued and alarmed him. Worse, there was something dark and arcane here, very old, and yet with a hint of familiarity. He now had no doubt that there was another spell here, at least one. Somehow, it seemed *incomplete.*

A significant aspect of identifying an unknown enchantment was deducing its intent, a far more difficult challenge than most would appreciate. Daegon could only determine that it was intended to do great harm, and that heat would be involved.

What completely stymied him was the *trigger.* What would activate the spell? Or was this the trigger to another spell, perhaps even more comprehensive and dire?

Enchantments were typically activated in one of three ways: by the direct and immediate action of the spell caster; by the remote and immediate action of the spell caster; or lastly, by a predetermined triggering event or circumstance that initiates the bound and pending sorcery.

Daegon was fairly certain that he was dealing with an example of the last. Despite his best efforts, he could determine no more. That alone was too ominous, and concerned him further.

He had no way of determining who was responsible for this nefarious sorcery; there was no trace of the caster's hand. However, he recognized that the essence of the spell was likely based upon the lore of the Old Ones. It was neither necromancy, nor something darker; but it was close, heavily influenced by the forbidden arts, and therefore very dangerous.

There was no way that the queen should ever be exposed to this potential danger—notwithstanding her orders to the contrary.

Daegon was quite loyal to Queen Mab. She had installed him in her retinue of mages and advisors despite the disdain and ridicule he endured from his elfin counterparts. Even though his vocation as an alchemist was not held in any sort of benevolent regard by the hereditary elfin adepts, it mattered little, since he now enjoyed her patronage—and her discretion. Only she knew of his other, more esoteric, sorcerous skills. He was certain that she valued his expertise because in her mind it gave her an advantage, an edge over any rival—regardless of old prohibitions. There were rumors of her influence concerning aspects of the dark arts, of course; but, as is often the nature of such speculation, most were nowhere near the truth.

However, one thing was certain; if something were to happen to her, it would not go well for him.

She must be warned!

ENTERING THE ROOM IN which Atrellan worked, Daegon waited just inside the threshold to be noticed and acknowledged.

Atrellan seemed determined to ignore him.

Moving into the very center of the room, Daegon cleared his throat and waited patiently. He was becoming quite irritated with Atrellan's apparent pettiness; especially in light of what he was coming to believe might well be a cleverly hidden conspiracy to do great harm to someone—perhaps even the queen!

Atrellan finally looked up, scowling in obvious irritation at the interruption. "Well, what is it? Have you exhausted your limited repertoire of magic? Or are you merely giving up? Not that it matters, for I have completed my report—"

"M'lord!" interrupted Daegon. "You cannot bring that body to the queen. You *must* not! I sense the traces of another, more sinister spell within the body of Boltar. The queen must not come near it!"

"*You* sense? You *dare* tell *me* what to do? You dare tell the *queen* what she must do? I knew it was a grave mistake to involve you in this matter—but *I* comply with the orders of my queen!"

Daegon's patience was at its breaking point. His words rashly burst forth.

"Atrellan, do not be such a *fool!* Great harm would come of your blind obedience! *She must be warned!* You *must not* bring that body before the queen!"

"Silence!" Atrellan thundered, storming to his feet.

"Do you think that I know not your intentions, Daegon? Of course you would prevent me from carrying out my duty! *You* would bring the body to my queen! You would claim *my* work for your own, despite *your lack of true ability! You* would worm yourself further into her good graces—and impugn me and my abilities! You *bumbling halfling!* I know you for the traitorous and opportunistic *cur* you are!"

Daegon could only shake his head and softly respond, "Atrellan, you are *beyond* an utter fool. Your insecurity and paranoia cloud rational thought. Tis so sad and pathetic. You will undo yourself in—"

Atrellan suddenly thrust out his hands and a cloud of sparkling green light enveloped Daegon in a tight column!

It was a strong stasis spell; Daegon could neither move nor speak. He silently cursed himself for not being more cautious with the temperamental elf—and more alert. Clearly, he had not anticipated that Atrellan would react so poorly, or dangerously.

Daegon's mind raced, but for the moment, there was little he could do.

Atrellan approached the column of green light, his face awash in evil satisfaction. He came to a stop about a full pace away and glanced at the floor of the chamber.

Daegon could shift his glance down as well. He was shocked to see that he stood in the middle of the large brass circle, its bright metal inlaid with runes of silver.

Gods be damned! How did I fail to notice this ring when I came to stand in the center of the room?

"Tell me again, Daegon, who is the *utter fool?* Did you really think that I would not be prepared for your bumbling betrayal and inept treachery? Oh, you cannot speak? Oh my, that *is* unfortunate. Perhaps it is best that you just *listen!* You see, it will be my sad duty to inform Her Majesty that her *pet alchemist* trifled with things he did not understand, and foolishly managed to banish himself to a forbidden realm in the wild—from which no living thing has returned!"

Daegon blanched at the elf's words.

Is this a foray into the dark arts? Just what does Atrellan intend?

Leaning slightly forward, the mage hissed, "Indeed, it requires a death to open the passage—and not just *any* death, but the death of a *sentient* being to open a gate of sufficient size. So, naturally the queen will have little choice but to assume the worst."

Atrellan was obviously savoring the moment, and added with a lyrical cackle, "Now, if you will be patient; I shall see to sending you on your way."

Atrellan opened his arms wide and began an incantation in an ancient elfin dialect. Tilting his head back at an almost impossible angle, his voice seemed to change, growing deeper and more guttural. His eyes rolled up in their sockets until only the whites showed.

A sheath of purple light sprang up from the brass ring, surrounding the sparkling green column of the stasis spell.

As Daegon watched helplessly, inky black tendrils slowly rose from the silver runes inlaid in the brass, and pulsed like sinewy veins throughout the purple encasement.

A mad gleam in his eyes, Atrellan stepped back, his countenance sporting a satisfied smile.

"Ah, excellent! Now, I shan't be but a moment. Do stay right there, won't you?"

In Atrellan's absence, Daegon tried to remember the incantation the old mage had used. It had been a mistake for Atrellan to assume that his victim was ignorant of ancient elfin dialects. Daegon had recognized the intent of the second spell immediately; it was an ancient and obscure form of transit spell. The inlaid brass ring was essentially used as a strong focusing aid, and helped to call upon some very old lingering energy which seemed to abound in this place. Daegon was fairly confident that he could defeat this spell *if only* he could move and speak; but, the stasis spell still held him mute and immobile.

However, one thing did confound him; what was the purpose of the silver runes and the black veins rising from them like denuded trees on a windswept winter's hill?

Atrellan reappeared with one of the weary acolytes in tow. The mage had the exhausted young elf discard his broom and stand near the wall of shifting purple light holding a black candle in either hand.

Atrellan touched the sharp tip of his athame to the wick of each taper; each was suddenly aflame. Cautioning the acolyte not to let any wax drip on the brass, Atrellan took up a position behind him and began to chant softly.

With an economy of motion that Daegon almost missed, Atrellan shoved his blade up into the base of the acolyte's skull—paralyzing him immediately. Maintaining a firm right-handed grip on the hilt of the athame, the mage deftly plucked the two candles from the dying elf's hands and snuffed them out. Then placing his left hand in the small of the acolyte's back, Atrellan simultaneously withdrew the blade and shoved the young elf forward into the purple light.

In a brilliant multicolored flash, Daegon gasped and succumbed to a numbing unconsciousness.

DAEGON WINCED AS HIS eyes fluttered open. He was nauseous, sore, and disoriented. He had no idea how much time had passed. He lay supine, staring up at an unfamiliar sky framed in towering pines, loose stones digging into his back.

Where am I? Am I all here?

A quick personal inventory reassured him as to the second question; but, as to the first?

He managed to sit up and take stock of his immediate surroundings.

He was sitting on a broad windswept ledge of exposed basalt that rose a few inches above tufts of ankle-high grass and sandy ground, just inside a meandering line of tall and widely spaced pine trees. Behind him, a conifer forest rose to hold deepening shadows, and no promise of safety. In front of him, a rolling plain of swelling hills, covered in long grasses pulsing in wind-driven waves, flowed toward the horizon. The sun seemed to be lowering in that direction and his shadow stretched out behind him.

Can I reasonably assume that direction is west?

He stood, a bit unsteadily at first, and took a deep breath; the air was cool and crisp. He tried to order his thoughts; the memory of Atrellan's trap flooded his awareness. He was stiff, but otherwise uninjured, and obviously no longer under the influence of the stasis spell.

He was alone; there was no sign of the murdered acolyte.

Remembering Atrellan's gloating words, Daegon realized that he truly was now in another realm, but he had no idea which one—no doubt somewhere in the *wild*. He recognized nothing.

A sudden gust of wind splayed his robe; there was a definite chill in the air. As he snugged his robe around him, a broad shadow suddenly flashed overhead. Glancing up, a moment too late, he saw nothing—then a second shadow blotted out the sun. He saw a bird with a massive wingspan glide swiftly above him, and then flare its wings to slow its flight just beyond the treetops of the thickening forest.

That was a huge bird! Has it landed? It could not have been far. Should I? Perhaps just a quick look? After all, I need to know more about this place; and, this is the first sign of any animal life.

Noting the position of the sun and the basalt ledge, he cautiously set off through the conifer forest. He made an effort to maintain a straight course, and frequently looked back, committing the view to memory in order to facilitate his return.

He had not gone far when he pushed aside some tall ferns and peered into a large circular clearing bounded on its circumference by a series of massive standing stones. Several pairs of upright stones were capped with more thick slabs laid horizontally across their tops—*lintels?*

Daegon sensed something here—*power*, or remnants of a very old and very strong power once concentrated here. Of that, something remained; some sort of residual wild energy lingered.

A scraping and rustling drew his attention upward as he crouched low in the lee of an upright slab. He gaped in awe. He had found the birds, huge vultures perched upon the stones like morbid statues in dusky plumage.

Fortunately, he had not been discovered. He peered up at the six great carrion eaters as they stared, completely focused, across the clearing in earnest patience.

Daegon could hear a series of grunting and snuffling sounds that seemed to come from the other side of the clearing, but he could not see past a large mound of earth in its center. Staying to the rear of the stones, and thus carefully avoiding being noticed by any of the vultures, he crept around the perimeter until he could see beyond the earthen mound.

His breath froze in his throat—*wolves!*

A pack of very large and thick-bodied wolves worried the torn flesh of a massive corpse. Slashing at its ripped belly, they tugged forth slimy ropes of steaming entrails.

Daegon could not identify this animal. It resembled a much smaller, coarse-haired, tree-dwelling creature he had once seen in a dense jungle on a tropical island in the Realm of Mer; a slow moving leaf-eater that the islanders called a *sloth*. But this monstrosity was thickly furred and larger than a carriage with a four-horse team. It must have been formidable in life. It had stout legs, and long arms ending in paws that held incredible claws, sweeping scimitar curves longer than a man's arm.

Daegon was reminded of the largest bears he had seen, but this short-faced beast was easily four times that size, a true giant.

Had these wolves brought down such a creature? Had it been much of a battle? Perhaps so—there lies a wolf that does not move, a long bloody gash along its side. And yet there limps another nearby as it waits to feed.

Daegon looked on in awe, not realizing that the wind at his back carried his scent toward the feeding pack.

One by one the wolves stopped eating and raised bloodied muzzles to the breeze. The largest male stood and scented the air. He only had to look to two of the lower ranked members of the pack, and they rose and started moving off in different directions, their noses in the air.

In a matter of a few heartbeats, realization dawned. The two wolves had Daegon's scent and were slowly stalking his hidden position from different angles. Even the stoic vultures took notice of the change in lupine behavior and watched with growing interest.

Daegon was in serious trouble. He knew he had no hope of outrunning the wolves, and there was nowhere to hide. Even climbing upon one of the great stones would only expose him to the oversized vultures; they could shred him as easily as the wolves. He needed to do something—soon!

His eyes fell upon the furry corpse.

Could I? Is it even possible? Given the lingering energy of this place, perhaps? It would be a serious drain on my system. What choice do I have? I must survive! I must be bold!

Clearing his mind of doubt and fear, he boldly stepped forth from concealment.

The two stalking wolves stopped in their tracks, extended their muzzles and tasted his scent. They sensed no fear, and that was sufficient for them to pause in caution.

Daegon raised his arms and spoke in a firm unhurried cadence; the wolves' ears pricked up at the sound of his voice.

The arcane incantation was in ancient elfin, and was intended to gather any ambient energy into a focused dark spell. It would take a few moments to muster the strength, and craft the intention of the sorcery, a time in which Daegon would be physically vulnerable—but he had no choice.

As Daegon began to feel the ambient energy gather, it became evident the wolves felt something as well. The other members of the pack began growling and snapping at the air. The two wolves focused upon Daegon were not immune; their fur stood on end and their fangs were bared. Each took a step forward and settled into a muscle-bunching crouch—an instant away from a leaping attack.

Daegon closed his eyes, uttered the final words of the incantation, and sent an almost visible wavering mass of virulent energy into the massive corpse.

The huge body shuddered; the nearest wolves yelped and leapt back.

At the sounds of surprise and distress from their pack-mates, the two wolves threatening Daegon twisted their heads to look over their shoulders.

Feeling spent and weakened, Daegon stepped back unseen and watched in shocked fascination from behind the shelter of a standing stone.

The great furred beast moved, rolled to its knees and tried to rise.

The two wolves ignored Daegon and raced back to join their pack.

The giant sloth pushed up, balancing on its hind legs, and uttered a mournful cry to an uncaring sky.

The wolf pack rushed in, teeth slashing at the back of the sloth's legs. The beset beast gave a strangled howl of rage and fought back, swinging those murderous claws in vicious arcs. A wolf went flying, crumpled against a stone, and lay still. The huge sloth spun about, slashing at its tormentors with surprising speed. Trying to lunge and step to one side, the enraged giant tripped upon a dangling loop of its own intestines. As it fell, two wolves renewed the attack, rushing at its throat—only to be batted away by a massive backhanded swipe.

The great sloth glanced at its entangled guts, and with a series of sweeping swipes of its claws, cut away several lengths of rope-like intestines.

Gaining its feet once more, this mountain of furious fur shrieked its defiance—an unholy gleam in its red eyes.

Growling ominously, the remaining wolves began to back away.

A vulture, bolder than the rest, unwisely chose that moment to sweep down and grasp a glistening piece of severed intestine. A lightning slash of the sloth's huge paw reduced the scavenger to an explosion of viscera and feathers. The remaining vultures immediately took to panicked flight, scattering skyward.

In that moment of distraction, the surviving members of the wolf pack melted into the forest.

The giant pain-maddened sloth roared in frustration and followed, slashing at trees and rending underbrush as it crashed through the forest in erratic pursuit.

Daegon leaned against the stone, close to exhaustion, but pleased with the results of his necromancy. However, casting the spell had nearly drained him. He would need time to recover—but he could not stay here. He would have to make his way back to his arrival point; he would rest there.

WALKING BACK TOOK LONGER than it should have, for he was winded and weary. Nonetheless, Daegon plodded on until he eventually stumbled into more familiar surroundings.

He sat for a long time on the rocky ledge and pondered his predicament.

How is it that Atrellan knows of this place? Has he disposed of any other enemies in this fashion? This appears to be a most deadly realm, indeed—the perfect place to ensure the elimination of one's rivals. However, tis not without bloodying one's hands, nay, and at the cost of a sentient life.

Daegon stood and stretched his stiff and aching muscles. He needed to find water; and, he knew that hunger would be upon him soon enough. He scanned the westward plains, hoping for any signs of a stream—and saw movement.

A group of large grazing beasts moved slowly toward the south, their path more or less parallel to the tree line. He had never seen their like; brown shaggy coats, and a pair of long uneven tusks jutting straight forward from their cheeks. Some of the beasts even had smaller tusks jutting from their lower jaws as well. Their long flexible noses were utterly strange to him; but, something triggered a memory.

As an alchemist, Daegon was a fairly learned individual. Somewhere in his reading and research, he had found descriptions of similar beasts—*elephants*—although the specifics differed considerably. He remembered them described as *grey* and *thick-skinned* rather than having brown shaggy coats or an extra pair of smaller tusks sprouting from the lower jaw. He recalled that their long flexible noses were called *trunks*, and were capable of prodigious strength. He was relatively certain that these beasts were *not* elephants, but perhaps something closely related.

As he watched, fascinated, he noticed other, more subtle movement along the flanks and to the rear of the slow moving herd. Something stalked them in the tall grasses, something acting as a pack.

Perhaps more wolves? No, I think not.

The herd kept up a steady pace; but the *hunters,* as Daegon began thinking of them, moved in sudden spurts, freezing in place if a herd beast looked that way, or raised its trunk to sample the air from that direction.

As Daegon watched, the lead herd beast suddenly stopped, raised its trunk, and trumpeted a strident warning.

Ah, a shift in the wind must have betrayed the scent of the hunters.

The herd had become distended, but nonetheless they began to move purposely into a tight mass. The larger beasts faced outward, and the smaller, presumably younger offspring, were shepherded into the protected center.

Unfortunately, several members of the herd had not yet attained the safety of the group. One lone adult moved with difficulty, walking somewhat briskly but with an exaggerated limp, and sounding a plaintive cry that bordered on panic.

The attention of the hunters became riveted upon this lagging and clearly ailing animal, while the rest of the stragglers reached the safety of the herd.

As the pursuers closed around the lone straggler, Daegon got a better look at a pair of the hunters.

Lizard-like in appearance, they stood erect on two robust rear legs; Daegon estimated that they were about shoulder high to him. Large oblong heads jerked in brief and sudden movements on long thick necks, revealing subtle flashes of color—*rows of feathers?* There were no shoulders to speak of, but a pair of short arms ending in hand-like claws jutted forth from the upper body. A long tapering tail seemed to counterbalance the bulk of the body as it stood on its two hind legs.

They were fast—incredibly so.

Daegon gasped when the two hunters suddenly turned and ran in opposite directions; they were lost from his view in seconds.

Their strategy became apparent to him in the next few moments.

The hunters intended to force their selected victim further away from the massed herd and closer to the tree line. At first, it appeared that their quarry was complying in its frantic panic, actually coming much closer toward Daegon's position. But suddenly the herd beast spun around, faced the two hunters dogging its heels, and trumpeted a defiant challenge at its pursuers.

The hunters stopped in their tracks, and Daegon could hear them *chittering* at each other.

They were communicating!

Something had drastically changed; it was clear the hunters knew it.

In the next instant, the herd beast lowered its head and charged, bellowing what could only be its war cry.

The lizards leapt straight up—higher than a man could reach—and flashed wickedly sharp foot claws at the charging beast, before bounding out of the way.

Their threat display did nothing to alter the charge. This herd beast was no ailing or weakened animal—this was a robust adult in its prime, full of furious fight.

Daegon realized the entire display of frailty, the limping and plaintive cries of panic, had been a diversion, a ruse to allow time for the weaker members of the herd to reach safety. But the danger was far from over for this beast;

now it had to make it back to the herd on its own. And there were at least eight hunters, perhaps more, that would do their best to prevent that from happening.

Daegon watched in awe as the hunters executed what had to be a choreographed attack.

A pair of hunters simultaneously rushed in from the side and leapt at the near flank of the charging beast. They slashed viciously with their oversized toe claws, and bounded away. The herd beast altered course to that side to fight them off, only to be attacked in the same manner on its opposite side. This pattern was repeated until the herd beast seemed to sense that it was running in a large erratic circle, getting no closer to the safety of the herd. Then it just stopped, long shreds of bloody hide flesh dangling from its heaving sides, almost as if it was taking stock of the situation—perhaps getting its bearings.

With a sudden speed that belied its size, the beast lurched to one side, swinging its massive head in a quick arc. The long tusks scythed through the tall grass and two hunters were thrown through the air, falling awkwardly to earth only a stone's throw from where Daegon stood frozen into immobility.

One of the hunters regained its feet and shook its head. Daegon dared not move. The lizard loudly sniffed the air and scanned the area; but, Daegon apparently remained undetected.

The other hunter that had fallen near the first tried to rise to its feet but immediately collapsed, hissing in pain. The first regarded its comrade curiously, jutting its head forward to sniff at the injured lizard—only to be savagely snapped at by the downed hunter. The wounded lizard thrashed about, hissing and biting at the air to keep his former fellow hunter at bay. Strings of bloodied saliva arced out across the tops of tall grasses, drooping in putrid loops from splattered stalks and seed heads.

In the midst of the confusion, a tawny blur flashed by at the far edge of Daegon's peripheral vision—instantly followed by another. A chittering squeal was abruptly cut off, followed by the sound of something large desperately flailing about in the tall grass.

Then all went still; there was no trace of the lizards.

Daegon dared not breathe.

The tall grass parted, and the largest predatory cat Daegon had ever seen stopped before him not a half-dozen paces away. The feline's chest and shoulders were more than twice the width of his own; and a pair of huge fangs, as long as his forearm, gripped the limp bloody throat of one of the lizards. A rustle in the grass announced the arrival of another similar cat, although slightly smaller than the first, the second lizard firmly gripped in its crimson jaws.

The pair of great cats regarded Daegon with mild curiosity. Strangely, he felt no fear—only staggering degrees of awe and amazement.

Both cats sniffed at him, and seemed to decide that he presented neither threat nor interest in their kills. The larger, a male, gave a short guttural cough and moved off at an angle, heading into the forest. The female followed, watching Daegon carefully. They disappeared into the deepening gloom; their heavy prey burdens presenting no apparent hindrance.

Daegon had the distinct and disturbing sense that the female had marked his location and sampled his scent, perhaps as prey for a future hunt.

Looking again to the west, he saw that the solitary, but brave, elephantine beast had finally succumbed to its hunters. The remaining six reptiles were busily worrying at the still warm carcass, while the closely packed herd moved off to the south.

Gazing back at the scene of the recent drama of life and death, Daegon was surprised to see the six remaining hunters snap their heads up in unison and stare at the forest to the south of his position. Scenting the air, they made neither sound nor movement.

With a bloodcurdling roar, a massive reptile erupted from the southern edge of the forest and bore down on the site of the kill. Similar in appearance to the hunters, but easily five times their size, the thundering lizard covered the distance in a matter of seconds.

At the first sight of the huge predator, the hunters fled, scattering in different directions. One was too slow—snapped up in crushing jaws in an instant. The rest disappeared into the tall grasses.

The huge, bloody-jawed, reptile flung the dead hunter aside, abandoned the chase, and stalked to the carcass of the herd beast. Lowering its great head to the remains, it carefully sniffed the body. Seemingly satisfied, it urinated on the carcass, and then again in many spots within the immediate vicinity. Finally, it stood over the carcass and let loose a rumbling roar, no doubt declaring ownership of the territory and the kill.

Daegon waited until it began to eat, and then slowly slipped further into the pines. He would not go far; he had yet to permanently mark the point at which he entered this realm, something he could not overlook. No doubt it was a fixed portal, one that supposedly could not be opened from this side; but then again, every enchantment had some sort of loophole. He surmised how it could possibly be done. However, even with his special skills, he was going to need some help—help from another realm.

Arranging that was going to be the problem.

For the moment, he had to find a safe place to spend the hours of darkness. Shadows had grown longer and the sun was already beginning to sink below the horizon. Considering what he had witnessed in broad daylight, he shuddered to think what horrors the night might harbor. One glance in the direction of the darkening forest was sufficient to convince him that he could forgo searching for water until the morning. The nearby taller trees offered the only semblance of temporary sanctuary.

Oh well, this wouldn't be the first night spent in the boughs of a tree—better than in the belly of a beast. Truly, this is the most dangerous realm I have ever seen. Atrellan, you and I shall have a reckoning. But, first things first—survive the night.

Laboriously ascending a rough-bark pine, Daegon knew he was in for a restless night.

THE TEMPERATURE DROPPED considerably throughout the night; his robe was hardly sufficient for adequate warmth. His involuntary shivering was not entirely from the cold. The sounds of nocturnal predators—and worse, the dying screams of their victims—were not conducive in the least to any sort of peaceful repose. His nerves understandably frayed, he was nonetheless determined to survive.

Since he could not sleep for more than a few fitful minutes at a time, wedged as he was between two stout limbs and the wide trunk of the towering tree, he passed the time wrestling with the problem of getting out of this realm. And by the first rays of the dawn's light, he had formulated the essential outline of a vague plan—desperate, to be sure, but a plan nonetheless.

Blowing warm breath into his cupped hands and rubbing them together, Daegon regained some dexterity in his fingers, stiffened from the frigid night air.

He fumbled within his robe and brought forth a small soft leather pouch. Probing within the pouch, he drew out a dull, unpolished gemstone, an amethyst the size of a large acorn. This was no common purple jewel; this ancient gem had been part of a dragon's hoard.

The sound of distant thunder drew Daegon's attention to the south. A dark line of heavy clouds was visible on the distant horizon; occasional flashes of lightning and subsequent rumbling within the roiling mass heralded a stormy day. A light breeze sprang up, no doubt a precursor of storm-chased winds to come.

Daegon would welcome rain; he could slake his thirst without having to venture into the forest in search of water. Of course, food was another matter, as his growling stomach reminded him.

Daegon looked up in time to see a flock of crows winging to the northeast, riding the breeze ahead of the front. He realized they would likely seek shelter within the edge of the forest to find a protected roost and ride out the storm.

For the first time since his rude arrival in this realm, he smiled.

Carefully returning the amethyst to his pouch, he watched the crows glide past the tree line and settle into the canopy of the forest. He marked the spot; his smile broadened.

Fate or chance had offered an opportunity—were he shrewd enough to seize it. His plan no longer seemed quite so vague or desperate.

He began the long careful descent to the ground; it would not do to sustain an injury from a fall. No indeed, since he already had a busy day planned—assuming, of course, he could avoid being eaten.

CH 5

MARK SAT IN ATLANTA'S crowded airport and silently cursed the weather. His connecting flight was delayed, unable to land because of a raging afternoon thunderstorm that was showing no signs of abating. His plans did not include Mother Nature throwing such a bombastic fit. He could only sigh in resignation; there was nothing he could do about it.

He had already called Delafaire Farm and spoken with Stacy and his cousin, Ellen; so, they knew he'd be arriving later than expected. He'd promised to call again when he knew his actual departure time from Atlanta. Propping his open briefcase on his knees, he removed his yellow legal pad and began to draft some notes. He had already accomplished a great deal; but, he would still have a busy week ahead of him.

His firm in New York had readily granted him a leave of absence; in fact, they were quite interested in establishing ties with existing law firms in Louisiana. Considerable opportunity was thought to follow throughout the reconstruction phase of the post-hurricane initiatives along the Gulf Coast. In fact, to be coldly rational, large infusions of federal *disaster recovery funds* meant there would always be comprehensive legal issues to resolve. Mark understood his firm's motivation. However, he had no intention of being sucked into that morass; his priority was a more family-based agenda.

He had done quite well—far better than he might have dreamed—in the discreet disposition of the selection of rare coins he'd taken to New York. His associate, the hobby-numismatist, had quietly managed to secure almost $325,000 for the assortment of highly desirable specie from a very discerning, select group of collectors. Even after setting aside enough to pay the anticipated taxes on the profit, this windfall would virtually eliminate the tax lien, and ensure the viability of Delafaire Farm for the immediate future. Beyond that, his draft of the articles of incorporation would establish a business enterprise at the farm, which would hopefully create an adequately sufficient cash flow to profitably sustain itself commercially, and help maintain the farm.

He scribbled a series of appointments he'd have to make for the coming week: a meeting with the family's attorney, Claude Fornier, to finalize the incorporation and initiate applications for the required tax and business licenses; a meeting at the bank to establish the appropriate accounts; and a meeting with Sheriff Frank Tatum to satisfy the outstanding tax lien. There would be other logistical requirements, of course, but he would deal with them as they arose.

Looking at his notes, Mark thought of certain issues that he dared not write down.

Yeah, like why was Miska now at the farm?

Neither Ellen nor Stacy was willing to discuss with him the specifics of Miska's arrival and protracted visit—at least not over the telephone. He would have to wait until he was back in LaBorde.

And what of this summons that Ellen had received, to attend a Council meeting?

This meeting was in less than a week—six days. Mark had no doubt that she intended to go; but, surely she would not go alone. Had she told Hawk? Of course, she would tell him; and Hawk would insist on accompanying her.

Mark realized that he was determined to go as well.

THE KITCHEN PHONE AT Delafaire Farm rang; Stacy answered in the midst of its second trill.

"Hello? Oh, hi Mark, I just knew it was you! That's great! No, of course we'll pick you up. Six-twenty, right? Okay, sweetie, we'll see you then. Bye-bye."

Millie and Ellen looked up from their tea and smiled at Stacy, whose beaming face couldn't have been any brighter.

"Well, Mom," said Ellen, tongue firmly in cheek, "I think we're going to the airport. Can we pick up anything for you?"

"No thanks, dear—just your cousin," Millie chuckled.

Stacy spun on her heels and announced, "I've got to get ready—I must look a fright! Give me ten minutes!"

"Uh, Stacy," Ellen said, "Mark won't land for almost two hours. You have plenty of time."

"Oh, that's right! Now I've got time to shower—my hair's a mess!" she declared, tousling her disheveled blonde locks, which only served to enhance her smiling pixie-like countenance.

As Stacy disappeared from the kitchen, Millie remarked, "I'm so happy for her—for them both. Can you see it, too?"

Struck by her mother's insight, Ellen realized that she, too, could see the change in both Stacy and her cousin. They *were* different, almost as if they completed one another; they were truly happy together. And like her mother, Ellen was happy for them.

"You know, I think I can," mused Ellen. "I think they're good for each other."

"Yes, they are—and it'll be nice to have Mark back here." Millie's smile faltered. "Have you seen the news—that horrible murder near Alexandria? It gives me the creeps! I'll feel better having Mark staying with us again."

"I saw something in the paper—just a blurb, not a whole story. Was there more on TV?"

Millie shrugged. "A bit more. They found the body of a man who'd been tortured, and a woman is missing. And I swear, Ellen, that smarmy on-camera newscaster absolutely gleamed luridly when he reported it. And then, he inferred that it was extremely *ominous* that the authorities wouldn't comment or answer any of his questions—like we're all in *grave danger* or something. Did Hawk say anything about it?"

"No. Come on, Mom, you know he doesn't really talk about his work—especially not about specific case details."

"Oh, I know, dear. I was just curious. Is he still coming for supper Wednesday evening?"

"Oh, yeah, he'll be here," Ellen smiled. "That reminds me; he asked if he could bring anything—some wine, maybe?"

"Sure! In that case, tell him to come early. The chef is not above sipping a little taste of the grape while she cooks!"

HAWK GLANCED UP AT the wall clock in the squad room and realized he would be late for Wednesday night supper. It was four o'clock in the afternoon; the meeting was about to start.

The room was crowded. Quite a number of investigators from other agencies had come at Sheriff Tatum's invitation. Both shifts of Chantilly Parish Sheriffs Department CID detectives were present.

The assembled investigators were milling about, casually visiting with friends and colleagues. Despite the restrained light banter, the mood was serious. Conversations dwindled to a respectful silence as Captain Miller entered, trailed by Deputy U.S. Marshals Todd Simmons and Willis Hebert.

"All right," announced the captain, "we'll get right to it. You all remember the request that went out to all the Louisiana Sheriffs from Sheriff Picard in Lafayette regarding the double homicide in Carencro?"

"The one with the *Colombian neckties?*" asked a voice from the back of the room.

"That's the one," the captain acknowledged. "Well, there are some new developments. I'll let Deputy Marshal Simmons fill you in. Todd?"

"Thanks, Lou. As y'all know, the Alexandria PD had a homicide discovered yesterday morning. The victim, a white male, 30 years, has been positively identified as Pierre Broussard, AKA *'Sprocket',* who is no stranger to law enforcement."

Todd's partner, DUSM Willis Hebert began passing out mug shots of the decedent as Simmons continued.

"Broussard has an extensive criminal history; mostly drugs, vehicle thefts, and petty larcenies. He's known to us as an old associate of Theodore Rasmussen, AKA *'Teddy Pots'*, for whom we have a warrant, which is why Broussard was on our radar. Broussard was currently on state parole for a distribution conviction, and was living on the west side of Alexandria. Yesterday morning, on a routine home visit, his state parole officer found Broussard's body. His corpse was bound with wire coat hangers and duct tape to a chair in the adjacent garage. There was evidence of pretty extensive torture; Broussard had a *Colombian necktie*. The P.O. further advised that Broussard shared the house with a woman; and at that time, she was missing."

"Did you say '*was* missing', Todd?" asked Trey.

"Yes, Sergeant, *was*, as in the past tense. She was found late this morning; deceased, tortured, likely raped, and also had a Colombian necktie."

The silence was thick in the crowded room. DUSM Simmons opened a file and rummaged through several reports before continuing.

"The woman's body was found by a unit of National Guard engineers grading roads in a training area of Camp Beauregard, just inside Grant Parish. So, the National Guard/Army CID is involved, assisting Grant Parish Sheriff's Office."

"Let me interject," cautioned the captain, "that nothing about finding this woman has yet been released to the media. Grant Parish S.O. and Army CID will coordinate with ongoing investigations. We've also been in touch with Alexandria PD, Rapides Parish S.O., and Lafayette Parish S.O.; all agree we need to keep some information confidential. So, aside from the official statement by the Alexandria PD yesterday about finding the victim of a homicide, we're going to hold off on releasing any further details on any of these related cases."

"We agree, as well," acknowledged Todd. "There are far too many similarities for these cases not to be linked. The Colombian neckties are too distinctive, damn near *signatures.* We'll get into that later."

"The first two were in Carencro, right?" asked a state police detective. "Did the Lafayette Sheriff's Office release any details about the Colombian neckties?"

"Only to law enforcement—not the media," Captain Miller assured him. "But we all know that with anything this potentially sensational it's only a matter of time before something leaks. For now, let's keep it on a *confidential/need-to-know* basis."

"Do they have an ID on the woman, yet?" asked Hawk.

"They do," answered Willis Hebert, stepping forward. "And that is why we are here. She is Patricia Brewster, white female, 24 years, with a misdemeanor record. And, she is the estranged niece of the late Fenton Brewster, our former potential OCDETF witness, who is now one of your open cases, a suspected suicide, as yet unconfirmed."

"Now, understand," Simmons cautioned, "that the late Patricia was not what we might call one of Fenton's favorite nieces—a *black sheep*, even within the Brewster clan. While working as an exotic dancer at one of his clubs, she was skimming the till and even tried to blackmail him; the details are vague. He didn't react well. He fired her, and put the word out no dealer was to provide her with *any* drugs. Some older intel had suggested she might be a drug user; but until lately we didn't know for sure that she was seriously addicted, a stone meth and heroin junkie."

"As it happens," offered Willis, "DEA was watching who they suspected might be her heroin connection in relation to another case; but, she hadn't been around that target for a while. Based on street CIs and routine surveillance, DEA is pretty sure that Patsy was getting most of her crystal from Teddy Pots, through her live-in boyfriend, Sprocket, maybe heroin, too. But that was speculation; they had no concrete evidence for either drug.

"Broussard's parole officer was in the DEA loop, but Broussard was pretty low key and appeared to break no laws. The P.O. couldn't violate him on a technical issue unless Broussard flunked a urine test, they found drugs in the house, or they caught him in the company of another felon. So, the interested agencies met and decided to wait and see what the P.O. could turn up to use as leverage to encourage Broussard to cooperate with us to find Teddy."

"And we would have remained patient," quipped Todd, "that is, until yesterday, when Broussard was found dead."

"That nickname, *Sprocket*, rings a bell," observed an Alexandria PD detective near the back of the room. "I think he was a suspect in a motorcycle theft, years ago. As I recall, we took the original theft report near the airport. The owner of the stolen bike only vaguely knew this suspect as 'Sprocket', but he was convinced this guy was involved. Thinking this might be related, we passed it on to Louisiana State Police, who were working a stolen vehicle ring. I never got called for court, so I don't know what happened with the case."

"We do." Todd lifted a document from the file, and answered as his partner sipped from a coffee mug. "You were right; it was related. However, Broussard was not among the indicted, although he was clearly involved. LSP didn't have a tight case on him, so he walked—but seven others were ultimately convicted. Naturally, those who went to jail assumed Broussard wasn't prosecuted because he cooperated. He hadn't, but his fellow thieves assumed that he'd turned informant."

Simmons sipped his coffee and continued.

"About four years ago, Broussard got arrested during a *buy-bust* sting in Shreveport and pled to a reduced charge of possession with intent to distribute. He did two and a half years of a four year sentence. He had to be kept in administrative segregation for his whole bit; the word was out that he was a *snitch*. He made parole, and has been low profile in Alexandria ever since."

"Until yesterday," observed Willis.

"Yeah," agreed Todd. "Something is up; the timing of these homicides is curious, with the possibility of a link we shouldn't overlook. We think there's another layer to all this, a bigger picture.

"Early this afternoon, our tech wizards and CSI tech, Cassie Spenser, from Chantilly Parish S.O., completed decrypting the files recovered from the computers and storage media belonging to another homicide victim, the hitwoman, Suzi Origami—another open case. We went over the decrypted data pretty carefully and found what we think is another hit list; the name 'Patsy B' appears on it. 'Patsy B' was Patricia Brewster's *stage name* as an exotic dancer. Somebody, maybe *Uncle Fenton*, had enough and wanted her taken out. This entry was in one of the last files Suzi encrypted, so it's not likely that she got around to doing anything about it. We know Suzi was killed before Patsy died."

"As far as we know," added Willis, "Suzi did all her own *wet work*. There's nothing to suggest she may have subcontracted a hit. We're certain she and Teddy Pots had an arrangement, most likely body disposal. That would explain why he appears to have been her only consistent contact—aside from her primary client, George Papadolis, AKA Papa George.

"So, Teddy Pots is the only consistent link in several of the these cases. And if we're right, our best guess is that someone else is now hunting Teddy Pots, uh, besides us. Bear with us; we'll explain."

Willis nodded to his partner.

"We know from latent prints," Todd began, "that Teddy was in the funeral home/lab outside of Lafayette. We have two bodies with specific mutilations in Carencro, just north of Lafayette. We don't know if there's a solid connection between Teddy and the bodies in Carencro. On the other hand, we can't ignore the two recently discovered bodies with the same mutilations, in Alexandria and north of Pineville, and the fact that, according to DEA intel, Teddy knows both of those victims."

"Now, you've gotta ask," posed Willis, "why would anyone hunt Teddy? As far as we know, he's got no money, no influence—nothing. He's a cockroach scurrying around the underside of reality. He's only got one talent in his sorry life—he's one *helluva* meth cook."

"So, let's assume," offered Todd, "that Teddy was definitely involved in that meth lab in the funeral home; but, maybe he wasn't there at the time of the raid, or slipped away before it went down. Now he probably knows it happened—it'd be hard to miss the media coverage. So, he's either on the run, or gone to ground. Remember, Teddy knows how to do a major lab; but, he doesn't have the bankroll to set one up. Someone had to put up the funds; and more than likely, someone had to broker the deal.

"From what DEA has determined, there was some serious front money involved. The source wasn't the current owner of the funeral home, Rudolf Broussard—no relation to Sprocket, who's broke and a closet crack addict. His mortuary business is on the borderline of bankruptcy. So, the funds came from somewhere else.

"But the lab blows up—no product, no cash flow. Now, these *financiers* want—and expect—a return on their investment; somebody's gotta pay. So, the questions mount up. Who's gotta pay? Who's gonna collect? How much? Who would have put up that kind of money? And, who could've brokered such a deal?"

"Fenton Brewster, as the broker?" Willis offered. "Sure, we all know that fits; but we also know he's now out of the game—dead. We have no doubt he was in it up to his eyeballs, probably even brokered the deal himself; but we all know he can't be our killer. So, who else? Well, of course Papa George comes to mind; he's fronted cash to Brewster on occasion, but nothing of this scale. Word on the street is that Brewster already owed Papa George too much, so there's no going back to the well. The fact is there's not a trace of evidence or intel that links Papa George to this lab deal. And we know his *cleaner*, Suzi, is out of the picture before these killings go down."

"It's becoming pretty clear," Todd pointed out, "that there's definitely another party involved in the initial financial commitment for the lab. Logically, only these investors would have a vested interest in finding Teddy—the only surviving link to the lab operation. Through him, we suspect they hope to find whoever has the deep enough pockets to cover the loss of their investment—and probably then some."

"Wait a minute," cautioned the captain. "Do you mean that these graphic killings are being done to send a message—to intimidate whoever was behind Brewster, to recover their *investment?*"

"Yeah, we pretty much think so, Captain," Todd agreed. "This was an expensive major lab effort, capable of many millions of dollars worth of production in a relatively short time. And that time factor significantly minimizes the risk—set up, cook, ship, and disappear."

"But there are always risks," Willis countered, "and the broker must be in a position to offer some level of assurance, like a *bond.*"

"A bond?" asked another voice from the back of the room.

"Yeah," Willis answered. "Think of it like this—there's this disgruntled investor who wants to make an insurance claim because his promised product has been destroyed and he's out all of his front money. But since the broker's dead, he's got to find whoever backed the broker, and his only link is this frightened little cook who's running or hiding."

"So that's why the bodies were left to be easily found, with the signature mutilations," Trey deduced. "The killer or *killers*—my gut says there's more than one guy—*want* the word to get out. They *want* Teddy to know! They want him to *run*, because then he's exposed and easier to find! And when they snatch him up, they can squeeze him, to move up the ladder."

"But you know," Todd observed, "that tells us something about our killer or killers, doesn't it? They don't understand how New Orleans works, or have any idea who Brewster typically went to for financial backing, do they? These boys ain't from around here, are they?"

"Nope," agreed Willis. "We're thinking that they might be from *way south* of here. We talked to Eva Quantrell at DEA, and she pretty much agrees. The *modus operandi*, the torture for information and then the Colombian necktie, is a ruthless and distinct cartel signature. They typically want it known that they have a long reach."

"If it *is* one of the cartels," Todd added, "they'd typically send a team, a four to six man unit, usually ex-military—what the *juntas* used to refer to as a *death squad*. These are not nice people.

"And there is the possibility of another twist. At the moment, we think there is only one cartel involved. However, there are multiple drug cartels, and they are often in competition with one another."

"Unfortunately," cautioned Willis, smiling slightly, "we have no solid evidence. This is a lot of speculation based on uncorroborated intel and what we *do* know so far. There are still a lot of unanswered questions."

"Of course," observed Captain Miller dryly, "now it all fits if you consider Papa George's known M.O. It's common knowledge on the street that he'd move in on any profitable operation that he'd have backed or developed any interest in. Now if Brewster couldn't repay an old debt, or turned up dead, Papa George would step in on whatever Brewster was up to and liquidate whatever he could find, or run with the operation. It's pretty clear that our killers evidently don't know that—at least not yet."

"Right you are, Captain," said Willis, no longer smiling. "We don't think they knew*;* but, we don't know what Patricia Brewster may have known and told them—and you can be certain that she talked.

"That leaves us in an awkward position because, unfortunately, as of right now, no one has a line on Teddy *or* Papa George. The killers may well be a step or two ahead of us, I'm afraid."

"So," began Todd, "we've shared everything we've got—which isn't as much as we'd like—but we've exhausted our leads on Teddy Pots. Admittedly, it's only a hunch that he had any recent contact with *Sprocket* or *Patsy*, but we think the odds are pretty good. He doesn't have many locations where he can go to ground. There are places in Shreveport and Monroe, but our people up there have them under tight surveillance."

"Everybody is looking for Papa George," Willis said with a sigh, "thanks to the outstanding material witness warrant in NCIC and the wanted posters in circulation; but he seems to have disappeared. Since he's still an OCDETF target, all agencies are encouraged to check all investigative files for any intel regarding any contingency plans Papa George may have made—assuming he had some, of course. Also check your files related to Fenton Brewster and Patricia Brewster for anything related to Papa George.

"We realize y'all are pretty familiar with your own files. Do any of your sources know of anything like a *safe house* he might have used, or prepared, in Chantilly Parish, or anywhere else?"

"Just that ranch that was seized recently, pending a forfeiture action by the federal court," observed Trey, "but y'all already know about that, right?"

"Yeah, we do," sighed Willis. "We'd sure appreciate it if y'all would keep an ear to the ground on this. Finding and arresting Papa George is an OCDETF priority."

"And don't forget," Todd added, "We'd sure like to find Teddy, too—before the competition does."

BY EARLY FRIDAY AFTERNOON, the humidity over the Toledo Bend Reservoir lay like a smothering blanket on the landscape. The warmth of the merciless sun cooked up a suddenly potent thunderstorm that chased boaters and fishermen off the turbulent chop with malicious glee. The storm stalled over the slate-hued water for several hours, giving the area a thorough drenching before wearing itself out in the late afternoon. By sunset, the heat had abated by only a few degrees, and the cloying humidity was worse than ever.

A lone crow flew an erratic northerly course along the eastern bank of the reservoir. Landing awkwardly atop a tall dock piling, it attempted to preen its worn and wet plumage; but, it carried its head at such an impossible angle, that much of its effort was fruitless. Furtive movement on shore drew its attention; the stoic corvid watched with listless eyes.

As shadows bled into the greying dusk, four men crept silently into positions of concealment around the large house overlooking the reservoir. Two more quiet men watched from a nearby tree-covered hill; one held binoculars to his eyes, as the other held a small microphone and depressed the transmit key in a series of small *clicks*. The four hidden men crouched down and disappeared from sight.

To the rear of the house, a broad deck faced the water; a set of short steps descended to a weatherworn boat dock. A pair of yellow porch lights brightened to life casting a soft golden glow upon the wet boards of the deck; damp shadows fled over its edge.

A lone figure stepped casually through a sliding glass door, onto the deck. The flare of a match and the subsequent small cloud of smoke betrayed a thin man enjoying a cigarette. As hidden eyes watched, another person, a tall woman, stepped onto the deck and joined the smoker.

They held a seemingly urgent, whispered conversation. The man took a deep drag, dropped the cigarette to the deck boards, and irritably ground the butt beneath his heel. Without another word, he preceded the stoic woman back into the house.

The watcher with the binoculars made a small flat sweeping gesture with his hand, and the other man responded with another series of radio clicks. The four hidden men relaxed and settled in to wait.

They were patient—very patient. Until the command was given, they were prepared to spend the night in these concealed positions. But if their information was correct, they would neither remain hidden, nor outside for long.

THE TALL WOMAN, LING, pushed a protesting Teddy Pots ahead of her as she went in search of Papa George. She found him in a lower level room sitting before a keyboard and a rack of security camera monitors.

"Quit pushing me, damn it!" Teddy complained. "All I did was go out on the deck for a smoke. What's gotten into you?"

Ignoring the fidgeting meth cook, the bodyguard addressed her putative boss. "Sir, we have visitors—men hidden near the trees."

George stood and asked, "How many?"

"At least two, whom I sensed. But, I would think two more, downwind of the house. So, let us assume four."

"Boss, I didn't—" began Teddy.

"Shut up, Teddy!" interrupted George, turning toward the door. "Vito! Get in here!"

A moment later, George's driver and occasional muscle filled the doorway, his right hand inside a loose jacket draped over his arm. The blunt muzzle of a suppressor poked out, pointed at the floor.

Ling stepped past him into the hall, only to return a moment later with her two silent goons, Bubba and Iggy.

George addressed them all. "We have uninvited guests on the grounds. As far as we know, they don't know that we know they're here. We don't know who they are, or why they're here—but I don't think it's the neighborhood welcome wagon. So, I need one of them alive. *Capisce?*"

Teddy decided that this was a good time to remain quiet and inconspicuous; but, his nerves were jumping. As he pressed his back up against a wall, Ling shot him a look that did little to calm his fear. Then she *smiled* at him—a feral *I smell your fear* grin!

George opened a hidden panel in the wall that revealed an impressive display of guns; rifles, shotguns, and pistols. He selected a short-barreled assault rifle, a Colt M-4, for himself, and an assault shotgun, a Franchi SPAS 12, which he tossed to Vito. George nodded to Ling and inclined his head toward the rack of firearms.

Ling just smiled and shook her head. "I will have no need of any such weapons."

Teddy shuddered at the eager tone in her voice.

George closed the panel and pointed at him.

"Teddy, you stay here, in this room. Watch the security camera monitors, and *touch nothing!* Vito, you're in the front room, where you can see the front door and the head of the stairs. No one, except Ling and her muscle, gets in, or down here. I'll cover the back room that accesses the deck and the kitchen door. Ling, you and your guys will have to deal with these *trespassers* outside. I'll need one who can talk. Now, let's go!"

With her two goons in her wake, Ling slipped soundlessly back upstairs to the main level.

Teddy was just relieved that she had left the room.

STANDING WITH GEORGE before the sliding glass door in the darkened great room, Ling looked out at the deck and decided on a strategy. All she really needed was a distraction; her two minions would be perfect.

She turned and faced them. "You will each go out onto the deck. Go to the far opposite corners. Each of you will then light and smoke a cigarette. Be at ease and relaxed. You will stay there until I tell you otherwise."

George watched as she slid the door open and the two men followed her instructions to the letter.

She slid the door closed, placed a finger to her lips, and leaned closer.

"Turn on no lights. I will go out the kitchen door; lock it behind me. This should take no more than a few minutes. Whatever you hear, do *not* go outside. I will tell you when it is safe to do so."

He nodded. "Got it. Remember, I need one alive."

She grinned, turned and seemed to vanish in the dark; only the ghost of her predatory smile lingered as an afterimage.

He heard the kitchen door softly open and close; he went and locked it as instructed.

ONCE OUTSIDE, LING melted into the night.

A few moments later, a large dark feline form emerged from a thick stand of ferns, and scented the cloying night air. With a graceful lope it disappeared downwind, into the trees.

THE HIDDEN WATCHER, crouched amidst reeds close to the water, had a clear view of the two men leisurely smoking in the warm amber glow of the porch lights. He was certain that his comrades, who were hidden even closer to the house, had them under surveillance as well.

Neither smoker fit the description of their quarry. There had been another man who had stood on the deck for a brief time earlier, physically a better fit perhaps; but, none of his team had seen enough to make a positive identification. The man they sought was supposed to be alone. They had no way of knowing how many people were in this house. Until they at least knew that much, they would continue to watch.

Snug in his right ear, a small molded earwig was his communications link to his teammates. Unfortunately, it also tended to mask any ambient sounds coming from his right rear quadrant.

He never heard her approach.

A crushing weight slammed him face-first into the muddy shoreline. He instinctively tried to roll to one side and get his face out of the muck. The weight on his back shifted, and his neck was seized in something like a warm wet vise. His right arm wedged under him, his hand found the pistol grip of his short assault rifle, still pinned beneath his chest. He tried to bring the muzzle to bear, but the pressure on his neck suddenly increased. He felt his skin being punctured. There was a ferocious jerk—he heard the bones of his neck break. His legs went into spasms, but he felt nothing—not even pain.

His sight slowly dimmed and he died.

She moved on.

THE NEXT MAN SHE ENCOUNTERED was standing in deep shadows behind the wide trunk of a cottonwood tree. In his left hand, he held a parabolic microphone pointed in the direction of the two men visible on the deck. A thin wire went from the microphone to a small box on his belt, and another went from the box to an earbud in his left ear. His right ear held his communications earwig. His AK-74 was slung across his back, muzzle down and safety engaged. He kept adjusting a dial on the small box with his right hand, no doubt trying to pick up any conversation between the men on the deck; but, they remained silent as they smoked.

She sat on her haunches, invisible in the gloom, and watched him for a long moment. It was obvious that he had not heard her; he could hear very little around him with both ears effectively plugged. She had approached from downwind. She was certain he did not know she was there; she savored the moment.

Something about him changed.

She could almost sense that the hairs on the back of his neck had risen; some primordial survival sense had awoken. He knew he was in grave danger.

His right hand drifted to the holstered pistol strapped to his thigh, and he tensed in readiness. With practiced speed, he spun around, drawing his pistol, a blunt suppressor protruding from the muzzle.

He found nothing!

He scanned the nearby darkness, but could see nothing. Still alert, he holstered his pistol and turned back to his assignment.

As he aimed the microphone once more toward the deck, a thick black paw whipped forth from the foliage above and smashed his head into the rough bark of the trunk.

Stunned, his knees gave way and he slid down against the tree, dragging his cheek the length of the rough bark. He groggily dropped the mike and fumbled for his slung rifle, only to be jerked back and flung down, one arm twisted beneath him. A huge paw thumped upon his chest, pinning him to the ground.

He dug at his holster with his free hand, but a crushing force seized his wrist. He could no longer feel his right hand. Had there been sufficient light, he might have seen that he no longer had one. He tried to draw a breath, no doubt to scream, but his face was suddenly covered by a moist maw.

Her jaws closed slightly and ripped upward, with a wet slurping sound; his face came away from his skull.

He gurgled in pain and shock for almost a full minute, and then lay still.

She reclined near the body and calmly licked the blood off her paws and forelegs.

IT TOOK A FEW MINUTES for her to work her way around to the other side of the grounds. She would have to stay more alert now; it was likely that the other watchers knew something was wrong. But it was unlikely they had any idea what was stalking them in the darkness.

She found the next man behind a fallen tree.

He watched his immediate area carefully, with his rifle ready at his shoulder. Although he could see the two men on the deck, it seemed to her he paid more attention to the shadows in his vicinity.

She sensed movement to her right, so she faded to her left and sought the deeper shadows. Soon enough she saw him, the fourth man, heavily bearded and carrying a scoped rifle. He had crept closer from upwind of her position, so she hadn't scented him. He gave some sort of recognition signal—coded radio clicks—and then joined his comrade. This was a complication; it would be foolhardy for her to attack two at once.

With her enhanced feline night vision she had no difficulty seeing the subtlest of small movements. She watched patiently as they communicated with hand signals; then she understood. Having lost communications with the other two men, one of them would have to go and check on their comrades.

She almost purred aloud; this would work to her advantage.

To her surprise, both men stood and carefully made their way toward the tree line. After a moment, she rose and followed silently.

At the edge of the wooded area, the men split up. The bearded one moved to the left, his likely intention to move along through the trees and find the other men. The other man moved off to the right, found a well-concealed vantage point, and settled in to observe the men on the deck.

She waited to be certain that the bearded man had walked out of earshot, and then quietly stalked the other man's secluded position.

She found him, his back to her, frantically keying his microphone in that coded clicking they used.

Then she saw it—a mirror! He had seen her! He was bait!

She instinctively dropped to a crouch as bright pain seared across the tip of her shoulder—a silent bullet had narrowly missed her, slicing into the underbrush. She spun to one side, her belly hugging the ground, as the man she had stalked spun and opened fire.

There was little sound other than the metallic clacking of his weapon's action and a series of *phfft-phfft-phfft—another suppressor!*

His burst barely missed as she instantly bounded away.

Melting into the shadows, she realized that the bearded man had doubled back and flanked her from upwind. He was good; she hadn't heard a thing. It was only thanks to her finely tuned survival instinct, and a bit of luck, that his lone shot hadn't done more damage.

Both men were using suppressed weapons, typical of professionals; worse, these two knew what they were doing. But they were *not* using silver bullets; her wounded shoulder was already healing.

Nevertheless, she was angry that she'd been caught unaware by such an old trick. But, then it *did* make the game a bit more challenging; she was going to enjoy this.

She immediately began hunting the first shooter, the bearded man. She found his scent trail; he was trying to get upwind of where he thought she was.

She had a surprise for him.

RAPHAEL MADE HIS WAY to the crest of a small brush covered mound and surveyed the area below him; nothing moved. He had a clear field of fire. He keyed his mike rapidly in the agreed upon code to advise the team leader of his current position and ask that the observer scan the area with the night vision goggles.

Something was in these woods—something like a big cat. He'd gotten a shot at it; but, he thought he'd missed. Juan had fired a burst, too; but, he'd missed as well. It was still out there, and it was screwing up their mission.

Nothing seemed to be going as planned; everything was wet, and the radios were acting up. Miguel and Emilio were still out of radio contact.

He froze—did he hear whimpering? Was someone crying? There it was again, from somewhere behind him.

He rose and peered into the gloom. Then he heard it clearly, a woman sobbing. He pushed aside some brush, eased past a thorny bush, and saw her in the gloom, a woman huddled on her knees—completely nude.

He was taken aback for only an instant; but that was long enough for her to smile at him, raise the suppressed pistol, and put a bullet through his open mouth.

JUAN STAYED VERY STILL, straining to hear any change in the night sounds around him. He glanced at the deck occasionally to see the two men still standing there staring into the night. His radio had been quiet for the past ten minutes. Normally that would not bother him; long periods of radio silence were common on these missions. But something about this one unnerved him—there were even wild animals in these woods!

Something had tried to sneak up on him! He and Raphael tried to trick it. Each shot at it, but he didn't think they hit it. It ran away. He hoped it stayed away!

Raphael had moved to a higher position where he could see more of the house, and watch Juan's back in case that animal returned.

He'd be glad when they finally stormed this house and *questioned* these people. That was always his favorite part; and the team always let him have his fun. He grinned in anticipation.

What was that? Had he heard something?

He glanced at the deck and was surprised to see that the two men were gone. Had they gone back inside? How could he have missed their movements?

He'd become distracted—that was not allowed. If this mission failed because of him, the entire team would be punished—severely. He would concentrate, focus on the mission.

What? He *had* heard something, behind him?

He stared into the darkness and slowly realized he could see a woman's face!

It seemed to hover in the night—then she smiled at him, a malicious, smugly satisfied smile.

His arms were suddenly grasped and yanked to either side—the two men from the deck! He felt a sharp blow to the back of his head, and collapsed like a rag doll.

UNDER THE HARSH FLUORESCENT lights of the cavernous garage, the unconscious man lay on the concrete floor, his hands tied behind his back and a length of cloth wrapped as a blindfold. His weapons and clothing had been taken from him. A trickle of blood had clotted on the crown of his head and crusted in his matted hair.

He lived, as evidenced by his shallow breathing.

Vito and his boss stood over the prisoner. The man's back, chest, and arms were liberally covered in amateurish and crude tattoos, clearly of jailhouse or prison origin. George curled his lip in disgust. He gestured to the pile of clothing on the floor.

"Vito, when he comes to, begin the interrogation. Depending on his cooperation, give him pieces of clothing and let him dress—but no boots. Keep him barefoot. He's only to see you, and you'll do all the questioning. Otherwise, keep him blindfolded. You know what information we need—get it, but keep him alive."

"You got it, Boss."

ABOUT A MILE TO THE east, two men, the team leader and the observer, stowed their gear in a muddy SUV and climbed in. They did not speak; there was no need. They had lost their men; the mission had failed. They had to make a report—not that they expected their bosses to believe them—they weren't even sure just what to believe.

And then, there would be an accounting.

GEORGE FOUND LING ON the darkened main level, standing at the glass doors and staring out at the night. Most of the storm clouds were scudding off, revealing a waxing moon risen over the eastern horizon. The porch lights were now off, so the deck was hidden in the moon shadow.

Ling seemed to be musing in her stillness, focused on some private thought. For just a moment, George was reluctant to disturb her, but she must have sensed his presence, and turned her head toward him. "Yes, sir?"

"The bodies?" he asked.

"Being buried in the woods, as we speak—only three—but there must have been others. We found no vehicle. Clearly, you are no longer safe here."

He sighed heavily, and came to stand beside her.

She remained stoic and returned her gaze to the night.

Peering into the dark, he responded, "Perhaps not, but then again, I'm not sure I was the intended target. Vito will find out."

Ling smiled. "Should he need any assistance . . ."

George returned her smile. "I appreciate the offer, but it probably won't be necessary."

"As you wish," she acceded. "What shall we do with their weapons?"

"Vito will clean them and place them with our own hidden collection downstairs. Otherwise, it is best that no further trace of these men be found. I'm sure you understand."

Ling only nodded, keeping her attention on the night.

Her intense focus prompted George to ask, "What is it in the night that holds your interest so?"

"Oh, that bird," she said. "A crow, I think. I saw it earlier, just after the storm. It was on that tall piling at the dock. It didn't move until a few minutes ago. Now it stands on the deck railing by the steps."

"Crow?" repeated George, squinting into the darkness, "I don't see *anything.* Are you sure?"

"Quite sure . . . I, uh, have excellent night vision, sir. Perhaps when the moon rises higher, you will see. It is in the shadow now."

"Shouldn't a crow be roosting? They aren't nocturnal, are they?"

"I don't believe so, sir, or at least so I thought," she answered, her voice trailing off. "There's something about this bird that is not right . . . something that unnerves me."

Now George was truly surprised. "Something unnerves *you?*"

She turned her head to him and said, "It has *dead eyes.*"

"My, you really must have good night vis—" His breath caught in his throat as the memory of another bird with *dead eyes* flooded his mind.

Dead eyes . . . Could it be?

Before he could begin to dwell on that line of thought, another sensation at the front of his skull demanded his attention; of course, he recognized it instantly. But he dared not open himself to it—not yet—he had to be alone.

"Sir? Are you all right? Are you not well?" Ling asked, suddenly concerned.

"It . . . it is nothing," he assured her. "I'm fine. I need to be alone, to rest for a little while. I'll be in my room. Please see that I am not disturbed—for any reason."

"Of course, sir. Can I get you anything?"

"No, thank you. And Ling, see to it that no harm comes to that crow. If it flies off—that's fine. But I have a hunch that it'll still be here in the morning."

He left, and she resumed staring out at the night.

ONCE IN HIS ROOM, GEORGE calmed himself and stood before a mirror. He saw no signs of the night's events on his clothing or countenance—it would suffice. He closed his eyes and allowed himself to be open to her summons. When he opened his eyes, he saw a transit globe materialize before him. He pressed inward without hesitation.

He was once again standing in a broad solitary cone of light; the Lady Diere, resplendent in a shimmering red gown, stood before him. He did not miss the hint of distraction that flickered across her brow just as he smiled and bowed deeply, holding the low position until she acknowledged him.

"Well, George, I see your manners are improving. You may rise."

"M'lady, I stand ready to serve you," he said smoothly.

"That is well, for the hour draws nigh," she remarked, with a suggestion of concern in the lilt of her voice.

"Yes, m'lady?"

"You are of course aware that you are to appear before the Council in less than two days. You have received your summons and the appropriate instructions," she stated with conviction. It was not a question.

"I have, m'lady. I am ready."

"Good. I will permit nothing to interfere with my plans. To that end, I have a very important task for you, which must be performed *before* the Council meeting—without fail. Much is at risk. Do you understand?"

"Of course, m'lady, what must I do?"

"A simple thing, actually . . . You are to seize Ellen Doyle, the Steward of the Grand Portal of the Realm of Man, and prevent her from attending the Council meeting."

George's jaw dropped; any semblance of courtier manners fled him.

"You want me to *what? Kidnap* Ellen Doyle? To *what?* Keep her from attending the Council meeting?"

Diere's face took on an ugly cast as she leaned forward and hissed, "Mind your speech, knave—lest you lose that tongue!"

Sufficiently cowed, he responded respectfully, "Forgive me, m'lady. I was, uh, surprised. Please, tell me how I am to do this thing."

"Very well . . . Listen carefully." She flicked at a trace of lint on her sleeve, apparently mollified. "First of all, you must understand that she is not to be harmed—inconvenienced, perhaps—but not harmed. Do you understand?"

"Yes, m'lady, I understand."

"I will provide you with certain enchanted implements to facilitate your task. It must be done tomorrow; the Council meets the next day. Look around you; this is the place you shall bring her. She will come to no harm here; in fact, she will be released and returned to her home, *after* the Council has met. By then, it will be too late. You will occupy the Chair of Man, and any objection she might raise would be moot, and untimely."

"*What?* She would object? Prevent me from acquiring the power of the Chair of Man? I'll show that bit—"

"Manners, George, manners!" Diere interrupted. "Oh yes, she would denounce you as a wanted criminal in your home realm, which would, of course, disqualify your candidacy. And we simply cannot have that, now can we?"

"No, m'lady, we *will not!*" He hoped his tempered manner of speech would please her, despite his smoldering determination. "Now, what of these 'enchanted implements' you spoke of?"

It did not occur to him that his unvarnished eagerness to acquire any semblance, or even mere trappings, of power might only serve to annoy her.

She regarded him in silence for a moment. He missed the subtle rebuke.

"Patience, George . . . I assume you will have minions to call upon to assist you in this task. They must also understand that the Steward is not to be harmed. And know this; I will hold *you* responsible. I will provide such assistance that bringing harm to her would be considered willful disregard of my instructions. Am I clear?"

"Yes, m'lady," he responded evenly. His patience was wearing thin, but he was careful to mask his growing frustration.

"Good . . . Now, watch carefully." She extended her hand, palm up.

Before his eyes a ring materialized, a large topaz in a yellow gold setting. He stared in covetous wonderment; but he dared not reach for it uninvited. Nonetheless, blatant avarice gleamed in his eyes.

"This is a unique ring," she confided. "This topaz was once part of a dragon's hoard and is capable of holding powerful spells. It now contains a transit spell that will bring you to this place—you and anyone whom you are touching. To activate the spell, merely twist the gem's setting; you, and those you touch, will be enveloped in a transit globe and deposited here. Activate it again, and you will return from whence you came. Do you understand?"

His eyes agleam, he nodded. "I do, m'lady, of course."

She hesitated before saying, "Good . . . You may take the ring."

"Thank you, m'lady," he whispered, holding the ring up and watching the light refract within the stone.

"Now, George, this is rather important. It would be best if the Steward does not see you, and never learns that you are responsible for her period of *inconvenience.* So, I have prepared another set of spells that are intended to obscure one's identity and surroundings, and ensure a level of compliance. It is a kind of mild stasis spell mixed with a shadow-fog spell."

"Yes, m'lady?" His avarice would not be contained; his eyes brightened in anticipation.

She sighed in resignation. "Observe."

Lady Dire held her open hand forward once more, and a soft bag of dark purple leather materialized on her palm. She loosened the drawstrings and shook out a few glass balls the size of marbles; a confusion of bright colors roiled within the small spheres.

He stared in wide-eyed wonderment, so easily enraptured by the simplest of small magics, as she held one between her thumb and forefinger and explained.

"Each of these glass balls holds a single combined set of spells. All you need do is break it at the feet of an individual and that person will be enshrouded in shadow-fog; he or she will neither see nor hear anything outside the fog. The stasis aspect of the spell renders them compliant. They will walk wherever you direct them, or they will stand stock-still until the entire spell wears off—and that can take two days."

His eyes widened, but he remained silent as she continued.

"I have added one more twist to the combined spells, an *aversion ward.* Anyone looking directly at someone under the influence of this shadow-fog spell will not *want* to see them, so effectively, they will *not* see. However, be warned that a very determined individual can sometimes manage to do so. Do you understand?"

"Yes, m'lady, I do," George said thoughtfully. "So, if anyone interferes with me, I can use one of these balls to take them out of the game; and nobody will even see them for a couple of days. That's brilliant!"

"Why, thank you," she said dryly, "I am certain you meant that as a compliment."

"Oh, of course, m'lady, of course." He groveled, already planning to save a few of these little surprises for future use. And that thought prompted his next question.

"Ah, forgive me, m'lady, but how many of these balls are in that bag? The Steward may well be surrounded by many people."

Diere hefted the pouch, as if gauging its weight.

"A dozen are in this bag; that should be more than enough for this task. I know that the new Steward has taken up residence in the former Steward's home, Delafaire Farm. And as far as I know, she lives alone, with two canine guardians. Do not underestimate these guardians. I think these spells would work upon them as well, but perhaps for not as long a time. You may now take the bag."

He did so, clutching it to his chest, unable to completely mask the greed lurking behind his eyes. "Thank you, m'lady. I don't see any problems that I can't deal with. Is there anything else?"

"Only this, George . . . Know that the crucial time is upon us. All my—*our* plans come to fruition within the next twenty-four hours. You have been well prepared and know your role. Fail me in this matter and I shall be most displeased."

"You may rely on me, m'lady."

"I do, George, I do . . . Very well, you may return and make your preparations."

With a simple gesture, she dismissed him.

A MOMENT LATER GEORGE was back in the bedroom of the house on Toledo Bend. He slipped the bag into a dresser drawer.

He found the house dark and quiet; more time had elapsed than he'd thought. He wandered into the main room, stood before the glass doors, and tried to order his thoughts.

Diere expected a great deal from him; he had yet to figure out how he could capitalize on that. He knew that she expected to control him; but, that wasn't on his agenda. There was an angle to be exploited here—he just needed to find it.

The moon was now almost directly overhead, and the deck was awash in bright moonlight. He stared unfocused into the night.

Tap . . . tap . . . tap . . .

George looked down—and stopped breathing.

The awkward crow stood on the deck, immediately outside the sliding door, tapping its beak upon the glass.

George had forgotten about the crow; but it all came back in a rush. Looking over his shoulder to be certain he was still alone, George unlatched the lock and slid the door open.

The crow did not move; it just stared blankly at him.

George stepped out onto the deck and slid the door shut. The crow looked up at him with a crooked, silent gaze.

"You remind me of a poem, from high school. I don't suppose you can say *nevermore*? No? Hmm, you do have *dead eyes* . . . I wonder . . ."

The ebony corvid stared at him in silence.

"Oh well, I'm going to sit down. Make yourself comfortable, my feathered friend."

George wheezed as he wedged himself into a narrow Adirondack chair on the deck.

To his sudden surprise, the crow leapt up upon the wide arm of the chair, and began making small gagging sounds. George watched in astonishment as the bird regurgitated a lump of something—something that sounded surprisingly solid as it thumped onto the arm of the chair.

In the moonlight it looked like a rock. Too big, he thought, to be what a crow would want in its crop. Upon closer examination, he realized it was a *gemstone!*

Plucking a handkerchief from his pocket, George picked up the stone and started to clean it off.

Suddenly, it was as if an electric shock went through his hands. He couldn't move; he felt paralyzed for a moment, and then it passed like a frost melting away.

Then he heard the voice—*Daegon's voice*—in his head.

Greetings M'lord George. I trust my messenger has found you. I am in dire need of your assistance, as soon as you are in a position to aid me, clandestinely of course. But I pray it will not be long—I am in grave danger. Take good care of my crow, you will need him very soon, I hope. I will describe in detail what you must do. Now it will take some time to explain, so make yourself comfortable . . .

George looked up at the nearly full moon and sighed. He then squirmed a bit in the cedar chair and realized that this might be as comfortable as he was likely to be.

Holding the purple gem snugly, he willed his attention on the stone.

Very well, Daegon . . . I'm listening . . .

CH 6

DESPITE THE LATE HOUR, Queen Mab of the Dark Elves was still in a protracted meeting with her Avatar to the Council of Realms, Darius, Earl of Tanist. Unknown to most, he was also the head of her secret police and intelligence service; and as such, he was under considerable pressure.

In recent months, the queen had become increasingly suspicious and short-tempered in response to a smattering of vague gossip concerning an alleged secret plot to usurp her rule. Of course, Mab—who had attained her throne through similar treachery and assassination—increasingly believed that an undercurrent of conspiracy was running rampant amongst the other Great Houses within the Realm of Dark Elves.

Unfortunately, Darius' investigations had turned up little more than idle speculation or wild and clearly unfounded rumors. This did nothing to restore the queen's confidence in the security of her reign—or in him.

She had been lately preoccupied with deciphering some sort of list, presumably names of hidden traitors, ostensibly secreted within an enchanted scroll. Darius knew of no evidence to support such notions, despite his queen's anxious hopes.

However, Darius did know that Atrellan, the Senior Magus, had acquired the dubious scroll, and would no doubt manipulate the scenario to further ingratiate himself with the queen.

Darius had little regard for Atrellan and his petty court intrigues. As for the mysterious scroll, which would supposedly expose this *grand conspiracy*, Darius held even less faith in such fanciful things.

In fact, Mab's escalating paranoia was making Darius' job far more difficult than it need be. He needed her to be focused and on top of her political game—right now. The next meeting of the Council was to be held in approximately thirty-six hours; there was much to discuss in preparation.

He sensed that the queen was somewhat distracted, growing more impatient as their meeting dragged on. A number of issues had yet to be addressed; and some, he knew, could not yet be resolved.

It promised to be a long night.

The soft knock on the door of her chambers came as yet another unwelcome diversion.

Darius sighed patiently; he should have expected another interruption.

At Mab's gesture, her ever-present warrior-bodyguard answered the door, and returned to announce, "Majesty, Senior Magus Atrellan awaits your pleasure."

Her expression immediately brightened. She gestured that he be admitted.

"It is about time! Bring him before me! Darius, you must stay. Perhaps we will now have some answers to a most pressing issue."

Atrellan came forth and bowed deeply before his queen, holding his tongue until she deigned to acknowledge him.

"Rise, Atrellan, and tell me your news," she commanded, her impatience evident.

"May it please Your Majesty," he began subserviently, "I have done as you have commanded; completed the examination of the body of Boltar, and brought it here, to your palace. It now lies in a guarded room off the Great Hall. I found two spells upon the corpse, and each is designed to have an effect only upon the corpse."

"I have waited long for this moment!" She clasped her hands before her breasts, as if in prayer. "So, we may now discover the hidden contents of the scroll you recovered from these traitorous conspirators, and ferret out those who would disrupt the peace and tranquility of our fair realm, may we not?"

The Earl of Tanist realized, of course, that her question was rhetorical.

However, Atrellan apparently did not, and clearly felt a response was warranted.

"Indeed, Your Majesty! My skills will reveal all!"

Darius kept silent. He had long harbored serious doubts about the competency of this well-regarded mage; but, this was not the moment to air them. He noted that the queen had not asked about Daegon, nor had Atrellan volunteered any information about the alchemist.

Now that is curious . . . She had set both of them to this task.

The queen gestured to her guard, who brought forth a small ornate chest and held it before her.

Pulling at a delicate necklace of tiny golden links that disappeared into her cleavage, she produced a dainty ruby-encrusted key. She unlocked and opened the box; the scroll lay within. Satisfied, she closed the lid, and turned to Darius.

"M'lord Earl, if you would be kind enough to carry this chest, we shall accompany Magus Atrellan to this guarded room. And there see, at last, what secrets this scroll has to divulge.

"Atrellan, you may lead on."

The senior magus bowed and did as instructed; the queen, her bodyguard, and the earl followed.

A PAIR OF MAILED AND armored guards snapped to attention as the queen and her retinue entered the modest windowless room. Twin torches held in elaborate sconces on each wall provided excellent illumination with a minimum of shadows. There, upon a polished wooden table in the center of the room, lay the body of Boltar.

At a gesture from the queen, the two guards withdrew and took up positions immediately outside the door, pulling it shut quietly.

Mab motioned to Darius; he held forth the chest. She opened the lid, removed the scroll, and held it out to Atrellan.

"You have assured me that this task is within your abilities. So, take this scroll, Atrellan, and do what must be done. I will have its secrets—now."

The mage took the scroll and approached the body.

This was Atrellan's moment; and, he was loath to let it pass without appeasing his flair for the dramatic. After all, a critical part of maintaining his image as the most accomplished adept in the realm was the timely deployment of his well-honed sense of skilled showmanship. So, with deliberately paced slowness, he stood near the body and carefully unrolled the scroll—but it steadfastly remained blank.

Nonplussed, he announced, "The enchantment holds, and can only be broken by actual contact with the intended recipient."

"Then *do so!*" Queen Mab urged, her growing impatience obvious to all.

"Of course, Majesty, immediately," he acquiesced, sensing he may have overplayed his theatrics a bit.

As he laid the open scroll across the length of Boltar's body, a vague mist rose from the parchment. As he peered closer, ancient runes, painted in brownish streaks of old blood, slowly appeared.

Atrellan turned toward Mab and smiled. "My Queen, writing now becomes visible!" He quickly turned back to the steaming scroll.

The excitement in his voice was contagious. The queen, her bodyguard, and the earl all took a step closer, their fascination exceeding their caution.

"What does it say? You *can* read it, can you not?" she demanded, her voice tinged with eagerness, her hands unconsciously clenching.

"Ah, soon, I think, my queen, very soon . . ."

Atrellan's response trailed off. He stared in disbelief. Even as the symbols became more distinct, he realized that he could *not* read these ancient runes. He had never seen such arcane scripts before this moment.

And worse—*they moved!* The runes flexed and pulsed as he watched! His panicked mind raced—*failure!* He could *not* so inform the queen! But he had to tell her *something—*

Darius suddenly called out, interrupting Atrellan's anguished train of thought.

"Majesty! The mist!"

They looked up in shock. The vague mist had coalesced unnoticed into a large nebulous bubble that shimmered ominously and gradually expanded to encompass most of the room, including its occupants.

Darius dove for the door and tried unsuccessfully to tug it open. The elfin bodyguard joined him, but their combined efforts were futile—the door would not budge.

In some sorcerous fashion, the shimmering mist-bubble had effectively sealed the room.

Queen Mab reached out and snatched Atrellan by the shoulder. Spinning him around, she screamed with full fury directly into his ashen face.

"What is the meaning of this? What treachery is this? Answer me!"

Words failed him as recognition dawned.

This mist conveys a hidden spell! But what? Aha, a simple yet enhanced transit globe, an ancient version, to be sure—and a trap! I must dispel its energy before it activates!

Twisting away from her grip, Atrellan opened his arms and began a hurried chant, invoking the strongest magic he knew. Along the damp walls, the shimmer of the entrapping mist began to pale, its strength slightly diminishing.

However, the infuriated queen, clearly incensed at his apparent impertinence, would not be ignored. Leveling an accusatory finger at the mage, she commanded, “Seize this traitor!”

The earl and the bodyguard instantly complied, pinning Atrellan’s arms to his side—disrupting his focus and breaking his concentration.

Shocked, Atrellan sputtered, “No! No! M-m-majesty . . . I-I must—”

The mist-laden transit globe suddenly opened a portal directly into the heart of a raging volcano. Molten lava, seething under untold pressure, surged into the room!

The queen’s dying screams startled the posted guards beyond the heavy door. As they sprung to action, trying fruitlessly to push into the room, the wooden door burst into flames and shattered. The billowing pyroclastic flow immediately immolated the hapless guardsmen.

Churning lava roiled forth and began to engulf the lower levels of Queen Mab’s palace. Anything flammable was incinerated in hellish flares as the inexorable tide of brimstone consumed all in its path.

The screams of the panicked and dying punctuated the incessant roar of the resultant firestorm. Even the very stone of the walls began to succumb to the intense heat of the flow, cracking, spalling, and some simply melting.

In blinding panic, desperate courtiers and servants scrambled up crowded staircases to flee the furious inferno below. Choking smoke, laced with demonic light, rose in dusky billows throughout the upper floors. Support beams failed in sequence; successive levels began to buckle and collapse into the central lava-fueled pit of unholy conflagration.

No one escaped. Fires, lava, searing heat, and insidious clouds of noxious gases claimed all within the crumbling walls of Queen Mab’s castle.

Death ruled absolute.

LADY DIERE PULLED BACK from her scrutiny of the crystal orb, the ancient incantation she'd been reciting dying on her lips. The devastating scene of death and destruction depicted within the sphere was morbidly fascinating. She was inescapably drawn to watch the manifest chaos that she had so painstakingly orchestrated over so long a time.

Her predatory patience had been the key to the effective execution of such a long-term strategy. Subtle plan upon plan, patient schemes of intrigue and diversion—all had now come into play and served her purpose. She sensed that her goals were almost truly within her grasp. However, she knew all too well that much remained to be done; and, time was of the essence.

Of course, she reasoned as a wickedly smug smile stole across her face, if time permitted, she could always use the orb to look back in on the continuing destruction of the *late* Queen Mab's *former* palace. After all, that insidious transit spell would hold the infernal portal open for an entire hour.

In truth, making any use of the scrying orb was a calculated risk; there were significant inherent dangers. In rare moments of personal reflection, characterized by complete candor and objectivity, she admitted—if only to herself—that reliance upon the orb was perilous, and seductively addictive. And worse, potentially tragic results were eventually very likely assured.

She dismissed such thoughts with a shake of her head, waved her hands over the surface of the crystal, and mumbled an arcane incantation. The fiery scene within dwindled to a flickering amber speck and winked out.

Satisfied, she left the hidden room and made her way to her chambers. Signaling to a servant, she issued several instructions, the last of which was to send for Malvana and the captain of her guard.

The captain arrived first.

"You called for me, m'lady?"

"I did, Captain. You are to double the guard, immediately! Then summon the Elders of the House of Hawthorn to an assembly in the Great Hall. I shall address them within the hour. I have just learned that a great catastrophe may have befallen our beloved queen. The fate of the throne, and our House, may be in jeopardy. The elders must be so informed. That is all. You may go."

"At once, m'lady," he replied bowing deeply, and then hurried to his task.

As soon as he had passed through the doorway, Malvana appeared and bowed. She appeared somewhat disheveled, attired in a robe and nightgown; obviously, she had been recently roused from sleep.

"M'lady, you sent for me? How may I be of service?"

"Ah, Malvana . . . Come in, child, and forgive me for having you woken at this hour. I fear I have some bad news for you. Come and sit with me on this divan."

As she complied, Diere took the girl's hand and explained that she had just received news of Queen Mab's demise, and unfortunately, that of her father, Darius, Earl of Tanist.

Malvana blinked several times and apologized.

"M'lady, please forgive me; but, I do not understand. My father is *dead?* And the queen, too? B-but *how—why?* "

"My child, I do not yet know the *how* or *why* of these things; but I assure you, I shall investigate these matters thoroughly, and deal with those responsible. I suspect some nefarious plot to wrench the throne from the House of Hawthorn is at the heart of this tragedy. We do not know why the House of Tanist was targeted as well. For now, you must be strong in the face of such adversity. Fear not for your own safety, for you are under *my* protection."

Diere took considerable time with her, displaying uncharacteristic compassion, until she was certain of Malvana's comprehension and acceptance of the situation—per Diere's carefully crafted description.

When Diere sensed that the young elfin maid was appropriately vulnerable, and susceptible, she spoke at length of how the realm was about to go through significant and unavoidable changes.

"No doubt we shall all be called upon in this terrible time of uncertainty; many will be destined to play greater roles. I know there will be burdens I must now shoulder—perhaps even the throne, should the fates so decree."

Finally, to allay the girl's obvious trepidation, Diere declared, "I swear to be patron and protector to you, Malvana, no matter what the future may hold; in return, I ask only your unswerving loyalty. Do you understand—and agree?"

Confused and still shaken at the news of her father's death, Malvana dropped her eyes and murmured breathlessly, "Yes, m'lady."

ELLEN POURED ANOTHER cup of coffee and looked over her shoulder at her mother and Stacy, who were busy with some project on the kitchen table.

"Anybody want more coffee? I'm pouring; there's half a pot here."

"No thanks, I'm good," replied Millie, using a ruler to draw straight column lines on a pad of paper.

A pair of clipboards, holding freshly lined paper, lay on the table.

Stacy waved an empty mug in the air and nodded affirmatively. She had a bite of bagel in her mouth and was chewing dryly.

Ellen took the mug and refilled it. Passing it back to Stacy, she asked, "So, what are y'all doing?"

Millie answered, sparing Stacy the indignity of trying to speak with her mouth full.

"What we should have thought to do sooner, a complete inventory of the gardens. We don't really know everything that's growing here; so, today we're going to make a list. We have to know what we have, so we can see what we need. Understand?"

"Oh," Ellen said, as the significance dawned on her, "of course, for the business. Hey, have you thought of a name?"

Stacy held up a finger as she swallowed. "Of course, silly—*Delafaire Farm*—what else? That's what's on all the paperwork Mark prepared. Now all we have to do is design a logo and a label. Got any ideas?"

"Gosh, no . . . I haven't even been thinking about the business," Ellen admitted. "I've been so busy with the journal and all the research material; I guess I've been preoccupied. I'm sorry."

"Don't you worry, dear," soothed Millie. "You've got a lot on your mind. We have this covered. We all decided to give you some *space*, what with this Council meeting coming up, and all. What are your plans today?"

"Well, I *do* need a break. So, I thought I'd take the dogs for a long walk; I think they're overdue for one."

At the sound of the word *walk,* both dogs, who until that moment appeared to have been sound asleep near the old stove, raised their heads and stared alertly at Ellen in obvious anticipation.

Stacy cackled aloud, pointing at the Chows. "Ah ha! Now you've done it! You wrote the check, now you have to cash it!"

Ellen grinned and shook her head in surrender. "Okay, okay! Where's Smokey? I haven't seen him all morning."

"Oh, he followed Mark out to the garage," Millie explained. "Miska came by early this morning; he and Mark were going to work on the truck."

That caught Ellen unaware, prompting her to question her own ears. "What—Miska? Miska is going to work on the truck? Did I hear that right?"

"Yep," offered Stacy. "It turns out that Miska has a fascination for motor vehicles; so, Mark is going to show him how they work."

"Oh, really?" Ellen grinned. "*This* I gotta see!"

"Just stop by the garage on your way—and don't laugh," warned Stacy, smiling. "Mark thinks he's a pretty good teacher; so, be nice."

Ellen grabbed a bagel and motioned to the dogs to accompany her.

"Aw, now Stacy, don't fret, I won't hurt your *significant other's* feelings."

She was gone from the kitchen before Stacy could find anything to throw at her.

ELLEN FOUND MISKA AND Mark in the garage, their feet protruding from underneath the elevated Ford truck perched upon stout jack stands. The dogs briefly sniffed at the men's trouser cuffs, then wandered around the interior of the garage. Ellen squatted down at the side of the truck and greeted the erstwhile mechanics.

"Good morning, gentlemen! And just what are you guys up to?"

"Oh, hi, Ellen," Mark answered, as he rolled his mechanic's creeper out from under the truck, and sat up. "We're going to change the oil in the truck. I'm giving Miska a crash course in motor vehicles."

"No pun intended, I hope," she teased. "Well, Miska, are you learning anything? I didn't even know Mark was such an accomplished teacher."

Miska scooted forth on another creeper and grinned broadly in answer. "Ah, Lady Ellen, he is a wonderful teacher! He has promised to teach me how to drive!"

"Uh, Miska," cautioned Mark, "Remember what I said about calling anyone *'Lady'* or *'Lord'* here?"

"Oh, yes! Forgive me—I forgot. My apologies, Miss Ellen," the big man said, suitably chagrined.

"I'm not offended, Miska," Ellen assured him. "I think Mark has a point. It's important for you to blend in. In this realm, such overt courtesy is far too rare; it would be noticed and remembered."

"Unless we were in the United Kingdom," Mark cautioned, "and addressing certain members of the relevant nobility, right Miska?"

The big man bobbed his head. "Yes, I remember."

"I guess that could happen," Ellen admitted, somewhat impressed with Mark's teaching efforts, "if we were to go to the UK, or folks like that were to visit us. Of course, I imagine they'd be introduced as such and then use of those titles would be appropriate. But in general here at home, where we have no hereditary nobility, titles aren't used; so, you'll have to be a bit careful. Just being polite is fine."

"I understand, Miss Ellen," Miska replied, his smile infectious.

Ellen grinned as well. "Okay! Now, where's Smokey? I'm taking the dogs for a walk and sometimes Smokey likes to go, too."

Mark pointed to the Chevy Biscayne where Smokey lay recumbent on the hood, quite comfortable in the soft glow of a warm sunbeam. The cat lifted his head to consider Ellen for a few seconds, and then returned to his rest.

Mark chuckled and offered, "I think that was a *'no thanks—morning nap, don't you know'*. You all go ahead; he'll keep us company."

"All right, see you later," she tossed over her shoulder as she and the dogs headed for the wooded trail.

THE AIR WAS STILL COOL in the shade of the forest canopy; echoes of birdsong brightened the sylvan ambiance.

Ellen was content to daydream as she walked. Max and Sophie ranged out before her, happily crisscrossing the path in an instinctive pattern unique to their kind.

They had been on the trail for nearly half an hour when the dogs stopped and returned to Ellen's side. She started to move forward, but Sophie leaned against Ellen to keep her still. Ellen realized that the forest had become quiet. She opened her sense of awareness and felt a concentration of energy coalescing before her.

Not ten paces away, a transit globe materialized, hovering over the leaf-strewn trail. This orb was opaque rather than clear, and somewhat different from all those she had seen before. For some reason, she was not alarmed, perhaps because the dogs did not react as if this were a threat. She watched as the globe settled on the path, and expanded to the height of a tall man.

It was, in fact, a tall man who stepped forth.

Gallenius!

The Storm Haven mage smiled, bowed from the waist, and greeted her formally.

"Lady Ellen, please forgive this intrusion, this unannounced visit, but I bear urgent news from the Guildmaster."

"Greetings, Gallenius, and welcome to Delafaire Farm—that's what we've decided to call my home, since it's going to be a working farm business."

"Ah, I see. We are alone, I trust?"

She nodded. "We are, but for my canine companions. So, your news?"

"Of course, m'lady. In response to your request, we have arranged a meeting with representatives of those races who had frequent dealings with the former Steward, your Aunt Maude, those who were helpful to her, here at Domaine Delafaire—oh, I beg your pardon, *Delafaire Farm*."

Ellen smiled in return. "It is only an updated name, Gallenius. Nonetheless, know that you are always welcome here. But I did not expect that the Guildmaster would arrange for a meeting with those who helped Maude until *after* the Council meeting. Is something wrong?"

Gallenius lost his smile, and his shoulders sagged a bit. His voice sounded tired but laced with a subtle desperate urgency, as he nodded slowly.

"We fear so, m'lady. We have reason to believe that there are forces that would rather not see you attend the Council meeting. They may even do you harm to prevent it."

"Oh, really? Who, and why?" Her brows dipped, her voice firm and determined. She thought she might already know the answer.

"We suspect the Lady Diere, and Queen Mab of the Dark Elves; but we have no firm proof." He paused, as if marshaling his thoughts.

She sensed there was more. "Go on."

He hedged, and shrugged in resignation.

"There is a complication; we have lost contact with *certain assets* who were placed within the palace household of Queen Mab. If Diere and Mab had something planned, we believe it may already be underway. Your safety may be in jeopardy. We felt we had to warn you and offer what protections we might."

Her face expressionless, she simply said, "I see."

Gallenius opened his palms. "M'lady, could you possibly defer attending this Council meeting?"

Ellen considered what he was asking for only an instant. She had already determined what must be done—come what may. She would not be denied. Setting her jaw, she offered a firm response.

"Gallenius, you and the Guildmaster must know that I appreciate your concern; but, I feel no need of *protection.* I *must* attend that meeting. And I think you already knew that, didn't you?"

"Yes, m'lady, but we had to ask—and we do understand your commitment. For that reason, the Guildmaster arranged for a meeting, as you requested, with those who worked with Maude. However, he did so now, so you might see that there are those among the realms who would be your friends and allies. With your permission, I shall bring them forth; they await my call at Storm Haven."

He concluded his remarks with a sweeping gesture at the transit globe.

"You mean to bring them here, now?" Ellen asked, surprised.

"Yes, m'lady—it would be best, for time is fleeting."

"Very well, Gallenius." She smiled, sweeping her arms open to encompass the forest. "I would be happy to meet them here."

Gallenius nodded and faced the globe. He whispered a soft incantation that included a series of names, and then stepped back a pace.

A willowy elfin maiden, her ashen white hair braided over an alabaster shoulder, and clad in gossamer layers of pale green, stepped delicately forth, and stood to one side. She was immediately followed by a stout man, only two-thirds of Ellen's height, ruddy faced with broad shoulders and a thick grey beard, wearing a broad-belted leather tunic and rough leggings. In his hand, he carried a soft blue cap that would cover his greying locks.

Another man stepped forth, much taller and paler than the first, and smiled toward Ellen. While his smile seemed endearing, his appearance was anything but—the man was unusually ugly. His eyes bulged and he seemed to lack a chin. His nose was a mere twin-slitted bump, and he seemed to breathe mainly through his generous mouth. His unusual clothing was crafted from an irregular series of slick green and black panels that resembled seaweed, stitched together to form a sort of tunic that fell to his knees. He carried a bright red cap in his webbed hands.

The last person to step forth from the transit globe was a petite and shapely woman of stunning beauty, wearing a short sleeveless shift that only enhanced her voluptuous assets. However, her pointed ears and webbed fingers betrayed her exotic otherness.

Gallenius stepped forward, bowing slightly. "Lady Ellen, Steward of the Grand Portal of the Realm of Man, may I present your visitors?"

"Please do, Gallenius."

As he introduced them, each bowed to Ellen. Not knowing the precise protocol, she bowed slightly in return—which begot amused and pleased smiles among her visitors.

"This is Maura of the House of Ash, of the Realm of the Light Elves. She is among those who have taught young Light Elves the ways of growing things—in her realm as well as yours, at Delafaire Farm. They hope to renew the arrangement they enjoyed with Maude.

"This is Rolf Ravensward of the Dwarven Guild of Brew Masters and Distillers, of the Realm of Dwarves. They too worked with Maude, and hope to do so with you.

"This is Finley of the Merrow Clan of the Mer, from the Realm of Mer. They were great friends of Maude, and frequent visitors to the deep freshwater lake at Delafaire Farm. They hope to establish a similar friendship and visitation arrangement with you, as the new Steward.

"And lastly, this is Selene, also of the Realm of Mer. Selene is an *undine,* um, a sort of *water elemental,* and a dear friend of ours."

Ellen acknowledged them and said, "I welcome you all to my realm and my home." She gestured to the dogs and added, "This is Max and Sophie, my friends and companions."

"And honored guardians," added Gallenius, with a wink and nod to Ellen. "We are acquainted, from when they served Maude."

"Of course," Ellen acknowledged. "Please understand that I fully intend to establish and maintain the same arrangements you all enjoyed with my late aunt, Maude Delafaire. As of this moment, I consider it done. Please feel free to visit, and do as you have done before.

"But, you must consider this; you should know that I do not reside alone at Delafaire Farm. My mother, Millie, my cousin, Mark, and my friend, Stacy, all live here as well. There are others who also visit my home, whom I trust and have taken into my confidence. I do not have secrets from those I hold dear. They are aware of the existence of the other realms; a few of these people have even visited other realms. They are aware of other races' existence. They will also know of your presence here.

"I tell you this because circumstances are now different from when Maude was Steward. My friends and family will keep your secrets, and, to the best of their abilities, protect you. Now, if this revelation in any way affects your decision, I will understand. Do any of you have any questions?"

The visitors looked to one another in a protracted silence; then, Finley of the Merrow Clan stepped forward and prepared to speak. He opened his wide mouth several times and then licked his thin lips. Ellen was comically reminded of a fish out of water, but she was utterly surprised when he finally spoke. His voice was remarkably inconsistent with his appearance—a clear melodious tenor, with the slight lilt of a brogue.

"Be ye at ease, m'lady. Your candor does your ladyship's reputation fair justice. That which ye've chosen to share with us upon this first encounter has already been made plain to us all by the Guildmaster—who holds yourself in no low regard, I might add. We ken the times have changed; and tis new challenges we'll all be facing. So, tis with this in mind that we all still came. And lest some here now would gainsay me, I think we all have no' changed our minds."

The others smiled in agreement, and one by one assured Ellen that they understood and accepted the changes in circumstances.

Gallenius brought the meeting to a close, reminding them to be circumspect in their actions over the next few days.

"Discretion is to be our path. The Council meets tomorrow night, and we must be aware of any threat to the Lady Ellen," he warned. "Please contact me immediately if you should hear of any such information—even the merest whisper or rumor."

All agreed.

Gallenius faced Ellen.

"Now, by your leave, m'lady, they shall return to Storm Haven, and thence to their respective realms."

"Of course," Ellen responded. "My friends, I bid you all a safe journey."

One by one, they stepped into the globe and vanished.

Gallenius, the last, paused at the event horizon.

"M'lady, I too must return. Please be cautious—we know not what to expect. We will help in any way we can."

"Thank you, Gallenius. Please convey my thanks and my regards to the Guildmaster."

PAPA GEORGE SAT SIPPING coffee out on the deck. The crow was still there, watching George from the nearby railing.

He sensed shadowed movement inside, his bodyguard. He smiled; if Ling thought she was the first to awaken that morning, she was mistaken.

As she slid the door open, he greeted her.

"Good morning, Ling. Are the others up yet?"

"Vito still snores; but, I heard movement from Teddy's room. My men are awake and dressing as we speak. We will leave this place today?"

"Yeah, Vito was successful in gathering information from our *guest*. There were two more men with them, who managed to elude us, so our location is certainly known by the cartel. They will return, of that you can be sure."

George sipped from his mug in a moment of reflection. In a casual gesture, he dumped the dregs of his coffee over the nearby railing and glanced at his bodyguard.

"As much as Vito has earned his sleep, we need to move; there is much to be done today. Please go wake him, and have everyone meet in the kitchen. Then I'll explain what we have to do."

As Ling went back into the house, George felt for the lump in his pocket, the amethyst, and looked at the crow. The bird simply hopped from the railing to the arm of George's chair and cocked its head inquisitively.

George held out a finger and the crow promptly balanced itself on the outstretched digit.

"Well, my feathered friend, it'd be best that you stay close to me now. We have something very special to do today."

Rising from his chair, he held the bird near his shoulder, and the crow stepped up and perched by his ear.

George stood looking out at the still water of the reservoir and sighed, the mug cooling in his hand.

His cup empty, but his plans jelling, he grunted and returned to the house.

He hadn't considered the impact of his entrance with the crow perched upon his shoulder.

Ling, her two stoic henchmen, Teddy, and a yawning Vito were milling around the kitchen—until they saw George.

Everyone stopped and stared.

Teddy broke the silence with a nervous laugh, saying, "Oh man, Boss. You look like that pirate—*Peg-leg somebody?*"

Vito squinted, wiped a hand down his face and corrected the fidgeting meth cook.

"Nah, Teddy, you mean *Long John Silver*, from Robert Louis Stevenson's *Treasure Island.* And he had a parrot, not a crow."

All heads turned toward the hulking driver. Even George wore an expression of amused shock.

"Why Vito, I had no idea you were so, uh, well read," George admitted. "You sometimes surprise me."

"Aw, Boss," the big driver groaned, "ain't no big deal. When I was a kid, I used to run errands for my great uncle, Salvatore, who had a pawnshop near the Quarter. He got hold of a collection of old comic books that I'd read when I got bored waiting around. I think they were called *Classic Comics;* that one was a good pirate story. I liked it."

"You mean *'Sal the Nose'*, the *fence* who ran numbers over on Carondelet Street? He was your *uncle?* You were one of his *runners* as a kid?" queried George, smiling.

"Well, yeah," Vito admitted. "He was really my mother's uncle. And he called it 'running errands'. He never got popped for taking numbers bets, just fencing stuff."

"So much for literature and history," interrupted Ling. "Sir, you indicated you wanted to explain the plans for the day?"

"Right," agreed George. "For now, just ignore the bird. As you know, this location has been compromised. So, we move to another safe house in Shreveport."

"The one I told you about?" interrupted Teddy.

"No, you idiot!" George fumed, rolled his eyes, and leveled an accusatory finger at the meth cook.

"How do you think the cartel found us here? They traced *your* movements! You didn't bother to tell us about your little stopover in Alexandria, or your visit with *Sprocket* and *Patsy B!* Oh yeah, Vito extracted that information from our *friend* last night. So no, we'll not be going anywhere you know about. I swear, Teddy, you just may be more trouble than you're worth. Is there anything else you've neglected to tell me?"

"N-no sir, Boss, no s-sir."

"Then shut up! All of you, just listen. There's some business I have to attend to today. And there's something that you all will be doing at roughly the same time—so listen up!

"Ling, you'll be in charge; I want you to kidnap Ellen Doyle, *without* hurting her. She's not to be harmed—do you understand?"

Ling, obviously shocked, only nodded her head affirmatively.

"Sir, who is she, where do we find her, and how do you want this done?"

George smiled and pointed to his bodyguard.

"Now *that* is the kind of response I like! What you need to know is that she is the sole resident of Delafaire Farm, which is about an hour from here. As to how I want this done—keep in mind that she is *not* to be harmed—I have something special to help you. Wait here."

He went to his room and returned with a purple leather pouch, from which he poured several small glass balls into his palm.

"See these? Each ball holds a chemical concoction that makes a kind of fog. Break one of these at the feet of someone and the fog sticks to them. I understand that they can't see or hear anything through it. And best of all, they become, uh, *easy*, you know, like *compliant;* you can lead them anywhere by touch."

"Uh, Boss, you mean we gotta *touch* that fog stuff?" Vito asked.

George shrugged. "Well, yeah, but don't worry, it won't get on you. It only affects the first person it gets on—and it doesn't come off. Oh, the effects wear off eventually. So, if somebody interferes with you, fog `em and leave `em—they'll come out of it in a coupla days."

"So," Ling said, "I assume we are to use this method of capture to kidnap this woman, because it will do no real harm? What then are we to do with her?"

George smiled, but the tone of his response was serious.

"Ling, your assumption is correct. However, once you bring her to me, I'll deal with her. Are there any more questions? No? Good, pack up; we are moving out, now."

Nodding to his driver, George added, "Vito, please bring our guest, too—I have a use for him. Keep him blindfolded and barefoot, and put him in the trunk."

WITHIN THE HOUR THEY were on the road. Teddy rode up front with Vito, while George and Ling discussed tactics in the back of the limo. Bubba and Iggy sat like silent statues in the jump seats.

George poured four glass balls from the purple pouch and handed them to Ling.

Ling smiled; she recognized the "chemical concoction" in the balls as a powerful set of blended spells, and realized that such sorcery was indicative of a very high level of skill. It was no shrewd guess that Lady Diere was the likely source of these glass balls—and the orders to kidnap the Steward. Although she had never seen her, Ling knew exactly who Ellen Doyle was. She also knew that Lord Addecus must be informed of this unexpected development at her earliest opportunity.

"These should be sufficient to make the grab, and deal with any interference," George explained. "I'm going to have Vito drop me off somewhere—I'm gonna take care of our *guest*."

Ling nodded. "I see, sir. And Teddy . . ?"

"He'll be coming with me." George pursed his lips. "Although, I have to wonder if he hasn't worn out his welcome. Anyway, while I'm busy, Vito will take you and your boys to Delafaire Farm. Make the snatch, and come back to pick me up. Now, any questions?"

"Will you be alone?" she asked, her eyes shifting to the back of Teddy's head.

George noticed her glance and responded blandly, "It is quite possible."

She smiled knowingly and nodded.

About twenty minutes later, George called out from the back seat, "Hey Vito! Pull into that general store up on the right. I need a few things."

HORACE TIPPET WAS GOING through the morning mail when he heard the tinkle of the small bell suspended above the front door and looked up.

A middle-aged gray-haired man wearing a windbreaker and dark slacks had entered and now stood near the front of the store, just kind of taking it all in.

Horace waved from behind his counter and called out. "Good morning! Good morning! Can I help you?"

"Huh? Oh yeah, hi! Wow, I haven't been in a store like this in years. Yeah, have you got any brass wire or something like that?" the customer asked, as he fumbled in his pocket for something. "It's gotta be brass though."

"Sure do, sure do! Two aisles to your left, almost all the way to the back in the crafts section. I'll be with you in just a minute, just a minute," answered Horace, feeling vaguely uneasy. Something didn't feel right; but, he couldn't put a finger on it. He went back to sorting the rest of the mail.

Years ago, the general store also served as a rural post office. Some local residents still picked up their mail there from an old wooden bank of locked boxes. The Tippets didn't mind a bit; a daily visit to the store forged firm bonds of friendship among their neighbors. And despite no longer being an official post office, the store was still on the mailing lists of most regional and federal law enforcement agencies as a recipient for certain notices, like sheriff's sales and wanted posters.

Horace hadn't heard her come from the back of the store, but his wife was suddenly there beside him. Carrie habitually wore a pendant that hung from her neck on a delicate silver chain; she now clutched the clear crystal stone tightly in her left hand. A sickly purple light seeped through the cracks between her fingers.

"What's wrong, Horace, who's here?" she whispered, showing him a peek at the gem.

"Dunno, dunno, only got one customer," he breathed and gestured toward the crafts section.

Unfortunately, Carrie couldn't see over the racks of merchandise, so she maneuvered around the back of the store until she could see the man.

Horace could see that the intensity of her glowing crystal grew as she got closer; and that its flare alarmed her. She backed away, unseen by the customer, and slipped into the office.

The customer evidently found what he was looking for and approached Horace. Placing a fist-sized spool of thin brass wire on the counter, the man pulled a wad of bills from his front pocket.

"Find everything all right? Anything else you need today?" asked a smiling Horace.

"This brass wire," the customer peered closely at the spool, "is about sixty feet, right? That ought to do it. Oh yeah, and can you give me ten dollars worth of quarters?"

"Uh, sure thing, sure thing. I'll be just a minute. I don't have that many quarters in the register right now—gotta get it from the office. I'll be right back, be right back."

Slipping into the small office, he found Carrie waiting for him. Soundlessly, she held up her glowing crystal and then pointed to a modest bulletin board on the wall above the desk. There hung the most recently received wanted poster, depicting George Papadolis in an old mug shot.

The poster said he was wanted for questioning in two murders. Horace had no doubt that this was the man now waiting in his store.

Carrie tugged Horace closer and whispered, "I'll make the call. You watch to see where he goes and what he drives away in. *No heroics, Horace!* You understand?"

Horace smiled and winked at his bride as he retrieved several rolls of quarters. She made a face at him; he knew that was just to let him know she meant business. He smiled and kissed the tip of her nose before returning to the counter.

"Here you go, sir, here you go, ten dollars in quarters." Horace smiled as he completed the transaction. "Thank you, and come again, come again."

He resumed sorting mail until he heard the bell's tinkle and the closing of the front door; then he slipped to the front window and stood to one side so as not to be seen. He watched as his most recent customer climbed into the back of a black limousine. The long car pulled out onto the narrow road and headed north.

Horace found Carrie in the office, on the phone. She looked up at him expectantly.

He said, "Black limo—dunno the make. I couldn't see the tag. It went north, definitely north."

She repeated his information, and promised the Sheriff's Department dispatcher that she'd stay near the phone. After she hung up, she opened her hand and showed her husband her crystal pendant—a gift from Maude. It was perfectly clear, no hint of color lingered.

"What does this mean?" he asked. "Has it ever done that before—ever?"

"No, and I don't know what it means," Carrie answered, suppressing a shudder. "I think those wards that Maude told us about were tripped. And *that* was a very bad man—I could feel it in my bones."

"Well, the poster says he's wanted for questioning on two murders—*two murders!*" Horace could barely contain his agitation. "B-but what about the crystal? I m-mean, shouldn't we tell somebody?"

"Like who?" Carrie scoffed. "Maude's dead."

"I know, I know," he said, "but what about her niece, Ellen—young Connor's friend?"

"Maybe," she mused aloud, "maybe both of them? I asked that lady at the Sheriff's Office to tell Connor what happened, and she said she would. So, maybe he'll call or come by? I hope he comes by."

"Me, too—me, too."

HAWK DID NOT GET THE message right away. He and Trey were in court to assist as extra security for a sentencing hearing in a domestic violence case that had tempers running high between two families. The proceeding was uneventful, but it took the better part of the morning. Hawk and Trey didn't return to the squad room until almost eleven.

Captain Miller waved them into his office as soon as he saw them.

"Trey, Hawk, y'all done in court? Good. We got an unconfirmed report of a sighting of Papa George—in a *limo* no less—out on Parish Road 157. Dispatch sent two patrol units, but so far nothing. Y'all go out to Tippet's and talk to Miss Carrie; she called it in."

"We're on it, Captain," acknowledged Trey, as they headed for the door.

THE REASON THE RESPONDING patrol units found nothing on their first pass up the length of the parish road was simple; George had Vito turn off the road a mile north of Tippet's store and drive a short way up an unpaved road that led past an old cattle pasture, overgrazed and fallow.

As far as Teddy could see, this was a pretty lonely spot; there was definitely nobody else around. He had no idea what was happening; but, he knew well enough to keep his mouth shut.

George had Vito stop, and pull their bound and blindfolded captive, Juan, out of the trunk. Pushing Juan into the pasture, Vito held him there while George climbed out of the limo with the crow perched upon his shoulder.

"C'mon Teddy, you're with me. I'm going to need your help. Vito, you take Ling where she needs to go. When she's done, come back here and pick us up."

Vito acknowledged his instructions, got back behind the wheel, and executed a difficult Y-turn with the overlong vehicle. Moments later, only the tire tracks and billowing dust of its passing betrayed that the limo had ever been there.

Teddy looked around at the desolate pasture, bordered on all sides by thick woods. He was understandably nervous; he was already on Papa George's bad side. And he knew damn well that whatever was about to happen to this blindfolded and barefoot *cartel shooter* was not going to be good. Hopefully, it would only happen to that poor guy; Teddy would much rather be a witness than a victim.

George pushed the bound man ahead of him for about ten paces, and then stopped.

Motioning Teddy over, George simply said, "Watch him, and don't let him try to run off."

Teddy nodded in acknowledgment and mumbled, "But Boss, I don't got no gun."

"You don't need one—now shut up!"

Teddy looked down and shuffled his feet, but soon forgot his scolding as he watched in fascination.

George took a wire spool from his jacket pocket and began to unroll the bare metal wire, forming it into a large circle on the ground, about six feet in diameter. He unwound the entire spool, laying out all the wire, making a little over three complete loops on the same circle.

Tossing the spent spool aside, George took a roll of quarters from another pocket and began placing them around the circle, right on the wire. When all the quarters were distributed, he stood back and considered his handiwork.

Then he took something else from his pocket, something too small for Teddy to see, and held it in his fist. George closed his eyes tightly in concentration. After a moment, he opened his eyes and rearranged some of the coins, getting their spacing just so.

When he was satisfied, he gestured to Teddy.

"Okay, bring him over here."

Teddy pushed the captive near the circle.

George held up a hand for him to stop. "Keep him right there. Now, Teddy, whatever you see, or whatever happens, do *not* let him move. Don't *you* move either, and stay *quiet*."

With the crow still perched upon his shoulder, George took his fist and held it to his forehead.

Teddy watched glimpses of purple light escape the cracks between Papa George's fingers as he started to walk slowly around the outer circumference of his newly laid brass circle. The gangster's lips moved and paused, as if he were listening to a voice that only he could hear, and then repeated the words. But Teddy could only hear a whispered incomprehensible string of mumbles.

As George completed his third trip around the circle, a purple mist began to rise from the wire. Soon it thickened enough to glow with its own pale violet light. Erratic black streaks began to rise from the silver coins like fine cracks in foggy purple glass.

George came to stand just behind the blindfolded man, and slightly to the right. He gestured to Teddy, directing him to move back.

His anxiety rising, Teddy gratefully complied, clumsily retreating several paces. He could barely maintain his balance. His breathing was rapid and shallow, and his knees were shaking badly. What Teddy was seeing was freaking him out—all his instincts screamed *RUN!*

But he couldn't budge; he was frozen to that spot.

Teddy didn't see the knife, but he heard the unmistakable *snick* of a switchblade.

Clearly George knew how to cut a man's throat. With an economy of motion, he stabbed deeply into the side of Juan's neck, severing the carotid arteries, and then slashed forward, through the jugular veins and softer tissues of the throat, avoiding the vertebrae entirely. Arterial blood spurted forth as George pushed Juan into the corrupted purple light of the circle.

The dying man simply disappeared.

George stepped back, and brought a finger to his shoulder. The crow perched upon the digit and stared crookedly into George's unfocused eyes, the irises laced with erratic purple and black streaks that pulsed with the rhythm of his heartbeat.

George spoke softly, but Teddy heard.

"Now, it is your time, my fine feathered friend. Go and find your master."

He held his arm out toward the circle, and the crow took wing—vanishing into the decadent purple shimmer without a trace.

George sighed heavily, turned to Teddy, and shrugged.

“Now, we wait.”

CH 7

SEATED IN THE FRONT passenger seat, Ling could see that Vito found the drive through the private forest of Delafaire Farm challenging in the big limousine. Since leaving the parish road, the unpaved surface and relatively serpentine path of the long driveway had demanded his full attention. She acknowledged the considerable skill required for such deft maneuvering with a nearly imperceptible nod—one professional to another.

When they reached the pecan orchard, Ling asked him to park the vehicle in a clear area between two huge trees. There the limo would not easily be seen, unless someone deliberately looked in that specific spot.

Ling fluidly exited the vehicle and scanned the immediate area. She stretched and scented the breeze. Finding nothing to alarm her, she gestured for Iggy and Bubba to exit the limo and join her.

Leaning at the waist, she addressed the driver through the open door.

"Vito, stay with the car. We will take it no further. I will take my men and scout the area ahead. If all is well, we will proceed with our task."

"Got it. I'll be here."

Rather than take the driveway, Ling led her men along the line of trees until she came to a thick copse of flowering mimosas.

"You will wait here, on this spot, until I return," she told them clearly.

The stoic men remained expressionless, and did not move.

She still had her reservations; however, at this point she had little choice but to assume they would do as they were told. Resigned, she slipped through the copse of mimosas and disappeared.

Minutes later, making her way in a stealthy crouch through a stand of tall irises, she saw movement in the distance. A woman, wearing a broad-brimmed hat and carrying a clipboard, was walking through rows of waist-high flowers. Ling settled in to observe, and noted that the lone woman—the Steward, no doubt—walked in a predictable pattern, right to left and then back again, covering the entire width of the planted field.

In the far distance beyond the woman, Ling could see parts of some buildings, probably the main house and barn.

She decided upon a simple tactic; and then watched for a moment longer to be certain her quarry did not change the observed pattern of behavior.

Returning through the mimosas, she found Bubba and Iggy right where she left them. She was uncomfortable delegating this task to these two, but she had no choice.

"Listen carefully," she began, and pointed in the direction from which she had just come. "Five minutes walk that way, you will find a woman carrying a clipboard. She walks back and forth across the field. Each of you will walk along the opposite edges of the field. Bubba, you will walk up on the left, along the driveway. Iggy, you will walk up on the right, along the tree line. Do not allow yourselves to be seen by the woman."

Ling paused to be certain they understood her instructions. Reasonably satisfied, she held forth her open hand; two small glass balls lay upon her palm. She gave one to each man.

She sighed in resignation and continued her carefully articulated instructions.

"When she gets close to either of you, throw this ball at her feet. It will break; and, she will be covered in a fog. You will then take her by the arm—gently—and lead her back to the car, where I will be waiting for you. Now go."

She watched with no small degree of trepidation as they departed. This was the most comprehensive set of instructions Ling had given these two. She was understandably concerned; but, as seemed to consistently be the case, she had little choice. With pressing business of her own to attend to, she wanted no witnesses. She moved silently into a denser area of trees.

Taking a small piece of notepaper and a pen, she hastily scribbled a series of runic characters. Then rolling the paper into a small tube and holding it before her face, she concentrated in gathering a small amount of ambient energy, just enough to form a tiny transit globe. Whispering her true name, she pushed the rolled tube into the globe. An instant later, she allowed the energy to dissipate; the little globe disappeared with a minuscule *pop*.

Cautiously making her way back to the limo, she found Vito leaning on a fender and smoking a cigarette. Neither of them spoke.

Vito raised his eyebrows in an unasked question.

Ling shook her head and shrugged her shoulders; they would just have to wait and see.

Moments later, Ling heard something to her left; Iggy came forth from the tree line, leading a fog-shrouded figure. The assassin sighed and released a ball of tension that was building in her chest.

As Vito opened the rear doors of the vehicle, Ling quickly assisted Iggy in placing his captive inside, and making her secure.

"Uh, Ling," Vito whispered hoarsely. "You'd better get out here."

"What?" she asked climbing out of the car.

Vito pointed toward the driveway; Bubba was leading another fog-shrouded figure toward the limo.

Ling was stunned!

Two women? Which one was the Steward? How are we to know? I've never actually seen her!

Bubba stood at the side of the car, awaiting Ling's next command. He had done exactly as he'd been instructed—and ironically, so had Iggy.

"So, what do you want to do?" asked Vito, without expression.

She knew he was actually quite relieved that this was not *his* screw-up.

"There were not supposed to be *two* women here," she spat. "But there were! So, we take them *both*—and let the boss sort it out. Get this one in the car and let's go!"

TEDDY WAS GETTING BORED. If he wasn't involved in cooking meth, his attention span was about half as long as a television commercial.

He'd been staring at the weird purplish light coming from George's circle for some time. While he hadn't seen anything for a while there, he sure *heard* some strange sounds; shrieking cries and distant roars, like feeding time at some zoo. That had made him *real hinky* at first, but it'd been pretty quiet for a while now. Even the boss had relaxed a bit.

"Boss, how long we gonna wait?"

George grunted and stretched; clearly he, too, thought this *was* taking longer than expected. "Until Vito comes back to pick us up, I guess."

"Not for nothin', Boss, but what if someone else comes along before Vito gets back? I mean, somebody uses this dirt road. Y'know farmers usually carry shotguns in their trucks—and we're all alone out here. And remember, I ain't got no gun." Teddy sincerely hoped he wasn't pushing his luck, but he *was* getting antsy.

"Hmm, that's true," mused George aloud. "Tell you what, come here."

Teddy stood before his boss, who handed him two small glass balls.

"You still don't get a gun, but here—be careful with these. I told y'all how they work, remember?"

Teddy nodded. "Yeah, Boss, I remember. Break one at somebody's feet and it'll fog 'em."

"Right. If you don't use them, I want these back when we get out of here—understand?"

"Right, thanks Boss . . . Hey, I hear something, like footsteps—fast feet!"

They looked around; they were still alone. Then they both heard it.

Someone was running as if their life depended on it. It was getting louder and closer!

Teddy paled and pointed at the circle!

The shroud of purple shimmer above the circle suddenly flared in a splash of violet light—a disheveled man tumbled forth, and literally fell into George's arms. Panting heavily, he couldn't catch his breath; his chest heaved. He kept trying to look over his shoulder, the fear evident in his wide eyes.

Teddy instinctively backed away, putting some distance between himself and this wild and frantic individual. And worse, the boss seemed to know this man! He was holding the poor guy up, and trying to calm him down. The man's hair was all matted and crazy. He was wearing some sort of long weird robe, all nasty and ripped, with mud and leaves all stuck to it. Who was he? Was this who—or *what*—Papa George was waiting for?

The gasping man managed to speak, but Teddy was almost too far away to hear more than a few panicked words clearly.

"M'lord George . . . tis you . . . th-thank the gods!" Gripping George's arm, the man looked over his shaking shoulder at the purple shimmering circle.

"Daegon, you're safe—calm down!" George urged, trying to free his arm from the frantic man's bony grip.

"No! Not safe!" Daegon screamed. "Must close the portal! Close the portal, m'lord!"

"But *how*, Daegon?" George spat, losing his patience and shaking the nearly hysterical man. "Your little jewel didn't tell me *how!*"

Daegon stared at George in disbelief. His mouth opened, but no sound issued forth. Confusion was writ large across his face.

"Uh . . . Boss?" Teddy hissed urgently.

George, entirely focused on Daegon, ignored Teddy.

"BOSS! Look!"

George looked up—and froze.

Two huge tawny and speckled saber-toothed cats stood just outside the shimmering purple light, cautiously sniffing the air. The massive cats looked about, taking their new surroundings in stride. They lifted their muzzles, evidently sampling the air and trying to scent their prey.

With a shock, Teddy realized that this guy, Daegon, *was* their prey.

DAEGON FINALLY RELEASED George's arm, mumbling, "Too late—too late—too late . . ."

George fumbled for his 9mm pistol and leveled it at the cats, his hands shaking. "What the hell?"

The saber-toothed cats reacted to the sound and movement. The larger one took a step toward the men.

George panicked, firing repeatedly; he emptied the magazine in seconds without realizing it.

Unfortunately, none of George's bullets struck either cat.

However, the strident sound of the gunfire did shock the felines into momentary immobility and confusion—but not so Teddy, who took off in a sprint. One of the cats noticed his headlong flight, and instinctively gave chase. But Teddy had a good head start; he was more than halfway to the trees.

The other cat began to stalk the two men.

Daegon began to slowly back away, but George stood his ground and carefully aimed at the predator. Time slowed and he began to experience a sensation like tunnel vision as the beast loomed closer.

George pulled the trigger, but nothing happened—the slide was racked back, held in place by the empty magazine. His mind raced as the cat continued to approach. He had nothing left but the small glass balls—would they even work on this beast?

What the hell—it's all I've got.

He dropped the pistol, grabbed a handful of balls from the pouch, and threw them at the saber-toothed cat.

Luck was with him; a ball broke upon one of the massive fangs. The surprised cat was soon covered in a vague grey fog. It did not move—it could not.

George and Daegon were equally surprised. Suddenly, Daegon pointed across the pasture to where Teddy was desperately trying to scramble up a tree—the other saber-toothed cat was almost upon him.

George shouted, "Teddy! Use the balls! They work!"

At a dozen feet above the ground, Teddy must have heard, for he paused in climbing long enough to fumble in his pocket. Just as the cat reached the base of the tree and crouched to spring, Teddy made his throw.

George and Daegon watched in awe as the second cat was suddenly enshrouded in the grey fog.

Teddy's throw had been true; but, he'd lost his balance in the process. He slipped from his perch, and fell heavily across another limb a few feet below. He was immediately covered in his own cloud of cloying fog.

George chuckled to himself, as he picked up his pistol.

"Hmm, the damn fool. He must have broken the other glass ball."

Daegon urgently tugged at George's sleeve and rasped, "You must close the portal! There are far worse things that may come through!"

"Fine!" George sneered. "Why don't you tell me *how?*"

Daegon gaped as the realization finally sunk in; and, he quickly explained.

"You must release the energy that maintains the portal—*you* confined and molded its purpose, and *you* must release it! Walk around it three times in the other direction, and focus on closing the portal by releasing the channeled energy. Think of nothing else—and do not come into contact with the light. The portal should slowly close as you walk, and the energy should be fully dissipated at the conclusion of the third circuit. It *is* the usual method."

George followed Daegon's instructions. He was more than midway through the second circuit when there was a shuddering impact and a deafening roar from within the circle. The sheaf of shimmering purple light bulged on one side, but did not rupture. Something tried to force its way through, but the portal was more than half closed.

Daegon cried out, "Ignore it! Keep going!"

George did so, desperately striving to heed the warning to *ignore* whatever raged on the other side. When he completed his third circuit, the circle went silent and the sickly purple light faded out.

Daegon dropped to his knees, his shoulders sagging, and mumbled, "Over . . . tis over . . ."

"Maybe," mumbled George, looking about anxiously. He found that the fog-shrouded cats were somehow difficult to see, even when he looked right at them.

How long would they remain in this state? We've gotta get out of here!

The crunch of gravel beneath tires and the muted purr of a motor caught his attention. Beyond the nearby tree line, the bright flare of sunlight reflected off chrome announced the return of the limousine.

George turned to a stunned Daegon and urged him to move.

"We have to leave—come with me!"

But Daegon did not move; he could only stare as the limo slowed to a stop.

Then George realized that Daegon had never seen a car before.

"Daegon, listen to me. That is only a vehicle, like a carriage—transportation. We ride inside, in a very comfortable compartment. Now come on!"

Daegon nodded in acceptance, then pointed behind him and asked, "But what of these beasts—and your servant?"

"*My servant?* Oh, you mean Teddy. He'll be fine in a coupla days. As for the cats, I don't know how long that stuff will hold them; but, they're someone else's problem now. Come on—we have to go!"

Vito got out and opened the rear door, raising his eyebrows as George ushered the filthy and disheveled stranger into the limo.

Meeting Vito's eyes, George merely shook his head—*no questions, not now.*

The interior of the limo was more crowded than George expected. Two fog-shrouded forms were strapped into the jump seats.

Ling and her henchmen made room for George and his new guest. Ling's nose crinkled at the lingering stench of fear coming from this disgusting stranger, but she kept silent.

Teddy's absence was equally conspicuous.

"Ling, why are there *two* fogged people, when you were told to grab *one*?" George asked her, his tone even but his frustration evident.

"Sir, your information was that she lived alone—but she was *not* alone. There were two women; so, rather than guess, we took them both. There were no problems; they saw nothing," Ling answered reasonably, as if this were the only logical course of action.

George considered her response, and had to agree. There was no way to tell which one was the Steward—the fog prevented that for at least two days—but she obviously hadn't been harmed. The other woman couldn't see or hear, so she couldn't identify anyone either. All in all, he reasoned, he'd managed to do what was required of him. Lady Diere should be pleased . . . *should be . . .*

"Uh, Boss," asked Vito, "where to?"

"Head for Shreveport—keep to the back roads."

ELLEN WAS LESS THAN a mile from home when she began to feel unaccountably anxious, despite the peaceful ambiance of the forest. The dogs seemed to sense her mood and they picked up the pace. In no time, all three were running for home.

When they arrived at the house, she found Mark and Miska in the kitchen, drinking iced tea and munching on toasted bagels.

"Hi El' . . . Is something wrong?" Mark asked, sensing her urgency.

"My mom and Stacy?" Ellen asked in a rush, still panting for breath.

"They're out in the gardens, listing plants or something," Mark said, his concern growing. "What is it? What's wrong?"

"I-I'm not sure," Ellen hesitated only a second, and then headed for the dining room. Calling over her shoulder, she asked, "When did you last see them?"

Mark rose and followed, Miska and the dogs at his heels.

"I guess about twenty minutes ago. Stacy was getting a couple of bottles of water and was going back out again just as Miska and I were coming in to get something to drink." Mark caught up to Ellen. "We've been in the garage working on the truck while she and your mom have been out there in the gardens most of the morning."

They reached the front porch and scanned what they could see of the gardens; but there was no sign of Millie or Stacy.

"I have this terrible feeling," Ellen said, uneasily, "that something is wrong. I can't explain it."

"I can see that something has gotten you upset," Mark said soothingly. "Did something happen on your walk?"

"Well, yeah . . . I met Gallenius, the mage from Storm Haven, and some people from some of the other realms. They sort of *popped in* for a short visit. He also came to warn me about some things. But that's not what's gotten me so worried—"

"He *warned* you?" Mark repeated, with alarm. "Let's go back inside. I think you'd better tell us everything."

Back in the kitchen she did so, as succinctly as she could; Mark and Miska listened carefully. When she finished, Mark only asked a few simple questions.

"So, Gallenius made no mention of Stacy or your mother? His warning was only for you? And the Council meeting is still scheduled for tomorrow evening?"

She answered his queries with nods or shakes of her head, her anxiety increasing incrementally. Her mother and Stacy had still not returned.

Miska sensed her distress and put his huge arm around her shoulders in a reassuring hug.

"Do not worry, Miss Ellen. It will be all right. Miska will protect you, and will help to find Miss Millie and Miss Stacy."

Mark had his cell phone to his ear. He pursed his lips in frustration and dialed another number.

A muted buzzing startled Ellen and she spun toward the sink—Millie's cell phone vibrated under a dish towel on the counter.

"Stacy's cell phone goes to voice mail," Mark announced; and then pointed, "and there's Millie's—"

"So? Would you need a cell phone to work in the garden?" she snapped, rolling her eyes in exasperation.

"Listen to me, Ellen," urged Mark. "Just calm down. We are not without our own resources, okay? Calm yourself and do your *thing*—you know, open your awareness and see if you can sense them. Give it a try, okay?"

He was right, and she was immediately grateful for his suggestion. She deliberately settled within herself and found her calm center. She opened her awareness in slowly expanding waves; filtering out those energies that she did not seek. It took a few minutes before she found them—clouded and fuzzy, but moving away.

"I sensed them," she said. "I think something is definitely wrong. They're moving away; and their energy signatures are somehow *obscured.* I think—no, I *know* this is *wrong!* I can't tell how far away they really are. We have to look for them!"

"I agree, but let's be smart about this," cautioned Mark. "Miska and I can search all the gardens very effectively, and do both sides of the driveway at the same time. If you'll stay at the house, you can monitor the phone in case they call. Stacy's probably got her phone—she doesn't go anywhere without it."

"But, I—" she started to object, but he cut her off.

"I'm not done! If you stay within earshot of the phones here, you can go out on the front balcony and use my field glasses—you know, my binoculars. From there you can watch our progress and scan for any sign of them all the way to the orchard. We'll signal you if we find anything. I'll have my cell phone."

"Okay . . . Yeah, that does make sense," she agreed. "Where are your binoculars?"

"My room—I'll get them."

Miska looked down at Ellen and said softly, "Do not worry, Miss Ellen, we will find them."

"Thank you, Miska. I'm sure we will," she agreed, but the uncertainty and stress in her voice was unmistakable.

With Max and Sophie flanking her, Ellen stood on the front porch balcony with Mark's field glasses to her eyes. She had no difficulty monitoring the progress of the search from that vantage point, until Mark and Miska went beyond the thick row of mimosa trees and into the pecan orchard.

She periodically opened her awareness, seeming to find her mother and Stacy at a slightly greater distance each time. She was convinced they were no longer on Delafaire Farm property.

Her cell phone rang.

"Ellen, it's Mark. We found the clipboards, in separate locations—and tire tracks, in the grass of the orchard and on the driveway. We're on our way back. Sit tight, okay?"

Sit tight? Was he kidding? I need to DO something! But what?

Something brushed against her ankle—Smokey. He had something in his jaws, the blue velvet bag that held the spectacles—Maude's special spectacles. He dropped the bag on her foot, and then pawed the bag.

She bent down and scratched behind his ears. He pawed the bag again.

"You want me to put the glasses on, don't you, Smokey?"

He promptly sat and stared up at her . . . *well?*

She slipped the delicate spectacles out of the bag, and settled them on her nose. She looked back to Smokey, for confirmation or approval—she didn't know which—but the cat now ignored her and began grooming himself.

She stood, groaning a bit as she straightened her back, and looked out over the gardens.

I wish I knew what had happened out there with my mom and Stacy.

At that thought, the view through the blue tinted lenses of the spectacles changed. Suddenly a section of the garden—the iris plantings—was magnified and came into sharp focus.

There was her mother!

A bald man in black wearing dark glasses seemed to have suddenly appeared and made a throwing gesture at her mother's feet. A thick cloud of some sort formed around Millie; and the man led her away, along the far tree line. Soon they came to what looked like a limousine; and two other people, a man and woman, put her mother in the car.

Another man, dressed like the first, approached leading another person cloaked in a similar sort of cloud—Stacy! She was placed in the vehicle as well. And then, the long dark car drove away, down the driveway and out of Delafaire Farm.

Ellen blinked; the vignette was gone. All she saw now through the spectacles were just the empty gardens of the present—not what had happened before. She removed the glasses and considered them in the palm of her hand.

Maude had cautioned her that she had not fully appreciated the spectacles—how right she had been. Now Ellen knew *what* had happened to her mom and Stacy, but not *why*, or by *whom—not yet.*

She was dialing Hawk's number when Mark and Miska trooped up the stairs and joined her on the balcony. She paused, held up the spectacles for them to see, and then quickly explained what she had seen through them.

"You're calling Hawk now?" Mark asked.

She nodded as she listened to the ringing.

HAWK AND TREY WERE concluding an interview with Horace and Carrie Tippet on the front porch of their store. The Tippets were certain that the man they had seen in their store that morning was George Papadolis.

Two sheriff's patrol units had twice run the length of Parish Road 157 without spotting the black limousine that George was reportedly riding in. The deputies were now parked at Tippet's store awaiting further instructions. Trey could not keep them from their other assigned duties much longer, each had calls backing up; and the dispatcher wanted Trey to landline her. He knew she'd tell him she needed those units back in service; and, he knew she was right.

He excused himself from the interview for a moment and walked over to the two uniformed deputies.

"Thanks, guys. Y'all can clear this scene; I'm sure dispatch has calls backing up. We'll finish up our interview here and be 10-8 ourselves shortly."

"Right, Sarge. Sorry we didn't find that limo," one of the deputies acknowledged.

"Well, keep an eye out—you never know," Trey cautioned, "and be safe."

Both patrol deputies acknowledged and drove away in different directions.

Trey was beginning to think the Tippets might have been mistaken. But just as he stepped back up on the porch, Horace produced a clear plastic baggie containing a ten dollar bill.

"This here's the ten he paid for the quarters with, this here. I didn't hardly touch it none, 'cept on the very edges, puttin' it in the bag, y'see. I figure y'all can get his fingerprints off'n it, and that'll ID him, f'sure, won't it? F'sure, right?"

Horace was obviously quite pleased with himself; his wife favored him with a satisfied smile. Trey had the sneaking suspicion that bagging that ten just might have been Carrie's idea; but, he didn't really care. This could be quite a break for the case.

"Excellent job, Horace!" Trey beamed. "Let me write you out a receipt for that piece of evidence—"

"Oh, that's all right, Sergeant—I trust you, I do."

Hawk laughed aloud, and Trey just chuckled as he explained, "I'm sure you do, Horace, but this is for the *chain of custody* of the evidence—documentation that supports the integrity of the evidence, *the paper trail.*"

Hawk's cell phone rang. The caller ID displayed Ellen's number and he excused himself to take the call in private.

Trey continued trying to explain certain rules of evidence to Horace, and make him understand that he might have to testify in court.

The next thing Trey knew, Hawk was tugging him off the porch, and apologizing to the Tippets—they had to go. Hawk briefly commented that they had a fresh lead on the black limousine.

HAWK SLIPPED BEHIND the wheel, and Trey reached for the radio—but Hawk stopped him.

"You need to listen before we call in and go 10-8," Hawk cautioned as they sped out of the parking lot.

Trey just shrugged, "I'm all ears, so?"

"That was Ellen calling. About twenty minutes ago, somebody in a dark limo snatched her mother, Millie, and her friend, Stacy, from the garden area at Delafaire Farm."

"So, now we have a kidnapping?" Trey assumed. "And a *dark limo* is involved. Papa George is allegedly seen in a *black limo.* That's too many coincidences for me. We're headed to Ellen's place now?"

"Yeah, now you can put out the call on the limo—as a kidnapping," Hawk said as he accelerated through the apex of a sweeping curve and activated the cruiser's blue strobe emergency lights.

"That's why the patrol units couldn't find the limo on 157—it detoured to Delafaire Farm," Trey deduced.

"Probably," agreed Hawk, "but the limo's not there now. It's somewhere on the road—*with two victims inside!*"

"Hmm, we gotta be careful how the dispatcher puts this out. I'm gonna get her on the phone."

Trey spent the next few minutes on his cell phone communicating with the dispatcher. Seconds later she commenced to broadcast a terse parish-wide lookout for the suspect limousine. Locating that vehicle was the priority—safely stopping it might be another matter entirely.

As Hawk deftly drove up the winding road, Trey reviewed what facts they now had. Finally, he realized what was bugging him.

"Hawk, Ellen told you they grabbed Millie and Stacy about twenty minutes ago, right?"

"Yeah, so they could be fifteen to twenty miles from here by now."

"True, but that's not what's bugging me. Why did Ellen wait twenty minutes to call you?"

"Huh?" replied Hawk. "Maybe she called the office, or 9-1-1 before she called me?"

"Nope, the dispatcher would have known, but she didn't. Everything I passed on about the kidnapping was news to her. The only other call about the limo was Carrie Tippet's original call earlier this morning."

"I dunno—about the twenty minutes, I mean," Hawk admitted. "When she called me, it didn't register, so I didn't think to ask her. I'll call her, if you want."

Trey thought for a second, and then said, "Yeah, it could be important. Call her and ask."

Hawk punched the speed dial on his cell phone and rang Ellen's number. She answered on the first ring.

"Ellen, it's Hawk . . . Yes, we're on our way—we'll be there in about ten minutes. Listen, I'm gonna put you on speaker. I gotta ask—"

He was suddenly interrupted by a frantic radio call from a patrol unit. The dispatcher tried to get the information, but there was considerable static and interference.

"Patrol 212, 10-9, repeat your traffic."

". . . 12 southbound past Miller's . . . He's running! . . . in pursuit . . . limousine . . ."

"Patrol 212, advise your 10-20."

". . . paper mill . . . back on 157 south . . ."

"Patrol 216, en route from LaBorde High School."

"Hey," exclaimed Trey, "that limo's headed right back for us. Stay northbound. We need to get to Truffant's farm and we've got him bottled up. I can't think of any turnoffs you could take a limo on!"

Hawk remembered his phone. "Ellen, I'm sorry—I gotta go!"

"I KNOW—I HEARD," SHE said hurriedly. "Please, be careful . . . I lov—"

But the line was dead; she hung up.

"What did Hawk say?" demanded Mark, nearly vibrating with tension.

"Uh, they have somebody pursuing the limousine—I could hear it on the radio in their car. How many limos are there around here? It has to be the same one!" she exclaimed.

"Yeah, gotta be!" He slammed a fist into his open palm. "Where's the limo now?"

"Um, going south on 157," she repeated. "They hope to get to Truffant's farm, so they can *'bottle him up'.* But I don't know where that is."

"*I* do; it's not far. I've seen it on the plat maps in the clerk's office. Listen, Ellen, stay here and man the phones. We need you to use your *special skill* to check on Millie and Stacy. As they come closer, or if they get separated, you should feel it! Maybe your glasses will show you something, too. We'll stay in touch by cell phone. Miska, come with me!"

She balked. "Wait, Mark! I'm going with you, I—"

He stopped and faced her.

"Ellen, think this through; what reason would anyone have for kidnapping your mother or Stacy? None, really. On the other hand, we already know that somebody doesn't want you to attend the Council meeting—remember? So, I don't think that Millie and Stacy ever were the intended targets; I think *you* were the intended victim. Call it a hunch, or intuition, but in truth it feels like something stronger, like I'm sensing someone's *intentions.* You have to trust me on this. I'm certain—it just *feels* right. Stay here, with the dogs, and be the communications hub. You'll be safe; and, we can keep you informed."

In fact, his explanation did feel right; and, she had to admit his strategy was wise.

"Very well, I'll stay. But you have to be careful—both of you!"

"We will—we promise!" With his pained smile and a confident wink, they were gone.

She went into the kitchen and saw the half-eaten bagel Mark had abandoned and the discarded shop rag on the seat of his chair. That reminded her that he and Miska had been working on the truck—which was still up on jack stands. Would they need any help getting the old Ford back on the ground?

She started for the back door when a strange throaty rumble stopped her in her tracks.

Now that's a new sound . . .

She pushed open the screen door and stepped into the yard as the rumble grew in volume.

Suddenly, the Chevrolet Biscayne roared out of the garage, into the sunlight. The flat-black vehicle reflected no light—it almost seemed to *absorb* it. It looked positively menacing just sitting there with a loping idle and subtle rocking motion. Mark sat behind the wheel, busily adjusting a restraint harness on his beaming passenger, Miska, who wore a smile that would do justice to an eight-year-old boy about to go on his favorite carnival ride. Mark noticed Ellen watching them, so he waved to her and gave a thumbs-up sign.

She smiled wanly and waved back as the *boys* in their *toy* roared away.

Please, be careful . . . and come back to me . . . all of you!

GEORGE'S INSISTENCE that Vito keep to the back roads was not the wisest course of action.

Any limousine, unless it was part of a funeral procession, was conspicuous on rural roadways; and, country folks don't miss a thing. As soon as the word had gone out that the Sheriff's Department was looking for a limousine, calls of reported sightings started coming in to 9-1-1 and the department's switchboard.

DEPUTY ANDY MERRIAM, operating Patrol Unit 212, was parked on the shoulder at the north end of Parish Road 157, preparing to run a radar speed enforcement detail on the nearby State Highway 71. He was waiting for an assigned motorcycle patrolman to meet him. Glancing in his mirror, he saw the grill of the northbound black limousine coming around a curve to his rear. The front end of the limo suddenly pitched downward as the driver saw the parked sheriff's car—a dead giveaway of a speeder slamming on the brakes.

Merriam's radio squawked, the dispatcher calling his unit.

"Base to Patrol 212. Citizen reports seeing a black limousine northbound on 157 from Paper Mill Road. "

"212 copies. I think I've got an eyeball on him now. He just stopped in the northbound lane of 157 just south of the 71 access cutoff. Standby . . . He's doing a Y-turn—black late-model stretch limo—now southbound on 157. I'm gonna close and try to read the plate. Please notify Motor 10 that I'm 10-6."

"10-4, 212. Advise you use caution—possible kidnapping suspect."

"212 copies . . . I'm closing . . . No joy—I can't read the plate. He's picking up speed."

"IS THAT COP STILL BACK there?" George asked, reluctant to turn his head to look.

Vito quickly looked in the mirror; the sheriff's car was closer.

"Yeah, he hasn't activated his lights and siren, at least not yet; but he's definitely interested."

Vito eased the accelerator down a bit and kept the limo just above the posted speed limit of 50 mph. The big car floated through the gentle curves smoothly.

"What do you want me to do, Boss?"

"Don't stop!" fumed George. This was rotten luck! He could not be caught in this vehicle with two kidnap victims. And Daegon—how would he explain *him?* His mind raced.

"Vito, listen . . . You gotta lose this guy—even if just for a coupla minutes. Let us—*all of us*—get out and get out of sight. Then you let this cop find you again. If he stops you, play dumb, tell him you got lost. The worst he'll probably do is write you a ticket for something, *capisce?*"

Ling just rolled her eyes and kept silent.

VITO GRIMACED. HE HAD serious doubts about *losing* this cop. The limo was fine for high speeds on a nice straight interstate, but this was a winding country two-lane with only a few straight stretches for passing. And worse, there were no shoulders to speak of; the land to either side of the road was heavily wooded, and deep drainage ditches ran alongside the pavement. This road would not suffer fools gladly.

But the boss had spoken, and Vito dutifully acknowledged.

"I'll do my best, Boss, but his sedan is better set up for this road than this limo. If it comes to it, I might have to *dent* him a little."

Catching Vito's eyes in the mirror, George smiled evilly. "I get it—do what you gotta do."

Vito concentrated on smooth speed, picking his lines to maximize late apexes in every curve, and then accelerating briskly without upsetting the suspension. He had the limo running between 80 and 90 mph with apparent ease, but that was about the limit for the road conditions—any faster in some of the turns and he could overtax the suspension and lose control. The sheriff's car was still behind him but the gap had opened significantly; almost a quarter mile now separated the two vehicles.

Vito saw that he was coming up on a southbound logging truck, and that a longer straight stretch of road lay ahead. Judging the distance, the truck's speed, the limo's present velocity and potential acceleration was the work of an instant—he floored the accelerator.

The big limo downshifted and leapt forward as the engine raced to redline. When the limo streaked past the logging truck, Vito caught a glimpse of the truck driver gaping in wide-eyed astonishment.

Vito looked as far ahead as he could, just *knowing* a curve was coming, and eased up on the gas pedal. The speedometer began counting down; 129, 125, 120, 110 . . . Vito ignored the digital gauge, keeping his eyes on the road.

The sweeping right curve came up quickly, but he was ready. He stabbed at the brakes repeatedly to bleed off speed and let the rotors cool before he entered the turn. He picked a line with a late apex, and as soon as he felt the vehicle's aft weight start to lift and shift left, inducing a bit of oversteer drift, he smoothly eased up, applied a bit more throttle to settle the suspension, and powered through the turn.

DEPUTY MERRIAM HIT his blue strobe lights, and reported that he was in pursuit. He had seriously underestimated the capability of the long limo, and the skill of its driver.

That good ol' boy was damned good!

The road turned and there was no way for the deputy to pass the logging truck without forcing it off the road and into the drainage ditch. The deputy's only option was to wait until he could see that it was safe enough to pass the truck in the next straight stretch. He got on the radio to keep the dispatcher advised.

MARK AND MISKA HAD driven out to Parish Road 157, but were uncertain whether to turn north or south, so they sat there at the intersection and tried to decide.

"Well, we are either ahead of the limo or behind it," Mark remarked. "If they're southbound, past this point, then we're behind them, and—"

"Hold," interrupted Miska, "Listen . . ."

"I don't hear any—"

"Quiet! It is hard enough to hear over the sound of this car," Miska urged.

"Oh, sorry," replied Mark as he turned off the ignition. The sudden silence was almost a shock of stillness.

Miska closed his eyes in concentration; then, he pointed out the passenger window.

"Something comes . . . There is a siren, but much further away . . . Something is chased!"

"Good ears, Miska," complimented Mark, as he restarted the Chevy, "but I gotta wonder if you're watching too much television—"

A long black streak flashed by—gone in an instant.

"Whoa! He's really moving!" Mark exclaimed, his head pivoting right and left. "But where's the cop? He should be here. Can you still hear the siren?"

"Yes, still far away—do we chase now?" Miska was grinning from ear to ear.

"Well," Mark temporized, "we'll just keep him in sight—so we can tell the police where he went. Hold on!"

Mark cocked the wheel to the left as he eased the clutch out smoothly. The old Chevy rolled onto the southbound lane of 157 with some slight fishtail motion as power overcame traction for just a second. Mark went through the gears fluidly, letting himself get a bit more aggressive, getting a feel for the drivetrain as he increased the power. Over the next few moments he became more familiar with the exceptionally tight suspension and the stiff ride; the old Chevy stuck like glue in every turn.

Mark realized the car's capabilities may well exceed his own driving skill—and he thought he was pretty good, having done some amateur racing in his college days.

For a full-size vehicle, the Biscayne was very light—the engine a torque monster. Mark could leave it in third or fourth gear and just *point and shoot*. The combination of power delivery and handling was simply an awesome package. He would have to be careful; this was no poseur hot rod. This was a serious business machine—it could hurt him if he forgot that.

Shooting out of a poorly banked S-curve, they were suddenly within sight of the limousine, several hundred yards ahead. Mark glanced at the speedometer needle holding just above 90 mph—he'd have sworn he was doing no more than 65 or 70 mph. He let his speed drop; he didn't want to get too close. After all, the idea was just to keep the limo in sight.

As the distance between the two vehicles increased, Mark caught the distant flash of blue lights in his rearview mirror, and eased further off the throttle, coasting near the vicinity of the posted 50 mph speed limit.

Like a wailing banshee, a sheriff's patrol car soon whipped past the Biscayne in hot pursuit of the speeding limousine. Both were soon out of sight on the winding country road.

Mark and Miska looked behind them, but there were no other police cars. They smiled.

"You know, I think that cop was alone," Mark speculated, a mischievous glint in his eye.

"And he might need some help—I mean *backup*," Miska eagerly concluded.

Mark laughed. "Ha! Now I *know* you've been watching too much TV!"

The matte-black Chevy accelerated brutally amidst the manic laughter of the two excited and determined would-be rescuers.

HURTLING NORTHBOUND in the unmarked cruiser, Trey slapped at Hawk's arm and pointed out a barely noticeable dirt drive in the midst of a thick stand of old pines coming up on the left. "Slow down, Hawk—there's Truffant's southern fire road! We can back in there and wait for them."

"Good idea," said Hawk as he abruptly slowed and slewed into the turnoff. He quickly backed the cruiser into position as Trey advised the dispatcher of their status. They settled in to wait and just listened to the chase over the radio.

The limo was still southbound, perhaps less than ten minutes from their location. A marked unit, Patrol 212, was in pursuit and had visual contact. The plan was to have another patrol unit deploy *spike strips* across the roadway in an effort to flatten the limo's tires. That unit, Patrol 216, was already in position, at the northern fire road of Truffant's Farm, about a mile north of Trey and Hawk's present position.

Trey stroked his chin, leaned forward, and peered through the windshield to the north, as far up the parish road as the foliage and overhanging trees would allow.

"What?" Hawk asked, turning his head to look in the same direction. "See something?"

"Nah, not yet." Trey sat back. "You know, Hawk, one thing concerns me about this *spike strip plan.* Don't most limousines use run-flat tires?"

"Oh, crap! I dunno, but I'd bet some do. Assuming this one does, what's plan B?" Hawk stared at his partner. "How does one stop a speeding limo?"

"Hmm, one improvises," Trey mused aloud, thoughtfully looking about.

VITO MANAGED TO KEEP the persistent cop from getting any closer than about ten car lengths, but he couldn't lose him. There hadn't been any other traffic, except for an old black Chevy that paced him for a few miles before that cop caught up to him again. Vito wasn't familiar with these roads, and he needed some sort of diversion or screen so he could get away. Another logging truck would have been nice, but now he was going to have to create his own diversion.

"Boss, I'm gonna have to *dent* this guy some, so you all hold on to something."

"Do it, Vito," George spat.

As the limo went into another sweeping left, Vito lifted his foot from the accelerator and the limo rapidly lost speed; but he stayed off the brakes to keep from illuminating his brake lights. A yellow warning sign indicated the turn eventually reversed into an ever-tightening right with a decreasing radius. Hidden by overgrown brush and out of view of the pursuing sheriff's car, Vito brought the limo to a stop, with the front end entirely in the oncoming traffic lane and the rear obstructing the other.

DEPUTY MERRIAM WAS closing the gap as the limo went into the sweeping left. These were *his* roads, and he knew he could take the upcoming sharp right easily at 40-45 mph. In his adrenaline-fueled excitement, he pushed the envelope and entered the blind right-hander at better than 50 mph.

He was suddenly staring at the rear of the stopped limousine! He slammed on the brakes and twisted the wheel to the left. His inertia was too great; the front tires locked and slid, plowing to the outside of the turn. The right front fender of his car clipped the left rear bumper of the limo and his car scraped with a harrowing *screech* down the entire length of the limo's left side.

Funneled off the road, the deputy's car plowed nose-first into the depths of the drainage ditch. Its momentum flipped the sedan end over end, barely clearing a stand of cypress saplings, and slammed to earth—wheels down—into the soggy muck at the edge of a shallow swamp.

The last thing Deputy Merriam consciously saw was the patrol car's air bag going off—belatedly—in his face.

VITO TURNED THE LIMO southbound once more and quickly accelerated away from the crash scene. Now he had to find some way off of this road; it would be crawling with cops in no time.

A few minutes later, he crested a sloped rise at breakneck speed and caught a flash of movement off to the right. A man in uniform had tossed something across the surface of the road—but Vito wasn't stopping for anyone or anything.

When he hit the spike strip, Vito smiled.

Ha! These are run-flats, baby—and worth every penny!

"Sorry about the rough ride, Boss; but I think we're clear of a tail, at least for the moment," Vito remarked, watching for George's reaction in the mirror.

"Good, now find a way off this road so we can . . . What the hell is *that?*" George shouted, pointing forward.

Smoke! A roiling wall of thick rolling smoke covered the entire road!

Vito stabbed the brakes, but the vehicle's velocity carried them into the blinding cloud before he could appreciably decrease speed. He could see nothing. He held the wheel and hoped the road stayed straight until he could get the vehicle stopped. He felt the crown of the road rise to the left and he instinctively steered to compensate.

He steered too much, too late.

The rear of the limo pitched heavily to the left; the left side tires slid off into the drainage ditch. The canted limo slammed to a jarring halt, the length of the driver's side firmly wedged against the wall of the ditch. The impact viciously slammed Vito's head against the door frame an instant before his air bag uselessly deployed.

He was out cold.

IN THE REAR OF THE limousine, George was the first to react. He was okay—but he knew Diere would not be pleased with him should the Steward come to any harm. He quickly made sure that neither fog-shrouded captive was injured.

He knew the police would be here any moment—he was determined *not* to be caught. He pressed against the door, but it wouldn't budge. The other door was crushed up against the wall of the ditch, and the cloistered gap separating the front seat from the rear passenger compartment was too small for someone of his size to climb through. He was trapped!

He looked to Ling for help, but she was dazed and rubbing her forehead. Daegon was in a state of wide-eyed shock. Only Ling's two henchmen and the fog-shrouded captives seemed unaffected.

The captives—of course! I still have an option!

"Ling, listen to me," he said urgently, "I am going to leave, and I will take these two and Daegon with me. You and your men will have to get away on your own. Leave Vito—let the cops find an otherwise empty limo!"

"W-what? H-how? W-why?" she tried to ask, her confusion evident.

Ignoring her questions, he unbuckled the seat belts of the two kidnap victims and pushed Daegon between them. Then, making sure he was in contact with all three, he produced Lady Diere's topaz ring, and twisted the stone's setting.

A multihued bubble expanded to encompass the four of them—and they were gone.

OF COURSE, LING IMMEDIATELY recognized a transit globe, but before she could react, it had vanished.

She cursed, then righted herself in the canted vehicle and tried the door; it was stuck. She braced her legs and applied her extraordinary strength; the jammed door popped open.

She cautiously peered out through the slowly dissipating thick smoke and scanned the immediate area. She could hear voices in the vicinity, but none very close. The authorities had not yet found the limousine. She dropped back inside and opened a panel on the front wall of the passenger compartment; a rack of weapons was displayed.

Handing short-barreled AK-74 assault carbines and extra magazines to Iggy and Bubba, she said firmly, "You will defend this vehicle; allow no police to approach it—no matter the cost."

She knew they were doomed; but in reality, they had outlived their usefulness. She would have rather enjoyed slaying them personally, but right now she needed a diversion. That her instructions most likely condemned the unconscious Vito as well, never even occurred to her—not that it would have mattered.

Levering herself out of the vehicle, she saw that more of the smoke was thinning out. She had to make her move now, before she lost the advantage of the poor visibility. She leapt to the pavement, and made her way into the woods.

THE OLD CHEVY SLOWED as Mark and Miska encountered the first tendrils of smoke questing through the trees and drifting across the roadway like grasping fingers.

Just before the upcoming turn, a marked patrol unit was angled across the road, its blue lights flashing on the roof bar, casting eerie formations in the twisting smoke. A uniformed deputy sheriff was crouched behind his car, the shotgun at his shoulder trained on something, a large vague shape in the smoke.

As Mark brought the Biscayne to a stop, well away from the sheriff's car, Miska awkwardly unbuckled his restraint harness and opened his door. He paused and sniffed the air.

"Smoke from burning pine . . . no, only *pine needles.*"

Suddenly he pointed off to the left, "Look, in the trees, someone runs away—only one person!"

"I don't see anyone, Miska. Damn, I can hardly see *at all!* The smoke stings my eyes!"

"No matter—Miska will follow and catch!"

With that, he was out of the car and disappeared into the woods.

Mark opened his door, fumbled with the release of his harness, and called out, "Miska! Wait!"

A sudden burst of automatic gunfire shattered the afternoon—staccato strobes of muzzle flash flared from within the thinning smoke.

Mark scrambled back into the Chevy and pulled the doors shut as answering *booms* from shotguns echoed through the trees. The constant sound of gunfire was deafening, punctuated by the dull pinging of rounds striking sheet metal and the whispered *tthhhipp* of a passing bullet's near miss.

It seemed to last forever; but actually, it was over in less than two minutes.

Mark peeked over the dash; the smoke had almost completely dissipated. He watched the deputy sheriff cautiously moving forward, his shotgun at his shoulder.

Mark could now clearly see the limousine, canted at a severe angle, obviously stuck in the drainage ditch on the far side of the road. The shiny black surface of the big limo was riddled with chips and pockmarks—bullet and shot impacts, defeated no doubt by some level of armor.

Two bodies were visible, both dressed in black. One lay sprawled facedown on the road, a short assault rifle gripped in his right fist and empty magazines littered about. The other body hung head down, half out of the open rear door of the damaged vehicle. Beneath the limp and blood-drenched hands of the suspended dead man, a shattered assault rifle lay on the roadway.

A few more uniformed deputies emerged from behind sheriff's department cars that had been hidden by the thick smoke. Approaching carefully, they disarmed and handcuffed the two men in black, and then called for paramedics.

At first, Mark thought that was strange, but then he realized that he didn't really know if those two were truly dead—despite appearances—and he had certainly seen stranger things.

The deputies searched the limo and announced that they found the driver. He had survived the accident and the firefight, but was unconscious.

"Mark! What are you doing here? Are you all right?"

Mark looked to the right and saw Hawk striding toward him, and he did not appear pleased.

"Hi Hawk . . . Uh, I'm fine—we were looking for Stacy and Millie, of course. Did you find them?"

"No, the limo is empty except for the driver and these two," Hawk tossed his thumb over his shoulder. "And what do you mean by '*we*'? Who is with you—Ellen?"

"No, no, she's at the house. Um, Miska was with me. But when we pulled up, he saw someone running off in that direction and he took off after him."

Hawk looked around to be certain they were not overheard and asked, "Just one—or were there more? Did *you* see anything? Like anyone else running away?"

"No, I couldn't see through the smoke; but Miska could. He said there was one; he chased him."

Hawk stepped closer and lowered his voice, "Mark, did Miska *change*?"

"Not that I saw; but, I wouldn't be surprised if he did. He'd be a lot faster and could track better."

"Great—that's just great!" Hawk stared at the ground. "All right. Mark, you have to get out of here—before the patrol guys get a good look at this car!"

"Huh? What do you mean?"

"I don't know why you came in the Chevy—but it wasn't smart! You don't even have a registration plate or an inspection sticker on it yet. Did you think the patrol guys wouldn't notice? This would be impounded in a heartbeat! This is a crime scene now. Go home. Stay with Ellen. I'll keep an eye out for Miska. Now you have to go!"

"Okay, okay, I'm going, but we really have to talk. I'll tell Ellen what's happened, okay?"

Hawk sighed. "No one else—this is official business now. I'll watch for Miska. So, go already!"

Mark started the Chevy and drove north.

FRUSTRATED AND ANXIOUS, Hawk stared into the woods and gnawed at his lower lip.

Miska, what did you see? Millie or Stacy? Where are you? Just who are you chasing?

CH 8

GEORGE, DAEGON, AND the two fog-shrouded captives collapsed in a confused pile upon the smooth stones in the solitary cone of light. Only darkness beckoned beyond the stark border of illumination.

George disentangled himself, quickly stood, and looked around.

She's not here. Thank the gods!

Tugging Daegon to his feet, he asked urgently, "Are you all right? Listen, you and I gotta leave this place—right now! I'd never be able to explain *you!* These two—they're all right; we'll leave them here. Damn! There was only supposed to be *one;* but, I don't wanna have to explain that right now, either."

Daegon found his voice. "Explain to *whom?* Where are we?"

"This," George said softly, glancing first over one shoulder, then the other, into the stygian void, "is a special place of Lady Diere's. I don't wanna be here when she arrives."

Daegon peered into the gloom, but said nothing.

George opened his fist. "See this ring? It's hers; I used it to bring us here. I'm sure she knows by now that I activated the spell it holds. I could use it again to leave, but it will only take me—*us*—back to where we came from. And right now, that would be a very bad idea—for both of us."

Daegon shrugged. "Then do not use the ring—transit us elsewhere. Or, is that a problem?"

"Yeah, you could say that," George groused. "I can't transit anywhere without help. She promised to teach me the necessary skills, but so far she hasn't done it."

Daegon smiled sympathetically. "I can see that your education has been sorely lacking, my friend. Fortunately, I can remedy that shortcoming. Put the ring away; I will share with you a secret."

George hastily pocketed the ring and looked up expectantly at Daegon's smug smile.

"There is a long forgotten transit technique that is darkly efficient and very powerful—but there is a price, a blood price one must pay on an annual basis. Of course, it needn't be *one's own* blood. But what is that to the likes of us—adepts skilled in those arts of which lesser mages fear to speak? Fear not, for I shall take us away from this place; that is well within my skills."

"But where will we go?" asked George. "I have to answer the Council's summons tomorrow night. I have no choice; Diere expects me to be there. She demanded it!"

Daegon soothed George's concerns. "You will attend, my friend. In the meantime, I have just the place in mind; in fact, I've thought of little else in the last few days. I have a score to settle with the one I hope to find there."

"That's fine with me," agreed George. "Now let's get the hell out of here!"

Daegon summoned a transit globe that was as black as the surrounding darkness. Pushing into the obsidian orb, he glanced at George and uttered a single word.

"Follow."

George did so without hesitation, eager to be away from Lady Diere's clandestine domain.

THE MUSTY DARKNESS did not abate, but George knew he was elsewhere. There was a scraping sound to his left, followed by Daegon's voice.

"One moment . . . ah, here we are."

Sparks flared and a candle sputtered to life. George and Daegon stood in a small room roughly hewn from bare rock; tables and bookcases were pressed up against the walls. As Daegon lit more candles, George saw that there was a large metal ring inlaid on the floor; he had a vague sense of déjà vu.

"No one seems to be here," muttered Daegon, clearly disappointed.

"Where are we?" George asked. "And who are we looking for?"

Daegon found a torch and held it to a candle's flame. In the brighter light, he swept his arm around the chamber.

"This is the lair and workroom of an elfin mage known as Atrellan, the fool who sent me into that perilous realm. I would return the favor; but first, I have to *find* him! This is only a small part of this place; there is much above and below us. I will search every nook and cranny for that traitorous bastard."

"Let's do it," rumbled George, "and then you can teach me that *transit trick*."

Daegon grinned evilly, and with torch held high, led the way from the chamber.

THEIR SEARCH TOOK NEARLY two long hours; they were thorough. From the highest parapets of the castle to the lowest pits of the dungeons, they found no one.

The larder had been well stocked; but, there was no sign of a cook or servants. The entire castle appeared to be deserted. The only living things they found were a few skittering mice and some well-fed horses in the stables.

Sitting comfortably in a pair of worn leather chairs, amid dusty books and scrolls in the small castle's old library, Daegon and George rested. Warming themselves before a smoky hearth that held a struggling flame feeding upon a mixture of green and seasoned wood, they sipped a mediocre wine from pewter goblets, and puzzled over the otherwise empty redoubt.

"So, Daegon, think—how many people did you actually see here before?" George prompted.

"Three," Daegon responded, staring into the weak flames. "Atrellan and two acolytes . . . No, that is incorrect; there was a fourth, Boltar—actually, his body, a corpse. That was the source of my initial disagreement with Atrellan. I suspect there were other servants, but I neither saw nor heard them."

"Well, you saw Atrellan kill one acolyte to open the portal, right?" George reasoned. "So, what happened to the other one? And where's this Boltar's corpse?"

"Oh, no!" cried Daegon, leaping to his feet, his mouth agape and the blood draining from his face.

"What?" George demanded. "What is it?"

"The body—Boltar's corpse—of course it is gone! I should have realized what that means. I warned him not to take it to the queen! The damned fool ignored me! I have to go to her!"

"Who? What queen?" George asked, rising to stand before Daegon.

"Queen Mab!" Daegon blurted. "I fear that idiot, Atrellan, has put her in great danger. The body is ensorcelled! Please understand that I must go! You can stay here until you must appear before the Council; you will be safe."

"Daegon, I get it. Go do what you gotta do. I'll be here until tomorrow evening; then, I'll have to go as well. I have my summons and the instructions; so, don't worry about me. Be careful, my friend."

Daegon stared out a mullioned window at the lowering sun. It was clear that dusk would soon be upon the land. He quickly drained the dregs of his wine, grimaced, and handed the empty goblet to George. "I can be at her castle by nightfall, but I must hurry!" He spun on his heel and ran for the stables.

George refilled his own cup, settled comfortably in the soft chair, and mused thoughtfully.

Whoever you are, Atrellan, you're in deep shit! I think Daegon is not someone to cross.

LING RAN THROUGH THE thickening woods until she could no longer smell the smoke or see any part of the roadway. She stopped to listen for any signs of pursuit, but she was fairly certain she had escaped unseen. The wind shifted a bit and she caught the barest hint of a scent, but the fickle breeze denied her a second taste. Nonetheless, she was fully alert, and decided to move deeper into the forest.

She had been moving quietly for almost an hour on a diagonal to where she believed the roadway lay when she came upon a game trail. Deer sign and the rough scratchings of a coyote's territorial markings were prevalent. This path would serve her well, and she began to follow its twisted course, the slightest bit of wind in her face.

The path wound down an incline to a streambed that held only a trickle of water. It was enough; she drank cautiously.

She heard something behind her. Her head snapped up; she squinted at the crest of the hill she had descended moments ago. A huge shadow now stood there and almost obscured the sun. She could not see well for the glare; but, she heard him perfectly well.

"So, I have found you at last," rumbled a deep bass voice.

She remained hunched over the stream, surreptitiously unzipped her light jacket, and slipped her arms free. As soon as the big man stepped forward to begin his descent, she initiated the *change;* a thick mist rose to obscure her.

She was eager. *It will not matter what he sees—he will not live to tell of it.*

In the matter of a few heartbeats, she had shrugged off any semblance of humanity. From the dissipating mist emerged the sable-furred panther, rippled with coiled muscle, and intently focused on this new prey, this human interloper.

Who stood there unafraid, and laughing . . . *laughing at her?*

The man had paused midway down the hill and pointed at her in his mirth.

"Oh my, what a *big* kitty you are. I can see you want to make this interesting."

She was slightly confused. Prey usually ran from her; and she relished the chase. She stalked him by moving to one side and gradually closed the distance between them.

To her surprise, he continued walking down the hill—*in her direction.*

She crouched, her shoulder muscles bunched in knots of explosive tension as her bloodlust rose. She'd rip out his throat—how *dare* he not flee from her! He would pay dearly for such insolence!

She sprang, her fury unleashed!

But her slashing claws struck nothing, her gaping jaws closed on empty air—she had missed him completely!

She twisted in the air, landing on the side of the hill; but, she could not see her quarry! Near the base of the hill a large pool of mist drew her attention. She scented the air in caution and scanned the area; the big human was nowhere to be seen, nor could she find his scent.

Suddenly a huge shape rose from the cloud of mist—a bear! Standing up on its hind legs, it towered over the streambed. It sniffed the air and immediately focused on her. Dropping down to all fours, the bruin stepped slowly from the dissipating mist, its great shaggy head wagging from shoulder to shoulder as it walked with a rolling gait.

The panther feared nothing—not even a bear—and this was a *very big* bear. In a single graceful leap, she was at the base of the hill.

Facing each other, the two predators began to move in a circle, mirroring each other's movements. Without warning, they suddenly charged, making slashing contact with a rumbling roar and a snarling howl of rage! Their movements were almost too fast to see. Each fought instinctively; slashing, ripping, and biting. The forest echoed with the sounds of their mortal combat.

A mighty swipe of the bear's huge paw sent the panther sprawling. She was instantly up—slightly favoring her left side—and crouched to spring. The bear reared up to meet the imminent attack, fury flaring in its eyes.

It appeared that the next encounter would surely be the last for one of these beasts.

Just as the cat sprung and the bear lurched forward to meet the attack, a stentorian voice called out, "Hold! Thisss inssstant! I command it!"

The snarling panther was suspended in midair, mere inches from the gaping maw and massive claws of the towering bruin—both beasts frozen in a terrible tableau of imminent savagery.

"Ling! Missska! I *forbid* you to fight!"

The stasis spell was enormously strong; yet, it barely held the combatants apart. However, the spell held; neither Were creature could move more than their eyes.

Lord Addecus stepped forth, his brow knit in concentration. He waited until he was certain both beasts were focused upon him, before he continued.

"You will both lisssten to what I have to sssay! Eventsss of great proportionsss are underway of which you are unaware. Ssso, you will ssstop thisss foolisssh-nesss and heed my wordsss!"

Addecus paused and looked around. Once certain that they were neither observed nor overheard, he spoke softly, but with urgency.

"Queen Mab of the Dark Elvesss isss dead—asssasssinated, I have no doubt! And I know that Lady Diere hasss ssseized the throne, and even now consssolidatesss her power and asssesssetsss. Ssshe hasss announced an invessstigation into the death of the queen—irony, indeed, borne of sssuch unmitigated hubrisss—a flimsssy façade for a purge of thossse ssshe may consssider disssloyal.

"Ling, your ssservice to George Papadolisss isss at an end. You will return with me to the Realm of Were. I ssshould have recalled you sssooner, but I did not foresssee thessse eventsss. Your messsage caught me unawaresss. To have George attempt to kidnap the Sssteward isss the puressst folly! We cannot be linked to thisss colosssal blunder.

"Ling, know that thisss werebear isss Missska of the Urssusss Clan. He may well be the key to deflecting sssussspicion of any involvement of our realm in the death of Queen Mab. He ssshall come to no harm—by you or anyone elssse.

"Missska, you are to remain in hiding—here, in thisss realm, for now. I know that Lady Leanan brought you here, and I believe it wasss a wissse choice. Ssstay here, until ssshe or I tell you otherwissse. I will now releassse Ling from the ssstasssisss ssspell and we ssshall depart."

He concentrated on Ling; the panther dropped gracefully to the ground and shook herself. She sniffed at the towering bear and then ignored him as Addecus abruptly demanded her attention.

"Hisssttt! Ling, there isss no time for you to *change.* We mussst go, now!" Addecus insisted, as he held his scaled hands apart and summoned a transit globe.

Without a backward glance, the Were adept and the black panther pressed into the shimmering orb and disappeared.

Suddenly released from the stasis spell, Miska dropped to all fours and shook himself mightily to loosen his tense muscles. Raising his muzzle he sniffed in all directions; Addecus and Ling were indeed gone. He glanced over at the streambed and saw that his clothes lay about in shredded tatters—he hadn't disrobed before the *change.*

He shrugged; he could easily stay in bear form until he got back to the cabin as the entire region was thickly forested. That would also help to more quickly heal his superficial wounds, especially the deep scratches across his forearms. In truth, both he and Ling would heal quickly from almost any injury—short of beheading—unless it involved silver. Recovery was much faster in animal form, but pain was nonetheless pain.

He set off through the trees, instinctively knowing the right direction, his movements deceptively quiet for a beast of his bulk. He did his best to commit Addecus' words to memory as he walked. He had understood all that was said, but did not fully comprehend what role he was expected to play.

Fortunately, he had friends; they might understand.

CAPTAIN LOU MILLER stood off to one side with his detectives, Trey and Hawk, as the tow truck operator activated the winch. The steel cable pulled taut and vibrated like an over-tightened guitar string; but, the limo didn't budge. The straining winch whined in frustrated protest.

"Gentlemen, I recommend standing somewhere else," Sgt. Melancon called out from near the CSI van. "If that cable lets go, it'll do some real damage."

The three men immediately appreciated the wisdom of his words and joined him at the CSI van.

Four technicians were busily storing gear in the cargo area, their initial work on the scene complete. The crews of two nearby fire department vehicles were stowing their gear as well. Yellow crime-scene tape cordoned off the roadway fifty yards to the north and south of the actual scene, and held back a small group of curious onlookers and impatient reporters. Two media vans had arrived earlier and set up satellite uplinks. However, no law enforcement officials would speak with any of the television journalists or reporters. Captain Miller would deal with them, but only when he was good and ready.

Before the arrival of the media, an ambulance had transported the unconscious limo driver to the hospital with a sheriff's department escort. The coroner's office had collected the two deceased gunmen, who had been readily identified as wanted fugitives, Wilson "Bubba" Cutler and Ignatius "Iggy"

Simpson. The detectives on the scene had already called the U.S. Marshals and the New Orleans Police Department and advised of the demise of their fugitives.

Captain Miller asked the CSI sergeant, "Mel, can you give me a preliminary report? I have to craft some sort of press release."

"Sure, Captain, but it's too soon for any details. Once we have the vehicle in our shop we'll know more, of course. The database shows it registered to a defunct nightclub/strip joint in New Orleans, one of Papa George's clubs that was flooded out by the last hurricane."

The captain nodded. "What do we know about the survivor—the driver?"

"I've got that. Gimme a second, Captain." Hawk flipped open his notebook and responded. "The driver's ID shows *Vitorrio Smith*—possibly an alias. The EMTs think he's got a bad concussion, still unconscious. He's en route to LaBorde General. Based on the name and DOB on the ID, no current NCIC wants, but we're pretty sure he's got priors. We'll know more about him when we run his prints and a complete criminal history."

"And no trace of our *alleged* kidnap victims?" the captain pressed.

Hawk started to flare at the implication, but Sgt. Melancon quickly spoke up.

"We don't know yet, Captain. The limo is full of latents, but we need the vehicle in our shop to properly process it. And by the way, the two recovered guns, the AK-74 carbines, have obliterated serial numbers, so we'll notify BATF when we get back to the office."

"That means we have the driver on *constructive possession* of altered machine guns; that'll be some leverage," agreed Trey. "Did your team find any dope?"

"Don't think so," said Mel, "but we don't know what this is—yet." He held up a clear plastic evidence envelope containing a pair of marble-sized glass balls. Swirling colors twisted thickly within each sphere.

Captain Miller interrupted to point out a white-shirted fire department official making his way toward the CSI van. "Trey, you need to have a talk with the Assistant Fire Chief. He's not real pleased with your idea to burn a bunch of pine needles across the roadway. It almost caught the brush along the ditches."

"Aw, Lou, I only did it because the one smoke grenade we had wasn't enough to obscure the road. And the pine needles were pretty wet—they made a lot of smoke."

"At this point I don't really care, Trey," the captain said firmly. "Now go explain it to Assistant Chief Dawson, and apologize if you have to—make nice and fix it. I don't want any problems with the Fire Department floating upstairs to the front office."

"I'll take care of it, Captain." Trey shrugged. "Don't worry about a thing."

As Trey walked off to intercept the fire official, Sgt. Melancon leaned against the open van door and asked, "What's the status with Deputy Merriam—is he going to be all right?"

Captain Miller sighed. "Thankfully, yeah. He's got a concussion and a broken nose. He was awake but groggy when the other units found him. I understand he was a real mess from the nose bleed. It looked a lot worse than it was."

"He's pretty lucky, Lou, considering what his car looks like."

"That's the truth," agreed the captain. "These other three units with the bullet holes—are you all done taking photos of the damage? I can't spare them as evidence; patrol division needs them back in service as soon as possible."

"Oh yeah, we're done. We've slapped some heavy-duty duct tape over most of the holes in the sheet metal. It looks like crap, but it'll hold until the patrol division can schedule repairs. However, 218 will need a windshield right away; it *can* be driven, but only to a glass shop," warned Mel. "It's ironic our guys couldn't put any holes in that limo—probably armored. We'll know for sure soon enough."

A metallic screech and the crunch of gravel announced that the tow truck had managed to free the limo from the steep drainage ditch. The operator began to hook up the damaged vehicle to tow it away.

Sgt. Melancon closed the side door of his van and said, "Captain, unless you need us for something else, we're gonna clear the scene and follow the tow truck back to our shop."

"Except for me dealing with the media, we're done here; your team can clear. The limo is evidence now, so stay with it to maintain the chain of custody."

The CSI sergeant nodded, climbed into the front passenger seat of the van, and motioned for the driver to proceed.

"Hawk, are those all the statements from the responding deputies?" asked the captain, pointing to a folder tucked under Hawk's arm.

"Yes, sir, it's all handwritten stuff," Hawk responded. "Some of the guys want to type their statements when they get back to the office."

"They needn't bother; these will suffice. Ah, here comes Lt. Withers; give the statements to him. He'll be doing the shooting-board inquiry paperwork."

Hawk handed the folder to the lieutenant. However, the captain wasn't done with him.

"Sit tight for a minute, Detective." Captain Miller held up a finger to indicate that Hawk should wait.

The captain drew Lieutenant Withers to one side for a few private words and then sent him to the hospital to interview Deputy Merriam.

Lou glanced at the growing crowd of eager reporters and sighed; he'd have to deal with them soon. Too much information had already leaked out; too many people routinely monitored the department's radio calls via scanners. There would be the inevitable questions about the alleged kidnapping—something his investigators hadn't yet confirmed had actually happened—and how this limousine was supposedly involved. Questions he couldn't answer if he wanted to. They were just going to have to settle for the old *ongoing investigation—unable to comment at this time* response. The media wouldn't like that. *Oh well . . .*

There was really nothing more to be done on this scene. He needed to release the state police troopers who had responded as back-up and get the road reopened to traffic. He was already dreading the paperwork this incident would generate.

The captain rejoined the waiting detective, and refocused on the primary issue.

"Hawk, we still don't have a handle on this kidnapping. I thought you and Trey were supposed to go to Delafaire Farm and take a statement from our complainant, Ellen Doyle. We found no kidnap victims in this limo. So, is she a witness or not?"

"Don't really know, Captain," Hawk admitted, somewhat reservedly. "We were on our way there when the chase call went out. We'll follow up."

A sudden burst of laughter drew their attention. They looked over to find Trey and the Assistant Fire Chief smiling and shaking hands. That situation certainly appeared to be well in hand.

Evidently sensing their eyes upon him, Trey turned and winked. Moments later, he bade the fire official farewell and strolled over to his captain and his partner. "Everything is *copacetic*, Captain, nothing to worry about." Trey grinned.

"Somehow, I think . . . " The captain shrugged and shook his head. "No, I don't want to know—just never mind. You and your partner have a statement to take. We still have a reported kidnapping on our hands, and we've been tied up on this scene for more than a coupla hours now. So, move out."

"Yes, sir!" Trey beamed, dragging Hawk toward their cruiser. "We're on it!"

DRIVING TO DELAFAIRE Farm, Trey remarked casually, "You know, Hawk, you ought to feel at least a little relieved."

"Me? Why?" Hawk asked from the passenger seat, obviously puzzled as he scribbled a reminder of the crime scene details in his notebook.

Trey smiled. "Well, whether you realize it or not, we just closed the Doyle assault/accident case. Y'know those two deceased gunmen back there? They were our other two perps from the Doyle case—Bubba and Iggy. That means that your girlfriend is no longer a potential witness. So, now I guess it'd be all right for you to date her . . . Oh wait—now she's reported a *kidnapping* . . . Hmm, I guess that makes her a potential witness—*again*—ethics considerations, don't you know. Gosh, it sure seems like the Fates are just plain determined to keep the star-crossed lovers apart—such sweet agony!"

"Why," pondered Hawk aloud, staring out the windshield, "do I get the distinct impression that my partner enjoys busting my chops?"

ELLEN AND MARK WERE on the front porch, looking worried and desperate for good news, when Hawk and Trey arrived just before sunset.

Unfortunately, the detectives had none.

Ellen knew Trey and Hawk had questions—she had questions of her own.

When all four of them were settled in the kitchen, she busied herself pouring mugs of fresh coffee; but her thoughts were still frantic. She tried to think of a way to explain to Trey just *how* she knew *what* she knew about Millie and Stacy's abduction. Hawk would understand the truth, of course.

But how could she make his partner understand? She knew well enough how the truth would sound to most people; but, Trey was a seasoned criminal investigator. He'd likely think she was mistaken, daydreaming—or worse, outright delusional! After all it hadn't been that long since she had suffered a head injury. Would the authorities want to hospitalize her again, her mental state now truly suspect?

What would Hawk think of her then?

Her train of thought was suddenly derailed as Miska, wearing only a pair of torn bib overalls, burst through the back door and made a bold announcement in his inimitable excitement.

"The Queen of Dark Elves is dead! Assassinated! Lady Diere has seized the throne! She tried to have Miss Ellen kidnapped by George Papadolis! Mark, I followed the one who ran from the long car, and caught her—Ling—a were-panther! We fought, but Lord Addecus of the Were showed up, and just *stopped* everything!

"He spoke of Queen Mab and Lady Diere! Then he took Ling back to the Realm of Were! He said I was to stay here. He knows of Lady Leanan . . . and, uh . . ."

Suddenly pointing to Trey, Miska asked, "Who is this?"

CH 9

AS DAEGON NEARED THE edge of the forest he could smell the stench of sulfur and other noxious gases. His horse shied and tossed its head. Daegon prodded the gelding forward and out of the shelter of the trees. He should have seen the parapets of Queen Mab's castle rising beyond the hills of the farmland before him; however, he saw nothing but a lingering cloud of sickly smoke, teased by roiling vents of hissing steam.

Cresting the final rise, Daegon saw no magnificent castle bathed in the golden light of sunset, only a massive rubble-strewn pile of steaming slag, and shimmering waves of intensely heated air rising from the slowly cooling mass of molten lava. Dead birds littered the ground between him and what was once his monarch's seat of power. In the field to his left a number of cattle lay dead, their stiff legs jutting into the air. Some had suffered obvious burns, but others were unmarked, no doubt victims of the more noxious fumes.

At the base of the hill, just off the road, a dozen elfin warriors milled about in the vicinity of two large cattle sheds. They appeared to be interviewing people and keeping a small crowd of onlookers, farmers and field hands from getting any closer, or from leaving.

Daegon nudged his mount on and descended the hill.

His approach had been noticed. At the base of the hill an elfin guard stepped out on the road and impeded his progress. "Hold, if ye please, good sir," the guard said firmly, reaching for the reins. "Tis not safe to go any closer."

"What happened here?" Daegon asked, mildly resentful at being stopped.

"Dismount, if ye would, good sir. The sergeant would like a word with ye. He'll be in the shed yonder."

Daegon was already anxious; the guard's tone and ready stance only disturbed him further. He was about to object when the guard made a gesture and three more mailed elves stepped forward and effectively surrounded his horse.

The first guard held tightly to the reins and added dryly, "The lads'll escort ye to the sergeant—now, if ye would, good sir."

Daegon said nothing as he dismounted and was escorted to the nearest shed. In the dim interior, he found the sergeant seated on a milking stool, an upturned barrel serving as an impromptu desk. A pair of stubby candles upon the barrel illuminated several parchments displayed before the frowning guard supervisor. He studied Daegon for a moment before speaking.

"Who are you, and what is your business here?" the sergeant asked gruffly.

"It is not your concern. I am on the queen's business. What happened here?" Daegon replied haughtily, his pique obvious.

The sergeant stood, looming nearly a head taller than Daegon. "That is what we would like to know. And we, too, are on the *queen's business!* So, I will ask the questions, and you will answer—one way or another."

The guard who had seized the horse's reins entered the shed, and urgently whispered in the sergeant's ear. The supervisor gestured and the guard left.

"So, I understand the mount you ride bears the Mage Atrellan's crest on the tack and saddle—"

"As well it should," interrupted Daegon, growing more impatient, "since it is his horse and tack!"

"I will ask you only once more," warned the sergeant ominously. "Who are you?"

"I am Daegon, Alchemist to Queen Mab of the Dark Elves. At her command, I and Atrellan performed a task. I am now returning to her service. Atrellan, um, loaned me the use of this horse. That is all I may disclose without further dispensation from Her Majesty."

The sergeant sat, leaned over the barrelhead, and studied a handwritten parchment. Shuffling through a large leather messenger's pouch at his feet, he withdrew a small scroll, and perused it briefly. He straightened and nodded to the guards standing behind Daegon.

Daegon was suddenly seized from behind. "What? How dare—"

"Daegon the Alchemist, it is my duty to inform you that you are to be detained and held for questioning by the Royal Inquisition, on the order of Her Majesty, Queen Mab LV. Put him with the others."

Daegon was shocked speechless.

What? Queen Mab LV? The fifty-fifth?

Stunned, he offered no resistance as he was pulled away and marched to the other cattle shed. He was thrown inside only to stumble over other prisoners in the darkened ramshackle building. A number of people groaned as he regained his feet and made his way to a wall.

Chinks between weathered boards allowed the dim light of dusk to illuminate the grey-faced features of the nearest prisoners. Through the rough slats, he could see the adjacent pasture, where the stiffening corpse of the herd bull lay as mute testament to the recent tragedy.

Daegon turned and surveyed those near him. Most were huddled within themselves, bearing ashen faces and numb expressions; more than a few were coughing and wheezing. Most of the prisoners were human, but a number of elves were also confined. The humans appeared to be work-hardened farm folk and herders, accustomed to hardship; however, it was clear these poor souls had recently been through something horrible, beyond which not even they could cope.

He noticed a sullen young elf in the torn livery of a messenger, sporting a blackening eye and a crust of dried blood below his swollen nose, sitting with his back to the adjacent wall.

Daegon approached and squatted beside him.

"Lad, can you tell me what is happening here? I have been traveling of late and find this all very strange. Why are you," he swept an arm about, "all of you, being held here?"

The boy, no more than a teenager, looked at Daegon suspiciously, and scoffed. "Hah, how can you not know? Why should I trust you?"

"Fine then, stay here and accept whatever fate awaits you at the hands of these warriors," Daegon replied, "but I have other plans. So, I shall be going."

He stood as if to leave the young elf, but stopped as a grimy hand gripped his sleeve. "Wait! Take me with you!" Then the boy added, "But . . . who are you?"

"I am called Daegon. Now, tell me what happened—quickly now!"

"You really do not know?" the youngster asked in the dying twilight.

Daegon merely shook his head.

The boy sighed. "Very well . . . I do not know much—I only saw smoke and flames from a distance. I serve as an apprentice messenger—tis my first year. I had completed my tasks and was returning to the queen's castle when I saw the smoke, and then flames as I came closer. Many animals were dead. It was hard to breathe. Soon these soldiers came, seized anyone they found, and questioned them—me, too—sometimes harshly."

Daegon grinned. "Would that explain your eye and broken nose?"

"Aye," the lad admitted, unconsciously touching his battered face. "I knew nothing, but that did not spare me a beating. They say the queen is dead, her staff and servants, too. These warriors talk among themselves; some whisper that it was foul sorcery, some say an accident—who knows? There is a new queen; the Lady Diere is now Queen Mab LV. She has declared an inquisition into the death of the old queen, the former Lady Celeste. All the staff, servants, and retainers of the old queen are to be detained and put before the Inquisition. Many whisper that anyone loyal to the old queen is in peril. These soldiers seize anyone, for any reason. All our lives hang in the balance."

His voice had drawn the attention of others in the cramped space, and a few braver souls echoed his comments.

"Aye, twas no accident—foul sorcery indeed, intended to kill the queen," mumbled a voice in the dark.

"An' all ` er mages an' magic cou' na stop it," clucked an old woman's voice.

"Her mages?" repeated Daegon. "What of Atrellan, the senior mage, was he with the queen—did he survive?"

"That pompous fop?" another male elf in the torn livery of a footman remarked, his disgust plain. "None within the inner walls survived; the rest of us beyond the outer walls fled. Fire flowed like a river, and the choking smoke killed with a single breath. Mage Atrellan was said to be with the queen; he is surely dead. No one came out of the heart of that—*that hell!*"

Slumping against the wall, Daegon felt the creeping tendrils of failure and despair.

Too late . . . too late . . . I am so sorry, my queen. Now I know—this was an assassination, and that Boltar's corpse was the key. And it is too late as well to visit my vengeance upon that fool, Atrellan! But who is ultimately responsible? Someone has played a most dangerous game, indeed. So, who stands to profit from such treachery? Ah, but the list is short; and the Lady Diere now reigns as the new Queen Mab.

Now only one question remains—did George know?

Looking around at the expectant faces turned to him in the darkening gloom, Daegon considered his situation, and the likely fate of all those now held in this shed.

No, I will not die here! As for the fate of these people, it will no doubt be as they suspect—of that I am certain . . . unless . . .

"Listen to me carefully. These guards mean to do us all harm—doubt it not! In a few minutes, full night will be upon us. There will be a great distraction among the guards—that will be your opportunity to escape. Flee into the hills and lose yourselves in the forest. But first, you must loosen some of these old weather-beaten boards in the walls of this shed. Do not remove them until the confusion is greatest, and then run from this place."

He pointed in the dimness to a few likely horizontal boards. "Start here, with these low ones."

The anxious prisoners needed no further urging; some men set to work immediately. Others stood by ready to help; no one was interested in staying behind.

Turning to the young elf, Daegon asked, "What are you called, lad?"

"Flynt, I am called Flynt . . . um, m'lord."

"Well, Flynt, you and I are going to arrange for the distraction. See this lowest board in this wall? Rap it with your knuckle."

"Aye, tis rotten—termites or post beetles have been at it. It crumbles to the touch!"

"Hush! Quietly now, remove it and see if you can slip through the hole . . . Yes, that's it—quietly now . . . Well done! Now, see the dead bull over there?"

"Aye, m'lord, tis much darker now, but I can see it."

Daegon slipped his hand through the opening in the wall. "Here, take this small knife and slice a bit of hide—about a finger's length—from that bull's carcass and bring it to me. Do not be seen! Hurry now!"

Flynt's eyes grew wide at Daegon's request, but he nonetheless followed the instructions. Several minutes later, he cautiously crept back with a bloody strip of the bull's flesh tight in his fist.

Pausing in a deep shadow along the wooden wall of the shed, the boy looked longingly across the barren pasture at the dark tree line.

Daegon saw, and knew that the lad considered making a run for it. Clearly it was too far; he'd be easily seen by these brutal guards and run down for sport. He must have had the wits to realize he had no chance without some sort of distraction. He mumbled a hasty curse, slipped back inside the shed, and surrendered the knife and the piece of hide to Daegon—who released the breath he'd been holding.

"Ah, well done, Flynt! Now go and check with the others to be sure all is in readiness. I must finish this task alone."

FLYNT WAS WELL AWARE that this stranger was about to perform some forbidden rite. Was he an *adept* of some sort? He was clearly no elf, so Flynt was sufficiently leery. The lad was more than happy to become useful elsewhere. He made the rounds of the others preparing for their escape and found that everyone was ready.

When he looked for Daegon, he saw the stranger huddled in a corner, his back to the rest of the room. Flynt started to approach, but hearing Daegon's mumbled incantation and seeing the soft glow of a sickly purple light coming from the immediate area near the hands of this dubious mage caused Flynt to stop in his tracks. He dared venture no closer, but watched in horrid fascination.

Moments later the purple light faded away and Daegon's shoulders slumped. He took a few deep breaths and rose to face the awestruck young elf.

"It will be soon," Daegon whispered loud enough for all to hear. "Stand ready to pull the boards free at my command. Then waste no time—slip through the wall and flee for your lives! Steady, now."

Slight sounds of movement in the field adjacent to the shed drew Flynt's attention. He peered through the low gap in the wall he had passed through mere minutes ago.

Something in the field was moving. A wide silhouette, blacker than the surrounding night, walked haltingly on four stiff legs toward the other shed.

A torch-bearing guard must have noticed the movement; Flynt heard him issue a challenge. The flickering light of the torch cast pale illumination and errant shadows, but gave the advancing bulk definition—the herd bull, its pace increasing. The alarmed guard shouted another challenge and warning. The reanimated bull focused its glowing fiery-red eyes at the elf; the guard's voice rose to a panicked shriek.

The other warriors came running; the bull charged.

Flynt tore his gaze from the bizarre scene as the bloodcurdling sounds of slaughter rose. He saw Daegon grin in the shadows, and heard this dark mage urgently utter the anticipated command.

"Now! Free the boards and flee! Flee for your very lives!"

The prisoners did so, as quickly as they could; but Flynt lingered, nearly invisible in a dark corner of the shed. His instincts screamed *run* but his mind urged him to wait and choose the safest path, away from the battle raging beyond these walls. He noticed that Daegon, too, stood still within the darkened shed, peering through a large gap in the wall, the reflected light of moving torches and many unintended grass fires dancing across his smiling face.

DAEGON WAS QUITE PLEASED with his distraction.

That he had likely sent most of the prisoners and the elfin guards to their deaths beneath the horns and hoofs of the ensorcelled bull bothered him not in the least. He had learned that which he had needed to know, and now it was time to depart this realm. In fact, it might be wise to avoid all the Council Realms for the immediate future, or at least until he could sort out some unresolved issues.

That was not a problem; he had long ago established a hidden stronghold in the wild, at a former redoubt of the Old Ones—or so he strongly suspected its origin. He was certain that it was unknown to anyone else; and, it would certainly serve admirably well now.

FROZEN IN THE DARKEST shadows, Flynt dared not breathe. Undetected, he watched Daegon in the flickering firelight as the dark mage spread his hands and summoned a pitch-black transit sphere and pressed within.

The dark orb shrank and popped out of existence.

Flynt shuddered; this had surely been *necromancy,* or some dark sorcery closely akin to it. No fool he, this would never be spoken of—to anyone. He gathered his remaining wits about him, and fled into the night.

TREY SET HIS COFFEE mug on the table and wolfed down the last of his corned-beef sandwich. Hawk and Ellen shared a concerned glance and sipped from their mugs. Mark and Miska each took another sandwich from the tray in the center of the table and commenced to polish off their second helpings.

All through the hastily prepared casual supper, they had shared the truth, to the extent that they could, with Trey.

Ellen refilled Trey's mug, and simply asked, "Well?"

Trey cocked his head and smiled.

"Well, I have to admit, that is one of the most bizarre and entertaining tales I've heard in a long time; but . . . "

"You don't believe a word of it," observed Hawk, dryly.

"I'm afraid not," Trey said smiling. "I'm sure you're enjoying putting one over on your partner, but it's not helpful right now when we have a case to solve. Can we get back to the alleged kidnapping—without the mystical flights of fancy?"

"Sergeant, every word we've told you is true," insisted Ellen, rising to her feet. "What will it take to convince you? What proof will you accept? The simple truth is that we don't have time for this—my mother and Stacy are in danger!"

Hawk put a gentle hand on Ellen's arm and nudged her to sit down. She did so, clearly unbowed.

Mark sensed her frustration and gripped her hand for a quick squeeze.

"Sergeant, if I may?" Mark began. "She did ask a valid question; what proof will you accept?"

"You mean to believe all you've told me? Well, I'm a practical man. Give me some solid evidence, sound scientific facts supported by empirical proof—something that will stand up in court, for example," Trey explained, holding his palms up in supplication.

Mark chuckled. "You sound just like I did—before I learned the truth the hard way.

"Look, Trey, this is all so new for all of us that I seriously doubt any identifiable supporting evidence is known to exist in the scientific community—not that there aren't a number of speculative theories. But the point is that we *do* have the proof—but it must be experienced to be fully appreciated. Perhaps if we were to show you, uh, *demonstrate* some evidence, would that be sufficient for you, at the very least, to consider the possibility that we speak the truth? Would you at least be prepared to keep an open mind?"

"Mark, I'm a professional investigator," asserted Trey, mildly affronted. "I always keep an open mind. But any evidence to support *this* story would have to be pretty impressive—and convincing."

Mark smiled and turned to Miska, who had finished his second sandwich. "Miska, my friend, could I ask a favor of you? Could you *change*—and do so in the presence of the good sergeant here?"

The request clearly surprised Miska.

"Friend Mark, that is an impolite thing to ask of a Were. But I realize you are unaware of this transgression. However, the circumstances are very unusual, to say the least." The big man sighed. "This is not something I enjoy doing on a full stomach. And it would be best—if I do this thing—that I stay that way through the night. It will help my healing process."

Mark clasped a hand on his friend's massive shoulder and reassured him. "Miska, I would not ask this of you if it were not important—you know that."

Miska smiled in return. "True, I do know. Very well, I will do this."

"Thank you, my friend."

Miska pushed back from the table and stood. With a wink for Mark, he said, "Please, do not let him shoot me—I just ate."

Ellen stood as well, but held up a hand.

"One moment, gentlemen. Would you mind doing this outside? I'd appreciate that.

"Miska, please feel free to join us for breakfast in the morning, um, on two legs, if you please, thank you. You all can go on out back; the overhead lights are on. I've already seen his transformation, so I'm going to stay here by the phone—just in case."

With Mark in the lead, the men filed out of the kitchen and into the yard.

Trey, bearing a confused expression of sympathetic accommodation mixed with a trace of apprehension, was the last to leave. As he closed the door gently, he heard its simple latch *click* home. That subtle sound seemed slightly distorted and disorienting—the final second recorded of his comfortable perception of mundane and ordered reality.

ELLEN GLANCED AT THE silent phone on the kitchen wall, knowing it would not ring despite her wishes to the contrary. There was no doubt in her mind that Millie and Stacy were no longer in this realm.

Before her thoughts could slip into despair, Smokey leapt up on the counter and casually sniffed at the empty sandwich platter. She reached out and scratched behind his ears; his purr was comforting.

"Looking for a little after-dinner snack—a little *lagniappe?*" she cooed.

At that comment, the dogs perked up their ears and looked at her expectantly from either side of the old cast-iron stove.

She couldn't resist chuckling and rummaged through the refrigerator for some cold cuts. Thin slices of cooked ham and turkey breast did the trick nicely. She filled their bowls and resumed her seat, her unfocused gaze once more settling upon the silent phone.

MOMENTS LATER, THE contentedly pleased pets, having made short work of their unexpected treat, suddenly alerted and stared at the back door.

The door swung open; Mark, Hawk, and Trey entered the kitchen.

Trey was ashen and unsteady; his eyes were wide with shock.

"Ellen," Mark declared, "I think Trey could use a drink. Where's the bourbon?"

"The end cupboard, top shelf. There's some Maker's Mark and Wild Turkey; will that do? Shot glasses are in the cabinet by the sink. We've got ginger ale and club soda in the pantry, if you want mixers or chasers."

Hawk grinned. "Oh yes, that'll work. And for the record, my partner and I officially just went off duty. But I'll stick to coffee; I'm driving."

Trey downed a neat shot without preamble and cupped a second between shaking hands.

Mark and Hawk looked on sympathetically, unable to hide their wry smiles.

"Whoa," breathed Trey, finding his voice. "Okay, I gotta admit, that was certainly impressive."

Hawk turned to Ellen and said, "I think Trey thought it was all an elaborate illusion—until Miska licked his face! That was priceless!"

Trey took a deep breath and stared at his partner. "I didn't think that was funny. But it was *so real!* I still don't understand how he did it—that's one helluva trick!"

"It was no trick, Trey," assured Mark. "It was a real transformation. And he is not unique; many beings in his realm have such dual natures, and can change shape at will."

"You know," offered Hawk, "something Miska said earlier got me thinking. This person he chased, Ling, he called her a *were-panther.* Trey, remember the crime scenes at the casino parking garage and the unusual DNA found there? I know how this sounds, but do you think, like maybe she could be involved?"

Trey sipped his drink, his hands now more steady, and his mind falling into the more familiar and comfortable mode of investigative analysis. The question was logical, assuming a heretofore unbelievable premise—of which he was still not convinced—and it potentially would seem to fit the circumstances suggested by the evidence at the scene.

And, to be honest, he had no better explanation at the moment.

Clearing his throat, he said, "I don't know what to believe, right now. But for the sake of argument, assuming this lycanthropy is truly real—that's what we're talking about, *lycanthropy*—then she would surely be a suspect. But we would need more corroborative evidence to place her at the scene; a DNA sample taken directly from her for comparison, for example. Then we'd have to establish motive, um, I guess." He stared into the refilled shot glass before him.

"Unfortunately," Hawk pointed out, "Miska says she's returned to the Realm of Were." Hawk sipped his coffee. "And then there's Lady Leanan, who's *confessed* to killing Fenton Brewster at the direction of Papa George. She's no doubt back in the Realm of Shadow."

Trey twisted in his seat, squaring his shoulders at his partner.

"Yeah, about that . . . Why didn't you tell me that Fenton Brewster wasn't a suicide? You *knew* we were spinning our wheels on that case!"

"Yeah, right—would you have believed me?" Hawk asked simply. "How could I tell you that a *vampire*, visiting from another realm, another universe, or whatever, carried out a *contract hit* on an incarcerated federal snitch in our jail? Would I still have a *job?* Or would I be placed on protracted administrative leave pending the results of my psychiatric examination?"

Trey didn't know what to say; Hawk's every word rang true.

"An open mind at this point, Sergeant—that's all we ask," reminded Mark.

Trey sat quietly, staring at his hands, wrestling with his thoughts.

If any of this were true, his perception of reality would be shaken to the core—but then, so would everyone else's—*if* it were to become common knowledge. But if true, how could it not become well known? Maybe it might be best if all of it were *not* true, but rather a set of fanciful delusions shared by a few fevered minds—mass hysteria or something?

He now clearly saw Hawk's dilemma; he *would* have been institutionalized had he told *anyone*.

But what if it were all true?

He had always trusted his gut instincts; but, this time—*this time*—he had no gut feelings to rely upon.

He sipped from the shot glass; the bourbon warmed his throat.

So, why shouldn't he believe his partner? That he trusted Hawk implicitly was a given; and Hawk seemed to accept all this without reservation.

Consequently, his decision was clear; for now, he'd trust his partner.

He knew one other thing for certain; at the very least, he needed to learn more, a great deal more.

Draining the last of his drink, Trey looked at each person around him in turn. There was no trace of duplicity or humor in their faces, only concern and determination.

"Very well, I will keep an open mind," Trey announced. "But, I warn you—we still have an open case. There are specific protocols we must observe in the course of the investigation which we cannot overlook or sidestep. But, I think we can be reasonably discreet in the process."

"Thank you, Sergeant. Is there anything we can do to help?" asked Mark.

"Well, as I said when we first sat down, our purpose in visiting this evening was to get a statement from Miss Ellen, as the complainant, about what she saw that prompted her to report a kidnapping," explained Trey.

"But there's the problem with Ellen seeing what happened—almost twenty minutes in the past—before she made the call," offered Hawk.

"But I told you," Ellen interjected, "I saw what happened through Maude's glasses. I'm not *lying! And I'm not going to!*"

"Of course not, El'—and we understand," Mark soothed. "But let me ask Hawk and Trey this; who else in your department knows about the time discrepancy?"

"Uh, no one actually," said Trey. "It hadn't come up. Hawk and I discussed it only after I called the dispatcher. So, I couldn't have mentioned it to her; and, I haven't talked to her or anyone else in the department since."

"Well, then," reasoned Mark, "I don't see that it *has* to be included in Ellen's statement. It is only relevant to those of us who are aware of, and understand to some degree, the capabilities of these glasses."

"But I saw what I saw by means of the glasses; and, it was too far away to see without them," Ellen objected.

"Quite true, Ellen," admitted Mark. "But is it not also true that you had a pair of binoculars—also known as *field glasses*—with you on the balcony at the time? And did you not look out upon the gardens with those glasses?"

As Ellen slowly nodded, Hawk and Trey looked at each other and began to smile.

"Oh, he's good," observed Trey.

"Yep, very good," echoed Hawk.

"So, Ellen," summarized Mark, "it is a fact that you saw certain events while standing on the front balcony, and making use of glasses. That is the crux of your statement, carefully parsed, and absolutely true."

Ellen frowned, thinking it through.

"Well yeah, Mark, strictly speaking, I suppose that is all true. All right, I can see that this makes sense. So, if Trey and Hawk are satisfied, I'm good with it," she conceded. "But now what do we do?"

"Well, we'll get busy," began Trey. "We'll need some recent photographs of Miss Millie and Miss Stacy. Hawk and I will organize a team of detectives to trace the route the limo took. We'll interview everyone who lives along that path in the hope they may have seen something. We can't overlook that your mother and your friend may have been dropped off or hidden somewhere along the route—because they weren't in the limo when we found it. You must understand that we have to look everywhere."

"Oh, I see. I have plenty of photos to choose from. You'll do that tonight?" she asked.

"Yes, actually, the evening shift already started," assured Hawk. "They begin with the scene—where the limo was found—and work backwards. That's why we need the photos tonight. I'll drop copies off with the evening-shift detectives, stop by the office to file our report and your statement, and then Trey and I will join the search first thing in the morning."

Ellen stood and walked over to a window; she stared silently into the night.

"What's wrong, El'? Are you all right?" Mark asked.

She sighed heavily and spoke toward the glass pane. "You won't find them. They are no longer in this realm. *He* took them somewhere—*somewhere else.*"

"*He?* Do you mean George Papadolis?" Hawk probed. "How could he do that?"

Ellen turned and admitted, "I don't know. Somehow, he can transit between realms. And I suspect he has help—maybe Lady Diere, as Miska said. But I do know *this*—to find Millie and Stacy, we may have to find him, George Papadolis, first!"

"No one knows where he is right now," Trey pointed out. "You know he's wanted, don't you? There's a warrant out for him; it's even in NCIC. Lots of people are looking for him."

"I know where he *will be* tomorrow night," Ellen said firmly, "because I'm to be at the same place, the Council meeting."

"That's true," Mark added, "his name appears on the meeting agenda, as does Ellen's."

"No problem!" Hawk beamed. "If we don't find Millie and Stacy by tomorrow evening, Trey and I will go with Ellen to this meeting, and take Papa George into custody if he shows up. Don't worry—we'll find out just what he knows about your mom and Stacy! Right, Trey?"

"Where is this meeting?" Trey asked. "Is it in our jurisdiction?"

"Good question," observed Mark. "I doubt it has even come up before. The Council meeting will be held in another realm, or another universe, if you prefer. But I suggest that we act as if we are completely within our rights to pursue and capture a fugitive criminal."

"What do you mean—*we?*" Trey asked.

"Oh, I'm going to the meeting with Ellen, too," Mark responded, smiling broadly.

Trey was about to offer Mark an argument when Ellen surprised them all.

"Actually, gentlemen. *I* am the only one invited. I was also told that I could bring an *appropriate escort* befitting my status as Steward. I think the three of you may meet that standard—provided you follow *my* lead."

"Huh? What do you mean?" Trey asked.

"Yeah, what do you expect?" Hawk pressed.

She shrugged, and waved a finger in warning. "You might not like it; but, you'll have to listen to me.

"I don't know exactly what to expect. However, I do know that we will be dealing with some very powerful races, some of whom may be hostile to us, and may have already been involved in trying to harm me. But that's not what I'm focused on.

"You must understand my priority here; I want to get my mother and Stacy back more than anything. If finding this Papa George is a necessary step, that's fine—I'm in. However, I'm gonna call the shots at this meeting. Now, if you can't do as I ask, I won't take the risk in bringing you. I'll go alone and do this on my own."

Hawk and Trey immediately objected, but Mark raised his hands for silence.

"I must concede she makes valid points," Mark admitted. "I, too, have been to another realm; so, I know she doesn't overstate in the least the potential dangers she may face. Coincidentally, that's also all the more reason we should accompany her. But she's right—she *has* to take the lead here, and she *is expected*. And it would be very unusual for her to appear without an escort, so these would be the perfect cover roles for us to play. Don't you see?"

Before Hawk or Trey could respond, Mark played his trump card.

"After all, only she can *transit* us—*all* of us—to the appropriate location, and home again."

Trey and Hawk exchanged hopeless glances. There was no more argument to be made.

Mark grinned. "Remember what I said, Trey; we have the *proof*—but you have to experience it to fully appreciate it."

Trey groaned in resignation, reached for the bottle, and poured himself another drink.

CH 10

ELLEN HAD NOT SLEPT well; her anxiety over Millie and Stacy had been nearly overpowering. Every time she shut her eyes she saw them in a succession of dire circumstances fueled by her escalating concern and rampant imagination. Only a state of emotional exhaustion finally seduced her conscious mind into a troubled and fitful sleep.

Morning brought no respite. Hawk had not called; so, she knew the overnight search efforts had been as she'd expected—fruitless. Rather than lie in bed and sink deeper into a puddle of worry, she knew she should *do* something; however, she first had to overcome this sense of frustration and futility that weighed her down.

Staring idly at dust motes blithely sliding across bright shafts of morning sunlight was enough of a mindless distraction to motivate her to get up and *do* something—*anything*.

Once moving, she realized she was hungry.

Dressed in shorts and an oversized T-shirt, she made her way to the kitchen with the dogs at her heels.

She found Mark and Miska finishing up passable servings of bacon and scrambled eggs. From the disheveled condition of the kitchen, it was evident that this was more of an experiment than accomplished meal preparation.

Mark poured a cup of overly-strong coffee and pressed it into her hands.

"Morning, El' . . . Before you ask, no calls. Can I get you some breakfast? I'm nowhere near the cook your mom is, but I can scramble broken eggs and burn bacon with the best of 'em. Sit down and let me fix you something."

She sat and mumbled, "Sure, bacon and eggs are fine. Do we have toast, too?"

"I toasted some bagels—will that do?"

"Yeah, whatever," she groaned, rubbing her temples.

"Are you all right, Miss Ellen?" Miska asked. "You do not look so good this morning."

"Why, thank you, Miska," she replied, the sarcasm wasted on the big man who grinned and nodded. "Truth is I slept like crap last night. I'm whipped."

"You'll feel better with some food in your belly," Mark assured her. "I'll pour you a glass of orange juice; that'll help, too. After breakfast, you might feel like taking a nap. You have to get some rest. You've got a big night ahead of you."

She smiled at his concern. "Let's just see how I feel after I eat your cooking, *Monsieur le Chef*."

The scrambled eggs were barely acceptable and the bacon *was* burnt. Thankfully, the toasted bagel smothered with strawberry preserves hit the spot. Ellen downed the last of her orange juice, giving only a passing thought to another cup of coffee, too strong by half.

However, Mark was right; she *did* feel better. Perhaps a nap was just what she needed; so, she'd forgo any more caffeine, especially that last pot of Mark's potent brew.

The dogs alerted, their tails wagging, moments before a brisk knock at the front door echoed through the halls of the house.

"I'll get it," announced Mark as he left the kitchen.

A muted jumble of concerned, yet familiar, voices heralded his return as Mark led a group of people bearing covered dishes and plates into the kitchen; Madeline and Armand Dupree, followed by Zack Johnson and his wife, Marie.

Mark introduced Miska as a visiting friend, whose grin broadened as new tantalizing aromas wafted from the covered containers. Ellen insisted on getting coffee—a fresh pot, of course—and tea for their guests.

Madeline reached out for Ellen. "Oh, you poor dear. We just wanted to come by and let you know that we are here for you. And we brought some food; nothing much, just some casseroles, a cake, and some cookies. You know, just something to have when you don't feel like cooking."

"Forgive me," said Mark, "but just how did you all know?"

"It's a small community," responded Armand with a wink. "Word gets around quickly. Have you heard anything from the authorities?"

"Not since last night," Mark admitted.

"Well, we're here now," assured Zack. "We'll keep vigil with you, and do anything you need done."

Dr. Latrice-Johnson pulled Ellen aside and quietly queried her patient. "How are you feeling? Any headaches? Are you sleeping through the night?"

"I'm fine, Doctor—I mean *Marie . . . sorry.* I'm sleeping fine; although, to be honest, I didn't sleep too well last night. I'm just worried, I guess."

Marie watched Ellen carefully, no doubt a quick medical assessment. "You do know how critical proper rest is, and how the proper balance of nutrition and exercise is helpful in times of high stress, don't you?"

Ellen just smiled and nodded, unconsciously tuning her out, until she realized that Marie had just offered to give her something to help her sleep. She actually was feeling the slightest bit sleepy, without the benefit of any pharmaceutical aid.

"What? Oh, no thank you, Marie. I just had a big breakfast. I think that's made me a little sleepy, so I was planning to take a nap."

"That's an excellent idea, Ellen," Marie agreed. "Why don't you go lie down—doctor's orders—and don't worry about a thing. I promise to wake you if anything happens, or if we hear anything."

RETURNING TO HER ROOM, Ellen pulled the shades down and lay upon the bed. Max and Sophie plopped down on the carpet between her bed and the closed door. She didn't really expect to sleep, but she knew she needed to try—otherwise she'd be dragging by this evening.

For some reason she felt more comfortable, perhaps even bolstered, by the arrival of her friends. Just knowing they were here seemed to help; she relaxed a bit. Of course, they had been Maude's friends first.

As she felt herself drifting off, she wondered if Maude had found them as warm and comfortable as she did . . .

. . . *Oh, of course I did, sweetie—they're the salt of the earth.*

. . . *Uh, Maude? Are we communicating telepathically in dreams again?*

. . . *So it would appear.*

. . . *Fine. Why do I get the impression that the Duprees and the Johnsons know more than they admit? Wait a minute—you told them things, carefully worded, like hypothetical circumstances, or story lines in a book, because some people can more readily accept truth if it's couched as fiction or speculation. And that sort of thing can inspire the right intellect to find the truth—and the evidence to support it.*

. . . *That's not a bad analysis. You're probably thinking that they were merely humoring me. Hmm, could be.*

. . . *Yeah, at the very least, I'll bet it was entertaining. But I think they really do understand. Zack can explain it in scientific terms that even I can understand.*

. . . *So, the mystery of the magic fades when explained in technical terms. Don't you find that just a bit sad?*

. . . *Yeah, I suppose I do. But I can't worry about this now—I have to find my mom and Stacy! What should I do?*

. . . *Well, Ellen, what do you think you should do?*

. . . I think this Papa George is the key. I know he works for Lady Diere—oops, I mean the new Queen Mab LV. It's even possible she's behind this whole mess—but if that's the case, that's another problem. I can't see how to challenge a queen. But Papa George? Yeah, I really do suspect he's the key, and maybe the weak link. I can't really say why, but somehow I'm certain he knows where my mom and Stacy are.

. . . So, you plan to confront him and expose him at the Council meeting—and then what?

. . . Trey and Hawk will bring him back here, I guess. And then we'll get the information out of him—somehow.

. . . Aren't you forgetting something, like the original reason for attending this meeting?

. . . Oh, of course, to introduce myself as Steward—and to prevent George from ascending to the Chair of Man.

. . . Quite so—don't lose sight of that in your quest to find Millie and Stacy.

. . . Maude, do you know where they are? Are they all right? If you know, you must tell me!

. . . I do not know; nor could I tell you if I did. Like most things, you must discover these truths on your own—as you well know.

. . . Can you at least sense if they're alive?

. . . Why would you ask that, child, when you already know? Have you not sensed them—although perhaps not in your home realm? Is that skill not among your own gifts?

. . . You're right, I'm sorry. I guess I shouldn't doubt myself. I should trust my instincts.

. . . Indeed. You can trust your friends as well; you know they are sincere and would do anything for you. It is nice to have people you can turn to.

. . . I know. For the moment, I just need them to be discreet and keep my secrets.

. . . Have faith; after all, they had no problem keeping mine.

. . . What? You mean they knew? What did they know? Maude?

. . . Time for me to go, Ellen. Time for you to wake up—the afternoon wanes.

. . . Maude, wait! We need to talk more—wait, please!

. . . Perhaps later, sweetie . . .

Ellen lost touch with her sense of Maude's presence, and slowly became aware of her surroundings. She was easing into wakefulness; and she actually felt well rested. She must have slept for almost six or seven hours; yet it only seemed like a short visit with Maude. A dream, of course, but she remembered it vividly.

The dogs nuzzled her, earning ear rubs and chin scratches, and went to stand before the closed door.

Propped up on her elbows, Ellen sighed. "I'll bet you guys are getting hungry. All right, I'm up."

She rose, stretched, and followed the dogs downstairs.

IN THE KITCHEN, ELLEN saw that someone had laid out a buffet style supper; warmed casseroles, platters of cold cuts, cheeses, and assorted fresh breads. A host of condiments were lined up on the counter.

Having already eaten, her guests were still seated around the long table, held in rapt fascination as Zack offered an explanation of what physicists thought one end of a wormhole would look like. Trey and Hawk were there as well.

She caught Hawk's eye and lifted her palms in the unspoken question . . . *any news?*

He joined her at the counter, stoically shrugged his shoulders, and slowly shook his head.

"We've found nothing so far, but we're undeterred."

She could sense his resolve to proceed with their plans to apprehend Papa George later tonight. His commitment and support were gratifying, and further bolstered her determination and sense of purpose.

Mark waved and pointed to the food, encouraging her to eat. She smiled and pointed to the dogs. He smiled and nodded, understanding she meant to feed them first.

Hawk winked at her, helped himself to a piece of pie, and tilted his head toward Zack.

"We've had an interesting conversation or two. Make yourself a plate and join us at the table."

As Hawk resumed his seat, she listened but only caught the last bit of what the astrophysicist was saying.

". . . so, the cylindrical end, or *terminus*, would most likely appear to the observer as a sphere or ball. Of course there's the question of size, that seems to be thought of as a relationship to the available energy expended to maintain stability and continuity—"

"But what would you *see—inside*, I mean?" probed Trey.

"Possibly nothing," Zack remarked, "unless there is a source of light, within the spectrum visible to the naked human eye, of course, at the other end. On the other hand, it may be perfectly reflective. And would then appear as a rather spherical convex mirror to the observer."

Ellen set full bowls of food down before the dogs and began to prepare her own plate.

Madeline joined her at the counter, as Zack's impromptu lecture droned on.

"Did you have a nice nap, dear? You look refreshed. You haven't missed anything; there's been no news of course."

"Yes, thank you, Madeline. I guess I really needed the sleep. I feel a lot better now."

"That's good—you'll need to be at your best tonight."

Ellen turned and looked directly in Madeline's eyes. "What do you mean *tonight*, Madeline?"

The kitchen grew very quiet. She'd been heard.

Madeline pursed her lips and sighed.

"Ellen, don't be upset. The truth is that we—Marie and Zack, Armand and I—were very close with your aunt. And Maude shared a great deal with us. She wouldn't exactly tell us *specifics;* but she'd confirm what we deduced. Do you understand?"

"Trust me, Madeline," Ellen said dryly, "I am quite familiar with the concept."

"The point is that we know what you're planning to do—confronting this man, George Papadolis, whom you believe had something to do with the kidnapping. I'll admit that I don't understand why Sgt. Bassett and Detective Redhawk are going along with this—it seems dangerous to me. But I know they are good men; they must have their reasons. We've been talking about it all afternoon. We want you to understand that we'll do anything we can to help."

"Remember the Middle Earth Society—our book club?" interrupted Armand. "Well, you're looking at the *core group*. I think we may have mentioned that Maude referred to us collectively as her *think tank*. We used to brainstorm lots of ideas and situations that she brought to the table. Sometimes it might have been a hypothetical political issue, some metaphysical speculation, or an outrageous plot twist for a possible work of fiction—even though we strongly suspected it may have frequently been a more factual scenario than she'd been prepared to admit. We pretty much knew she was much more than she appeared to be. Nonetheless, she was our dear friend, for whom we cared greatly—more than enough to respect her privacy."

"Just as we respect yours," Zack interjected smoothly. "Please understand that we are not probing or prying into your personal business. You don't have to tell us anything; we'll respect that. But you should know—with complete confidence—that anything you share goes no further than this *think tank,* a most appropriate appellation, in my opinion. And that any recommendations or guidance we may offer are based upon the most thorough analysis of the data on hand. We believe confidentiality to be sacrosanct in these matters. I will only add that we earned Maude's trust, and we hope to earn yours."

"Ellen, my concerns are specifically your health and welfare," Marie added with a smile, "and you are still my patient. I'm sure you're familiar with the concept of medical confidentiality between doctor and patient, in both the ethical and legal senses; it is an unswerving constant upon which you may rely. Whatever path you choose, whatever information you may elect to share, you may rely on my discretion.

"Now, all that aside, you are still recovering from a serious head injury. Consequently, as your doctor, I am concerned and thus urge you to take it easy during your period of recovery. Out of an abundance of caution, I don't want you doing anything strenuous—nothing physical beyond light, modest exercise for the immediate future."

Ellen and Mark shared a quick glance and tried not to smile—if the good doctor had known *half* of what her patient had been through since leaving the hospital . . .

Hawk coughed and found some sort of interesting spot on the ceiling to stare at, his tongue pressed firmly in cheek.

Ellen did not wish to offend her friends, but she was not prepared to share any more at this moment than she already had—perhaps later, after she'd had some time to consider the ramifications.

"Thank you, thank you all. I'm deeply grateful for all your concerns. But for right now, please understand that I'm preoccupied with getting my mother and Stacy back. So, let me get some supper—I am kind of hungry. And you all go on with your discussions."

Everyone mumbled assurances that they understood and urged her eat to her heart's content, devoid of any interruptions or questions. She smiled gratefully.

WHEN SHE HAD FINISHED, Mark approached her with a piece of pecan pie.

"A little dessert? This pie is wonderful. Let's have it in the library." He added *sotto voce*, "We need to talk."

"Oh, maybe a bite or two," she acquiesced, her curiosity piqued.

Once seated in the library, she asked, "Okay, what's up? I should be getting ready soon. How long before sunset?"

He looked out the window and said, "I think forty-five minutes, an hour at the most, I think. Where will we do this?"

"I thought out back, behind the cistern." She shrugged.

He leaned toward her. "Are you going to let our friends, *the Middle Earth Society,* observe our departure?"

"I hadn't thought about it," she admitted. "I'd only been thinking about how Trey might react. If they were to even see a transit globe, much less watch us use it, there's no turning back—they'll need to know the truth. Which raises the question; just what did you tell them while I was asleep?"

"Nothing specific about any other realms, or our *abilities.* But they definitely know more than we thought they did—thanks to Maude, most likely."

"Well, Mark, counsel me. What do you advise?"

Mark stared out the window before answering.

"El', I believe that at some point we are going to need their perspective, insight, and collective wisdom. We already know that we don't understand most of this. I don't think we ever will, without some serious help. To be perfectly candid, I think this may be the best help we could ask for.

"These are very intelligent and intuitive people. They'll arrive at their own conclusions, with or without our input. And time may be of the essence. So, it may be that it's really a matter of *when* we tell them. I think perhaps the real question is whether or not you are willing to trust their discretion—now, as well as in the future. This is really your choice; I recommend trusting your instincts. I can *sense* no ill intentions on their part; so, I advise trusting them, when *you* are ready."

"I see, thank you, Mark. I'll consider what you've said. But now, I have to change clothes and get ready; so you'll have to excuse me." With a strained smile, she left the library.

MARK RETURNED TO THE kitchen, uncertain if his well-intended and sincere advice had truly been all that helpful; clearly his cousin already had a lot on her mind.

Zack continued his commentary about Membrane Theory, and the propensity for parallel or alternative universes. ". . . and of course, a number of physicists are of the opinion that our own universe may have duplicates that are slightly *out of phase*, lightly overlaying our universe but entirely separate. This engenders speculation that there may be *multiple phases* of our universe arranged in some sort of layered order—not that this sits well with adherents of *chaos theory*—"

Trey raised his open hand in interruption.

"Hold on a moment! Forgive me, Zack. Can you go back a bit to the part about the *Laws of Physics* being different? What would be different?"

The astrophysicist nodded. "No problem, Sergeant. Ah, the laws of physics, what would be—or could be—different? The simple answer is that there is no way to be certain—not so simple, eh?

"If the differences were too great, life as we know it may not even exist. Proteins and amino acids might not synthesize; carbon-based life would be impossible. On the other hand, if the differences are subtle, we may not even recognize that universe as substantially different from our own. However, seemingly small things, slight aberrations with significant consequences, might be our only clues. For example, water may not freeze at zero degrees or boil at 100 degrees Celsius, that's thirty-two and 212 degrees Fahrenheit respectively. It's possible that green may not be the perceived color of chlorophyll, and photosynthesis may function slightly differently—"

"Or," interrupted Armand, a twinkle in his eye, "even simple matter and energy might be manipulated by some mysterious means we have yet to understand."

Zack rolled his eyes. "Really, Armand? You just had to slip the concept of *magic* in somehow, didn't you?"

"Why not?" countered the anthropologist. "It's fun, serves quite well as a pragmatic example of our limited comprehension, and keeps a potentially dry explanation from becoming too boring. Besides, I couldn't resist."

Zack sighed in amused resignation. "Ah, you never can—but I take your point."

"Huh?" Trey mumbled.

"You see, Sergeant, as my esteemed colleague has reminded me, we don't know what we don't know; at best, we're speculating in the realm of the theoretical. The truth is this; there is no way of knowing what differentiates another universe from our own without experiencing that universe and conducting comprehensive scientific analysis. Perhaps then we'd have some solid evidence, facts to rely upon."

"Well, that I understand," Trey responded. "But, bear with me. I guess what I'm really wondering is whether or not there could be people in these other universes. If so, how would they be different?"

Armand chuckled. "*People?* Why not? If life, as we know it, is environmentally possible in that universe, then it should be quite possible, perhaps even probable, that you'd find people living there. Now, as for their *differences*—who knows? They might appear completely normal to us—or not. And of course, we're normal, right?"

He snorted at his feeble joke attempt; his wife rolled her eyes and gently shook her head. He ignored her, cleared his throat, and continued.

"As Zack said, two or more universes could very closely mirror one another with only the slightest differences. Consider this, how do we know that we do not live in a virtual phase of another universe? Could this not be a *parallel reality*? Isn't it possible that in another universe a group of friends are even now sitting around a table discussing the possibility of *our* existence?"

That began a lively discussion that demonstrated just how fertile some peoples' imaginations could be. Many of the comments were inadvertently humorous. Some of the wilder speculations had Miska crafting impromptu puns that precipitated periodic wincing and spates of laughter.

ELLEN RETURNED, PAUSING at the doorway. In that moment, she smiled in appreciation at the warmth of good fellowship and purposeful camaraderie effusing from her kitchen. Her guests noticed her arrival and looked to her expectantly.

"I don't want to interrupt the party, but it's almost time to go," she announced, gesturing to the window.

The last vestiges of sunlight were draining away as the reddened orb slipped below the horizon.

Everyone rose from the table in anticipation. Trey and Hawk collected their gear and joined Mark and Ellen at the back door.

Facing Trey, Ellen asked, "Do you have a copy of the warrant?"

"Yes, actually there are two warrants, right here." He tapped a chest pocket on his utility vest. "One is for Papa George as a *material witness* in two homicides, and the other names him as a *principle* in the contract murder of Perry Wilkerson. The DA decided to move forward and seek a warrant on a bill of information and then take it to the grand jury for a later indictment. Just between us, I heard he was worried the media might break the story prematurely. Anyway, I have certified copies of both warrants."

She nodded and then turned toward the rest of her guests.

"My friends, I have made the decision to entrust you with the truth—inasmuch as I know it. Of course, nothing of this—*not a word*—may go beyond this core group, as I am sure you will come to understand. However, time grows short; so, further explanation will have to wait until we return. I don't know just how long we'll be gone, most likely several hours. Please, feel free to wait here with Miska. Make yourselves comfortable. But now, we have to go. Oh, you're welcome to watch our departure."

Ellen led the way outside; and of course, everyone followed.

Standing in the yard behind the house, she said, "What you're about to see, I'll be happy to more fully explain later. I just don't have the time right now; so, please hold your questions."

Ellen held the Council's invitation flat in her hands. Focusing on the parchment, she concentrated on drawing ambient energy to form a transit globe. As it gained substance and finally established itself, gasps of surprise escaped the onlookers.

Ellen turned to see wide eyes and open mouths transform into childlike delight and knowing smiles.

She had a sudden inspiration.

"Miska, while we're gone, why don't you tell our friends *your* tale—from the very beginning? I'm sure they'd love to hear your story."

The big man smiled eagerly.

Turning to Trey, she said, "Trust me, and do just what I do. We will press into this globe, one at a time, and then we'll be in another realm. Are you ready?"

At his nod, she disappeared into the globe. After only an instant's hesitation, Trey did so as well; Hawk and Mark followed.

The globe shrank and *popped* out of existence.

ZACK STOOD IMMOBILE, staring at the spot, and then stepped forth, his hands extended as if he might feel something there.

"If I hadn't seen it . . . Was it a wormhole—a dimensional warp—*what?*"

"Ah, twas *magic*," offered Miska, grinning broadly.

CH 11

ELLEN STOOD NEAR THE center of a broad balcony of polished granite. Flickering torchlight flared and pulsed, scattering lingering remnants of shadow across the wide expanse, and illuminating a low balustrade surrounding the massive porch. A huge wall of the same polished stone rose above the balcony and disappeared into the night. Alabaster figurines, evenly spaced along the perimeter, held stone torches; sparkling flares of blue and green cavorted within the overly bright flames. In each corner of the balcony, stood a brace of large statues—apparently some sort of winged gargoyles. Two more were placed near the building, to either side of a very wide, and overly tall, set of ornately carved crystal doors.

Mark, Hawk, and Trey stepped to Ellen's side.

"This is impressive," observed Mark.

"Are we *alone?*" asked Hawk.

No other persons were visible in the immediate area, but Ellen knew what he really meant. She concentrated and opened her perceptions. Almost instantly she knew.

No! We are not alone!

"Well, Trey, what do you think?" probed Mark, not unkindly.

"I don't know what to think," Trey admitted, "and I don't know what to say."

"Say nothing," warned Ellen. "We are *not* alone. Something else—no, *several somethings*, very old and sentient, are nearby. Our arrival has been noticed; someone is coming."

"What's nearby? There's nothing here but those big ugly statues," Trey whispered hoarsely, pointing into the corners.

"Don't point and don't stare!" Ellen hissed. "Remember, we are being watched."

"Ellen was invited," Mark cautioned, "so, let her do the talking. We're just her escort. If you do have to speak, keep in mind that *lord* and *lady* are common terms of respect, especially for any sort of nobility. Many attendees will be considered noble, certainly the official representatives of their realms."

Ellen knew that Mark's comment was largely for Trey's benefit, but it was just as well that they all renewed their focus on their undercover roles. It would be inappropriate for a personal guard to speak out of turn, if at all.

She saw that Trey and Hawk kept their eyes moving, making certain their glances took in the gargoyle statues. There was no movement, of course, despite the persistent dance of torchlight and shadow, but there was something nonetheless unnerving about those statues.

One of the great doors opened; soft amber light poured forth.

A diminutive figure walked toward them, slowly becoming more distinct in the torchlight. The flickering illumination revealed a small woman, clutching an open scroll in her hands. Clad in a brown robe trimmed with golden thread, she wore a soft conical cap with a golden tassel dangling from its lazily flopped point. Her poise and carriage suggested a certain dignity, and authority.

She stopped before Ellen and executed a brief sort of combined bow and curtsy. No taller than chest-height to Ellen, her voice was strong and clear, although quite highly pitched.

"On behalf of the Council, I bid you welcome. I am Madam Moya, Dowager of the Mayfield Brownie Clan, and Chief Clerk to the Council. I presume you are . . . " she consulted her scroll briefly, "Lady Ellen Doyle, Steward of the Grand Portal of the Realm of Man?"

"Quite so, Madam Moya. And these gentlemen," Ellen indicated with a sweep of her hand, "are my escort. I am pleased to make your acquaintance. And now?"

"If you please, m'lady, I shall show you to the rooms prepared for you," Madam Moya intoned, pursing her lips as she took in Ellen's dark slacks, short jacket, and white boat-necked blouse. "There you will find appropriate ceremonial robes. The meeting will not begin for another hour. If you like, I can arrange for food and refreshment to be brought to your rooms."

"Thank you, Madam Moya, but that really won't be necessary. We—" Ellen began, when another woman's voice sounded from the open door.

"Moya! Is that Lady Ellen—has she arrived?"

The speaker was walking swiftly across the smooth stones—another petite woman. However, this was no brownie.

Moya squinted. "Selene, is that you? You have interrupted a formal welcoming! Have you no sense of proper decorum?"

"Oh, Moya, be not so fussy! Lady Ellen is a *friend!* I did not want to miss her arrival!"

Ellen did in fact recognize the delicate yet voluptuous undine who now hugged Madam Moya playfully. She had been among those individuals Gallenius had recently introduced on the wooded path at Delafaire Farm. He had called her *a dear friend of ours*. There was clearly some sort of implication there. Ellen thought it might be best to go with the flow in this regard.

"Oh, Selene! I am so happy to see you," Ellen effused. "I did not know that you would be here."

"Oh, it is just one of those things, Ellen dear. One of Lady Orla's personal retinue is ill, so I am filling in—you know the Avatar of Mer would never travel without a full staff. So, here I am! Now, I most certainly do not want to interrupt my friend Moya's welcoming procedure—that would be rude, and she is such a stickler for proper protocol—so I shall just walk along with you. Besides, Moya gives a great introductory talk to first-time visitors—and I love to hear it."

"More like you love to *interrupt* it," corrected Moya, with a twinkle in her eye.

"Well, you do tend to leave out the juicy bits," teased Selene coyly, batting her eyelashes—no doubt for the benefit of the men, who hadn't taken their eyes off her.

"We would most certainly like to hear Madam Moya's talk," Ellen said as the group started walking toward the open door. "I am already fascinated by the grandeur and magnificence of this place."

Moya smiled as if she had been personally complemented. "Thank you."

"In truth," Selene teased, "my dear friend Moya does feel more than a little proprietary about the Council facility and its annexes. She loves to explain how the building came to be."

"Which I would, Selene, were you not interrupting me," the brownie scolded in mock annoyance.

"Oh, so sorry dearest Moya," the unrepentant undine cooed impishly. "Please, by all means do continue."

"Why thank you, Selene," Madam Moya retorted, a small smirk betraying her amusement.

"Ahem . . . Almost three millennia ago, the newly formed Council decided to erect a suitable place in which to meet. This realm was selected, in part because it was uninhabited, and because it is of exceptionally small size—nothing exists beyond a stone's throw of the outermost walls. The only permanent residents are contingents of the non-aligned races who were tasked by the Dragon Lords to serve certain functions for the Council; the Bogies serve as the messengers, the Gargoyles serve as the sentinels, and we Brownies serve as the administrative staff."

At the mention of *gargoyles*, Ellen saw Trey and Hawk exchange a shocked look of realization. Mark must have noticed their exchange as well; he glared at them and briefly shook his head to caution silence.

Hoping this *faux pas* had gone unnoticed, Ellen deliberately drew the brownie's attention.

"Please excuse my ignorance, Madam Moya, but what did you mean by *non-aligned races*?"

Moya smiled. "Lady Ellen, please feel free to ask questions of me or any of my staff. We Brownies find no shame in *ignorance*—only regret when one does nothing to overcome such a shortcoming. We love knowledge, and respect all those who pursue and protect it.

"Now, the term, *non-aligned races*, refers to those races who have not sworn fealty to either of the Courts of Faerie. In fact, one could say the race of Man is among the non-aligned, having never sworn such fealty. Does that adequately answer your question?"

"Yes, thank you," responded Ellen, in thoughtful reflection. Moya's comment had piqued her curiosity; clearly there was much more to learn about these non-aligned races.

As they passed through the gigantic doors, Moya continued with her presentation.

"The representatives, or avatars, of the member realms are afforded quite spacious apartments for themselves and their staffs in the annex buildings adjacent to the Council Chamber. We now stand in the Grand Reception Hall; the highly decorative walls depict historical scenes and selected works of art from the Council Realms."

Reciting a litany of diverse artists and pointing out their respective works on display, Moya led the group across the vastness of the Grand Reception Hall, coming to a stop before another massive set of closed crystal doors.

Upon closer examination, the visitors could see a profusion of delicately carved prismatic engravings that effectively rendered the crystal opaque. However, a suffused luminosity from within betrayed the presence of considerable illumination beyond the threshold.

Drawing their attention to the ornate doorway, Moya continued her lecture.

"I am sure you have noticed the size of many of the doors throughout the Council facility, which includes the Council Chamber and the Grand Reception Hall. They are sized to accommodate dragons, although we have not been visited by any of the Elder Lords in many centuries. Beyond these doors lies the Council Chamber."

As the brownie pushed on one of the huge doors, it swung open easily. A row of broad steps led downward to a large circular amphitheater in the Greco-Roman style. Dozens of strategically placed stanchions of wrought bronze held shallow bowls of dancing flames, illuminating the entire interior. Across the vast chamber another set of huge doors stood open; two sets of smaller doors were set equidistant in the left and right walls of the chamber.

Polished marble benches ringed the sloping floor of the domed space, descending in ever smaller concentric circles like inverse ripples in a pond lapping up against the central stage, a round dais supporting eight chairs evenly spaced about its circumference.

A number of brownies, administrative staff no doubt, bustled to and fro throughout the chamber in obvious preparation for the impending meeting. Many noticed the dowager of their clan conducting the visitors' tour, and bobbed their heads respectfully as they passed nearby.

Moya explained how Dwarven master craftsmen had labored for decades to create this magnificent building. Every realm had contributed something to the effort; raw materials, designs, and labor.

"I must also caution you that no spells will work within this chamber; it is heavily warded by the strongest of old magic, cast by the Dragons themselves. Of course, magic is permitted in other locations, like the private apartments of the Council members and staffs. In fact, most members and staff transit directly there, to and from their home realms. You arrived on Dragons' Perch, which is now used primarily for guests and visitors."

Drawing Moya's attention to the stage, Ellen asked, "May I assume that the chairs we see are for the representatives or avatars—the Council members?"

"Quite so, m'lady. Their respective staffs are typically seated on the benches immediately behind each member. Visitors may sit anywhere behind the staff. We expect a goodly number in attendance for this meeting. You and your escort may take seats anywhere to the rear of the Chair of Man."

"I understand," Ellen remarked. "Would you be kind enough to point out the Chair of Man? They all seem alike to me."

"Ah, of course, m'lady. Let us go closer, that you may see more clearly," Moya responded and began descending the broad steps.

They stopped about halfway down, and Moya pointed out specific chairs. There were discernible differences in the stout wooden seats; subtle carvings and runes covered most of the visible surfaces.

Ellen was at a loss to understand or comprehend their meanings.

"That one, the Dragon Chair, is vacant, and has been so for five centuries." Madam Moya's tiny finger pointed to another ornate chair. "To the right, in the Dwarven Chair, sits Svengard Thorenson, who serves as chairperson for this decade, a role that rotates amongst the members. Someone must conduct the meetings, you see."

"Of course, I understand," assured Ellen. "Please, do continue."

"Certainly . . . To the left of the Dragon Chair, the Chair of the Dark Elves is vacant—the Earl of Tanist, Avatar of Queen Mab, recently died. I would not be surprised if a new avatar is to be proposed at this meeting."

"I do not recall that being on the agenda that I received," noted Ellen.

"No, it was not on the published agenda," admitted Moya. "We were not aware . . . Well, suffice to say that these are extraordinary times."

"That is certainly an understatement," Selene observed dryly.

A wincing scowl marred the brownie's countenance at the undine's interruption. She sent Selene a withering glance, cleared her throat, and continued frostily.

"Ahem . . . The next chair seats Lord Varney of Shadow; and to the left sits Lord Talbot of the Were. The Chair of Man is next—vacant, of course—followed by the Chair of Mer, occupied by Lady Orla. The final chair seats Lady Rowan of the Light Elves."

"Thank you, Madam Moya, I am most grateful," said Ellen sincerely. "You have been very patient with me; this has been most enlightening. I presume it would now be best if we were to proceed to our assigned accommodations?"

"Yes, of course," agreed Moya. "Please, follow me, this way."

AS THEY LEFT THE COUNCIL Chamber, Trey nudged Hawk and cast an obvious glance at a narrow walkway high above, near the base of the domed ceiling. Hawk followed Trey's eyes and saw a host of gargoyle statues evenly spaced around the circumference of the space. Neither man felt the need to comment, as both understood the implications.

Moya led them to a large set of connected rooms, much like a suite. Illuminated by small glowing lamps that brightened as they entered, the visitors found simple but comfortable furnishings and a wide table in a common area. Bowls of fruit, loaves of bread, and wedges of cheese were laid out; another smaller table held exquisite crystal goblets and elaborately engraved carafes of cooled wine.

Moya spread her arms wide and said, "M'lady, I hope you find the rooms satisfactory. You will find appropriate ceremonial robes in the adjacent chambers. A page will come for you within the hour to lead you to the meeting. If there is anything you require, you need but ask. Now, I must be about my duties; so, if you have no further questions?"

"The accommodations are fine," Ellen assured her, "and you have been a most gracious, and informative, hostess, Madam Moya. Please, feel free to return to your duties. We will take our ease in preparation for the meeting."

Moya smiled, did her special little curtsy-bow, and vanished down the hall.

SELENE CLOSED THE OUTER door and came to stand close to Ellen.

"We have very little time," she whispered, and grasped Ellen's wrist. "You must come with me—quickly now."

Ellen resisted, deftly twisted her wrist free of Selene's grasp, and stepped back a pace.

"Not so fast, Selene! What do you want?"

Undines are stronger than they appear; so, Selene was somewhat surprised at the ease with which Ellen freed her wrist. Ellen was proving to be stronger in her resolve, and in her person, than she appeared.

Selene stepped closer and whispered, "You must understand. There is someone you must meet—information you need!"

Ellen tilted her head, but otherwise didn't budge.

Seeing that she had not convinced Ellen, Selene added softly, "The Guildmaster has arranged it. But we must go *now* and be back here before the page arrives!"

"The Guildmaster? I see—very well then," conceded Ellen, "but we *all* go!"

"No, Ellen," Selene insisted, hands on her hips. "You, I know; Gallenius and the Guildmaster vouch for you. These others, I do not know. And I would not jeopardize our resources."

"Selene, stop," Ellen said firmly. "These are people close to me; I trust them implicitly. Neither you nor the Guildmaster need have any concern regarding their trustworthiness and discretion. They go with me—or I don't go anywhere."

Selene stepped back and saw Ellen in a new light. This young woman was far more formidable than she had been led to expect. Selene now had to make a difficult decision; she realized she actually had little choice. Ellen could not go into that meeting without being fully informed—too much could be at risk.

"As you wish," Selene capitulated, and faced the entire group, "but I will have a binding oath of secrecy from all of you—know that lives will be put at risk! Do you—each of you—agree?"

"I speak for us all, and we agree," Ellen said firmly.

The men nodded their heads in agreement.

Hands on her hips, Selene rolled her eyes and shook her head.

"Forgive me, Ellen, but that is not good enough. No one can swear an oath for another."

Selene stood before each member of Ellen's escort in turn and coached each man in the articulation of a binding oath using his *true name*.

Within a few moments, all had complied—including Trey, another first for him.

Satisfied, Selene merely said, "Remain silent and follow me."

She stood before a large wall mirror, placed her hands upon its surface, her webbed fingers widely splayed, and softly recited a simple incantation. A series of ripples in the glass seemed to emanate from her hands, flowing ever outward across the mirrored surface as if it were liquid.

Her hands sank into the rippling glass.

Selene glanced back, and uttered a single word as she stepped *into* the mirror.

"Come."

Ellen looked to her companions, gave them a wry smile, and followed Selene into the ensorcelled looking glass.

The men followed without hesitation—even Trey, whose jaw had dropped in shocked surprise.

THEY STOOD IN A DIM passageway of smoothly finished stone that went off in three directions; one of which was a narrow descending staircase. Selene stood on the top step and motioned for them to follow her down. The stairs led to a series of landings that offered openings to other passages; but, the undine continued to descend.

Ellen wondered at the expanse of these passages, and briefly let her awareness expand. To her surprise, she realized the entire facility was riddled with hidden ways and secret rooms. There were no torches and no apparent source of illumination, but a muted half-light seemed to suffuse from the very walls. No doubt some very old magic was at work here.

Selene stopped at a landing and pointed to a passageway.

"We have descended to the level below the Council Library, which lies beneath the Grand Reception Hall, to what is commonly referred to as the *archives*. It is actually just a storage area, but this is where we will find Elsbeth, the former librarian.

"She is among the oldest of the Brownie Elders, and had served the Council for many centuries before her retirement. Now, as the self-appointed *archivist*, she sorts and maintains certain records, and knowledge, relating to the Council and its doings. Most here think she is an addled and harmless old pensioner puttering away down here amongst her piles and stacks of trivia, a bright mind gone dull with age and apparent senility—a façade that she is very careful to maintain. In truth, she may be aged, but her mind is sharp and quick. She is, without a doubt, one of the foremost information brokers of the known realms."

Selene paused and said ominously, "You are now privy to one of the Guildmaster's most closely guarded secrets—powerful knowledge that you are all oath-bound to protect."

Ellen simply said, "We understand. This secret is safe with us, I assure you."

Selene, her expression betraying nothing, remained silent. Instead, she turned to face what appeared to be a blank wall of the ubiquitous smooth stone, placed her palms upon its face, and softly recited an incantation. Her hands seemed to sink *into* the very stones.

She uttered a single word over her shoulder as she stepped *into* the wall.

"Follow."

THEY FOUND THEMSELVES in a space crowded with piles of dusty old books and parchments, stacks of discarded document folders, and towers of boxed scrolls leaning precariously overhead.

Ellen glanced behind her, thinking to find another mirror, but saw only an old bookcase stuffed to overflowing with a disheveled display of more erratically shelved papers and torn notes. Narrow footpaths, littered with loose scraps of paper, wound haphazardly among the cramped stacks and piles.

Ellen was surprised the clutter hadn't caved in upon itself. The very scope was overwhelming.

Ye gods! This looks like a hoarder's secret stash!

Selene led the way confidently through the maze of minutia and came to stand before a small, yet surprisingly clean, desk. There sat a wizened brownie, obviously a woman of great age, hunched over a tattered piece of parchment, a large magnifying glass in her tiny weathered hand.

Muttering to herself, she ignored her visitors, seemingly totally focused on some inconsequential scrap—the very picture of senility.

"Elsbeth," Selene said softly, "this is Lady Ellen, and these three are her personal escort. She vouches for them, and I have bound all by oath—I assume the implied responsibility. Time is short; we must return in a few minutes."

Elsbeth looked up for the first time and assessed her visitors. No befuddlement or confusion fogged her eyes or dulled the intensity of her stare. This was clearly an intellect to be reckoned with, razor sharp and quick to draw metaphorical blood.

Yet her voice was frail and its timbre infirm—great age still exacts a price.

"Greetings, Steward," Elsbeth wheezed. "I must be succinct, so please forgive my brusque words. Firstly, I have no news about your mother and friend; many are searching on your behalf.

"Your presence here places you in danger; others have recently arrived who may bear you ill will. This includes the Lady Diere, now Queen Mab LV; Lord Addecus of the Were, who is known to serve the schemes of Lady Diere; Lady Leanan of the Sidhe, who is accompanied by Lady Sabrina and the newly ascended Lord Gunther.

"I understand that the fledgling vampire Lord Gunther bears a particular animosity toward you and certain members of your escort, Lord Hawk and the Counselor. Of course, he knows nothing of the good Sergeant Bassett—yet. And lastly, another human from your home realm has arrived, George Papadolis, a pawn of Lady Diere's, who has been nominated for the Chair of Man, as you already know. You must be on your guard at all times."

This was unsettling news, to be sure, but it would not dissuade Ellen from her path.

"Elsbeth, I am very grateful for the information. I did not expect to find so many arrayed against me. I will be most careful, I assure you. But I will do what I must to find those who have been taken from me." Her determination was clear.

"I have only given you the facts as I know them, child," Elsbeth offered. "Now, hear my analysis. Aside from offering a new avatar, Diere's presence suggests that she will likely make an effort to further consolidate her hold on the voting bloc of the Unseelie Court, the Realms of Shadow and Were—in addition to subverting the Chair of Man.

"Now, as it happens, she does not know you are even here—at least *not yet.* Word of your arrival has been closely held—no, do not ask how, for I cannot compromise any further resources. I recommend that you be discreet and not flaunt your presence until it is to your advantage; that is also the safer course.

"You will be completely safe within the Council Chamber and the Grand Reception Hall; the sentinels will see to that. But be wary near the annexes of the other realms. It would be wise to be circumspect even within your current visitors' accommodations for those rooms are protected by only the simplest of wards."

"It may be best to avoid any of the other realms' annexes altogether," interjected Selene. "Each realm crafts its own wards for its assigned space, and such sorcery is typically among the strongest its mages can concoct—some of which can be quite dangerous."

Elsbeth smiled at Selene and said, "Sage advice indeed, Selene. I should have mentioned that as well. The annexes are considered as a part of the assigned realm; thus, the laws and any magic of that realm apply therein. The sentinels alone are immune; but, they do not interfere unless it is the will of the Council."

"I understand," replied Ellen. "It's like the embassy of another country. Uh, in my home realm we honor territorial jurisdiction much the same way. However, we were not planning on visiting another realm's annex, only the Council Chamber."

"That is a wise course of action, my dear," Elsbeth observed. "A final word, it is rumored that Titania, Queen of the Light Elves, may attend tonight's meeting. I strongly suspect that this is more than mere speculation. It would be very much like her to appear to personally take the measure of the new Queen Mab, the former Lady Diere. I do not know what to expect, but there is no love lost between the two. You would be wise to avoid them both during recesses in the Grand Reception Hall."

"The former Queen Mab LIV, and Titania had a number of agreements," Selene added, "some of which have been in place for decades. Now, all such bonds may be in jeopardy."

"Quite so," mused Elsbeth thoughtfully, "and all the more reason to tread carefully this night."

"Elsbeth, the time . . . " Selene urged.

"Of course, Selene, I have not forgotten," Elsbeth remarked dryly, as she stood.

Coming around the desk, Elsbeth took Ellen's hands in her own and said, "I am delighted to have met you, and your friends, Ellen. Remember to be careful in all you do and say here—assume the very walls have eyes and ears. Now you really must return. Selene will see you back to your assigned quarters."

"Thank you, Elsbeth, for everything," Ellen said gratefully, "but before I go, may I ask? Did you know my predecessor, the last Steward, my Aunt Maude?"

"Yes, child, I knew Maude Delafaire very well."

Elsbeth's smile encouraged Ellen's own in response, and she asked, "Would it be possible for us to talk, sometime in the future, perhaps under better circumstances?"

"Certainly, my dear, I would like that very much. Now go, you must!"

And so she did, the ghost of a hopeful smile lingering on her lips.

CH 12

THE COUNCIL CHAMBER was crowded almost to overflowing. Ellen and her escort found seats close to the front, several rows behind the Chair of Man. Clearly the beings seated around her were not from the Realm of Man. The colorful varieties of ceremonial robes and the subdued dissonance of different species' accents and dialects confirmed her observations.

She and her escort, mindful of Elsbeth's advice, kept their hoods up and their voices down—the better to keep their identities hidden, at least for the moment.

Directly above the central stage—actually more of a slightly raised dais—a softly glowing node of suffused light appeared, slowly growing in size and luminosity until the entire stage and its eight empty chairs were bathed in the gentle radiance. An anticipatory hush fell over the chamber as all eyes focused on the central tableau.

A soft chime echoed around the chamber and the audience rose to their feet in silence. Five individuals, attired in ceremonial robes of different styles and colors, made their way down a broad stairway and onto the stage. Each stood before an empty chair, facing the center. Their elbows bent at their waists, they held their palms up and gazed upward. One of the five, a stout, broad-shouldered individual, spoke in a clear stentorian voice.

"On this auspicious occasion of the Moon of Gemini in the Year of the Dog, the Council of Realms, in compliance with the Dragon Accords, is once again convened. Draw nigh to hear and be heard. The Council is now in session. I, Svengard Thorenson of the Realm of Dwarves, shall serve as chairperson and moderator. Please be seated, and come to order."

The audience resumed their seats in silence but for the rustle of robes and an occasional muted cough. As the Council members took their respective chairs, they were attended by aides and members of the Clerk's staff who bustled about distributing documents relative to the agenda.

Ellen recognized Madam Moya as she came to stand in the center of the dais.

The Dwarven representative acknowledged the Council Clerk.

"Ah, Madam Clerk, what business is first on our agenda?"

"M'lords and ladies," Moya began. "We have a special request, of an urgent nature, that does not appear on the Council agenda. Her Majesty, Queen Mab LV of the Dark Elves is in attendance; and, she requests that she be permitted to address the council on the matter of her avatar."

"Of course," responded Svengard Thorenson. "If there are no objections from the other members, we will hear from Her Majesty."

Taking his time, the moderator called upon each Council member by name, starting on his left.

"Lady Rowan?"

The Light Elf merely shook her head.

"Lady Orla?"

The Mer representative gave a dismissive wave.

"Lord Talbot?"

The Were Lord scratched his beard and shook his head.

"Lord Varney?"

The Vampire Lord slowly shook his head as well.

The chairperson continued, "I see there are none. In that case, the Council will hear from the Queen of the Dark Elves. Your Highness, if you please? The floor is yours."

Across the chamber and slightly to Ellen's left, a lone figure rose and flipped back her hood—Queen Mab LV. A dozen burly figures in dark robes rose around her as well. With an elegant gesture, she indicated that her personal guard should remain in place, and allowed a single individual to offer his arm and approach the stage.

Inclining her head to her escort, the queen said something and smiled—her escort pulled back his hood and let it drop across his shoulders.

A collective gasp went up from those seated around Ellen, startling her. She heard the shocked whispers that spread through the crowd like wildfire.

"Padraic the Rogue? It *cannot* be! As *consort?*"

"Duke Briar will be *apoplectic!*"

"Such nerve—she *flaunts* him!"

Ellen saw a reasonably handsome man of middle years; however, she was far more interested in the queen. This was the first time she had actually seen the Lady Diere, the newly enthroned Queen Mab LV—her apparent nemesis. The Queen of the Dark Elves was an undeniably beautiful creature, strikingly sensual, and yet, somehow aloof and cold.

Ellen's immediate reaction was confused, morbid fascination tempered by caution and distrust. There was an ominously dark, yet subtly seductive, energy about the elfin woman that Ellen sensed without any effort. The allure of such superficial beauty belied the hidden capacity for treachery and vindictiveness. Ellen intuitively pierced the perilously pleasing façade and recognized Diere as an adversary not to be underestimated.

The Dark Elf Queen's sole escort did not accompany her onto the dais; he stood at the edge, holding her cloak.

She strode to the center, resplendent in a clinging raven sheath with a scarlet wrap draped across her alabaster shoulders that seemed to caress her in the flickering torchlight.

"Members of the Council, and assembled guests," Mab began, graciously. "I appreciate the opportunity to address you. As you are aware, the former avatar of the Realm of the Dark Elves, the Earl of Tanist, is dead, brutally murdered along with my predecessor, my dearest cousin, Celeste, Queen Mab LIV. This foul act of treachery I shall thoroughly investigate and severely punish! No stone shall remain unturned—and those responsible, dealt with! I have been made aware of incriminating circumstances that cast suspicion upon, let us just say *certain others.*

"But, alas, I digress; this is a difficult time . . . please forgive me.

"I come before you today to propose a *new* avatar, *my* representative, for the Realm of the Dark Elves—the daughter of the late Earl of Tanist, the Lady Malvana. Surely, you can see the appropriateness of the nomination.

"Furthermore, I request that the Council proceed with an immediate vote on her proposed membership. According to the rules of the Council, she is eligible; and, she is present, should you wish to question her. In conclusion, I must tell you that as monarch of the Realm, I do not wish to see it unrepresented on the Council—for *any* length of time."

There was a moment of silence before Svengard Thorenson spoke.

"Your Majesty, on behalf of all Council members, I offer condolences for your losses. As for the nomination of the Lady Malvana as your avatar, she is indeed eligible and is well known to us. Thus, absent any objections, I think she need not be questioned; her father was a valued member of this Council. So, if there are no objections, we can proceed with an immediate election."

The moderator once again looked to each Council member in turn; none took issue with the proposal.

"I see that we have no objections. Very well, Madam Clerk, please proceed."

Madam Moya stepped forth, a large scroll in her hands.

Queen Mab stepped back to the edge of the stage, near her consort—but she did not leave the dais.

Moya stood in the center and read aloud from the scroll a recitation of the rules of election. Only a simple majority of the Council members present was required for a candidate to be elected to Council membership.

At the conclusion of her reading, Moya asked for each member's vote. In due time Lady Malvana was unanimously elected to the Council.

SVENGARD THORENSON affixed his signature to a succession of documents produced by Madam Moya.

The protocols observed, he rose and proclaimed, "The requirements having been met, the candidate found worthy, and the election to the Chair of Dark Elves conducted and completed pursuant to the Council rules, I ask the Lady Malvana of the Dark Elves to come forward, that the oath of office may be administered."

The elfin maid arose from the gallery, flipped back the hood of her cloak, and gracefully approached the dais, her bearing no less regal and assured than that of her mentor, the new Queen Mab. Glancing deferentially at her monarch, Malvana waited for Mab's subtle nod of approval before stepping upon the stage. A clerical brownie appeared at her side to take her cloak. Malvana stood demurely in an understated gown of pale amethyst trimmed in delicate black lace—a subdued counterpoint to the Queen's shimmering ebony ensemble.

Madam Moya gestured for Malvana to join her at center-stage.

Svengard Thorenson considered the young elf standing before him, her shoulders squared and mouth held in a grim line of determination—much like her father, whom the Chairman had personally liked and found to be a valued Council member. He sensed a bit of trepidation in her eyes, as if this was all too much, too fast—after all, she had only recently lost her father. However, her new queen had called upon her; and she had answered. He hoped the daughter of the Earl of Tanist was up to the task.

"Lady Malvana of the Realm of the Dark Elves, do you hereby agree to represent your home realm during your tenure as a member of this Council, and swear by Air, Earth, Fire, and Water to uphold the principles and policies of the Dragon Accords in your capacity as a member of this Council at all times and in all matters, and finally do you accept this binding oath by your *true name?*"

"I, Malvana of Tanist, of the Realm of the Dark Elves, do so hereby agree, swear by Air, Earth, Fire, and Water, and accept this oath by my true name."

The chairperson smiled and said, "Congratulations, m'lady, and welcome to the Council. Please be seated in the Chair of the Dark Elves."

The audience applauded politely as the newest Council member took her seat.

Queen Mab looked on approvingly, and then boldly stepped to the center once again.

Svengard Thorenson's brows knit in disapproval at this breach of protocol. He glanced quickly to Moya, who merely shrugged helplessly.

"Yes, Your Majesty," the chairperson acknowledged, somewhat reluctantly. "Was there something else?"

"Members of the Council, I thank you for honoring my request. Now, if I might bring up a similar matter that coincidentally appears on the Council's agenda, the vacancy of the Chair of Man."

The moderator did not normally permit—much less welcome—disruptions to the Council's set agenda. But this was a *queen*—indeed, one of the most powerful monarchs of the council realms. Discretion was well advised.

"Uh, Madam Clerk," the chairperson asked, "this matter is on the agenda?"

An aide stepped to the moderator's side and held forth a parchment for the chairperson to see. Thorenson wedged his pince-nez on the bridge of his nose and squinted at the document, deftly hiding his displeasure and growing resentment at the elfin queen's none-too-subtle manipulation of the Council's business.

"It is, m'lord," Moya responded. "A native of the Realm of Man, George Papadolis, has been nominated by the late Earl of Tanist, on behalf of the Realm of the Dark Elves, for the Chair of Man. The candidate was summoned before the Council for questioning and possible election this night. I am informed that he is present, and awaits the Council's pleasure."

ELLEN FELT HAWK TENSE as another robed figure stood among the seats behind the Chair of the Dark Elves and pulled back his hood—Papa George!

Squeezing Hawk's wrist, she whispered, "Patience! Don't do or say anything—let me handle this!"

The moderator cleared his throat irritably, his nose close to the parchment, and said, "So it is. Thank you, Madam Clerk. I suppose, if the other members have no objections of course, that we might take a matter out of order?"

He queried each member once again; as before, none raised an objection.

At a gesture from the chairperson, Moya called for the candidate to present himself.

Having been called forth, George ascended the stage and came to stand, in obvious deference, near Queen Mab.

Moya spoke briefly with George, and then stepped forward to address the entire Council.

"Members of the Council, pursuant to a summons duly issued by this body, the candidate, George Papadolis of the Realm of Man, is present as requested."

"I see, well then," Svengard Thorenson began, "if there are no objections, it appears that we may as well proceed—"

"But there *is* an objection—on behalf of the Realm of Man!" cried a voice from the audience.

Ellen was mildly surprised to find it was her own, and that she was standing, pulling her hood back to reveal her face.

"What? Who?" asked the moderator, obviously confused.

The other Council members looked at one another in surprise and then scanned the crowd for the source of the interruption.

Moya stepped forth and announced, "M'lords and ladies, the objection is raised by Lady Ellen Doyle, Steward of the Grand Portal of the Realm of Man. Her appearance here tonight is also on the agenda."

"The *Steward?*" seethed Diere in shock—loud enough to be heard.

George winced and seemed to shrink within himself, but otherwise did not move.

"Ah, I see. Lady Ellen, please approach," requested Svengard Thorenson.

Accompanied by her escort, Ellen made her way to the dais. She grabbed Mark's wrist and whispered, "You all must wait here at the edge until I call for you—just trust me on this!"

Hawk and Trey heard as well; they complied, albeit not happily.

The three men found themselves standing next to the man who had escorted Queen Mab, her silent consort.

Padraic smiled pleasantly and nodded, but otherwise ignored them, focusing instead upon the drama now unfolding in the center of the stage.

Ellen strode forth and took a position slightly to one side of George and Mab, who had not budged from the center.

The moderator addressed her courteously.

"Lady Ellen, thank you for coming. It seems we are taking a number of our agenda issues out of order this evening. It is an honor to meet and acknowledge the Steward of the Grand Portal of the Realm of Man. We welcome you. Now, you raised an objection?"

"She cannot raise an objection," spat Queen Mab, "she has no standing with the Council!"

"If you do not mind, Your Majesty," Svengard Thorenson said evenly, "the Council will make that determination. Lady Ellen, please explain."

"Thank you, m'lord. I was invited to present myself as the new Steward of the Grand Portal of the Realm of Man; and, I do so now. I must beg your indulgence for seeming to speak out of turn, but I would be remiss—to the honor of the Council and to the welfare of my Realm—were I not to object to the nomination of this man, George Papadolis, as the representative of the Realm of Man. His nomination was *not* made by my realm; and, it is *not* in our best interest. And lastly, I would be surprised that he is even eligible—this man is a wanted criminal, a fugitive from justice!"

George flinched as though her words were angry wasps intent on stinging him into submission. His eyes darted about—no doubt an instinctive reaction—impulsively looking for an avenue of escape.

Ellen was close enough to see Queen Mab surreptitiously stab an elegantly manicured thumbnail into the back of Papa George's hand to keep him focused and still. She'd drawn a crescent of blood—he stopped fidgeting immediately.

"Lies! Despicable lies!" Mab uttered in *sotto voce;* but, all on the dais could see that her venomous gaze askance at George boded ill for him, nonetheless.

Thorenson ignored the interruption and asked, "Lady Ellen, have you proof of this man's criminal nature?"

"I do indeed, m'lord," Ellen assured him. "I am escorted by two law enforcement officials of my home realm, who are tasked with the apprehension of

George Papadolis, and his production before a court of law. They bear official documentation that will attest to all that I have told you."

"Very well," Thorenson acknowledged. "Let them come forth and produce this documentation. Madam Clerk, if you would?"

As Trey and Hawk stepped up on the dais, Moya met them at the edge and accepted copies of the warrants. She spent a few minutes examining the papers.

Ellen took that opportunity to formally introduced Hawk and Trey to the Council.

"May it please the Council; I present Sergeant Trey Bassett and Detective Connor Redhawk of the Chantilly Parish Sheriff's Department."

"Ah, yes . . . Welcome, gentlemen," Thorenson intoned. "You may come forward."

They stepped up to stand just behind Ellen, and to either side.

George visibly leaned away from them. It appeared that only Queen Mab's presence and his fear of her wrath kept him from fleeing the stage.

"M'lord," interrupted Moya tactfully, "I have examined the documentation, and find that the facts are as Lady Ellen has described. This man, George Papadolis, is to be brought before a court in the Realm of Man on multiple charges of murder. He is clearly ineligible to be considered a candidate for Council membership."

"I see," Thorenson mused thoughtfully, as the other Council members looked to one another in mute surprise.

The chairperson turned to Queen Mab and added smoothly, "This candidate is clearly *not eligible*. Surely, Your Majesty, you were not aware of this man's nefarious past—otherwise his nomination would not have happened? Is that not so?"

All eyes fell upon the Dark Elf Queen, and the entire chamber seemed to strain to hear her response.

"Sadly, it was my *late* predecessor who, um, initiated the nomination process," Diere explained contritely. "However, I have no doubt she was *equally uninformed* of such disturbing news. Of course, I felt that I was duty-bound to complete her, um, current programs and policies."

The moderator nodded sympathetically. "Ah, yes, I believe we can understand. And now?"

"Harrumph . . . Now however, under the circumstances, I would withdraw our support for the nomination. Of course, I shall make further inquiries in this regard."

"You withdraw the nomination?" repeated the chairperson. "I see there are no objections. So be it."

"The minutes will reflect the nomination withdrawn, without objection, m'lord," assured Moya, in her capacity as Clerk.

"M'lord," Ellen said to Thorenson, "these law enforcement officials are prepared to immediately assume custody of this man and return him to the Realm of Man to face justice."

"No! He is in *my* custody," snapped Mab. "And he will remain so until I am satisfied with the results of my inquiries. It is bad enough that the Council must continue to function with another vacant chair—yet I must ascertain how such a poor candidate came to enjoy my late cousin's support, before I might consider nominating another."

Facing the fuming elfin woman, Ellen raised her palms. "Oh, Your Majesty, your concern is touching, but I believe this Council need not be further constrained by the continued vacancy of another chair."

Turning to Lord Thorenson, Ellen smiled. "I am certain Her Majesty is quite busy and has better things to do with her time. So, allow me to make a recommendation, as the acknowledged Steward and a citizen of the Realm of Man, that another candidate be nominated at this time for the Chair of Man."

"Now I see," seethed Queen Mab spitefully. "You seek the chair for yourself! Just like your predecessor, Maude Delafaire!"

Ellen bristled; but, kept her temper in check, and did not rise to the bait.

"Oh no, Your Majesty. On the contrary," Ellen responded blandly, "I would nominate another, a wise man known among us as the Counselor, Mark Paige."

That stopped the queen! "*Who?* Mark Paige? What game are you playing?" she hissed.

Ellen knew Mark was shocked, too. He had no idea she was going to do that. She saw him glance at Hawk and Trey, who were evidently equally surprised and simply smirked at him.

Directing her remarks to Svengard Thorenson, Ellen continued. "Mark Paige is of the Realm of Man; you will find him eligible. He is present and may be questioned. I *do* agree with Her Majesty, Queen Mab, in that the Council would benefit from filling the Chair of Man with an appropriate candidate as soon as possible. I submit that Mark Paige is the right man. May I call him forth?"

"Please do, Lady Ellen," the moderator acceded, the hint of a smile playing on his lips.

"I really must object," Mab interjected. "There is insufficient time to question a candidate—much less hold an election!"

"May I be heard, m'lord?" interrupted Mark as he came to stand with Ellen.

Hawk and Trey kept a wary watch on George and the very displeased elfin queen.

"Of course, please proceed," intoned Svengard Thorenson.

"May it please the Council, m'lords and ladies . . . I am Mark Paige, known as the Counselor, of the Realm of Man, and I shall be brief. I have not sought membership upon this Council, but if called upon by my home realm, as seems to be the case, I would so serve if elected. Of course, I would be happy to answer any questions."

He scanned the faces of the Council members. None spoke, so he continued.

"Now, Her Majesty, Queen Mab, has raised two objections; firstly, that the Steward has no standing with the Council and thus can neither recommend nor object to any candidacy for the Chair of Man and, of course, the inherent Council membership. May I ask, now that Lady Ellen has presented herself to the Council, as requested, as the Steward of the Grand Portal of the Realm of Man, and has been thus acknowledged and accepted as such, does she not now enjoy *standing* in the eyes of the Council?"

"Quite so," spoke the chairperson, clearly impressed with the logic.

He was not alone; most of the audience could see the slowly bobbing heads of the attentive Council members—all, that is, but for the newly seated Lady Malvana, who sat rigidly upright, staring at Queen Mab's scowling face.

"Then, I submit, m'lords and ladies," Mark continued, "that the queen's objection as to *standing* is moot. Such status, as has already been acknowledged and granted, is the sole purview of the Council, and not that of a member realm's monarch.

"Now, as to Her Majesty's second objection; that there is insufficient time for questioning a candidate and a subsequent election . . . I would like to point out that—at her insistence—the Council has already considered and waived the questioning of a newly proposed candidate, conducted an election, *and* seated a new Council member in the Chair of Dark Elves, all of which was *not* on the Council's published agenda.

"And now, an anticipated period of questioning of a candidate, and the potential subsequent election, which *do appear* on the published agenda, have also been rendered moot—the previous candidate having been found ineligible. So, I respectfully submit that there *is* sufficient time, as previously allocated, for any questioning of a candidate, *and* subsequent election to the Chair of Man. The Council would merely be following its published agenda and established protocols as planned. Thus, Her Majesty's second objection is likewise rendered moot."

"A most compelling argument, sir," commented Thorenson, trying not to smile. "I believe you may have swayed the other members of the Council, as well."

"He has not swayed *me!*" spat Diere furiously. "I am *Queen!* I will not have my will challenged by a mere human mortal!"

SVENGARD THORENSON winced at her outburst. He had little enough regard for this Dark Elf's behavior; her disregard for the long established traditions and protocols of the Council he found particularly distasteful. However, he was not so foolish as to underestimate her power and influence. She could be very divisive. He could not afford to ignore the damage a rift in the Council could do.

Her realm had traditionally controlled a voting bloc of three, to include the realms of Shadow and Were. Of course, it remained to be seen if *this* elfin queen could maintain that control. He needed to placate her, to some degree, to keep the Council together as a cohesive and effective entity.

He noticed the sentinels were paying particular attention to her. If she were to further escalate her tantrum, the gargoyles would physically remove her. That would be a most embarrassing affront to her personally, and likely precipitate unimagined diplomatic consequences.

The situation must be dealt with—deftly. The chair must always moderate, however challenging.

"Is this how you treat a *Queen?*" Mab fumed, her voice growing shrill. "Answer me!"

Before the moderator could form an answer, Lady Rowan of the Light Elves stood and addressed the Council.

"A point of order, my fellow Council members," the Light Elf said in a voice nearly musical, "but Her Majesty, Queen Mab, is not the only monarch present."

"Indeed?" asked the chairperson, as hope and relief flickered in his eyes.

"Quite so," remarked Lady Rowan, who gestured gracefully toward the crowded benches to the rear of the Chair of the Light Elves. "May I present Her Majesty, Titania, Queen of the Light Elves, and Monarch of the Seelie Court."

A robed figure stood and flipped back her hood, revealing a cascade of bright blonde hair and piercing green eyes. That she was beautiful was an understatement.

A host of individuals seated around her dropped to one knee among murmurs of "Your Majesty, Your Highness . . . "

With a bright laugh she gestured for her subjects to rise and resume their seats. She made no move to approach the dais.

"Welcome, Your Majesty," called out Svengard Thorenson. "Would you care to join us upon the dais?"

"I think not, Lord Thorenson—it seems a bit crowded at the moment," the bright queen said impishly. "Perhaps my esteemed *sister monarch* would consider returning to her seat, so that the Council might proceed with the business at hand? She and I have *so much* to discuss during the pending recess."

THE APPEARANCE OF TITANIA absolutely stunned Diere.

At some point, in her new capacity as Queen Mab, Diere fully expected to have to deal with Titania, Queen of the Light Elves, but not this soon. Titania was far too powerful an adversary to openly engage at this stage of the game. Diere was not yet ready; too much was happening, much too quickly.

Nonetheless, Diere was shrewd enough to play this dangerous game with the best of them—or the worst. Right now, she needed to stall for time, and avoid Titania.

"I greet you, *sister.* I look forward to speaking with you, soon," Queen Mab replied.

Titania merely smiled and tilted her head in acknowledgment, but the smile never reached her eyes. Without another word, she resumed her seat.

Turning to the chairperson, Mab announced, "At this time, I shall return to my accommodations; I am confident that my avatar will see to my interests."

Shoving George before her, she said to Padraic, "Put this scum under guard in our chambers."

"One moment, Your Majesty," called Svengard Thorenson.

The Dark Elfin Queen paused, half-turning toward the chairperson.

"The Council has not yet decided what is to become of this man. It appears that a member realm has a legitimate claim upon him. For the moment, he may remain in your custody, since we can understand that you no doubt have some questions for him.

"The Council will discuss this matter, among others now before us, *in camera*, during the recess."

Mab said nothing. Turning her back to the chairperson, she stormed from the chamber with Padraic and her guards at her heels. George was pushed unceremoniously along within the entourage, panic and desperation alternatively flashing across his face.

"LADY ELLEN," THE MODERATOR asked, "I wonder if you could make your *Counselor* available for questioning by the Council members in a closed session, in one hour?"

Ellen glanced at Mark, who grinned and shrugged.

"I believe I can spare him, m'lord," she said with a smile.

"Excellent! Madam Moya will seek him out and bring him before us."

"Thank you, m'lord," Ellen said. "May I inquire, will the disposition of the fugitive, George Papadolis, be decided as well? It is *vitally* important that we assume custody and question him at the soonest possible moment, m'lord."

"I think it quite likely, Lady Ellen," the chairperson answered, and then turned toward Moya.

"Madam Clerk, if there is nothing else of immediate concern before us? No? Excellent! Please announce a two hour recess; the Council members will meet in an executive session, *in camera*, in one hour."

"As you wish, m'lord."

Standing in the center of the dais, Madam Moya called out in her clear high voice, "The Council stands in recess for two hours! Refreshments are laid out in the Grand Reception Hall."

Ellen led her group off the dais, and started up the broad stairs. Finding themselves alone at the top landing, she turned to the men, and raised her eyebrows quizzically.

"So, food and mingling, or what?"

Mark shrugged. "I don't know. I'm not hungry; so, I don't really care. We can go back to our rooms or we can mingle. What do you want to do?"

Trey and Hawk kept their eyes roving; people were still moving about, but none were within earshot—or so it appeared.

A small webbed hand tugged on Trey's sleeve. He looked down in surprise and was lost in the depths of a pair of lustrous sea-green eyes that peered up from beneath the hood of a diaphanous aqua robe. It was a moment before recognition set in.

"Uh . . . Selene, is it?" Trey mumbled. "How did you— Uh, I didn't even see you until—"

"Selene? What are you doing here?" interrupted Ellen, clearly surprised at the undine's presence.

Without preamble, Selene pulled them into a tight circle and whispered, "Avoid the Reception Hall! Return to your rooms and accept no invitations. Elsbeth sends a message; 'Trust not Titania!' Now go!"

WITHIN THE CLOISTERED apartments of the Dark Elves delegation, George stood in fear-stricken paralysis before an enraged and pacing Queen Mab. Her silent fury boiled off of her in perceptible waves of virulent energy.

Flashing a hand in irritation, she commanded, "Seal the room!"

All but two servants hastily departed as elfin guards moved to block the only two exits.

Jabbing a finger at her consort, she seethed, "Padraic, I have no need of your services at the moment."

Padraic needed no further persuasion; so, he excused himself and found an unobtrusive niche in the hallway nearby. From there, he could easily hear whatever transpired in the room he had just vacated.

George clearly had no hope of escape; he knew that Diere could not have been angrier. He tried to give her a wide berth, but the room was far too small for his liking. Somehow, he had to calm her down, explain all this. It really wasn't his fault—surely she would see that.

"Lady Diere," he began.

"Silence!" she shrieked. "You shall address me as a q*ueen!* I am now *Monarch!*"

He winced and shied from her wrath.

She furiously shrugged off the ceremonial council robe and threw it aside in a heap. Before a servant could bend to pick it up, the queen pointed a long elegant finger at the garment; her fingertip briefly glowed and the robe suddenly burst into an unearthly flame. An instant later there was only a collapsing pile of ash and a lingering acrid smell.

George almost fainted; but her stern voice cut through his panic-fueled despair and held his tenuous attention.

"You were to have seized the Steward and placed her where I instructed—she was not to appear here! Obviously, you have failed—and you have done so for the last time!"

"M- m'lady—" He groveled.

"That is *Majesty* to you!" she screamed in his face.

"Your Majesty . . . I, uh . . . I thought we *did.* We took them *both*—she *had* to be one of them."

She spun on him, pointing the same dangerous finger, right between his eyes. "*Both?* What do you mean—you took them *both*? Explain!"

"M-majesty, you said that she'd b-be alone—but she wasn't. There were two women, and we didn't know what she looked like—I've never seen her! So, my people grabbed them *both.* I assumed one of them was her, so I took both of them to the place you instructed me to. I don't know how she got away, or whatever. That's all I know."

"Two women?" she repeated, somewhat befuddled—yet her anger was undiminished.

George's head bobbed up and down; he dared not speak.

"Where is my topaz ring?" she demanded.

George fumbled in his pocket and produced the jewel.

She snatched it from his hand and held it near a glowing lamp. Her expression darkened as she studied the deeper recesses of the stone. She turned on him once more.

"Have you misused my ring? Some of the spell's energy lies unspent, still contained within the gem. What have you done?"

"O-only what you t-told me to do, Y-your M-majesty." His shoulders hunched and his head hung.

"Do not lie to me!" she exploded, flinging the ring at him. It struck him on the side of his head, gashing his temple, and skittered across the floor into the hall.

George howled, crumpled to his quaking knees, and held his lightly bleeding scalp.

At the queen's gesture, her elfin warrior-guards rushed forward, snatched him to his feet, and wrenched his arms painfully behind his back.

In the hubbub, no one noticed Padraic stoop to scoop up the ring and secret it within his robe.

"So, you took *two women*, did you? Well, we shall see," she said ominously. "Put this fool in a windowless room under guard—no food, no water. I will decide his fate when I return."

She swept into the hall and noticed her consort lingering nearby.

"Padraic, attend me!"

FOLLOWING HER INTO her private chamber, Padraic closed the door and leaned against it in silence.

She sat at an opulent dressing table before a large mirror and regarded her reflection, catching his eyes as well in the glass. She spoke without turning.

"Padraic, I must go and see what this idiot has done. He has most certainly botched a delicate assignment. I shall not be long. No one is to know that I have briefly left this realm—especially Queen Titania. She will probably send an invitation, something social, I should think. But, she might just as well appear at our door. No matter—you must stall her! I am not yet prepared to deal with her. Tell the guards, um, that we are *indisposed and not to be disturbed!* You understand, do you not?"

"Of course, they will assume we are being *randy,* and protect our privacy." He smiled lecherously, purely for her benefit, pushed off the door, and stepped up behind her. "But tell me, what *are* you going to do about this fellow, George? He seems most untrustworthy. Will you let the authorities from the Realm of Man take him to face their justice?"

Her eyes, still locked on his in the mirror, flared.

"*That*, my dear consort, is *not* an option! He could tell tales that I would not have told. No, his fate will be something else entirely."

IN ANOTHER SET OF CLOISTERED chambers assigned to the delegation from the Realm of Shadow, Lady Leanan and Lady Sabrina sat sipping their preferred crimson libation from delicate crystal goblets, while holding a quiet conversation before a cold hearth.

"I must say, her control appears to be slipping," observed Sabrina. "No shrewd queen would let her emotions become so obvious, I should think."

"True," agreed Leanan, "but remember she is newly come to the throne; and, she was never one to be cautiously diplomatic. Still, she ought to know better than to offer such blatant opposition to the Council's plodding procedures. Such impatience can be fatal to negotiated diplomacy, and further compromise alliances."

"Do you think the Unseelie voting bloc is in jeopardy? Could she lose that influence?" Sabrina asked. "The possible ramifications of such a loss of face alone could be considerable."

"That is quite an understatement, my dear Sabrina." Leanan smirked in amusement. "Yes, that is indeed possible. I think Queen Titania senses that as a potential weakness as well. Titania will no doubt move soon to renegotiate certain agreements previously forged with the former Queen Mab."

Sabrina's hand went to the base of her throat. "Do you mean the Elfin Accords? In part, or perhaps in their entirety?"

Leanan's eyebrows rose. "Yes, the accords assuredly—but in their *entirety?* Hmm, that is a good question—a distinct possibility, I should think. If Diere, as the new Queen Mab, is not in firm control of the voting bloc, she will not be bargaining from a position of equal strength. Titania will no doubt wrest considerable concessions from her despite—"

A brisk knock on the chamber door interrupted Leanan's analysis.

The newly fledged vampire, Gunther, a black patch over his right eye, bowed from the open doorway.

"M'ladies, forgive the intrusion, but Lord Varney has arrived in response to your invitation."

Gunther stood to one side as the elder vampire lord entered the room, and bowed from the waist.

"Lady Leanan, Lady Sabrina . . . How pleasant to see you once again. How may I be of service to the House of Lamia?"

"Ah, Varney," Leanan said with genuine warmth, "it is good to see you as well. It has been too long, my old friend."

"May we offer you a libation?" said Sabrina, gesturing for Gunther to pour another warm sanguine draught from a dark green carafe.

“Thank you, but no,” declined Lord Varney. “Time is short. I am to attend the closed session in a few minutes.”

“Indeed, it is that session about which we need to speak,” Leanan said, as she motioned for Gunther to shut the door.

“Really? How so, m’lady?” Varney asked, curiously intrigued.

“You should know that Mark Paige, this *Counselor*, proposed for the Chair of Man by the Steward, is well known to us,” Leanan explained. “In fact, he is personally responsible for the slaying of Damien the Cursed.”

“Indeed? Is this Counselor strong in blood or craft—or perhaps both?”

“I would say most likely *both*. I know he was bitten by Damien,” Leanan explained, “and I know that he assimilated aspects of Damien’s power and skills upon killing him. I do not understand how that happened. The point is that he *was bitten*. That being the case, he should prove to be susceptible to certain *influences and persuasions;* that may prove to be in our best interests. So, it has been decided that the Realm of Shadow will not object to his election to the Chair of Man. Do you understand?”

“Quite so, m’lady, quite so,” Lord Varney acknowledged thoughtfully, and then asked, “Who else knows of this development?”

“Many know of his slaying of Damien,” Leanan admitted, “but none, other than us, know of the potential of the residual link to *our kind*. That information shall, of course, be closely held.”

Lord Varney smiled—not a pleasant proposition—and executed a subdued bow in deference to Lady Leanan.

“M’lady, I can readily see a number of scenarios in which subtle *persuasion and influence* upon the votes cast by the Chair of Man would be most beneficial to our home realm.

“In the final analysis, we must be pragmatic; some of us fully understand how potentially dangerous the Realm of Man could be. Therefore *any* control or influence over mankind is very desirable. Consequently, I understand completely, m'lady.

"And may I congratulate you on your statecraft—you would be a formidable diplomat."

While she knew his compliment was entirely sincere, Leanan easily sensed his unspoken and appreciably cautious thoughts . . . *For you are a most cunning strategist, indeed; therefore, around you, I must be wary.*

"Why thank you for your kind words, m'lord."

"M'ladies, I must beg your indulgence. If there is nothing else, I am expected for the closed session, and must depart."

"Our business is concluded, m'lord," Leanan assured him.

"Until we meet again, m'ladies," the Elder Lord acknowledged while executing a courtier's sweeping bow.

"Dally not, Lord Varney, for duty calls," Leanan said, raising her goblet in toast, with a smiling nod for him.

After Lord Varney had departed, Sabrina held up her drained goblet and pointed to Leanan's; Gunther hastened to refill them both.

Leanan noted that the scowl that had encamped upon the fledgling vampire's countenance since the first mention of Mark Paige, the Counselor, still persisted.

Sabrina posed a question. "M'lady, I remember that I was unable to successfully *persuade or influence* this Counselor on a previous occasion. What makes you think it would work now?"

Leanan set her cup down on the arm of her chair. "Unfortunately, that was not persuasion or influence; that was a rather clumsy attempt at an opportunistic *seduction.* No, Sabrina, take no offense; the fault was mine—not yours—a poorly considered strategy at the time. What we will need to focus on now, assuming his successful election to the Chair of Man, will be more deftly considered persuasion and influence, however subtle, regarding certain issues that may come before the Council."

Leanan could see Sabrina was not convinced. Clearly she still viewed the attempted seduction as a failure on her part—not to mention a blow to her considerable pride.

"Well, I for one would not trust him." Sabrina whined peevishly. "He talks too much; and he *insulted* me!"

"I shall rip his throat out, my beloved!" growled Gunther, his devotion eclipsed only by his hatred.

"Enough!" demanded Leanan. "Sabrina, you would do well to keep your fledgling under close control. I will not tolerate such outbursts any more than I would tolerate any disruption to our plans. Keep him well away from all those from the Realm of Man—lest you both come to know my unfettered wrath. Am I clear on this?"

"Yes, m'lady," Sabrina conceded contritely. "There will be no problems, I assure you."

She rose and curtsied before Leanan. "By your leave, m'lady?"

Leanan nodded, her face expressionless.

Sabrina crooked a finger at her servant. "Gunther, attend me now in my chambers."

Leanan watched as Gunther followed his mistress from the room. The stiffness in his neck and shoulders betrayed his rebellious inclinations despite his reluctant compliance.

Running a manicured fingernail delicately around the lip of her crystal goblet, she relished the soft vibrating tone and kept her thoughts to herself.

Gunther, you would bear watching . . . unbalanced . . . a tragedy in the making.

LADY DIERE, NOW QUEEN Mab LV, stared down in surprise at the two slumped figures collapsed against one another in the bright cone of light.

So, the fool really did seize two women—the wrong women!

Both were still obscured by a clinging shroud of cloying fog, wisps of which were starting to thin and dissipate. She looked more closely and determined that the spell would hold for at least another twelve to fourteen hours, plenty of time.

Well now, just who do we have here?

Leaning over the two captives, she spoke a soft incantation and waved a hand over their faces. The grey fog pulled back from their shoulders exposing their heads, slumped forward on their chests.

Grasping a handful of tousled blonde hair for leverage, Diere rocked one's head back exposing her face—an unconscious young woman she did not recognize. Diere let go in disgust.

However, when she looked upon the face of the other woman, she paused. Familiarity tugged at her memory; then, without a doubt, she knew.

Millie—the other woman!

Older, for certain, and perhaps a bit careworn, but this was indeed the woman for whom Padraic had deserted the elf over a quarter century ago.

Which means . . . this woman is Ellen Doyle's mother! I have the Steward's mother!

With another wave of her hand, the grey fog closed once again over the heads of the two unaware women. Diere realized that she had gained an advantage—despite the fact George had botched the task.

Now she just had to figure out how to best capitalize on this turn of events. A host of ideas bubbled forth in her mind, as a smug smile stole across her delicate face.

But for the moment, she had to return to the Council Realm before she was missed.

The newly inspired Queen Mab LV transited back to her assigned chambers.

PADRAIC LOUNGED UPON the bed, boredom his sole expression. He brightened and rose up on his elbows as she appeared.

"You were right! Queen Titania *did* send an invitation, by messenger. The guards did as instructed and refused to admit him. He left that scroll tube for you—there, on that table."

Mab upended the tube and unfurled the scroll; she read silently, her face expressionless.

Padraic waited patiently. He already knew the contents, but feigned mild curiosity nonetheless.

"Well, what does it say?"

"Be patient—I am reading!"

Finally, she rolled the scroll and slid it back into the tube. Tossing it aside, she shrugged.

"It is as I expected. Titania wants to meet to begin renegotiations of certain agreements between the Seelie and Unseelie Courts."

He swung his feet off the bed and sat up. "Is that all?"

She favored him with a lone raised eyebrow and scoffed. "Ha! It is more than enough, and much too soon. I am not yet ready; so, I must put her off. I am also certain that she expects this; so, now we commence the diplomatic dance.

"However," she mused aloud, tapping a fingertip to her elegant jawline, "this plays to my advantage. It gives me time, and that is my need right now.

"Have there been any other developments while I was gone?"

"None that I am aware of." Padraic tilted his head. "Do you think she may broach renegotiating aspects of the Elfin Accords as well?"

She paused, and scoffed once more. "Hmmph, probably—I must put her off as long as I can."

"I see. Have you come to any decision about this man, George?"

"George? Oh, no . . . not yet."

She looked away, as if distracted, and resumed her seat at her dressing table.

He sensed her mind was elsewhere; so, he remained silent for the moment.

Where had she gone? What has changed? What is she thinking at this moment?

He must wait to see what she might reveal.

She turned back to him, her expression grim and determined.

"Padraic, send messengers to Lord Addecus of the Were and Lady Leanan of Shadow; they are here with their respective delegations. Invite them to meet me here, in half an hour—sooner, if possible."

"I'll see to it," he assured her, but then cautioned, "I understand the Council will resume its public session in just under an hour. If you intend to attend, that may be cutting it a bit close."

"Rest assured that I shall be in attendance," Mab said firmly. "My preliminary meeting will not be that long in duration. You should be there when the Council returns; should I be delayed, you may inform me of that which I might miss. Now, go—send the messages."

LORD ADDECUS STRODE alone down the corridor in the direction of the apartments of the Realm of the Dark Elves. He had not been surprised at the new Queen Mab's invitation; he'd been expecting something of the sort.

However, he was concerned after what he had witnessed in the Council's opening session. The Steward, Ellen Doyle, had certainly upset Diere's original plan; and now, he didn't know quite what to expect next. If nothing else, this was certainly turning out to be one of the more interesting Council meetings in recent memory.

Rounding a corner he saw a lone approaching figure, someone familiar—the Lady Leanan.

As they continued walking, each looked around carefully to be certain they were unobserved. They met at the intersection of the final corridor that led to the Dark Elves' delegation.

"M'lady, you ssseem well," Addecus said. "Are we alone? I would dissspenssse with our public pretenssse of mutual animosssity and baleful bickering on thisss occasssion."

"I think so, m'lord," Leanan ventured. "You have come in response to *her* invitation, I assume?"

"Aye, I have. Ssshould we find it ominousss that ssshe now requestsss both of usss?"

"Perhaps, but I admit I *am* curious. Her plans have obviously fallen apart, thanks to the Steward. She now plans something else; so, somehow she needs us. To be candid, she does not merit our trust."

"I mussst agree. Her plansss invariably expossse our realmsss to sssome sssort of jeopardy. The moment of reckoning may be at hand. I am no longer inclined to bend to her will."

"Nor am I. However, I think we have little choice but to hear her out."

Addecus did not need to respond, for they had arrived at their destination.

They were admitted and led to Queen Mab's private chamber.

THE NEW QUEEN MAB LV smiled, greeted her guests formally, and then declaring a need for privacy, dismissed the servants and guards. Her guests stood before her in silence.

"I am glad to see that you are not at each other's throats—that is good. Time is short, so I shall be brief. You are to instruct your Council representatives to vote *against* this Counselor. I will find another for the Chair of Man. Our plan has only experienced a minor setback, as you shall see. The Realm of Man will be laid open for you once again."

"Majesty, with all due respect," Leanan began, "we all know that will not happen."

"Do not *dare* to contradict me!" Mab spat vehemently. "You will do as you are told!"

"I think not," Addecus retorted, "not any longer—and not without good reasssonsss."

"What do you mean? You know the plan—what more do you need?" Mab demanded.

"The plan to open the Realm of Man for *hunting* and *harvesting* is a fool's goal—*and you should know better!*" Leanan decried, all pretense of royal courtesy absent.

"Mankind hasss grown far too dangerousss! You can no longer tempt the more bloodthirsssty among usss with sssuch fantasssiesss," Addecus warned.

"But the plan—" Mab began.

"Your *plan,*" interrupted Leanan, "is *nothing!*

"Be content that you now sit upon the throne of the Dark Elves. You will have problems enough ruling your home realm. Nothing you can offer will compel us to do your bidding. And as for having our respective realms' representatives vote against the Counselor for the Chair of Man, votes will be cast only in the best interest of our home realms—*not according to your whim!*"

Mab's face darkened with fury; her voice grew frigid with barely controlled anger.

"You forget yourself, Leanan! I remind you that *both* your realms are clearly implicated in the treasonous plot to assassinate—to *murder*—my dear cousin. *Regicide*, no less! Were I to make open accusations, the administrations of both realms—and yourselves, personally—would be in dire jeopardy."

Addecus made a dismissive gesture and shrugged. "Then do ssso! We dare you! We know that thisss *treasssonousss plot* wasss of your crafting!"

"And that the death of your cousin, Celeste, the late Queen Mab," Leanan finished, "was carefully orchestrated and arranged by *you!* And, any clues that may tend to implicate anyone else—or any other realms—were also created by *you*. You have always coveted the throne, and now you have seized it—indeed, through treachery!"

"Ssspare usss any usssselesss attempt at denial," Addecus interjected before Mab could speak. "And know thisss—there isss *proof* of your involvement."

His confident assertion gave Mab pause, but she continued to refute the allegations. "I do not know what you are talking about! I cannot believe a word of this!"

"Whatever you claim to believe or disbelieve does not matter," Leanan pointed out with equally obvious confidence. "It only matters what the Council and the other realms will choose to believe. And they would hear a very interesting tale about a young Were, enticed to come to Shadow, where he was ensorcelled by a powerful elfin adept. Bereft of his *identity* and *true name*, he was dubbed *Boltar*.

"And events were set in motion that would ensure that a certain scroll and Boltar would come into the presence of the doomed elfin queen."

Addecus continued the narrative. "But your plan wasss flawed. You did not anticipate that the young Were would be missed, or that hisss family would sssearch—and find him! True, by then he wasss dead, but that did not alter your essstablissshed ssstrategy."

"Enough!" Mab decried, her hands balled into fists of frustration. "What do you want?"

She was furious—they knew far too much! They would not be so confident if this boast of *proof* were merely a bluff. If but a trace of this story were to circulate, even as unfounded rumor, it could seriously undermine her reign—not to mention the very tenuous hold she had on the Unseelie voting bloc.

"You can offer nothing we want, nothing we need," Leanan said quietly.

"You ssseek power for the sssake of having more," Addecus explained. "Our needsss are vassstly different. Our populationsss are in sssteady declinesss and have been for over a century. Your promissse to open the Realm of Man for hunting and harvesssting had an undeniable appeal for many in our realmsss—repopulation ssseemed posssible. But the reality would have been disssasssterousss!"

"A reality *you* should understand better than most," Leanan interjected. "After all, you and I—as *Dee Dee* and *Leigh Ann*—spent considerable time with Maude in the Realm of Man. Have you forgotten how ominous we began to find Man's *soulless magic—technology?* Can you possibly be unaware of the catastrophic destruction of which Mankind is now capable?"

Mab was silent. In truth, she had never considered anything beyond making an offer that would likely appeal to the masses and the more shortsighted administrations of the other Unseelie realms. Getting their cooperation was all she cared about. However, if just some of the things that she remembered from her infrequent visits to the Realm of Man around the mid-twentieth century were still true, then she had seriously erred in her proposed enticement.

And now, she knew that her hold on the Unseelie voting bloc was crumbling. Her threats and attempted coercion had been effectively countered and checked by the very races she had tried to manipulate. Even the scheme to usurp control of the Chair of Man had failed.

Worse, she was in danger of having her plotting further exposed if that worthless fool, George, were to fall into the hands of the authorities of the Realm of Man. Now, there was a loose end that had to be dealt with very soon—very soon, indeed.

Something nagged at her . . . another loose end?

When Addecus had mentioned proof, a synapse flashed dimly in her memory, and until this moment she hadn't realized its significance.

Of course—a witness! . . . Salidar? It stands to reason—he is known to both Leanan and Addecus. And he knows far too much! Indeed, he would be most damaging as a witness! But does he still live? Do they have him?

Mab's mind raced. She had given Salidar no thought after she had refused to ransom him from some pirate in the Realm of Mer. She assumed he was slain, as his captors had threatened.

But what if he had survived—and escaped? Was he now a witness against me? Would he even trust Leanan or Addecus? What if they do not have him? Is that more likely? He certainly fears both of them!

But whether or not he is this witness—he would go to ground. He would be all too well aware that he knows too much—a loose end, indeed. Where would he go? Surely he would try to hide from me—but where? Ah, yes, where indeed . . .

A smug smile slowly stole across Mab's face, as her mind crafted a most elegant solution.

"Addecus, Leanan . . . Please, listen carefully," Mab began reasonably, and then paused to be certain she had their full attention.

"I have reason to believe—no—I *know* why your populations are in decline. Your people are leaving your realms—*sneaking away!* They find succor and shelter in another realm; and they flourish there."

"Pah! How can that be?" Addecus scoffed. "The Council doesss not permit masss migrationsss of indigenousss populationsss from one realm to another. That would upssset the balance ordained by the Dragon Accordsss."

"We would all be aware of another Council realm growing so greatly in population," confirmed Leanan. "That is not the sort of thing that would go unnoticed."

Mab's smug smile returned, and she picked at invisible lint at the wrist of her sleeve as she spoke.

"Oh, I think it would go unnoticed if the *refugees* were fleeing to a realm outside the Council, a realm not subject to the scope of Council law and influence, a realm not entitled to Council *protections.*"

"What are you sssaying? That our ssserfsss, ssslavesss, and laboring classsesss have been essscaping to a realm in the *wild?*"

"Exactly that, Addecus," Mab confirmed. "And it appears to have been going on for over a century, perhaps even longer."

"And just how did you come to know this?" asked Leanan, unconvinced yet clearly intrigued.

Mab's smile faded and she said, "I had occasion to trace the movements of, um, a *servant*, whom I did not fully trust. A bit of sorcery was required; that servant never knew that I learned this secret."

Leanan pressed, "And why did you wait until now to share this information with us?"

"To be honest, I did not put it all together until just now. At first, I thought this place was merely a smugglers' den, a hidden place in the *wild* to trade and dispose of stolen goods. But as I probed more deeply, using certain methods at my disposal, I found that there were far too many beings residing in that uncharted realm to be merely an isolated den of thieves."

"How many?" Addecus asked.

Mab shrugged. "I did not try to count—many thousands, I am certain. I now have no doubt that these are *your* missing populace. Oh yes, I learned even more; the place has a name, *Storm Haven*."

"Just where is this realm of Storm Haven?" probed Leanan.

"Now, *that* information you must bargain for," Mab countered, folding her arms. "You have something I want: your continued cooperation and solidarity as the Unseelie voting bloc on the Council; and your *silence* as it relates to these *scurrilous allegations* about the untimely passing of my dear cousin."

"And in return, we get the location of thisss realm of Ssstorm Haven—and have free rein to recover our misssing property?" Addecus pressed, still unconvinced.

"Quite so," Mab assured him. "The Council will not interfere—this is a realm in the *wild*. You may do there as you please."

"I mussst admit, thisss will appeal ssstrongly to the Adminissstration of Were. However, I know they will not blindly follow your insssructionsss in regard to voting asss a bloc on Council isssuesss."

"Nor will the Administration of Shadow cast Council votes as you would direct. We will always vote in our best interest," Leanan insisted. "Now if that were to coincide with your intent on a given issue, then the Unseelie bloc would be seen as intact—that is the best you may hope for. Compliance will be coincidental, at best. So, you should come to expect disagreement on some issues.

"For example, the pending vote on the Chair of Man—you may as well put that from your mind. It is already a moot issue. Shadow will vote in its own interest."

However, Mab was not put off.

"Listen to me! I am offering a solution to the single most significant problem facing both of your realms. All I ask in return is cooperation in voting on Council issues, and your continued silence, of course."

"Neither the Lady Leanan nor I can bind our ressspective adminissstrationsss to your *voting* demandsss," Addecus reminded Mab, "even if we were inclined to do ssso. We can only convey your offer; and, we have already predicted the ressspponssse. Trussst me, that isss a foregone conclusssion.

"However, our sssilence in the matter of your cousssin'sss untimely demissse isss entirely another matter—one that I think may be more important to you than you would care to admit. Tell usss now, isss that not an isssue worthy of further negotiation?"

"Indeed," agreed Leanan. "The truth is that you need us—*our silence*—more than we need you. Now that we know about the existence of this realm of Storm Haven, it is only a matter of time before we find it on our own, as you well know. So, what is it that you are *not* telling us? What is it that may be worth our silence?"

Diere had never been a good negotiator; she was much more in the habit of making demands and having her every whim catered to. How ironic that now, as Queen Mab LV, she was compelled to *bargain* like a common merchant. Worse, she was dealing with two individuals who had always despised one another—and yet here they were, working in tandem like a shrewd brace of hagglers at a country market.

Mab was exasperated, her patience spent.

"Listen to me, you ingrates," she finally spat. "You might eventually find Storm Haven; but you will never breach its defenses! They are in a constant state of preparedness in the event of any attempt at invasion. As I understand it, those preparations are quite formidable. They will only be taken by guile, stealth, and surprise."

"And you have sssome way to accomplisssh thisss?" Addecus asked.

Mab's face slowly creased into the most sinister of smiles.

"Oh, yes . . . I most certainly do."

CH 13

GEORGE WAS FRIGHTENED and angry. He knew he was in serious trouble; but to his way of thinking, it wasn't his fault.

No, not *his* at all!

Diere's information had been faulty; and then Ling had to go and grab *two* women.

Hell! I wasn't even there!

None of this mess was his fault. Nonetheless, it was his life on the line—of that fact, he held no illusions. He knew the real problem was that he was no longer of any use to Lady Diere.

Oh, excuse me, I should say "Queen Mab". Oh man, what an ego—what a bitch!

Of course, he couldn't really fault her; because, in a slightly perverse way, he understood her. He would have no difficulty, no second thoughts, arranging the disappearance of someone who was no longer an asset, especially someone who knew too much, and had thus become a liability. He'd certainly done it often enough.

And now, to make matters worse—*cops!* Cops from his home world were here—*here in the Council Realm*—to take him back in handcuffs to face a court. He knew without a doubt that was something this new Queen Mab would never allow to happen.

He was a dead man; it was only a matter of time.

Sufficiently despondent, he sat on the edge of the bed in the small, windowless sleeping chamber and sighed heavily. Even if he could get out of this locked room, there were two elfin guards posted on the other side of the door, and another pair in the outer chamber. If, by some miracle, he could get past them, where would he go? He couldn't even transit out of this isolated

Council Realm unaided; Daegon had yet to show him how, even though he had promised.

The flame of the small oil lamp wavered as if teased by an errant breeze. However, the air was still; the door remained tightly locked. The flame rippled violently and twisted upon itself as it lost its saffron-amber glow and turned a sickly green with flares of sparkling purple within its heart.

Pressure steadily grew in the room. George felt his panic rising as he crabbed back across the bed on his heels and elbows. Wedging himself into a corner, he stared in disbelief as a small dark amorphous mass appeared, suspended in midair, near the middle of the room. It seemed to gain substance from the very shadows, slowly increasing in size and assuming a generally spherical shape.

When it was about the height of the doorway, it solidified into a glossy black ball reflecting the sole lamp's baleful light and George's stunned face—*a transit globe?*

A man stepped out of the sphere.

George gasped, *"Daegon?"*

"Aye, now be quiet! I can see you are in a spot of trouble. As you once rescued me, I would return the favor. But first, I have some questions."

George leapt to his feet. "Questions? We don't have time for this! When she comes back, she's going to kill me! We have to get out of here, now!"

Daegon shoved a stiff finger into George's chest. "Keep your voice down and listen! I found out what happened to my queen. It was no accident, or some bungled mistake with a spell casting by that fool, Atrellan! No! She was *murdered!* It was a deliberate *assassination!* I strongly suspect the elf who now holds the throne—this Lady Diere of the House of Hawthorn."

"Yeah?" George retorted sarcastically. "Well, she calls herself 'Queen Mab LV' now. And I wouldn't put the murder of your queen past her—that's what she plans to do to *me* when she returns. Now, can we get out of here?"

"Not yet," Daegon said firmly. "As I said, I have some questions. I know you serve this Lady Diere. What do you know of a plot against my queen?"

"Not a damned thing! Look, Daegon, I admit I did do some things for her—Lady Diere—but I don't know anything about your queen. I don't doubt that Diere did it; but do you really think that she would let me in on her plans—*especially to take out a queen?*

"Look, her purpose for me was to sit in the Chair of Man, where she thought she could pull my strings, you know? But now, even that deal is off the table; the Council declared me ineligible just because of some trifling legal issues back home. So now, I'm of no use to her—and worse, I know too much about some stuff she's involved in. So, she sees me now only as a liability. She has to get rid of me, which she will, as soon as she comes back here. We really have to go!"

"So, you knew nothing about the murder of my queen? You had no involvement in her assassination? You no longer serve this *usurper?* Is that correct?"

"Yes, correct, absolutely correct! Let's go!" urged George, gesturing to the black sphere.

"Do you agree to serve me, as my apprentice, as we once discussed?" Daegon asked evenly.

"Sure," George responded impatiently.

"Then so swear, in a binding oath, using your true name," Daegon insisted.

For an instant, George paused. Something about the solemnity of Daegon's voice alerted his instincts that this was no idle request. But all along, George had wanted to learn more magic—and magic was power. Could this be just what he really wanted?

"And you'll teach me—the magic, I mean?" he asked.

"I will, my apprentice," Daegon narrowed his eyes, and added, "*if* you give me your oath."

"Very well," shrugged George, who then swore as Daegon instructed. "By the Powers of Air and Earth, Fire and Water, I, George Papadolis, hereby swear to serve you, Daegon, as your apprentice, until you teach me all about magic. Will that do?"

"Oh yes, quite well," answered Daegon, a sinister smile spreading across his face.

"Great! *Now* can we leave this place?" George kept glancing at the dark transit globe.

"Not yet," Daegon said, stroking his chin. "It would not do—not without leaving a calling card. You say this pretender, Lady Diere, will return here, for you?"

"Hell, yes! What are we waiting for?"

"There are guards outside this chamber?" Daegon asked casually as he pointed toward the locked door.

"Yeah, two big warrior-elves . . . Why?"

Daegon smiled ominously. "Hmm, they will do. Alert them—call them in here."

"What? Are you *nut*—" George started to babble.

"Silence! Do not question me!" fumed Daegon. Purple sparks flared in his dark eyes. "Just do as I say! Watch and learn, apprentice, watch and learn. Now, call them!"

ELLEN AND HER COMPANIONS arrived back in their assigned quarters.

Trey and Hawk started making plans related to taking Papa George into custody.

Mark gestured Ellen aside for a quiet, and overdue, conversation.

"El', I wished you'd have let me know you were going to propose me for the Chair of Man. That nearly freaked me out! I'm already on edge over Stacy and your mom; you know I'll do anything to get them both back safely. I guess I'm trying to say that you didn't have to *blindside* me."

"Oh, Mark, I know, and I'm sorry about that. I would have told you ahead of time, but the truth is that it was a kind of *sudden inspiration*. I mean, let's face it—it's the kind of thing you'd be great at. We both know it. And it was just the right move to keep Queen Mab off balance. You have to admit, she was not pleased to see me, was she?"

"Oh, I think we can agree on that point!" Mark chuckled. "That further suggests that she is at least cognizant, if not directly involved, with the kidnapping."

"Hmm, have you picked up on any intentions from her—or anyone else for that matter?" Ellen tilted her head.

"No, to be honest I haven't really tried," he admitted. "I'm a little leery about the warning we heard that no magic supposedly works here. I don't want to trip any alarms, or offend our hosts."

"You know what? I'm not so sure that warning applies to passive abilities," Ellen mused aloud. "I think it's intended to restrict the overt casting of spells and the like. If you can feel something passively, without deliberate intention and overt effort, it may not be a problem.

"I let my awareness expand when we were being led by Selene through the secret passages—which are quite extensive, by the way—and I didn't seem to trip any alarms. For what it's worth, I think you should just keep it in mind—just in case the right circumstances present themselves."

"Look, El', I just don't want to mess anything up," he confessed, and bared his heart. "Sometimes all I can think about is Stacy—how much I don't want to lose her. I'm sure you feel the same way about your mom, you know?"

"Yeah, well, maybe not the *exact same way*," she teased, "but I know what you mean. It seems like I've just recently found my mom again; I don't want to lose her."

They were interrupted by a soft chime at the chamber door. Madam Moya had come for Mark; the Council was ready for him.

Trey and Hawk wished him luck.

Ellen pecked him on the cheek and teased, "Just be a lawyer—they won't comprehend a thing."

Mark smiled. "They don't call me *Counselor* for nothing!" With a wink, he mimed straightening an imaginary tie, turned and followed Madam Moya from their chambers.

LATER, MARK RETURNED to their assigned rooms to find his companions in hushed conversation with three individuals he did not know; a demure female elf wearing a pale-yellow diaphanous ceremonial robe, a gray-bearded dwarf in a heavy blue robe trimmed in ornately carved leather, and a tall lanky man, of unfortunate appearance, with bulging eyes and a wide smiling mouth, attired in a green and black robe, and holding a bright red cap in his webbed hands.

Ellen smiled at Mark's entrance and rose to greet him.

"Oh, I'm so glad you're back, Mark! How did it go?"

"Uh, fine, I guess," he responded with a hint of reticence.

"I knew it! Didn't I tell you? I can't wait to hear all the details," she exclaimed, patting his cheeks.

"Of course," he retorted, grasping her hands, "but later. Now aren't you going to introduce me to our *guests?*"

"Oh, I'm sorry." She chuckled and tugged him across the room as the guests stood.

"My friends, this is my cousin Mark, also known as the *Counselor*. Mark, let me introduce Lady Maura of the Light Elves, Rolf Ravensward of the Dwarves, and Finley Merrow of Mer. Please, everyone sit down, relax. We have at least twenty minutes before the Council resumes its session."

Ellen took Mark's hand. "I'll explain the significance of our visitors' presence. First of all, our guests *aren't really here*—understand? This is a very informal and *unofficial* meeting as far as the Council may be concerned."

"Uh, fine, whatever you say, Ellen." Mark acknowledged with a shrug, his curiosity growing.

"Good. These are the people I told you about, who Gallenius introduced me to yesterday morning on the forest path. We can trust them."

Mark nodded. "I understand. But why are they here, now?"

Ellen smiled. "To confirm that we have reestablished the agreements and bonds that they originally formed with Maude. Each of them arranged to be included in their respective realms' delegation to this Council meeting, thereby providing the opportunity for all of us to meet without any unwelcome scrutiny or suspicion. I'll explain more later, but for now, let me tell you a little about our friends.

"Lady Maura teaches and trains young elves in the ways of all manner of plants. Per the agreement with Maude, Maura and her students tended the trees, plants, and flowers of the farm; in return, they were granted free access to the entire property—especially the old growth forest. Their very presence lightens the heart of our forest."

The delicate elfin maid smiled and demurely lowered her eyes, as Ellen continued.

"Rolf Ravensward is a Master Distiller of the Dwarven Guild of Brew Masters and Distillers. Remember the still we found in the cave in our forest?

Well, it will be up and running again in no time. Rolf tells me that it would be an honor if we would consent to sampling the Guild's finest products distilled in our forest."

The stout dwarf smiled mischievously and winked at Mark, who couldn't help but chuckle in return.

Trey and Hawk grinned broadly and bobbed their heads.

"Finley Merrow of Mer has overseen the general health of the ecosystem of our deep freshwater lake, a favorite place to visit for his people—a sort of vacation spot for their families. They will renew both their oversight and their frequent visits."

Another voice, musically liquid, interrupted. "I hate to disturb you, but time grows short. All should return to their delegations before they are missed."

The voice was Selene's, who stepped forth from an open hidden panel in the wall.

The guests rose and nodded to Selene, and then bade Ellen and her companions farewell, acknowledging that in all likelihood they would not visit with her again until she returned to Delafaire Farm.

Selene was the last to disappear into the hidden passage, but she paused and smiled at Mark.

"By the way, congratulations, Counselor. It seems the Council members were rather impressed with you during your questioning session. We expect that there will only be a single vote against your ascension to the Chair of Man."

Mark was clearly surprised. "But, I—uh, I mean, but how do you know? It was only ten or fifteen minutes ago that I left that session."

Selene only smiled wryly. "Elsbeth already told you; 'assume the very walls have eyes and ears'. Now, I must go."

The panel slid silently back into place, absent any trace of the hidden door.

"Mark, don't look so shocked. I assume that is good news," Ellen reasoned. "Now can you tell us what happened? You were in there for over half an hour."

"Well, yeah, I assume I can talk about it—I mean, I wasn't told otherwise. I just sat in a single chair before all the Council members, who were seated at this long table, in a closed room. They asked questions; and I answered. It was as simple as that."

"Yeah, but what *kind of questions?* What did they ask?" probed Hawk.

Mark scratched his head. "Mostly about what I knew about the other realms, and whether or not I personally could perform any *magic* or *sorcery.*" He shrugged. "I know how that sounds—I thought it was a little ridiculous, too. But they were *serious.* They wanted to know how many other people in our world—the Realm of Man, I mean—know about any of the other realms. Let me see, what else? Oh yes, how our system of justice worked, and how I felt about that. You know, it was a lot like sitting through a *voir dire* session in court."

"Anything else?" asked Trey. "Did they ask anything about George Papadolis?"

"No," Mark said thoughtfully, "they didn't. In fact, I got the impression they were deliberately avoiding the subject while I was present. I was finally excused; so, I left the room. No one else left; so, I assume they were still in session and took up the discussion about Papa George once I'd gone."

"Did the kidnapping of my mother and Stacy come up at all?" asked Ellen, a hint of strain in her voice.

"No, I'm sorry." Mark shook his head. "Nothing was said. Do you think *I* should have said something? Or about that we think Papa George has something to do with it?"

"No, it's best that we don't tip our hand at this point," Trey cautioned. "We really don't know who on the Council can be trusted, so it's best not to appear overly anxious to get our hands on Papa George. We don't know for certain who else may be involved. Look at it this way; officially we've made a legal claim, on the record, before a governing body. I don't see how they can deny it. If necessary, once Mark is seated as a full member, he can bring more pressure to bear if they seem reluctant to rule in our favor."

Once again a soft chime announced a presence at the door of their suite, a brownie from the Clerk's staff, who formally announced that the Council would reconvene its session in a few minutes.

As they prepared to return, Hawk drolly observed, "Well, it seems we're not going to have to wait too long to see if Mark has a new job—and if Papa George gets some nice new stainless-steel jewelry."

A pair of handcuffs dangled from his outstretched finger.

Trey scowled, trying not to smile. "Put those away, young grasshopper. Premature celebration often leads to karmic disappointment."

"Hmm, profound," Hawk teased. "Was that Confucius?"

"That was your sage and most wise sergeant, Detective," Trey responded solemnly. "Now, let's go."

SVENGARD THORENSON called the Council back into session. The chamber was as crowded as before, and it took a moment before the audience settled and the inherent rustling of stragglers finding their seats appreciably diminished.

At a gesture from the chairperson, Madam Moya stepped to the center of the dais and announced that Mark Paige of the Realm of Man was to present himself before the Council. When Mark joined her, she favored him with a small smile and left him facing the moderator.

"Mark Paige, known as the Counselor, of the Realm of Man," intoned Svengard Thorenson formally, "be it known that the Council finds you to be an acceptable candidate for election. If elected, you will be seated in the Chair of Man, and assume all powers, duties, and responsibilities related to the representation of your home realm. Do you understand, and are you willing to proceed at this time with the election?"

"I do understand, Lord Thorenson, and I am willing to proceed."

The moderator polled each Council member. As Selene had predicted, the only vote against Mark was cast by Lady Malvana of the Dark Elves.

QUEEN MAB SAT WITH Padraic at her side in the first row behind her avatar. Her face had adopted a slight scowl at Svengard Thorenson's opening remarks, and it had yet to leave her countenance. Her attention was no longer focused upon the formalities unfolding upon the dais.

There was nothing more she could do to prevent Mark's election to the Chair of Man. She was angry and frustrated that this aspect of her plans had been derailed—all thanks to Ellen Doyle. However, she was not one to lament over her failures; she had to focus on salvaging what she could from the mess George had made. How could she still capitalize on the kidnapping of the Steward's mother?

Padraic leaned closer and whispered, "You appear distracted. Is all well, Majesty?"

She merely shrugged and ignored him, as general applause erupted throughout the chamber when the newest Council member formally took his seat in the Chair of Man.

The moderator's next words galvanized her attention.

"Madam Clerk, we will now address the issue of the ineligible candidate's disposition. Is the former candidate, George Papadolis, present?"

Moya quickly scanned the seats in the rows near the Chair of the Dark Elves; the ineligible candidate was not present.

Lady Malvana, obviously not happy with what was about to transpire, spoke up resignedly. "M'lord, that man is being held in our custody, pursuant to the order of Her Majesty, Queen Mab."

"I see. Very well, we can and shall proceed without him," Svengard declared. "The Council discussed this matter at some length in the closed session, and it has been determined that the Realm of Man has a legitimate and legal claim on this man. It has been further determined that, notwithstanding the position taken by the Realm of Dark Elves, and in consideration of the recent opportunity they have had to question him, it is in the best interest of the Council Realms that he now be turned over to the authorities of the Realm of Man, represented here by two law enforcement officials who bear the appropriate documentation. Accordingly, Lady Malvana, the Council directs you to so inform your queen, and arrange for the transfer of custody of the person of George Papadolis to the sentinels."

Lady Malvana remained silent, looking desperately aside for guidance from Queen Mab.

A wave of shocked gasps and low murmurs flowed across the assembly as Diere rose in a huff and stormed from the chamber, Padraic and her guards in her wake.

THE CHAIRPERSON IGNORED the rude breach of decorum, and turned instead to Mark, who was now seated in the Chair of Man.

"Lord Mark, please arrange for the law enforcement officials to meet the sentinels on the concourse at the entrance to the enclave of the Dark Elves. There they may assume custody of their prisoner."

"At once, m'lord," responded Mark, as he made a gesture to Hawk and Trey.

THE DETECTIVES ROSE and left the chamber, with Ellen close on their heels. They wasted no time in going directly to the entrance of the reception hall of the Dark Elfin Enclave.

Four very large and immobile gargoyles stood facing the open doorway; they were so still they could have easily been mistaken for statues. One, with a hooked beak and large pointed ears, turned, raised a broad clawed hand at the end of an overly long arm, heavily roped with sinew and muscle, and stopped the three companions from crossing the threshold.

He remained silent, and stared deeply into Ellen's eyes.

Startled, she balked as thoughts not her own seemed to form in her mind. Then she understood—he was warning her of the danger.

Hmm, some sort of telepathy?

"Hawk, Trey! Listen, we have to stop, here. We can't cross that threshold—it's *warded*," she warned.

"What? You mean *magic?* How do you know?" asked Trey, with more than a trace of frustration in his voice.

"Well, I remember that Selene mentioned it when we visited with Elsbeth." She pointed to the sentinel. "But, I think he just told me, and saved us from making a potentially serious mistake."

To the huge gargoyle, she added, "Thank you."

The massive sentinel nodded once and turned back toward the entrance. He and another sentinel stepped across the threshold. There was an immediate *zap* and the smell of ozone; but the two gargoyles were unaffected and continued to move deeper into the reception area. The other two remained just outside the threshold, as still as stone.

Suddenly, screams and unholy howls of rage erupted from a dark hallway beyond the reception area, followed by sounds of close combat and chaos.

The two sentinels who had entered rushed toward the hallway, just as a bloodied Padraic emerged, staggering under the burden of Queen Mab, unconscious and bleeding.

"Unh . . . They come . . . behind me," he gasped to the sentinels as he plodded forward under the weight of the queen. "Two guards . . . turned on her . . . attacked us . . . other guards are fighting them, but nothing stops them . . . some sort of spell, I think."

The sentinels assumed defensive postures at the hallway entrance and maintained an intense focus on the sounds of the struggle that were growing ominously closer.

"This way!" Ellen cried out to the wounded man, her urge to rush to his aid nearly overpowering. "Come to us! We can't cross the threshold—you must come to us!"

He looked to her, hefted his burden, and struggled forward.

Something flew over him from the hallway, spewing an arc of crimson spray. Thudding on the polished floor, it bounced and rolled near the threshold—the wide-eyed, decapitated head of an elfin guard.

Accompanied by a prolonged shriek of utter madness, a blood-soaked figure with dead eyes—wearing the tattered remnants of an elfin guard's uniform—emerged holding a headless body above him on stiffened arms. The corpse was still spurting blood in ever-diminishing pulses from its ravaged neck. With seemingly little effort, the guard howled and threw the body at the nearest sentinel, who stumbled back under the impact.

Another bloodied and gore-stained elfin guard staggered forth from the chaotic inner sanctum of the Dark Elves, dragging the dismembered leg of another victim, the raggedly shredded thigh trailing bright streaks of warm blood. One of the guard's eyes, ripped from its socket in recent combat, dangled on his blood-slickened cheek like a macabre ornament. A huge gash had cleaved the crown of his skull from ear to nose; swells of glistening pink brain matter bulged out, a mortal blow. Nonetheless, this hulking bespelled guard rocked his head back at an impossible angle and uttered his own anguished cry of tormented rage. He then slowly started swinging the sundered limb like a club, in wide, gore-splattering arcs.

Padraic, chest heaving and sucking deep breaths, crossed the outer threshold and dropped to his knees.

Trey and Hawk, keeping a wary eye on the two demonic guards, eased the wounded woman from Padraic's arms to the ground.

Ellen began quickly checking the elfin woman's injuries. A scalp wound had bled freely but was now only a trickle, and a dark bruise was forming on her opposite cheek. Worse, a set of deep slashes descended from one shoulder down the back of that arm. The bleeding was considerable; but, it appeared the artery had been spared.

At that moment, the two ensorcelled guards spotted their quarry.

Shrieking with rage, they advanced in a determined lurching stagger toward the wounded queen—only to be blocked by the two sentinels, who were immediately attacked.

The fight was vicious and brutal. The guard swinging the bloody leg ruthlessly hammered at a gargoyle who could not block all the blows as he fell back. Another sentinel tried to grapple with the other berserk guard, but the blood-slickened elfin armor offered no purchase, and the sorcerously enhanced strength of the cursed guard seemed more than a match for the gargoyle's own.

Despite receiving a host of mortal injuries, the relentless guards slowly pushed the two sentinels back, the battle coming ever closer to the semiconscious queen.

The remaining two sentinels leapt to their comrades' aid, joining the furious fray.

His hand on the butt of his holstered pistol, Hawk shouted, "We have to move her! They're getting too close!"

Looking around, Ellen spied an invitingly open door across the wide expanse of the concourse and pointed. "There! Let's get them both inside and secure that door!"

Trey scooped up the injured queen, as Hawk helped her exhausted consort to his feet.

"I am fine," Padraic muttered tiredly, nonetheless grateful for the assistance. "All this blood . . . is not mine."

With Ellen urging them on, they made it to the dubious safety of what appeared to be an empty storage room of some kind.

Ellen took a last look down the concourse and saw reinforcements en route; more of the large sentinels running, and a handful of smaller gargoyles flying on stubby leather wings. Closer, she noticed that a number of other people began to appear from side corridors, drawn by morbid curiosity toward the disturbance.

Ellen shut the door, cursed that there was no lock, and turned her attention to the wounded.

Despite his blood-splattered robe, Padraic had no open wounds, but his hands and arms bore blossoming bruises. A lump the size of an egg was rising on the crown of his head. His back to a wall, he slid down to a sitting position and held his throbbing head, his elbows braced upon his knees.

As Ellen had already assessed, Queen Mab's injuries were more severe, but not life threatening. Taking a large bandanna from Hawk, she busied herself bandaging the queen's arm snugly enough to stop the bleeding.

"SIR . . . SIR?"

Padraic heard a voice at his shoulder, the older of the two men, he thought.

"Sir, can you tell us what happened?"

Padraic's head lolled to one side, resting on his crossed forearms. Through half-lidded eyes, he stared at Ellen as she ministered to Mab's wounds. Here he was, within an arm's reach of his daughter—*his daughter!*

"Sir, stay with us now," the voice said firmly as Padraic's eyes drooped. "Can you tell us what happened?"

The younger man stooped to Padraic's other side and pointed.

"Some head trauma here, Trey, probably a concussion. We have to keep him conscious—don't let him nod off."

"Right," agreed the first voice.

"Sir, can you tell us your name? Come on, now, you heard Hawk; you might have a concussion. So, you have to stay awake—talk to us. We need to know what happened. Let's start with your name. Can you tell us your name?"

Padraic wearily lifted his head. He considered the two men hunched over him.

Trey and Hawk? Ah yes, the policemen from the Realm of Man.

He intuitively understood they were only trying to help. He mustered his strength.

"I am Padraic . . . She, Queen Mab, went to . . . the room in which the man, George, was kept under guard . . . She had four of her guards with her. I heard screams and a loud commotion. I ran to the sound . . . She was on the floor, dazed from a blow, I think.

"Her four guards were fighting with the two guards who had been watching the prisoner—he was nowhere to be seen. These two guards were bespelled somehow; their strength was incredible, not even mortal blows could stop them . . .

"I tried to lift the queen and carry her from the room, but I was battered from behind and found myself briefly drawn into the melee. I managed to get free, and tried again to remove the queen. As I got her to her feet, one of the berserk guards grabbed for her and slashed the back of her shoulder and arm. She fainted and I managed to carry her out, toward the main entrance.

"I think all of her loyal guards were slain, and the other two came after the queen. They meant to kill her—of that I have no doubt."

Trey leaned closer. "Okay . . . Now you said there was no sign of the prisoner, more precisely that 'he was nowhere to be seen'. Has he escaped?"

"I do not know, but I suspect so," Padraic admitted.

"Hey guys," Ellen interrupted urgently, "I think she's coming around."

MAB ROLLED HER HEAD from side to side and groaned. Her head hurt and her arm throbbed. She opened her eyes, but for a moment saw only vague shapes. Her vision cleared, and she realized with a shock that she was looking into the concerned face of Ellen Doyle, the Steward.

"Where . . . where am I?" Mab asked, groggily. "What happened?"

"You are safe," Ellen said.

Padraic crawled to her side. "Majesty, you were attacked by ensorcelled guards, and you have been injured. But you are now safe, I believe—at least for the moment."

Hawk went to the door, opened it a crack, and carefully peered outside. After a moment of careful observation, he turned quietly to the others. "Actually, we may all be safe. I think it's over; there's a crowd near the scene now."

"Majesty," Padraic urged, rising slowly to stand, "we must get you to a healer."

"You will both need medical attention," stated Ellen. "Hawk, is it safe enough to leave here?"

He pulled the door fully open and stepped beyond, returning a moment later to confirm his assessment. "Yeah, it's over. The sentinels have the guards restrained. In fact, you may want to see this."

Ellen offered her hand to Mab, "Can you stand . . . uh, Your Majesty?"

She ignored Ellen's offer, and instead pulled herself up using Padraic to steady her stance.

Trey asked Padraic, "Sir, are you all right?"

Forcing a smile, Padraic responded, "I am fine, thank you. Please, lead on. I am sure we are all ready to leave."

Trey nodded to Hawk, who led Padraic and Queen Mab out of the room and across the concourse.

A FEW PACES BEHIND, Trey leaned toward Ellen and whispered, "He's an all right guy; but she doesn't seem to be the grateful type, does she?"

Ellen just shrugged; she'd been thinking much the same thing, but remained silent.

More whispers preceded them and the crowd parted as Queen Mab, leaning heavily on Padraic's arm, was recognized. They made their way toward the center of the gathering.

There, no less than a dozen sentinels restrained the two ensorcelled guards. A number of aloof individuals, wearing the robes of mages, stood in close consultation before the two captives. To one side, stood the Council members, including Mark—who visibly relaxed when he saw that Ellen, Hawk, and Trey were unharmed.

Svengard Thorenson stepped forward and was about to address the assembled adepts, when the two bespelled guards spied Queen Mab.

Howling in anguished rage, they strove to break free of the restraining sentinels and attack the Dark Elfin Queen once again. But the sentinels proved too strong; it became evident after a few moments that the doomed guards' struggles were in vain.

Suddenly they went rigid. Harsh green light shone forth from every wound and orifice. It was as if a flaring verdant fire was consuming both of them internally. The mob of spectators drew back, as a wave of heat singed some who stood too close. The shafts of light turned to a malignant purple and grew in strength, but the sentinels did not release their grip on the prisoners.

There was a sudden *whooshing* sound, an incandescent flare of blinding purple light.

The sentinels were left holding only handfuls of crumbling grey ash. The ensorcelled guards were gone—immolated from within.

The shocked crowd was deathly silent and apprehensive as a stunned Svengard Thorenson joined the mages in hushed conversation. More than a few souls cast furtive glances periodically in the direction of the Dark Elfin Enclave.

The Dwarven Lord gestured for a sentinel to attend him, and spoke softly to the gargoyle. The sentinel then motioned to his companions, and they all filed silently into the enclave.

Thorenson then saw Queen Mab, and approached her solicitously.

"Your Majesty, I have sent for healers. Can you help us to understand what has happened here?"

Mab stood a little straighter, eschewing Padraic's supporting arm, and mustered her dignity.

"Two of my own guards attacked me. I went to *question* the human, George Papadolis. Two guards assigned to hold him in custody went berserk, as you have seen."

"Indeed, Majesty," he agreed, "but what of this man—was he slain as well?"

"I do not know," she admitted. "Both of the traitorous guards were within the chamber in which he was being held, but I did not see *him*."

The sentinels emerged from the elfin apartments.

Thorenson excused himself and went to meet them. After a few brief moments he stepped forward and consulted with the mages once more. Finally, he turned and addressed the crowd.

"Your attention, please . . . The sentinels have searched the Dark Elfin Enclave and have found no living thing. Sadly, all those within have perished. There is no sign of the man, George Papadolis, and it may be that he escaped. I will not mince words. We all saw what we saw, and many among us know what it means, and what it portends. This was no doubt a foul act akin to *necromancy!* Some aspect of the forbidden Black Art was conjured *here*—in the very heart of the Council—in blatant disregard for the most sacrosanct restriction of the Dragon Accords!"

A collective gasp rose from the crowd. Lord Thorenson shuddered and seemed to shrink slightly within himself as he continued to speak.

"I am saddened beyond words . . . I, like you, am offended and alarmed at such ominous temerity. At this time, I ask that you all return to your chambers, and give these matters your full consideration. The Council will reconvene in one hour, and we would like to hear any constructive thoughts and suggestions—through your representatives, of course—in regard to this dire event and what it bodes for our future."

As the crowd began to disperse, the healers arrived and immediately began tending to Queen Mab and Padraic.

SVENGARD THORENSON approached Ellen and drew her off to one side.

"Lady Ellen, I am told that we have you and your escort to thank for the timely rescue of Queen Mab and her consort. Indeed, that you simply disappeared with them as the danger drew nigh?"

Ellen shrugged. "Well, Lord Thorenson, we did what anyone would have done, I'm sure. But we hardly 'disappeared'; we merely sought refuge in a convenient room directly across the concourse."

"Room?" asked the Dwarven Lord. "What room would that be?"

"Why, that one," Ellen explained as she swept her arm up to point at what now appeared to be a blank wall. "Um, I thought it was right over there . . . but now I don't see it."

"Perhaps you were confused in the excitement, m'lady," he offered sympathetically. "It is really of no consequence. I only needed to ascertain that you did not invoke a *transit spell* within these walls. As you were told upon your arrival, transit spells may only be used in designated arrival and departure areas, or within the member realms' enclaves. Any attempt to do so elsewhere would be frustrated and defeated by certain wards in place throughout the common areas of the Council Realm."

"You may rest assured, m'lord, that I made no such attempt," Ellen responded coolly. "Madam Moya was quite clear in her introductory remarks. I would not presume to disregard the rules of the Council."

"If you please, m'lady," he said contritely, "I intended neither rebuke nor criticism, and certainly no offense."

"None taken, m'lord," she replied graciously, allowing her gaze to slide past him and consider the blank wall across the concourse.

"Then, if you will excuse me, m'lady," he bowed briefly and signaled for a passing brownie to attend him.

Ellen took several steps toward the vast expanse of the now blank wall.

There had been a room there—its door open and inviting, just when we needed it . . .

NEAR THE ENTRANCE TO the Dark Elfin Enclave, Trey and Hawk pulled Mark aside.

"Listen, Mark," Trey whispered, "we need to get in there and see for ourselves. Could you approach the chairman, Svengard Thorenson, for permission to conduct our own search of the *crime scene?*"

"Sure, no problem," Mark agreed. "Come with me."

Unfortunately, the Dwarven Lord could not help them.

"Counselor, please understand that only the Dark Elfin Queen can grant such access and suspend the protective wards. But as a gesture of goodwill, allow me to accompany you and convey your request."

However Queen Mab, still with the healers, refused—without explanation—and turned her back.

The Dwarven Lord pursed his lips in disapproval and slowly shook his head. The three men could see that Thorenson had had about enough of this Dark Elf's disrespect, but that he dared not rebuke her.

Thorenson nodded sympathetically to Mark and the detectives, shrugged his shoulders, and walked away.

A FEW PACES AWAY, PADRAIC, ever observant, had missed none of that exchange. He saw that Trey and Hawk were clearly irritated with Mab's refusal. They mumbled something to Mark, who smirked but chose to keep silent and led them away from the Dark Elf.

Padraic thought it graceless for Mab to snub their rescuers under the circumstances.

Apparently, he was not alone.

A light female voice, like a spring breeze through lilacs, teasingly chided Queen Mab.

"Oh my, *dear sister*, I would think you would find it rather *impolite* to decline a request from those who may have just saved your life. But then again, you *poor dear*, you are hardly quite yourself these days, what with all this *bother* with which one must now contend."

As the healers wrapped a poultice of herbs in a bandage around her wounded arm, Mab turned her head to see Queen Titania of the Light Elves standing behind her.

"You will forgive my momentary lapse of courtly manners, *sister,*" seethed Mab, "but as you can clearly see, I have been injured."

"Oh dear, how *distressing*," oozed Titania in mock sympathy. "Does this mean you will not be available for a meeting this night? We really do have *so much* to discuss."

"Perhaps some other time, *sister*," Mab responded, in equally mock earnestness. "I fear that I would be *such* poor company in my present condition. I am certain that you understand."

"Alas, as you wish," Titania conceded, and added, "One must take care of one's health. Holding on to a throne can be so *precarious*, can it not, *sister?*"

Padraic could almost hear Mab grind her teeth as Queen Titania turned in a swirl of diaphanous skirts and strolled away.

UNFORTUNATELY, ELLEN had missed this exchange between the elfin queens.

Scanning the crowd, Titania suddenly altered her course and came before Ellen.

"Why, Lady Ellen, is it not? I am so pleased to meet you." Titania's greeting held little warmth.

"Good evening, Your Majesty." Ellen mimicked Madam Moya's clever combination of bow and curtsy. "This is indeed an honor."

"My congratulations on your appointment as Steward," the queen said blandly. "You must come and visit me in the Realm of Light Elves, perhaps even attend the Seelie Court. Now, you really *must* visit—say two days hence?"

"Majesty? Forgive me," Ellen stammered, "but did you say 'two days hence'?"

Titania merely raised a single eyebrow, as if she did not believe she was just asked to repeat herself.

Ellen noted the unconscious gesture of privileged conceit, but continued as if she had not.

"If so, with all due respect, Your Majesty, I must decline—the issue is the *timing*. Unfortunately, I am presently dealing with a personal crisis of significant magnitude. You see, my mother and a close friend have been kidnapped. I am sure you can understand that right now I am entirely focused upon finding them and bringing them home safely."

The Light Elfin Queen appeared to be hardly interested.

"Well, whenever you can get away, I suppose. But visit, you must. The *last* Steward and I were so *well acquainted.* Ah, here comes my entourage. Now I really *must* be off. *Ta-ta.*"

Turning about, Titania was swept away by a gaggle of fawning courtiers and sycophants, who disappeared down the concourse like a pretentious flock of preening parrots.

Mark appeared by Ellen's side. "What was that all about? Wasn't that Queen Titania of the Light Elves?"

"That was her, all right," acknowledged Ellen. "And I just got invited to visit her in the Realm of Light Elves. Oh yeah, and to attend the Seelie Court, too."

Mark smirked. "Really? What next?"

"EXCUSE ME, LADY ELLEN?" Padraic interjected. "Please forgive me, but I wanted to thank you and your friends for helping Queen Mab and me in our moment of need."

"There is no need to thank us, uh, Padraic, is it?" she said sincerely. "We were happy to help."

Padraic stood there for a moment, relishing the sight of his daughter—who, he was coming to appreciate, was quite an exceptional young woman. Part of him longed to tell her, but he knew that was most unwise—it would only put her in more danger, and she was playing in perilous enough leagues already. Nonetheless, the smile he gave her was sincere and genuine in its warmth.

"If you would indulge me, Lady Ellen. Forgive me, but I could not help but overhear Queen Titania's invitation to visit. You should know that an invitation to *attend the Seelie Court* is viewed by many as tantamount to an invitation to *join* that court by swearing fealty thereto—a situation I would recommend avoiding. Whether it be the Seelie or Unseelie Court, swear fealty to no one."

"One moment, Padraic," interrupted Mark. "I was told that you are the consort of Queen Mab of the Dark Elves, she who also rules as the Monarch of the Unseelie Court. Is this not true?"

Padraic smiled. "Quite true, Counselor."

"Yet you just warned against swearing fealty to either of the Faerie courts. Did you not?"

"I did. In the realms of Faerie, my young friend, not all is precisely as it seems. Now, I must bid you both a good night. Be wary and well."

With a smile and a wink, he turned and strode away.

"NOW, *that* was interesting," mused Mark aloud. "He certainly wasn't as I expected."

"Which sort of proved his point," Ellen observed dryly. "But I don't get it. He seems to be a really nice guy—what does he see in *her?*"

"Well, there's no accounting for taste," he teased. "And speaking of which, here come Hawk and Trey."

Ignoring his teasing jibe, she frowned askance at her cousin. "Yes, and they don't look happy."

Trey's scowl did not fade as he explained the roadblock they'd hit in trying to investigate George's possible—no, *probable* escape.

Hawk's mood was no better. "Papa George is gone. I don't know *how*, but he's definitely gone."

"But where could he go? None of the Council worlds would harbor him—not even the Dark Elves, after what happened to Queen Mab," Ellen observed.

"Well, the only other realm he knows is his own," Mark noted. "He'd certainly know how to hide there, wouldn't he?"

"How would he get there?" Trey asked the obvious question. "Can he just *transit* like Ellen can, or would he have to have some sort of help? Does the Council's invitation have anything to do with it—I mean, he was invited, right? Consider this; there were instructions included with the invitations to get the invitees here, so it stands to reason that there must be some means of returning them home. Do you follow me?"

"Yeah," Mark agreed, "but he was *summoned* rather than *invited*. I've learned that there's a considerable distinction."

Trey nodded thoughtfully. "I can appreciate the difference. But, any summons I'm familiar with—and I've seen and served more than a few in this job—always comes with some sort of instructions. So, why wouldn't this one?"

"You may have something there, Trey," Ellen said, "but I think he would have to have the summons in his possession. Do we know if he did?"

"No, and that's part of the problem," complained Hawk. "We can't get into where he was staying, or where he was being held, to conduct a search for clues. Queen Mab refused to cooperate."

"Speaking of getting into places," Ellen began, gesturing behind Trey and Hawk. "Can you find the room we ducked into?"

"It was right in the middle of that wall," insisted Hawk, as he turned and pointed to the solid wall across the concourse.

Trey slowly nodded in agreement, with furrowed brow. "What was it—another secret passage, or something?"

"Maybe," she conceded, "but I wanted to be sure we all saw the same thing. It appears we were seen during the rescue, and thought to have just *disappeared.* Anyway, it seems that's what was reported to the Council chairperson. Apparently, no one knew about *that room,* or could see it.

"Lord Thorenson just asked me a few minutes ago if I had invoked a transit spell during the rescue, despite the prohibition against magic in most common areas. But, I think what he was more concerned about was that the old wards are still working as intended. He relaxed only when I assured him that I hadn't tried a transit spell and told him about the room; but then, I couldn't point it out to him. He suggested that I was just confused about the location. I didn't get the impression that he knew otherwise. I really think he doesn't know; and, he is sincerely worried about the wards."

"That would suggest," Mark reasoned, "that the Council's control of this realm may not be as comprehensive and complete as it appears, or as they would have us believe. And if that's the case, it logically follows that there may be other forces at work here as well."

"Well, somebody certainly helped us," Ellen remarked dryly, "I seriously doubt it was just *luck.*"

"Be that as it may," warned Trey, "it doesn't help us find Papa George."

Hawk's expression soured as his partner continued.

"In all candor, I think there's little more we can do here," said Trey in resignation. "The best lead we've got, as Mark said, is that he might go back home to hide. So, unless someone has a better idea, we should probably get back and look for him."

"I can't go—at least not right now," Mark interjected. "I have to attend the rest of the Council meeting; and, I still have to deal with some logistics. Madam Moya will open the Enclave of the Realm of Man for me; it's been closed since Maude's last visit. Anyway, you don't have to worry about me getting home. As a full member of the Council, I can share in the power reserves—magic of some sort I assume—made available to its members. This just means that I, as a Council member, can now freely transit between any of the Council Realms. Of course there's a bit more to it, but Moya is supposed to show me the ropes, so to speak."

But Ellen was still concerned. "Are you sure you'll be all right, staying here, if I take Trey and Hawk home?"

"I'll be fine," Mark assured her. "Besides, it'll give me time to have another discreet visit with Elsbeth to ascertain if her information network can shed any light on Papa George's disappearing act."

"That's a good idea, Mark. You might ask her about that mysterious room, too. But, above all, be careful," warned Hawk. "How long will the rest of the meeting run? Beyond that, how much more time will you need?"

"I'm not really sure. Look, if I'm not back by morning, feel free to come looking." Mark chuckled.

"Count on it," Trey confirmed and nodded to Ellen. "Besides, I think I could get used to traveling like this." He grinned and nudged Hawk. "Let's get going."

Ellen held up her hand and said, "One last thing... Keep in mind what we all witnessed with those two guards; they were *dead*, and yet they rampaged like berserkers of old Nordic legends! Nothing stopped them, until they just self-destructed somehow. As Lord Thorenson said, that was likely *necromancy*, the manipulation of the dead, a form of black art long forbidden. But somebody used it—and I don't think it was a coincidence that it happened around Papa George's apparent escape."

"Wait a sec," cautioned Mark. "Are you suggesting that he—"

"Papa George? No, I seriously doubt that he has the necessary skills," Ellen countered, "but it's clear that someone does. I think Papa George is somehow involved; and, I suspect so is someone else. We should not discount that he may have help—very dangerous help; and, at this point we have no idea who."

"Oh man," groaned Trey, "doesn't *necromancy* mean, like uh, *zombies?* So now, we've got *zombies?* What next?"

"And probably a *zombie master*—don't forget," Mark added facetiously.

"Oh yeah! So that means *head shots*, right?" offered Hawk, with a grin.

Ellen was not amused; they were getting off point.

"All right, very funny. I'm glad you're all keeping up your sense of humor. Seriously, let's stay focused, guys! Look, I'm sorry; but I'm tired. I'm also scared and worried sick. My mother and Stacy are still missing—kidnapped! Possibly by people with this kind of power! And I just don't want anyone to get hurt!"

Staring into their solemn faces she squared her shoulders.

"Now, on that cheery note, let's go home."

Coming Soon

The tale continues in STORM HAVEN, Vol. IV of THE STEWARD.

Fallout ensues following forbidden necromancy within the diplomatic precincts and hallowed halls of the Council itself!

Elfin queens are at odds!

Papa George is a fugitive from justice and Lady Diere's vengeance!

Storm Haven, the hidden realm, is compromised and under siege by the forces of Shadow and the Were!

Stacy is injured and Hawk is missing!

Worse, almost all is Ellen's fault.

About the Author

M.D. Ironz is the pseudonym of a former government official, based in an undisclosed location in North America, and now serving as a confidential consultant on matters of intelligence, security, and investigations.

www.ingramcontent.com/pod-product-compliance
Lightning Source LLC
Chambersburg PA
CBHW030537310726
48979CB00010B/1939/J

* 9 7 8 1 7 3 3 7 5 9 4 4 1 *